Raves for John Ramsey Miller's spellbinding novels of suspense

Inside Out

"John Ramsey Miller's *Inside Out* needs to come with a warning label. To start the story is to put the rest of your life on hold as you obsessively turn one page after the other. With a story this taut, and characters this vivid, there's no putting the book down before you've consumed the final word. A thrilling read."
—John Gilstrap, author of *Scott Free*

"*Inside Out* is a great read! John Ramsey Miller's tale of big-city mobsters, brilliant killers and a compellingly real U.S. marshal has as many twists and turns as running serpentine through a field of fire and keeps us turning pages as fast as a Blackhawk helicopter's rotors! Set aside an uninterrupted day for this one; you won't want to put it down."
—Jeffery Deaver, author of *The Vanished Man* and *The Stone Monkey*

"[Full of] complications and surprises . . . Miller gifts [his characters] with an illuminating idiosyncrasy. This gives us great hope for future books as well as delight in this one." —*Drood Review of Mystery*

"Twists and turns on every page keep you in phenomenal suspense until the last page. Superb novel."
—*Rendezvous*

The Last Family

"A relentless thriller." —*People*

"Fast-paced, original, and utterly terrifying—true, teeth-grinding tension. I lost sleep reading the novel, and then lost even more sleep thinking about it. Martin Fletcher is the most vividly drawn, most resourceful, most horrifying killer I have encountered. Hannibal Lecter, eat your heart out." —Michael Palmer

"The best suspense novel I've read in years!"
—Jack Olsen

"Martin Fletcher is one of the most unspeakably evil characters in recent fiction. . . . A compelling read."
—*Booklist*

"The author writes with a tough authority and knows how to generate suspense." —*Kirkus Reviews*

"Suspenseful . . . Keeps readers guessing with unexpected twists." —*Publishers Weekly*

Also by John Ramsey Miller

The Last Family

Inside Out

And look for

SIDE BY SIDE

in September 2005

upside down

John Ramsey Miller

A Dell Book

Dell

UPSIDE DOWN
A Dell Book / July 2005

Published by
Bantam Dell
A Division of Random House, Inc.
New York, New York

This is a work of fiction. Names, characters, places, and incidents either are the product of the author's imagination or are used fictitiously. Any resemblance to actual persons, living or dead, events, or locales is entirely coincidental.

ISBN 0-553-58340-9

Printed in the United States of America
Published simultaneously in Canada

www.bantamdell.com

OPM 10 9 8 7 6 5 4 3 2 1

To my father, Rev. Rush Glenn Miller.

If a better man exists, I have yet to meet him.

Acknowledgments

Thanks to my agent, Anne Hawkins of Hawkins & Associates, NYC, and my editor, Kate Miciak, who introduced me to Faith Ann Porter, and whose patient guidance and support have been crucial in the Winter Massey series. My thanks also to Nita Taublib and Irwyn Applebaum, and all of the people at Bantam Dell who worked to make sure *Upside Down*'s best foot was put forward.

I apologize for any and all inaccuracies in this book. My wife and I lived in New Orleans for ten wonderful years, and it seems that my characters keep insisting I go back down there to refresh my memory and accuracy since the city changes things without consulting me. When practicable, I am faithful to actual locations, businesses and the street names, but sometimes accuracy is inconvenient and begs for alteration.

Thanks to my dear friends in New Orleans: Nathan Hoffman and his wife, author Erica Spindler, and to William, Stephanie and Garrett Greiner for their hospitality while Susie and I were doing research for this book.

I appreciate the help of NOPD's Captain Marlon Defilo, Homicide Lt. James Keen, Sgt. John Rice, the Assistant Commander of Homicide.

Thanks to the copilot and engineer on the Canal Street ferry, the USS *Thomas Jefferson*, for patiently answering my "what if" questions without calling Homeland Security.

To my friend, fellow author John Gilstrap, whose sense of humor never fails to cheer me up, and whose understanding and love of our craft always inspires me to try harder.

Heartfelt thanks to all of the doctors and staff at North

East Medical Center's George A. Batte Cancer Center in Concord, N.C., who saved my wife Susan's life.

Thanks to childhood friends, Johnny Ward and Larry Levington, and to the revitalizing effects of their company. Thank God for the C.H.S. Memorial Gramling Art Class Wildlife Sanctuary & Gun Club—where the woodstove is hot, the conversation is easy, the wine plentiful, the cigars smooth, and the deer couldn't be safer.

I wish I could individually thank all of the people who inspire me and support me and those people who are my friends. I cherish every one of them. They know who they are, and I do too.

upside down

1 Baton Rouge, Louisiana
Friday / 4:01 A.M.

From ground level, the automobile graveyard looked boundless. The moon was like an open eye that, when it peered through holes in the clouds, was reflected in thousands of bits of chrome and glass. After the four figures passed under a buzzing quartz-halogen lamp set on a pole, long shadows ran out from them, reaching across the oil-stained earth like the fingers of a glove.

The quartet entered a valley where rusting wrecks, stagger-stacked like bricks, formed walls twenty feet tall. One of the three men carried a lantern that squeaked as it swung back and forth.

The woman's tight leather pants showed the precise curve of her buttocks, the rock-hard thighs, and the sharply cut calf muscles. A dark woolen V-neck under her windbreaker kept the chill at a comfortable distance. The visor on her leather ball cap put her face in deeper shadow.

They stopped. When the man fired up his lantern, hard-edged white light illuminated the four as mercilessly as a flashbulb.

Marta Ruiz's hair fell down the center of her back like a horse's tail. In an evening gown she could become an exotic, breathtaking creature that made otherwise staid men stammer like idiots. "How far now?" she asked. Her accent had a slight Latin ring to it.

"Not too far," Cecil Mahoney said, looking down at the much shorter woman. An extremely large and powerfully built man, Mahoney looked like a crazed Viking. His thick bloodred facial hair so completely covered his mouth that his words might have been supplied by a ventriloquist. He wore a black leather vest over a black Harley-Davidson T-shirt, filthy jeans with pregnant knees, and engineer boots. His thick arms carried so many tattoos that it looked like he was wearing a brilliantly colored long-sleeved shirt. Silver rings adorned his fingers, the nails of which were dead ringers for walnut hulls.

The other two men were dull-eyed muscle without conscience or independent thought. Cecil Mahoney was the biggest crystal methamphetamine wholesaler in the South and the leader of the Rolling Thunder Motorcycle Club. Stone-cold killers pissed their pants when a thought of Cecil Mahoney invaded their minds. Few people could muster the kind of rage required to use their bare hands like claws and literally rip people into pieces like Cecil could.

The three men didn't see Marta as a physical threat. How could such a small woman harm them—kick them in the shins, bite and scratch? They had seen that she was unarmed when she stepped out of the car and put on a nylon jacket so lightweight that any one of them could have wadded up the garment, stuffed it into his mouth, and swallowed it like a tissue.

They turned a corner, moved deeper into the yard.

"Over there," Cecil said.

They stopped at the sharply angled rear of a Cadillac Seville with its front end smashed into a mushroom of rusted steel. Marta's sensitive nose picked up the sickly sweet odor, folded somewhere in the oily stench of petroleum and mildewed fabric, of something else in decay. One of the henchmen lifted the trunk lid while the other held up the lantern so Marta could see inside.

"Careful you don't puke all over yourself, little girl," Cecil warned.

Marta leaned in, took the corpse's head in her bare hands, and twisted the face up into the light. The way the skin moved under her fingers told her a great deal. There were two bands of duct tape surrounding the head; one covering the mouth and nose and another over the eyes and both ears. It made the features impossible to read, which was now irrelevant. Other than hair color, this corpse was not even close to the woman she had come to identify and to kill.

"Where's the reward?" Cecil grunted.

"The money is in my car's trunk, but whether or not it belongs to you is a question I can't yet answer," Marta told him.

"That's her, and I'm getting that reward."

"Perhaps, perhaps not."

"Okay, gal, you've seen her enough."

The low position of the lantern made Cecil look even more menacing—his small water-blue eyes glittering. He used a lot of what he sold. From the start he had made it abundantly clear to Marta that dealing with a woman was beneath him. His first words to her had been that he didn't know why anybody would send a "split tail" to do important business. He had referred to her as a "juicy little thang." If she played this wrong, she would be raped and murdered in some unspeakable manner. She knew the piece of trunk cheese was no more Amber Lee than Cecil Mahoney was the Son of God. The needle marks on the dead woman's arm alone were enough to tell her this girl was some overdosed waif. It followed that the envelope Amber had in her possession would not be there. Marta hoped Arturo was having luck tracking the woman in New Orleans.

"You failed to mention that she was dead. Why is that?"

Cecil's patience was thinning. "Bitch choked on her own vomit. Look, honeypot, a hundred thousand clams was the deal. So stop with the questions. Let's go get my money."

"It wasn't a dead-or-alive offer, Mr. Mahoney. There were questions that we needed to ask her, and can't now. My boss expects accuracy in the information he receives from me. You said that she was alive. When did she die?"

"It's damn unfortunate. Boomer found her dead yesterday evening choked on puke. Ain't that right, Boomer?"

The man holding the lantern nodded. "I found her dead yesterday. Choked on her puke."

"I wonder how she gained so much weight in so few days."

"Well, she's just bloating up 'cause it's hot in a car trunk."

"Hot in there," Boomer agreed.

The temperature had not risen above fifty-five degrees in the past two days. "Take *it* out," Marta told the men.

"What the hell for?"

"It will be abundantly clear to you, Mr. Mahoney, when they take *it* out."

"Get old Amber out, then," Cecil ordered. Boomer put the lantern on the ground and both he and the third man reached in, wrestled the body from the trunk, and dropped it to the oil-crusted black dirt like a bag of trash. In the lantern light the men looked like depraved giants. As Marta squatted beside the corpse, she pinched her cap's brim as if pulling it down and withdrew from it a wide matte-black double-edged ceramic blade that fit inside the bill. She palmed it, holding the blade flat against her forearm. She knew what was going to happen in the coming few seconds just as surely as if they had all been rehearsing it for days. "You are right, Cecil, it doesn't smell so good. Like it's been dead longer than one day."

"Bodies," Cecil said. "Who can account for spoil rates?"

She shrugged. "You have a knife?" She held out her right hand, palm up.

"Knife for what?" he asked.

"A knife, yes or no?"

She didn't know how much longer Cecil would allow this charade to run. Still entertained, he reached into his vest pocket and placed a stag-handled folding knife in her hand. She opened it using her teeth and tested the edge for sharpness with the side of her thumb. Much better than she would have hoped. *A man and his tools.*

"You could shave your little pussy with it," Cecil muttered.

Nervous snickers—six fiery, obscene pig eyes.

She reached out suddenly and sliced through the duct tape, laying the corpse's cheek open from the jaw to the teeth twice to form parentheses that crossed at the top and bottom. She jabbed the blade into the flesh and lifted out the plug in the same way one might remove a piece of pumpkin to make a jack-o'-lantern's eye. The dark purple tissue was crawling with what looked like animated kernels of rice.

"Aw, man!" Boomer exclaimed.

"You're trying to pull one over on me," she chastised.

"Hell, honey," Cecil said, "I never was too good with times and days and all. I'm better with arithmetic like adding up you and this corpse and getting a hundred thousand in cash money." Cecil and the other two men had her boxed in, the open trunk at her back. That was fine, she wasn't going anywhere.

Marta remained on her haunches, tightened her leg muscles, and bounced up and down gently so maybe they believed that she was nervous. She would have preferred to be barefoot, because she had gone without shoes for most of her life and felt more secure that way. The sharp clutter in the junkyard made that impractical. "You think you are getting a dime for this fraud, you're even a bigger moron than people say you are."

"How about I dump you and the maggoty little whore in the trunk and take the cash?"

"What will you tell my boss's men when they come to find me?"

Cecil slipped a revolver from behind his back and held it by his side, barrel down. He cocked the hammer, probably imagining the sound intimidated her. "That you never showed up. Must a run off with his cash. Or I'll say, 'Just kiss my ass.' Boys, I think it's gonna be plan two."

"What is plan two?" she asked. She was aware that the man on her left had pulled a pistol from his coat pocket. The man called Boomer had something in his right hand. She didn't care what it was, because unless they all had grenades with the pins already pulled, they might as well be holding tulips. She turned Cecil's Puma knife in her hand so the blade was aimed up.

"Plan two is the old 'snuff-the-Beaner-cunt' plan."

"You aren't man enough to snuff this Beaner, Cecilia Baloney." Her next words were hard as Arkansas stone, certain as taxes. "And as a woman I resent the C-word coming from the rotten-tooth stink-hole mouth of a stupid, syphilitic, dog-fucking redneck puke." Keeping her left fist in shadow, she twisted the flat blade she had taken from her cap into position.

The other two men sniggered at her insult, which infuriated Cecil. "Watch it happen . . . you stinking wetback blow job." As he raised the gun up, she launched her light body into the air, slicing, the Puma up through Cecil's right bicep like an oar's edge through still water. Before his handgun hit the ground, Cecil had spun and fled for the front gate, howling and holding his useless arm.

Marta spun a full revolution, a whirling dervish with her arms extended so that one blade was much higher than the other. After the spin, she squatted between the confused men. Balanced on her haunches, she looked like a jockey on the home stretch—her elbows out like wings, her hands in front of her face level with her chin like she was pulling back hard on reins. Instead of leather leads, the wetly lacquered blades radiated out from her fists. Knowing the men were no longer a threat, she focused straight ahead, her eyes following Cecil as he ran through the valley of wrecks.

The nameless third man pulled his hands up to his neck, perhaps to see what the sudden blast of cold against his throat meant. His scream gargled out from a new mouth below his jawline. He stamped his boots a couple of times like he was marching in place to music and collapsed. His feet quivered as though he was being electrocuted.

Boomer dropped to his knees and stared at the bloody pile growing on the ground below him. When he turned his eyes to her in disbelief, she smiled at him.

She said, "That was the Beaner cunt's plan number one." She stood and, laughing melodiously, loped out into the dark after Cecil.

By the eerie lantern light, the kneeling man worked to gather up the steaming mess that had slid out of him and put it all back.

2 | New Orleans, Louisiana

Faith Ann Porter yawned and looked over at the venetian blinds for any sign that the sun was rising. Her watch's display read 6:13.

The small reception area always smelled like a place where somebody really old lived. The space was strictly a prop, because there was no receptionist. Usually Faith

Ann's mother could hardly afford to pay the office rent, much less hire someone to sit there at the desk to greet the few people who ever came there. Not a single one of her clients had ever been to visit her, and the fact was that the vast majority of her mother's calls were outgoing. Even so, it was absolutely necessary to maintain a professional office.

The upper part of the front door to the five-room suite, which was at the end of the hallway, had a frosted glass panel in it where each tenant's name had been hand-painted backward on the inside since 1927, the year the building had been constructed. At that moment, Faith Ann was lying prone, peering through the brass mail slot, watching the fifty feet of hallway between herself and the elevator lobby. Not that she believed the mysterious woman was going to show up this time either. Most likely she'd been awakened and dragged all the way down here before dawn for nothing.

"Watching won't make her get here one second sooner. If she sees your eyes looking out at her from down there, she'll think we have rats. You shouldn't snoop," Kimberly Porter said from the door.

"You just told Mrs. Washington that you liked my inquisitive nature. You said my curiosity shows intelligence."

"You were listening in on the extension while I was talking to your teacher!"

Time to change the subject. "I bet you got me up early for nothing. I'll be sleep-deprived when I get to school . . . for nothing. I'll bet you a dollar she won't even show up. I'll bet you another dollar if she does she's just some lunatic trying to get money for some old letters she probably scribbled up herself, knowing you'd do anything to save Harry Pond."

"Horace," Kimberly corrected automatically. "If she's right, he's really not guilty."

"You think everybody you represent is innocent."

"I don't think any such thing. There are lots of other lawyers with investigators who try to prove innocence. When that fails, they call me."

"To do legal mumbo jumbo. Hocus-pocus high jinks. Pick a card, Your Honor." Faith Ann plopped onto her back and clapped her hand to her chest. "No sir, that isn't really an ace of hearts, I say it's a two of clubs, your honor. So, since it isn't the ace at all, like you thought, my client is *not* guilty."

"You little monkey!" Kimberly said. She leaned down and tickled her daughter's ribs.

"Child abuse!" Faith Ann said, laughing, squirming, and trying to push her mother's hands away.

Kimberly straightened. "What I do is not trickery. Horace Pond might be one in a hundred. This is exactly why there shouldn't be a death penalty. It is preferable to—"

" 'Free a hundred guilty people than punish one innocent one,' " Faith Ann interrupted. "Like freeing a hundred criminals to go out running around doing crimes is going to happen. You know most people don't agree with whatever old jerk it was said that. Uncle Hank, for one."

"For your information, Miss Know-It-All—that 'whatever old jerk' was Supreme Court Chief Justice Earl Warren of *Brown v. the Board of Education*. And I know Hank Trammel does too agree."

"Then why does Uncle Hank have a sign on his office wall that says LET NO GUILTY MAN ESCAPE? You know who said that?"

"I somehow doubt it was Earl Warren."

"Old Hanging Judge Parker. He hanged men as quick as his marshals could round them up."

"I believe that sort of behavior is precisely why Earl Warren said what he did." Kimberly walked from the reception area.

Just as Faith Ann was about to get up and follow her mother, she heard the elevator door open, so she looked out through the mail slot. Sure enough a woman stepped out. It had to be *her* because her mother's office was the only one on the fourth floor except for an eyeglass repair shop run by a frowning man who just came to work when he felt like it. People didn't bring their eyeglasses, either. The glasses came by UPS and the mail, from optometrists all over the city. Lots of times, boxes and mailing envelopes containing broken glasses sat in the hall outside his door, waiting for him to show up. Faith Ann made it her business to know what was going on around her at all times.

Faith Ann called out over her shoulder urgently, "Mama!"

"I'm coming," her mother called back from her office.

The woman, who was rapidly approaching the office on high heels, reminded Faith Ann of a movie star, probably because of the scarf that seemed to be there to keep the balloon of blond hair from rising right off of her scalp. Her cinched-up trench coat accented a narrow waist and substantial breasts. Faith Ann's eyes locked on the rolled-up manila envelope protruding from her shoulder bag, which the woman was gripping like she expected someone to run up and try to snatch it. She removed her sunglasses and shoved them into the pocket of her coat.

Faith Ann stood and pulled open the door for the woman just before she reached for the knob, which startled her. Faith Ann was instantly assaulted by a wave of sickeningly sweet perfume.

"You look rather young to be a lawyer," the woman said, trying to make a joke. Her brown eyes hardly rested on Faith Ann at all as they darted around the room.

"My mother is the attorney."

"You're what, sixteen, seventeen?"

"Twelve." Faith Ann didn't let on that she knew the woman was being all hokey with her, trying to make friends or something. "You can hang your coat up," Faith Ann offered, pointing to the standing coatrack.

"I'll just keep it on." Faith Ann was disappointed that she wouldn't get to see what kind of outfit was under it. The woman's eyelashes looked like spider legs, and her brows were arched lines that had been carefully drawn on her forehead, maybe with a sharp-pointed laundry marker. Faith Ann just couldn't help but stare at her.

The woman looked relieved when Kimberly appeared in the doorway. "I'm Kimberly Porter, Ms. Lee. I see you've met my daughter, Faith Ann."

"She's just cute as a bug. I'm sorry," Ms. Lee said, "could you lock the door?"

"Nobody ever comes here this early," Faith Ann said.

"Of course I can," Kimberly answered.

Faith Ann turned the deadbolt herself. She was amazed at how calm and professional her mother was acting. Faith Ann knew that what her mother really wanted was to jerk that rolled-up envelope out of Ms. Lee's purse and rip it open to see if it really was "explosive eleventh-hour evidence."

"Call me Amber," the woman said and put her hand on the envelope like she'd caught Faith Ann thinking about it. "I'm sorry I've been so vague about things, but you'll see I have good reason. Do you have the *thing* we discussed?"

She means money, Faith Ann thought.

Kimberly nodded. "Come into my office," she said, leading the woman into the hall and into the first door on the right. Faith Ann started to follow, but her mother's raised brow stopped her. "Faith Ann, you go do your homework in the *kitchen* while I meet with Ms. Lee."

"I already did it all."

"Well, then paint me a picture I can frame."

"I don't have my art stuff here."

"Well, then draw something with a pencil." She raised her brow and through clenched teeth said, "*Please*, Faith Ann."

As soon as Kimberly closed the door, leaving Faith Ann in the hallway, she scooted down the hall and turned into the next doorway, which opened into the conference room. She stopped in her tracks when she saw that her mother was closing the other door in her office, which connected the two rooms. The conference room held a large table with eight wooden office chairs around it that the building's owner had robbed from other vacant offices as an added incentive to get her mother to move into his building. The shelves were loaded with her mother's law books, most of which were full of cases you couldn't be a lawyer without knowing. Stealthily, Faith Ann slithered down on the floor, placing her ear as close to the crack at the bottom of the adjoining door as possible. It was a heavy wooden one and might as well have been a vault door for the sound it allowed through—or so her mother believed. Being an adult, Kimberly had never bothered to lie down and put her ear to the crack to make sure nobody could listen in.

"I'd like to record this," Kimberly's professional voice said, "if you have no objections. It'll help me later, and it will simplify things down the road when I am in front of the Governor."

"If you want to, but I wouldn't trust the Governor," Amber's voice said. "I mean, I've personally seen him in the club. Jerry owns half the cops—all the ones that run things. He could never have pulled off doing what he did to Judge and Mrs. Williams and framing your client without the police being involved. Nobody in this state can be trusted—especially not in law enforcement. After he found out I had this, the police put out a warrant for my arrest, for embezzling of all things. Jerry did that easy as snapping his fingers. If the cops get me, I'll be fish food."

"Don't worry, my uncle is a U.S. marshal. He'll be in town late this afternoon. He is on a first-name basis with the Attorney General of the United States. I doubt your Jerry owns *him*."

"I guess he'd be all right . . ."

"Let's start by having a look at your evidence."

Faith Ann heard the contents being removed from the envelope, followed by the familiar muttering that signaled her mother was giving her undivided attention to something that she believed was very important.

"Who is this Jerry?" Kimberly asked, sounding like she did after a long run.

"You're obviously not from around here. Anybody around here would know who he is."

"Is he a gangster of some sort?"

"Well, yes, but not so's you'd know it by the papers . . ."

"Dear God!" Kimberly blurted out. "Is this *him* in the picture? This is sick."

Faith Ann realized that she was holding her breath and exhaled slowly. This was great! Of all the neat conversations she'd ever spied on, this one was better than all the others put together.

"This *isn't* a hoax," Kimberly stammered, sounding confused. "Forgive me for ever doubting your claims, but in cases like this people often say they have evidence exonerating a death row inmate—especially at the eleventh hour. They almost always turn out to be . . . less than helpful. No, I've seen the crime scene pictures and this is the same room and those are the same people. But they are both alive in all but two of these."

"The negatives are in there. I don't know much about photography, but I don't think you can fake those. So, is it worth a grand so I can get out of town until he's in prison?"

"Why did he make these? Why did he keep them? This is insanity."

"You're right. No person in their right mind would have." Amber continued, "I can't hardly sleep a wink without seeing those pictures in my head."

"And he knows you have these?"

"Yes, he does. It's a long story."

"I've got time."

Faith Ann was so fascinated by everything she heard during the next couple of minutes that she was still lying on the hardwood floor absorbing the information when Kimberly suddenly opened the door. After having to step over her daughter, she pulled the door closed and lifted Faith Ann up off the floor with the hand that wasn't holding the fat envelope full of evidence. "I guess you heard all that, Miss Nosey-Britches?" she said in a low voice.

"I dropped something."

"It's a clear violation of professional etiquette to eavesdrop."

"Why did you tell her that fib— Uncle Hank was coming tonight?" Faith Ann asked accusatorily.

"Because it's true."

"No, it isn't. Today is Friday. They're going to be here tomorrow—Saturday."

"They're coming in tonight. They're staying at a guesthouse and having dinner with some old friend of Hank's. Then they're coming to see us tomorrow."

"Can I see the pictures she brought?" She knew asking was a waste of breath. Her mother had already commented on how horrific they were. Faith Ann had heard tales of mayhem and murder since she was old enough to understand the adult conversations going on around her. Every capital case her mother took on came with lots of boxes, most of them containing crime scene pictures taken by the cops. Faith Ann looked through those whenever she got a chance, despite her mother's best efforts to hide the graphic files. "Pretty please?"

"Absolutely not!" Kimberly went over to the copier and, one after the other, put each of the eight original photographs facedown on the glass, then pressed the button to make copies of the pictures. Faith Ann couldn't see any of the images, which was infuriating. No dead judge and his wife, no rich killer named Jerry doing something truly horrible to anybody. Of course Faith Ann didn't *want* to see anything like that, but as a lawyer in training, she needed to study all of the legal evidence she could.

Kimberly gathered the photocopies from the bin. At the table, she slid the copies into an envelope, added a glassine sleeve containing dark strips of negatives, and sealed it by licking the glue strip and pressing it closed. Faith Ann's heart sank. Kimberly put the curved original photographs back in their envelope. She swung away the corkboard adorned with pictures of her clients to expose a wall safe that some doctor had used once upon a time to store his drugs. Kimberly opened the safe and took out a stack of bills, which she put in her pocket.

"I want your word of honor that you will not attempt to open that envelope," she scolded. "I want your absolute word of honor."

"I give you my mile-high word of honor," Faith Ann said, knowing that the envelope was sealed, which placed snooping inside it outside her tampering abilities. She made the appropriate X motion with her trigger finger. "I cross my heart and hope to die and stick a needle in my eye. I will never look at those pictures unless you tell me to."

"There are times to be curious and times, like now, to refrain from snooping. Tell you what. I'll fill you in on all of this after Horace Pond is free. Word of honor. And, Faith Ann, I *am* so very proud of your intelligence and . . ."

The two distinctive voices originating from the office changed Kimberly's expression to a look of terror. The voices weren't coming under the door into Kimberly's office, so they had to be carrying down the hallway, meaning that Kimberly's office door was open like the conference room door.

"Hide!" Kimberly whispered, pushing her down under the table.

Faith Ann obeyed instantly, climbing up into the hard seats of the chairs parked under it. This was a place she had hidden before to annoy her mother—make her think she wasn't in the office. Faith Ann knew that as long as she was quiet, and nobody pulled the chairs out or got down on all fours, it was the safest place available. She got in there just in time. Her mother had just shoved her backpack under the table, when a man jerked the adjoining door wide open. From her hiding spot, Faith Ann saw him from the waist down. Beyond him Amber sat in the chair in front of the desk, her face ashen with blind terror.

"Who are you?" Kimberly demanded. "How dare you come in here like this? Put that gun away before there's an accident."

Gun? Faith Ann thought. *Why does he have a gun?*

"Get in here," he ordered, like he hadn't heard her. "Amber has been a very, very bad girl," he chided. "Jerry would like to have back the private property she stole from him." His calm voice had a Spanish accent. He didn't sound at all like somebody who would break into the place and be holding a gun.

"It's in her hand," Amber told him, pointing at the manila envelope containing the real pictures.

Kimberly held it out to him. "Take it and get out." She didn't sound afraid at all to Faith Ann.

"Is anybody else here?" he asked, taking the envelope from her.

"No," Kimberly said. "But my paralegal volunteers will be here any minute. I suggest you take that and go. Up to this moment you haven't committed any crimes we can't forget about."

"Amber, you show this to anybody else? Make copies?"

"No! No, I haven't," Amber stammered. "Please?"

"There a back door?"

"No," Kimberly told him truthfully.

Amber blurted, "She *can't* say anything on account of attorney-client privilege. You've got the pictures. It's over."

"Lawyer lady, did you make any copies?"

"I intended to, but I didn't have time," Kimberly told him, her voice full of false regret.

Faith Ann, terrified he would see them on the table, reached up, felt for the envelope, and pulled it to her.

"He threw me out," Amber whined. "I only wanted him to take me back. Just tell him I'm—"

Amber's words ended with a dull pop followed by her chair turning over. Kimberly screamed out. Faith Ann pressed her hand over her own mouth so *she* wouldn't. Faith Ann saw her mother dart around the desk and grab the phone, but the man moved and blocked her view of what happened next. Faith Ann heard two of the pops and the sound of two things hitting the wooden floor—her mother and the telephone. When the man bent down to pick up the three empty casings, Faith Ann stared at his profile. All he had to do was turn his head and he'd be looking straight at her—no more than fifteen feet away. The manila envelope seemed to be glowing, surely he would see it!

Frozen in place, Faith Ann fought back the terror that had seized her, trying to remember what her mother had drilled into her. *In an emergency, stay calm. Never panic. Fear freezes you and it can kill you, Faith Ann. Always follow your instincts.*

After snagging the shells, the man straightened. He went around the desk, aimed the gun down, and to Faith Ann's horror fired one more time. As he bent down to collect the final casing, she glimpsed the manila envelope curled up in his coat pocket. He came into the conference room and stopped at the edge of the table—opening and slamming the top of the copy machine. Faith Ann focused on the hem of his long coat, on his gray pants with sharp creases and cuffs and his shiny two-tone shoes. He went through the things on the table above her; scattered papers fluttered to the floor.

Faith Ann pushed away the thought of what his gun might have done.

You can't find me.

I'm not here.

Go away.

Don't look for me.

I'm invisible.

As if commanded by her thoughts, the man left the room.

She listened to his footsteps as he checked the other rooms down the hall. After he looked in both the vacant office and the kitchen, he hurried back up the hall and left through the front door.

Faith Ann lay there trembling in silence for a very long while, afraid his closing the door was a trick designed to flush her out. Then she slipped down onto the floor and came out from under the table on all fours. "Mama?" she said, testing the sound of her voice.

The only sound inside the office was the steady beeping of the telephone, off its hook behind the desk. The smell of cordite, which reminded her of shooting cans with Uncle Hank, mixed with Amber's gardenia perfume.

Faith Ann could hardly see through her tears. She had never seen a real dead person before, and it was terrifying.

Amber was sprawled out on the threadbare Oriental carpet where the chair had dumped her. Her face was bloody, but Faith Ann didn't focus on that—didn't want to look at the person who had brought this horror to the Porters.

Slowly Faith Ann rounded the desk and stared down at the ruined woman she loved more than anyone on earth. The terrible reality of it slammed into her, giving her the sensation of being hollowed out and filled with superheated air. Scared she would faint, Faith Ann inhaled sharply, fighting to remain conscious.

Cold-blooded murder. This is how it comes—all of a sudden, out of the blue. Nobody warns you. A door opens and there it is. Mama, this is exactly what your death row men did—those friendly-looking men on the corkboard who can smile at your camera like saints, even though one day they did something just like this to people just like you. Faith Ann knew she shouldn't be hysterical.

The large red stain on her mother's white blouse was so bright and wet it seemed to glitter. The pearl, run through with a thin gold chain—a Mother's Day gift from Faith Ann—rested in the hollow of Kimberly's throat.

Faith Ann dropped to her knees, placed her hands on her mother's chest, and pressed down hard. Air hissed, and bubbles rose from her chest. Her face was so pale. . . .

Faith Ann put her mouth on her mother's and blew in, trying to make her all right. That made more bubbles, and Faith Ann was crying so hard she couldn't see. She tried to wipe away the tears, but she wiped blood across her face, tasting it.

She screamed.

Faith Ann reached up to the desk and found the box of tissue there, pulled several out and wiped her eyes and face.

No lifesaving effort would matter. After she had wiped her eyes, Faith Ann studied Kimberly's face. It was slack, her mouth open the way it did when she slept on her back, her eyes partly open, the irises rolled back.

Faith Ann knew her mother wasn't ever going to say anything—never again tell Faith Ann that she loved her, or scold her for goofing off. Faith Ann ignored the hole in her mother's forehead and, closing her own eyes, kissed her warm cheek, inhaling the familiar, comforting scent of her. She could almost pretend that her mother was sleeping. Faith Ann understood that she was now suddenly all alone, and she didn't care if the man came back and killed her too while she was kneeling there.

When she became aware of a wet warmth and saw to her horror that she was kneeling in a growing pool of her mother's blood, Faith Ann shrieked and jumped back. And she knew that she really *did not* want to die.

Tell me what to do, Mama.

She alone knew why the man had killed her mother and Amber. Kimberly's client, Horace Pond, was being executed at ten P.M. on Saturday night for two murders the man in the pictures did.

Today is Friday. Tell me what to do, Mama. Please.

Faith Ann felt herself growing lighter, the fog in her mind clearing. It was almost seven o'clock. Later, Napo, the law student from Tulane who was helping her mother on the Pond case, would come.

Faith Ann's mind locked on something else. *The killer took those pictures! He stole the Pond evidence!*

The negatives! Faith Ann straightened and hurried into the conference room. She looked at the corkboard, meeting the basset hound eyes of Horace Pond, an aging, narrow-shouldered man who actually *was* that one innocent man in a hundred. She pulled a chair over to stand on, opened the corkboard door, and rolled the numbered dial. *Three times around to thirty-one. Left to sixteen and right passing ten once and stopping at it next time.*

She heard the snap as she twisted the lever and eased the heavy door open. She opened the cigar box, gathered up the remaining currency, and stuffed the wad into her jeans pocket before closing the door and replacing the corkboard. She reached to her hiding place, pulled her backpack up onto the table, took out the textbooks, and slipped the sealed envelope into it. The plastic bag containing her mother's rain poncho was in there, as was the lunch her mother had made her and a bottle of water. Then Faith Ann went to the bathroom.

She screamed at the sight in the mirror of her blood-smeared face. She used a bar of soap to scrub her hands and face. As she washed, the water running to the drain turned red. Faith Ann started crying, and she slumped over the sink and let the grief enclose her. Only when the tears stopped flowing did she dry her hands and blow her nose into a paper towel.

I can't call the police.

Jerry owns the police.

Tell me what to do, Mama.

Faith Ann went into the conference room, grabbed her backpack from the table, and went out into the hallway. She paused at the door to her mother's office to take one last look. When she did, she noticed a faint reflection from a steadily blinking red light. She hurried to the desk and moved the loose papers covering her mother's cassette recorder, which was still running.

The killer missed it! When she recorded interviews, Kimberly liked to cover the machine up so people would forget it was sitting there. That way they'd be less self-conscious, she'd told Faith Ann.

Faith Ann couldn't believe her luck. She pressed the Stop button once, then pressed it down again to eject the tape, which she put inside her backpack next to the sealed envelope containing the photocopies and the negatives.

Everything her mother and Amber had said was on that tape.

Faith Ann leaned over and touched her mother gently on the cheek. "I love you, Mama."

That said, Faith Ann went straight out through the front door and was gone.

3 | Charlotte, North Carolina

Often when Winter Massey sat still for a period of time, his right foot would grow numb and tingle. In order to restore the feeling to it he had to get up and walk. The lingering nerve damage was the only thing left over from being shot a year earlier. The entrance and exit scars were islands of white scar tissue on the front and back of his right thigh. He had been on crutches for six weeks after he was shot and had used a cane for another three. The injury made sitting at a desk to fill out reports, and stakeouts conducted while sitting in cramped spaces, rather unpleasant. Few things blew a surveillance more effectively than for a watcher to get out of a parked vehicle every thirty minutes or so to walk around in circles before getting back in. He still participated in his favorite activity, fugitive recovery, but no matter how many fugitives he apprehended, Winter Massey would always be best known for his ability with a handgun.

Over a year had passed since Winter had been wounded. At that time his reputation had been such that he could have chosen to head up any marshals office in the country or have any position near the top of the United States Marshals Service organizational chart he wanted.

The name Winter Massey had been golden, but now he was burned out on playing cops and robbers.

Doctors said the dead spots in his leg and foot would regain sensation and his circulation would vastly improve in time. At thirty-seven, he could still run ten miles without breaking a sweat, but he would never again compete in an Ironman contest. Considering all he had been through in his career as a deputy U.S. marshal, just being alive put him among the luckiest people on earth.

He had left I-85 and was on I-77 negotiating the sweeping left-hand turn when his cellular rang. As he straightened the Explorer's path, and with the Charlotte, North Carolina, skyline looming before him, he looked down at the displayed name and number.

"Hey, old man," he said, after opening the phone.

"Just a courtesy call to remind you about lunch," Hank said.

"Sean said she'd be finished at her doctor's in the BB&T building by eleven," Winter replied. "I'm about six minutes out on I-77."

As he hung up, his cellular phone rang again. He didn't check the caller I.D. "Yeah?"

"*Yeah* what, Massey?"

Winter smiled at the sound of his wife's voice.

"So, what did Dr. Wanda say?" he asked. Sean hadn't been feeling well for a couple of weeks, and Winter had finally convinced her to visit his doctor, a youthful blonde with an enthusiasm, an infectious smile, and a talent for making everybody feel like they were her only patient.

"Dr. Wanda said, 'Get dressed, you perfectly healthy young lady,' and she wrote me a prescription to head over to the café for lunch with my favorite man."

"What about the—?"

"Jesus, Massey. I'm fine. Okay? Did you finish the letter?"

"I did." He glanced at the console to the letter addressed to the director of the United States Marshals Service—a letter he had spent a week drafting to make sure the tone was perfectly pitched, respectful, and that the resignation it announced was clearly stated. Everybody understood his decision and there were no hard feelings or regrets. The letter was a formality, because he had already told the director, Richard Shapiro, that he was going to accept the offer from Guardian International Security. The company had offered him an enormous salary, yearly stock options, and about a hundred attractive perquisites they figured were necessary to close the deal. Winter would have been insane not to take the executive position that would allow him to lock his carry weapon away in his gun safe. Sean, who knew how dangerous his job had become, had been deliriously happy when he made the decision.

"I can't wait to get you on the slopes and teach you how to ski," she said. "You're gonna love it."

"I know how to ski," he said.

"Water skiing isn't the same thing as snow skiing, Massey."

"You teach me to snow ski and I'll teach you a thing or two in the chalet."

Her laughter was glorious.

Although Sean and Winter had only been married for eight months, he felt as though he had known her his entire life. They had met when Winter joined a witness protection detail and was charged with protecting a professional killer who was going to testify against an aging mobster. Sean had been married to the killer, and when the operation turned deadly and went as wrong as things can go, it had been Sean Devlin whose life needed protecting and only Winter who had been in a position to save her. That had happened a little over a year before. After their shared experiences—each having trusted the other and after each had saved the other's life—neither of them wanted to be apart from the other.

Winter believed that he had twice been married to perfect women, who had both been his closest friends. His first wife, Eleanor, had been killed in an airplane crash four years earlier. For three years he had lived with a deep grief that was only made bearable because of his love for their son, Rush. After Eleanor's death Winter's mother, Lydia, had moved into his home to help him raise his son and both of them took immediately to Sean.

After a short formal courtship, Winter had asked Sean to marry him, and she had accepted. Winter still thought daily about Eleanor, but he knew that Eleanor would have wanted for him to love someone and to again be loved by them. Someone who would be a good and nurturing mother to her son. And Winter knew that she would have approved of Sean.

"Hey, Massey, you know what?"

"No, what?"

"You know *what,*" she said, hanging up.

"I love you too," he said before he put the phone in his pocket.

He hoped mailing the letter would lift a great weight from his shoulders—that leaving the badge behind might somehow cause the ghosts of the people he had killed to vacate his mind.

He repeated a familiar prayer. *God, please release me from my guilt and give them peace. In return, I promise that if there is any possible way to avoid doing so, I will never take another human life.*

Winter Massey had asked God for favors before. He understood that although He had the power to do so, God might not take the deal.

Until 1802, Charlotte had been a sleepy community founded in the 1750s by Scotch-Irish Presbyterians and German Lutheran farmers. That year, a farmer named John Reed discovered that a yellow rock the size of a shoe, which he had unearthed years earlier with his plow blade and had been using as a doorstop, was in fact a gold nugget. Until the California strike at Sutter's Mill in 1848, the mines in North Carolina supplied all of the gold used for coinage by the United States. The railroads made Charlotte a commercial hub. After the mines played out, textile and tobacco barons like the Cannons and the Reynolds turned the area into an industrial center. As a consequence of enterprising individuals, the banks filled up with money and began an expansion that had never stopped.

When Winter arrived at 10:55, the City Grill was nearly empty. He took a corner table near a front window. Five minutes later, Hank Trammel, who had been Winter's boss until he'd retired six months earlier, had been his superior officer, his mentor, and had become his closest friend, swaggered into the room like a sheriff in a Western movie, replete with a charcoal-gray handlebar mustache and gold eyeglasses with small round lenses and wrap-around earpieces.

Hank Trammel was walking proof that being from south Texas wasn't something you could easily scrape off your boots. Although he hadn't lived there in over thirty years, Hank dressed like he still ranched in south Texas. Rain, shine, hell or high water, he wore cowboy shirts, khaki pants, sharp-toe boots, a hand-tooled belt with a turquoise-laden buckle the size of a man's fist, and a string tie. On formal occasions, he wore patent leather boots with his tuxedo. He had given up golf but had in his closet a pair of fire-engine-red Tony Lamas with metal spikes.

Hank was a substantial man who, at fifty-eight, still

wore his hair in the same flattop he'd had in high school. Both his grandfather and father had died from gunshots. His grandfather had been ambushed by cattle rustlers, and his father, a Texas Ranger, had been shot in the back by a teenager on a thrill-killing spree. On duty, Hank had always carried his father's gun in the same hand-tooled high-rise hip holster. Trammels were stone-tough people who lived hard lives because they didn't know any other way.

Hank crossed to Winter's table, dropped his "Lyndon Johnson" Stetson on the wide window ledge next to a potted plant, and sat with his back to the glass.

"We ran into Sean outside, and she and Millie went to go powder their noses," Hank said. "She's smoking a cigarette."

Millie Trammel was a secret smoker. Hank had quit, and he acted like he didn't know his wife still did, and she acted like she didn't do it. It was sort of a sanctioned denial game.

A waitress with curly black hair and a silver bead on one side of her nose swept up and stopped in front of the men. "Our wives are joining us," Hank told the young woman. "We'll all have tea."

"Sweet tea?"

"What, darlin', don't I look sweet enough to you?"

"Don't pay my grampy any mind," Winter told her. "Sweet tea."

The waitress walked away.

"So you're really doing it?" Hank asked Winter.

"Yep."

"I'd hoped you would change your mind."

"No way. You're retired now, so why the hell do you care whether I'm still on the job? Ain't like there aren't fifty to take my slot."

"I was looking forward to having you nearby in my golden years. In case I have a stroke and need somebody to bathe me, change my diapers." Hank wiped his head as though there was some hair over his ears that needed pushing back. "I suppose Virginia or Maryland is close enough. You're going to miss the job."

"I owe Rush and Sean my nights and weekends. And I've just been plain lucky for just too long. The odds of me walking away from another scrape like the last couple is slim. I've seen enough action to last me awhile."

"My old daddy always said the only man you can't ever walk away from is one you kill."

Without any words to add, Winter just shrugged. He didn't want to talk about the weight of the dead men perched on his shoulders. It was something no amount of churchgoing, psychiatry, or emptying bottles could lessen. Neither self-defense nor heat of battle made the slightest difference in the anguish that killing brought a normal man.

"Massey, I have to say that the idea of you teaching ex-football players how to protect executives whose biggest threat is not hitting a green in regulation gives me some pause."

"It's done. I stuffed my resignation letter into that blue box right out there before I walked in. As of November the fifteenth, I will be a civilian."

"Then congratulations," Hank said, extending his hand across the table. "Those security guys want the best, that's what they're getting. I told them so back when they called me."

"Millie excited about the trip to New Orleans?"

"Ask her yourself," Hank said, rising from his chair.

As Hank's wife and Sean crossed the room together, Winter was aware of men's heads turning, their eyes following Sean. With her height, shoulder-length raven hair, almond-shaped golden eyes, slim build, and elegant features, she looked like a model. He stood and pulled a chair back from the table for her. Hank went to do the same, but

Millie waved him off and seated herself. "It's much too late to make anybody believe you're a gentleman, Hank Trammel."

Millie Trammel was five-one, weighed maybe ninety pounds, and wore her hair in a salt-and-pepper pageboy.

"Winter, I was just telling Sean you'll have to bring Rush and come out and have dinner with us when we get back. Next Saturday."

"So tell us about the trip," Winter asked Millie.

"It sounds exciting," Sean offered. "New Orleans is wonderful this time of year."

"We're leaving from Greensboro, which saved us a fortune, and getting in around three this afternoon. A friend of Hank's, Nicky Green—"

"You've heard me talk about Nicky," Hank interrupted. "Nicky's the one put the skunk in—"

"Please," his wife interrupted, "not that story *again*. He's only going to be there for one night."

"Millie only acts like she doesn't like Nicky. He's a laugh a minute."

"I can like Nicky for one night every few years. Actually he means well. He's just a little odd."

"Eccentric," Hank said. "He's a private eye. Works mostly for oil companies, that sort of thing. They kinda like his eccentricities, and he does good work. Travels all over the world."

"I recall you talking about him," Winter said.

"And you need to meet him one of these days real soon. His father was my commanding officer in Nam—boy grew up on Army bases. Nicky's forty, I think. Was a Western nut from childhood. Always wanted to live in the Wild West, and he used to get me to tell him all about what it was like growing up on the ranch. He did a four-year stint with the Army, but he didn't fit. Now he lives outside Houston, in Big Spring."

"He's an urban cowboy who's never ridden a horse in his life," Millie declared. "He has the accent and he dresses like he just stepped off the stage at the Grand Ole Opry."

"He drives a '65 Caddy convertible and he rides a Harley some. He's allergic to horses," Hank said defensively.

"He's bald, right?" Winter asked.

"From childhood," Millie said. "There's a name for it."

"Profeema, or propizza, or something," Hank offered.

"Alopecia," Sean said.

"No brows, not even any eyelashes," Millie continued. "It takes some getting used to. He looks surprised all the time. Always has a toothpick in his mouth, like he's just had a steak dinner. Awful."

"Well, it keeps him from smoking," Hank said. "How many people would put a skunk in the window of a motel room to flush out a cheating wife and her paramour?" He laughed as he thought about it. "Pair of 'em come out the door naked as baby mice and stinking to high heaven of skunk pee. Has it on video. I've seen it."

"So after a fun-filled night spent with Nicky reliving his experiences once again, we'll be spending the rest of the time with Kimberly and Faith Ann."

"Rush is very fond of Faith Ann," Sean said.

"If he told us to ask you to tell her hello for him once, he said it a hundred times," Winter told the Trammels.

"And Faith Ann's real fond of him," Millie said, chuckling. "That girl doesn't make friends easily. She's so independent and smart, it puts off most children her age. Kimberly was the same way. Knows what she wants. She wanted a child, but she didn't want a husband to complicate her life. She wanted to be able to pick up and go wherever her work led her."

"The Kimberly Porter Electric Chair Crusade and Traveling Sideshow," Hank said, drawing a frown from his wife.

"They've lived in interesting cities, like Houston, Dallas, Nashville, and New Orleans. It hasn't hurt Faith Ann one little bit," Millie said.

"Faith Ann has a built-in bullshit meter that would turn a seasoned Texas Ranger green with envy," Hank added.

"Hank Trammel!" Millie chided.

"Rush can't wait for her to come back up this summer. They instant message daily, e-mail constantly. He's been planning things for them to do," Sean said.

"We won't be here this summer," Winter reminded his wife.

"Rush and I have discussed that. Hank and Millie can bring her to Washington and stay with us. I'm sure she'd like to see the Smithsonian, the Air and Space Museum, the White House. It'll be fun."

"We would love to do that," Millie said. "That child's too energetic for me alone."

"Let's plan on it, then," Sean said. "How's Kimberly's practice doing?"

"She's struggling a bit, I think," Millie said.

"Kimberly Quixote," Hank said. "Always looking for a windmill to tilt at. And dragging Faith Ann along to hold the spear."

"Lance," Millie corrected. "I'm not always sure how I feel about things like capital punishment. But Kimberly has always known exactly how she feels about everything. She's an immovable object when it comes to her convictions. She isn't always hitting you over the head with her opinions, like *some* people."

"Her legal cases barely cover her living expenses. Soon as she starts getting herself a reputation—and she does win more than she loses—she moves somewhere else and starts over on sexual harassment or age discrimination or some danged liberal cause."

"I think it's good for Faith Ann to understand that believing strongly in something like justice is far more rewarding than making money practicing more profitable kinds of law," Millie countered. "And Faith Ann has never wanted for anything."

Hank told Winter, "All the Porter women since Texas belonged to Mexico have been cute as puppies, smart as whips, and as thickheaded and set in purpose as a mule lashed to a grist wheel."

Winter noticed Sean was being quiet, smiling but seemingly caught up in her own thoughts.

The waitress came to the table to take their orders. Hank contemplated the girl and leaned back slightly. "I knew this waitress once who reminds me of you. She wore a perfect three-carat diamond stud in her nose that an oilman gave her for a tip. Oh, it would catch the sun and would light up like a prairie fire. And this was before having things stuck through the side of your nose was at all common."

"That so?" the girl said flatly.

"Hank?" Millie's voice carried a note of warning.

"Well, one day at a chili cook-off at the state fair she went to sneeze, pinched her nostrils shut, and that diamond stud shot across the field like a bullet. Bunch of us got down on our hands and knees spent all afternoon searching through the grass for that rock."

"Hank, that's a terrible story," Millie groaned, shaking her head.

"But it has a happy ending."

"You found the diamond?" the waitress wondered.

"Heck no. She got the insurance she kept up on it and bought herself a pickup truck and a padded steel barrel and became a rodeo clown. But best of all, that hole in the side of her nose grew back in so you'd never guess it was ever there," Hank said, winking at her.

"I think we best order now," Millie said.

"Yep, the noon rush will be starting up any minute," Hank said.

"I meant while we still have appetites," Millie said, frowning.

4

Paulus Styer sat alone at a table twenty feet from where the two men and their wives were eating lunch. His gray ponytail hung over the collar of his button-down shirt. He tapped his fingers softly on the table and stared down at a folded newspaper beside his bowl of chili. Although he appeared to be reading and listening to music through earphones leading to a Walkman resting on the table before him, the small tape machine was actually an extremely sensitive, narrow-field listening device picking up everything the two couples said. After they finished eating, he followed them out, passing by them as they were saying their good-byes on the sidewalk.

Styer was a lifelong competitor whose professional life consisted of one chess match after another, and like any grand master worth his salt he was always plotting his assault on the next king he was sent after. He had been at this match, doing his own last-minute daily field study, for a solid week. That week had come only after studying his opponent's dossier, which had been gathered from every source imaginable by the best researchers and analysts in the world. He had spent two weeks prior to arriving in the United States studying those files, committing them to memory. The research phase was necessary to complete an assignment and assure his success. His style of working an assignment was time-consuming, but his success ratio ensured that he had free rein to be as self-indulgent as he liked. *What was Trammel's word for this Nicky Green fellow? Eccentric.* Oh yes, Paulus Styer was eccentric. Why work if it wasn't fun? What was the point of walking up to someone and putting a pill in the back of their head—running an awl through their medulla? An ex-marine could do that sort of thing for ten thousand dollars a hit. When you were paying for perfection, you wanted a guaranteed elimination, and cost was a secondary consideration. Paulus Styer, lovingly referred to as Cold Wind, was your man.

A block away, he climbed into his rented car and opened his laptop. Seconds later he was on the Internet, via cellular modem, accessing his e-mail account.

There was an English text message waiting.

Please furnish ETA on next delivery.

He hit Reply and clicked inside the message box:

Going to New Orleans. Advise client that the job will be completed in the next few days. Require immediate file on Nicky Green / a private investigator from in or near to Houston, Texas. I require two unconnected heavy-lifting assistants and an assorted #9000 tool kit plus vehicle on arrival. Flying this afternoon / Direct flight arrives in New Orleans around 4:00 this day from Greensboro, NC.

He closed the computer. Terrorists had made it virtually impossible for a legitimate, hardworking professional to travel with the tools of his trade. Having to have his weaponry delivered to the job sites was a maddening inconvenience.

He had spent several weeks in New Orleans four years earlier after an assignment which left him with wounds to mend. He chose New Orleans in order to listen to some Dixieland and to tour the places of interest he had read about. He had enjoyed himself and was glad he was returning there to work. The city would be a perfect environment for a hunt. He was tempted to charter a flight and beat them to New Orleans, but he decided it would be best to stay close to the Trammels and begin setting up the board.

A cold wind blows in the City of the Dead.

5 | New Orleans, Louisiana

Arturo Estrada was on cloud nine as he strolled into the River Club, where the cleaning crew was hard at work getting the place ready for the Friday-night crowd. His client, Jerry Bennett, was a short man who resorted to a girdle to hold back his expansive gut because he was too lazy to do the exercise that remaining trim required. Bennett sat at a table near the main bar, doing business with a woman who appeared to be a sales representative. There was an open sample case beside her leg, and several open bottles of wine stood on the table, along with stemware for sampling. Bennett saw Arturo, but he ignored him the way he might any other employee.

Arturo strolled straight back to the office in the rear. Jerry Bennett wasn't technically his boss, but he paid Arturo a seventy-five-thousand-dollar yearly retainer in cash that included odd jobs like making more difficult collections, plus a generous bonus for jobs like the one Arturo had performed that morning. In a good year, Arturo made a hundred and fifty thousand dollars from his one client.

For difficult assignments, Arturo picked a partner and Mr. Bennett paid the tab. It had been a good relationship for five years, mostly because Arturo had always achieved positive results and Bennett had never once tried to stiff him.

After Arturo had spent ten minutes cooling his heels in the expansive office, Jerry Bennett strolled in. Although his face was the hue of burnished copper, the white skin on his neck and the backs of his hands gave away the fact that his tan was pancake. The collection of fur-thick black hair of his toupee didn't match the mixture of gray and brown chest hair framed in the V of his perfectly starched white shirt. Arturo supposed that nobody had ever mentioned he looked like a silly old woman who made an effort to retain a youthful appearance but only managed to fool herself.

"Mr. Estrada, I have to go right back out there. I'm considering changing the house Merlot. And, with a nice enough order, I might just get a slice of that little wine representative. A vixen, a vixen for sure."

Arturo wasn't sure what a vixen was, but he assumed it had to do with sexual acts. "Good-looking sales rep. And she can give you an alibi for this morning, Mr. Bennett. Not that you need one . . . now."

Bennett's gray eyes blazed with excitement. "You found Amber! You did, didn't you? And you got *them* back?"

In answer, Arturo reached a gloved hand inside his coat, slipped the curved envelope out, and placed it on the desk. Bennett opened the flap and slid the photographs out just far enough to see the top one. Then he counted the corners to make sure they were all there.

"I caught up to her at some lady lawyer's office. The lawyer didn't make copies."

"You're sure?"

"Absolutely. I came in before she made any. I looked around. I don't know what Amber told her, but I know she was there only a couple minutes alone with her. It is possible the lawyer called somebody, but it won't matter, since you have everything back."

"Why did she take it to a lawyer?"

"I found out from one of the girls at the Moonbeam that Amber might be staying with a friend of hers named Erica Spicer. Erica was real helpful. She told me Amber was going to sell those to some lady attorney who's representing the man who's going to die for whacking the judge."

Bennett searched his mind for a name. "Kathy Porter?"

"It was Porter. I guess—"

"Kimberly," Bennett interrupted. "Kimberly Porter?"

Arturo nodded. "I guess since the blackmail thing didn't pan out, the lawyer was Amber's last shot at cashing in."

Bennett nodded slowly. "Yeah, that was the only move left. Myself, I'd have gone to the FBI with it, but that Porter bitch would have waved those papers in front of television reporters and then handed them to the FBI."

"She told me what building Amber was going to—"

"Who told you?"

"Erica, Amber's pal. I almost caught up to Amber before she went in. I had to wait until the janitor left the lobby. He never saw me and there's no security cameras there."

Bennett narrowed his eyes. "What about her pal Erica?"

"She had a little kitchen accident involving a toaster oven and some spilled milk."

"Good work, Arturo. As always. You're the best, kid. With the one notable, close-to-home exception."

Marta. Arturo's heart dropped. "None of my business, sir, but I'd destroy those," he said, gesturing at the envelope. "Souvenirs like those could prove very expensive."

Bennett raised an eyebrow. Then he unlocked and opened a desk drawer and removed a thick envelope, which he handed to Arturo. "I added what I owe Marta."

"The police have probably found them by now," Arturo

said. "The lawyer mentioned she had some volunteers or other coming in."

"Yeah," Bennett said thoughtfully. "Executions bring bleeding-heart pricks out of the woodwork. You earned your bonus. Take a few days and kick back. Bring a date to the club and dance. Invite Marta Ruiz. Class up the place."

"She doesn't like noisy rooms." He started to leave but turned at the door. "Marta didn't find Amber," Arturo said. "I did. I guess her fee was a waste after all."

"Well, Marta didn't find Amber, but she did handle some unpleasantness this morning. I wish I could afford to employ her full-time. It's nice to know she's around for the *big* jobs."

Arturo felt the burn of jealousy. It was a bitch the way everybody overestimated Marta's ability. She was good, but not as good as her reputation. The thing he did was man's work. People weren't afraid of Marta, she had no presence. *It wasn't her who got Amber's evidence.*

Arturo left the office knowing that Bennett was a seriously bent gear, and he was far too attached to his filthy old pictures to ever destroy them. Not that Arturo gave a damn. What Bennett did or didn't do about those had nothing to do with him.

6

Faith Ann Porter sat cradling her backpack to her chest as the streetcar made its way up St. Charles Avenue. Faith Ann and Kimberly had lived in New Orleans for a little more than a year. She stared down at the damp knees of her jeans and thought about her mother, whose blood was staining her clothes and skin. How many times the two of them had ridden those few miles together during the past months. Sometimes they rode the streetcar for the sheer pleasure of the experience, sometimes because the five-year-old Dodge Neon had some problem. Faith Ann knew the transportation routes, because weeks before she had moved here she'd gathered as much information on New Orleans as she could so she wouldn't be a stranger. Research, her mother always told her, was crucial preparation.

Faith Ann felt an involuntary tear rolling down her cheek. She swiped it away with the back of her hand. She didn't have time to feel sad. She looked out the window to see where she was. *Just one more stop.* Faith Ann wondered if she should go to school, act like nothing had happened, and wait for the principal to send for her. She imagined herself walking into the office, where two cops would be standing there to inform her that some crackhead had murdered her mother along with some big-breasted client named Amber Lee.

She couldn't risk it. She had to remember that the cops were her enemies and they had ways of tricking people with lies. Even if Amber hadn't said so, Faith Ann knew from listening to her mother that the police and prosecutors had their own agendas. You couldn't trust most of them.

Hank and Millie Trammel were her only relatives. Millie was her mother's older sister and about the nicest person you'd ever hope to find. Hank was big and could be intimidating, but he was always nice to her and her mother. She held on to the thought that very soon Hank and Millie would be there to take care of her.

Faith Ann let her mind focus on its image of Horace Pond, her mother's client on death row. He was merely a picture on a corkboard and a small voice heard once over the speakerphone in her mother's office. She noticed that her fingers were trembling and she clenched her fists. She needed to form a plan—to decide how to spend the time until her relatives came, but all she could come up with was to go home and change clothes. At home, it would be easier to think. At home it would all be better. She would be safe at home.

Faith Ann felt the streetcar slowing for her stop and she stood. When it stopped, she climbed down from the cabin, stepping onto the neutral ground. It was just three blocks to her house.

7

New Orleans homicide detective Sergeant Michael Manseur turned onto Camp Street and pulled up behind one of the white prowlers whose doors were appointed with a decal depicting a five-pointed star set in a crescent moon. He switched off his flashing blue light and moved it from the dashboard to the floorboard. The day was warming rapidly, the sun shining, but the weatherman had promised a cold front would be pressing through later that afternoon. Temperatures would drop into the fifties by evening. Manseur had caught the call so he would be the primary on this one, a doubleheader called in by a law student. With luck, this one would be a slam dunk and he could go back to one of the eight active cases on his plate.

Manseur grabbed a new spiral murder book and checked his pocket for the Cross pen before he stepped from the Impala, locked the door, and walked into the old professional building. A uniformed patrolman standing in the lobby pointed him to the elevator and said, "It's on four."

The detective pressed the button, and as he waited for the cab to descend he sneaked a sideways peek at his image in the gold-veined mirror tiles glued to the wall of the run-down office building. What he saw was a shortish man in a crumpled brown suit who was tapping a spiral notebook impatiently against his leg. He looked at the overworked, overweight, underpaid detective—a sad reflection. Behind his back, people sometimes called him Froggie, not because he was of French ancestry but because his face was wide, his lips thick, and his eyes seemed to bulge more than other people's did. He could see skin between the cables of dishwater-blond hair that he carefully combed over to hide his baldness. For years he had promised himself that one of these days he would invest in a hairpiece, but so far there was always something more important requiring his and his wife's salaries. But he knew that there were four things that were very special about him. The first three were his wife and two daughters, and the fourth was that he was an extremely good detective.

The ride to the fourth floor was slow, the cables supporting the car creaking, the motor laboring. The carpet under his wingtips was stained, the wood-panel walls scarred, the certificate of worthiness made illegible by the scratched plastic lens that protected it. Finally the cab stopped, and Manseur stepped out into a foyer whose floor was comprised of thousands of little white tiles. The border was formed of double black lines of small black tiles, accented at regular intervals with left-facing swastikas. Even though the tiles were laid into place a decade before Hitler adopted the symbol as his logo, forever trashing it, it was unsettling to see it used decoratively.

Manseur turned right and headed for the open door at the end of the dimly lit hallway, where uniformed cops were gathered. He heard the voices and put on his game face as he neared the crime scene.

He entered the reception room and cast his frown on a police sergeant, who was leaning back in an old chair and had his feet on the desk, telling a joke. "The fuckin' son of a bitch said he *likes* his coffee half full of hot sauce! I swear to—" The sergeant cut off the story and scrambled to his feet when his eyes met Manseur's. The other two patrolmen, who had been laughing, were struck mute. Their faces went red.

"What's the deal here?" Manseur asked the sergeant. His New Orleans accent made the word *here* sound like *heeyah*.

The cop opened his notebook. "Two female vics, forty-seven and forty-three. Multiple bullet wounds, probably from a .38. No brass. One is Kimberly Porter, the forty-seven-year-old. It's her office. The other is Amber Lee, forty-three years."

"Did anybody touch anything?"

"My people know better. The first officer was sure they were dead and came right out. Porter's law student, Napoleon Ferris, called 911 at 7:10. He's in the kitchen now cooling his heels. The janitor saw him come in, and a minute later he came flying down the fire stairs screaming bloody murder. Ferris swears he came straight here from breakfast at the Camellia Grill."

"How did you identify the vics?" Manseur was writing everything down in his own brand of chicken scratches and symbols.

"Ferris is last year Tulane law. He knew Porter from being a legal volunteer. Seems students can handle cases in their last year of law school. And I recognized Amber Lee. There's an outstanding warrant out for her—"

"Warrant . . . for?"

"Embezzlement."

"And how did you know her?"

"From the River Club. Amber's worked there for years and I think was the manager, sort of. I'da never figured her for a thief, but Mr. Bennett himself filed the charges."

"You knew her from the River Club," Manseur repeated, interjecting a fleck of suspicion in his words.

"I did some security work for the club back in the day," the sergeant said defensively.

Manseur didn't know Jerry Bennett personally, but he knew *of* him. Bennett was one of those "special friends" of the police department, the mayor, the aldermen and fire departments. That meant he was both rich and generous and carried a gold badge the sheriff gave him that allowed him to carry a firearm and could be used in Orleans Parish to avoid traffic tickets—and he would never have to pay one or appear in court, if he got one.

Like most cops, Manseur had accepted his share of *lagniappe* from merchants during his eighteen years on the job. As a patrolman he'd turned a deaf ear when a benefactor's car was begging for a parking violation. Sometimes he'd stopped a driver who was going a little too fast, maybe had suspicious breath, and let the guy skate. He had fixed tickets when it didn't matter. But proudly, he had never compromised his oath to protect and serve the citizens of New Orleans.

"Where's Detective Bond?" the sergeant asked. Larry Bond was Manseur's partner.

"Larry's in Baton Rouge. His father-in-law died. Be back Monday afternoon. Can we get back to this?"

"Sure thing." The sergeant nodded. "Janitor saw Porter come in around six with her daughter. Lee came in fifteen to twenty minutes later."

"Where's the kid?"

The cop shrugged. "Janitor didn't see her leave, but she wasn't here when this happened."

"And you know that, how?"

"She didn't call 911 or run to find help. He says she sometimes catches the bus to school from the corner. Her name is Faith Ann. There's a picture of her on the mother's desk."

Manseur finished making his notes and underlined the child's name. Beside it, he wrote two question marks. One represented discovering where the girl was when this happened, the second was to remind him to find out all he could about her. He would assume for the present that the schoolgirl wasn't here when this took place.

Then he went to the first door down the hallway and looked into the office. He could see both bodies from the doorway. Porter was to his right, the body lying limp behind the desk. Amber Lee's corpse lay to his left, facedown in front of the desk. Another ten feet behind Ms. Lee's corpse, a second door stood open. Before he entered the office, Manseur took a pair of shoe covers and a pair of surgical gloves from his jacket pocket and put them on.

When a seasoned homicide detective looked over a crime scene, it would start to come alive. As he gleaned more information, the film that was the crime came into increasingly sharper focus, edited so that all of the collected elements defined the drama.

Was Lee in this office to get help with the embezzlement charge?

He noted how she'd fallen and studied the pattern made by bits of blood and tissue on the floor and desk. He formed an image of Ms. Lee sitting in the chair and the lawyer sitting behind the desk. Since he couldn't yet make a determination of the perp's size or sex, he visualized a featureless silhouette standing beside and behind Amber

Lee, aiming a gun at her head. He noted the position of the purse, that the flap was closed and latched.

He squatted beside Ms. Lee and, using the bare end of his Cross ballpoint, parted her teased hair to examine the entrance wound located above and behind her left ear. The stippling and burned hair around the small round wound told him that the muzzle had been very close to her head. The exiting bullet had made a silver-dollar-size hole.

Could be a .38, a .32 revolver. If someone picked up their cases it might be a .380 or even a nine millimeter. That was something the medical examiner could tell him. *For whatever reason, you weren't looking at the killer when he fired.* He leaned down and noted the tracks on her left cheek made from tear-melted eyeliner. *Were you aware of the perp standing there? Were you crying because you were afraid? Or were you upset and didn't see him—or her?*

Carefully, Manseur looked at both of her hands and under the nails. Nothing. Done with Amber for the time being, he stood and went around the desk and looked down at Kimberly Porter. The dead lawyer's name, but not her face, seemed familiar to him, he wasn't sure why. He was fairly sure that he had never faced her in a courtroom.

There were two holes in Porter's blouse, located so close together they almost formed a figure eight. There was a third hole in her forehead—a safety shot. It made him wonder if maybe she was the main target, had been shot first. No, he was reasonably certain based on the splatter pattern that Amber hadn't been cowering in the chair but sitting upright, her face pointed at the desk. He saw the phone beside the lawyer, and in his film he imagined her holding it—perhaps trying to make a call, before or maybe even after Amber was shot.

He saw blood on the wall behind the desk and judged that Kimberly Porter was standing when she was shot in the chest. Her missing loafer was several feet away, resting against the baseboard. *Did you kick at your killer? No, it came off while you were rushing around the desk. You made it to the phone and picked it up before the killer fired. You went down, pulled the phone off the desk, and then he came around the desk and shot you again to make sure. Two that close together, fired from six, seven feet away, means he was a marksman and he was also a calm one. Two in the ticker, one in the head. A professional? Some client you didn't get results for? Someone who needed to keep one of you from doing or saying something?*

Manseur was in the zone. The film was running in his mind and everything else was a million miles away. He was visualizing paths of travel, bullet channels that when charted would define angles, distances, and even put a nearly exact height to the perpetrator.

He studied the desk. A framed photo of a smiling girl—a young face that reflected equal measures of cheer, confidence, and intelligence. Faith Ann Porter was maybe ten, eleven years old in the picture, had long strawberry-blond hair tucked behind her ears, big blue eyes. Also on that desk sat a Sony cassette recorder whose door stood open, revealing an empty tape chamber. There were several unopened cassettes stacked on the credenza and an open package for one on top of the desk. He looked in the trash can. The cellophane wrapper for it lay alone in the bottom. He made a mental note to search for a tape, but he was certain it had been removed by the killer.

When he looked back down at Porter again, he saw something else. There on the far side of and beside the body, barely visible in the puddle of coagulating blood, were two distinct circular impressions. *Knees.* Manseur imagined the killer kneeling there, but knew that a killer wouldn't get his or her knees drenched accidentally. *No way a pro would do that, and I'm dealing with a pro.* On the hardwood, just beyond the threadbare carpet, he saw something both interesting and alarming. There were circular, patterned tracks where someone had tracked blood away. The partial prints looked to have been made by a small sneaker. Faith Ann Porter must have seen her mother's body, and it would have been the girl who'd knelt beside her mother, her knees planted there when the blood was still running out from under the corpse.

Manseur had a daughter who was about Faith Ann's age. His mind raced as he tried to re-edit the film using new information. Was the young girl the motive for the killings? She may have seen it happen or not. The thought struck him that the child might have been abducted by the killer. Maybe she was wandering the streets in shock. Maybe she was fleeing from the killer. Maybe he took her somewhere else to silence her and she was already dead. But why not just kill her here? He had to find out all about Faith Ann Porter and do it very soon.

"Sergeant!" he called out.

"Yes sir?" the policeman answered from the hallway.

"Search the building. Top to bottom. Roof to basement. Have units sweep the neighborhood. Get a description of what the Porter girl was wearing. Issue an APB on her. Find out what school she goes to, see if she showed up there. Send a unit by the Porter house to see if she's there. *I need to get a search warrant for the residence.* You know the drill." He was barely aware of the sergeant parroting his orders into the radio.

Manseur followed the bloodied tracks. They led to a corkboard and appeared in the seat of a chair resting under it. Pinned on the board was a photograph of someone Manseur *did* recognize. Anger filled his hollow stomach. Horace Pond. A two-bit sack of crap who had murdered two people who caught him rifling their house.

Now he knew why Kimberly Porter's name was familiar. She was the conniving bitch who had been trying to keep that perverted piece of murdering shit alive. Horace Pond was going to die Saturday night, and no magic this lawyer could have performed could change it.

Manseur couldn't help but smile inside at the thought of that little low-life weasel taking the needle in thirty-eight hours, but he wished the powers that be had grandfathered in a nice long ride on a lightning bolt straight to hell. He was staring into the eyes of a dead man when the sergeant interrupted.

"Janitor said that there's a wall safe behind that corkboard. He says Porter had the combination changed when she moved in. And the crime scene unit is downstairs."

"Tell them to hold off for a few minutes."

Manseur used his pen to open the corkboard. Peering closely at the brass lever, he could see loops and swirls stamped there in dried blood. On the floor at the end of the table, someone had dumped out three textbooks and a composition notebook from Holy Cross School for Girls. "Sergeant, she attends Holy Cross uptown. Let's get this safe cracked open."

Manseur walked out and turned right. In the kitchen, a bored patrolman leaned against the counter watching over an ashen-faced and delicate-looking young man who sat slumped at a small table. He stared down at his clasped hands, the thin fingers of which were tipped by immaculate fingernails. Manseur sat down across from the young man, and when the kid looked up Manseur studied his eyes and knew the kid wasn't his killer.

"How well did you know Ms. Porter, Napoleon?"

"I've been helping her with two of her capital cases. I knew her sort of well. We weren't friends or anything like that."

"You weren't friends?"

"She was sort of all business."

"Husband? Boyfriend?"

"I only know they lived alone."

"What can you tell me about her daughter?"

"Faith Ann? She's smart as a whip. Doesn't talk much. I've only been around her up here a few times. She's kind of quiet. Shy, I guess."

"She and her mother get along all right?"

"They were super close. Kimberly always treated Faith Ann like an adult. She's way beyond kids her age in lots of ways. She can talk to you about most subjects."

"Did you know the other woman," Manseur asked, "Amber Lee? Could she have been a client?"

Napoleon shook his head. "Kimberly only does—did appeals on capital cases, so she wasn't a client. I guess she was either related to an inmate, or . . ."

"Or?" Manseur saw something change in the boy's eyes.

"She could have been the one who has been calling the office."

"Calling about?"

"A woman has been calling to talk to Kimberly. Wouldn't give her name. Kimberly mentioned she claimed she had evidence that one of the inmates on The Row was innocent and that she had conclusive proof of who was guilty. Kimberly said she thought the woman wanted money for whatever she had. Nuts come out of the woodwork any time a case is in the news or an execution date is coming up. Far as I know, her last call was Wednesday. I left early yesterday, so she might have called back."

"I didn't see a computer in the office." Manseur made a note to request a list of the dead lawyer's incoming and outgoing calls for the past thirty days.

"Kimberly had a laptop. She carried it back and forth from home. There's a printer both places. She was sort of frugal-minded. Drove an old car, wore the same clothes. But she was the best. She saw things that are invisible to most lawyers. She could have made big bucks. But Kimberly believed in justice, not money. You know what I'm saying?"

"Yes," Manseur said, closing his murder book. "I am intimately familiar with the syndrome."

8

Marta Ruiz felt as if she was standing between heaven and hell as ten high-pressure nozzles—five each on opposing walls—assailed her. She stood naked in the center of the stone-tiled shower stall as cold water stung the front of her body and hot scorched her backside. Her mind was far away, her thoughts as unfocused as the eyes of a newborn. Unless she was in a completely safe place, as she was now, Marta could ill afford the luxury of letting her mind wander. In her line of work, safe places were rare. The house, which she shared with Arturo, was located in the woods north of Lake Pontchartrain miles outside Covington, Louisiana.

Marta turned off the jets and dried off using a thick towel. She stood before the full-length mirror and studied the most important weapon she owned—her chiseled and finely tuned body. The first and most important rule in her line of work was to stay in fighting trim. When she wasn't on a job she spent several hours a day in her well-equipped gym, working out on the Nautilus machines to maintain her strength. Her five-foot-five-inch frame was as close to perfection as diet and exercise could make it. She maintained a balance in her muscle structure because being too bulked would slow her and limit her range of movement, while having too little muscle would cost her strength and stamina. She swam laps in the pool behind the house, ran ten miles a day, practiced gymnastic exercises to give her stamina, balance, and strength. She kept up her proficiency with a wide variety of weapons. She could slow her heartbeat and hold her breath for over three minutes. She maintained her peak condition—pushed herself because her clients paid a lot of money for perfection.

Part of her regimen included training in absolute darkness, using the sounds and scents of her adversaries for orientation. Her sparring partner was a sixteen-year-old neighbor boy who lived a half mile up a dirt trail that ran along the Tchefuncte River. On those days the boy came, Marta wore a blindfold and went weaponless, while he used a bamboo sword and tried to hit her as many times as he could before she disarmed him. She would pay him five dollars for every blow he delivered until she took the sword away. He had never made more than five dollars, but he kept trying harder, which she appreciated. Like a blind person, each time she played the game her hearing and other senses took the place of her sight.

She smiled at her mirror image. At twenty-nine she could still pass for a teenager. If she wore her hair short it would be easier to take care of, but she loved her long hair and so did men, which gave her an edge more important than an ability to disguise herself. She studied her face and how her hazel eyes, heavy black eyebrows, high cheekbones, strong chin, and full lips worked together.

Marta put on a plush robe, wrapped her hair in a towel, and went into the bedroom humming. Hard hands grabbed her from behind. The intruder locked his forearm tight around her middle, and pressed a blade against her throat. His body odor assailed her nostrils, but under that there was a very familiar scent.

Marta grabbed his wrist, pressed her fingers against the

back of his hand, and disarmed him. Effortlessly, she now held his trademark switchblade to his throat.

"Poor baby," she crooned teasingly. "Did the little girl get the better of you?"

"Okay, I give up," he said.

She kissed him full on the lips, both cheeks, and on his smooth forehead before handing back his knife.

"You have been sweating, Arturo," she said.

"It was a long morning."

She stood, pulled him to his feet, and embraced him. "Come and take a shower, Arturo. We can spend a few minutes talking. I've hardly seen you all week."

Marta led him into the bathroom, and while he took off his clothes she set the water to cascade from the overhead nozzles.

"How did you do that?" he asked, perplexed.

"I read the instructions. They are in the—"

"The contractor should come show me again. I wasn't paying attention to him before."

"I'll show you," she told him.

While he stood under the water soaping himself and singing, Marta picked up his soiled clothes and dropped them into the hamper. She would wash and dry them later, as she always did. As he lathered his body she sat on the deep stone counter with her legs crossed and admired him. He was the only man she had ever loved—ever cared about at all. "Are you hungry?"

"No. Just tired."

"I'll cook you something. I've got some of the wine you like and I picked up some prime steaks."

"I got a triple this morning," he said.

She shrugged. "So did I. That prick Cecil Mahoney and two of his little geckos. I just pinched off their teensy little heads."

"I didn't think that pig was telling the truth, but

Bennett did. Mahoney was insane. Anyway, I found Amber and got back the envelope. And I brought your fee. Bennett was pleased by your triple, even if it wasn't the right triple."

"I'm happy he was pleased," she said sarcastically.

"He invited me to bring you to his club tonight, but I told him you are a simple girl who doesn't care for noisy places."

"What I don't care for is bad food, boom-boom music, watered-down drinks, sweaty people, and flashing lights. And I especially don't care for your boss. He should work in a circus."

"He pays me good money and I have complete protection, which doesn't exactly hurt you."

"I handle my own protection. And I prefer working for different clients and taking the assignments I want to take. The money is better than working for a single person."

"Less long-term security," he argued.

"Nobody who needs our services can offer long-term security."

"So you don't want the piddling amount Bennett sent to you? Twenty thousand is not bad for killing the *wrong* people."

"It was good exercise. I helped only because I love you, Arturo. As always, I will back you up. Not for the money, but because you need me."

"I'll keep the twenty then."

"I will take the money and invest it, because you will only waste it on toys you can't be bothered to learn to operate. You are too impatient, Turo. That is a bad thing."

She stared at the lines of scar tissue scattered over his torso, made by knives, and the four familiar bullet wounds, left from three separate incidents. "You are like an alley cat, Turo. But for your battle scars you would have a perfect body."

"I think of my scars as a road map of my life."

His offhand comment filled her with sadness. "It isn't how you learn something, it's how you use the knowledge."

"Always preaching," he said curtly. "Church is out. I don't need your advice. I am a man, a professional, so let's drop it."

He cut off the water and dried himself with the towel she tossed him. After he had combed his hair and wrapped the towel around his waist, she said, "Even with the scars, you are just too pretty. Those long eyelashes, the brows, those big golden eyes, and lips any woman would kill to have for herself."

He tensed at the reference to femininity, as she knew he would. But it was true.

Arturo took her face between his hands, kissed her hard on her lips, and stared into her eyes. His amber-colored eyes held her soul and he knew it. "You love me."

"I love you, Turo."

"Love is a weakness. It will get you killed, Marta. That is my sermon to you." Arturo turned and left the bathroom.

After they ate the steaks Marta cooked for them, and while she washed the plates, Arturo sat at the table smoking a cigarette.

"I thought you quit," she said, concerned.

"I quit all the time," he answered. "I'll quit again tomorrow."

"It's bad for your wind."

"It relaxes me. I work hard so I deserve to feel good."

"Things that feel good aren't always good for you."

"You know, you should preach on television." He crushed out the cigarette and turned on the big plasma-screen set. A reporter was standing in front of an old building.

"Look!" he said excitedly. "I made the news!"

". . . And we understand that police are searching for a twelve-year-old girl, one of the victims' daughter, who my sources inside the police department tell me might have witnessed her mother and another woman being murdered. Authorities are not releasing the names of the two victims yet, but as soon as they notify next of kin I hope to have that for you. If you are wondering how the police can effectively enlist the community's help in the search for a young girl whose name they won't *release, so am I. It looks like it's going to be up to the department to resolve this. New Orleans detective Michael Manseur is leading the investigation. He should be familiar to New Orleanians as the detective who arrested Terrance Woodhouse last year for the murder of . . ."*

"FUCK!" Arturo screamed. "There wasn't no kid! I searched the place. It's a trick."

The telephone started to ring.

"Fuck!" he yelled. "That's Jerry. What I'm going to do, Marta?"

Arturo stared at the ringing telephone like it was a rattlesnake.

9

Faith Ann removed her clothes and dropped them into the hamper in the hall bathroom. Then she sat on the edge of the tub, swung her legs in, and turned on the water. As she scrubbed her mother's blood away with a washcloth, tears ran down her cheeks.

She mustn't be sad, she told herself. She had to think things through. It was as though her mother was talking to her, because she had always talked to her, advised her. *First thing is I can't trust the police. I have to get the evidence to someone who can stop the execution. Okay, Mama said that's Uncle Hank, because he knows the judges and the attorney general. He is coming here this afternoon to see his old friend.*

She thought hard about what her mother had said and remembered only that Hank and Millie were staying at a guesthouse. Maybe she could still catch them at home. She needed Uncle Hank to tell her what to do next.

Faith Ann dried off and went to the den, where she picked up the list of telephone numbers her mother kept on the side table. She lifted the receiver and dialed Hank's number. It rang three times and the answering machine picked up. Millie's gentle voice asked for her to leave a message. "Y'all, this is me, Faith Ann. I don't know where you're staying. I need to know because can I see you as soon as you get here because it is really, really important."

If Aunt Millie and Uncle Hank were on the way they wouldn't get the message. How would she find them? She would have to call guesthouses and ask if the Trammels were staying there. She fought down a sob. She lifted the yellow pages book and opened it.

The doorbell's melodic tones froze her. She stood there in only her panties, phone in hand, afraid to breathe. After a few seconds there was a pounding on the door and a voice calling out, "This is the police, is anybody home?"

A second voice, that of a woman, joined in. "Faith Ann Porter, are you in there?"

Faith Ann backed slowly up and peered down the hallway. Through the sheers, which filtered the light coming in through the glass panel in the front door, she could make out two dark shapes.

More banging.

A barely audible discussion for several seconds.

The doorbell rang again.

The police twisted the knob, and for a panicked second

Faith Ann was sure she hadn't locked it. But she had, and turning the knob was a waste of the policeman's energy.

The dark forms seemed to shrink as the two police left the porch.

Heart thundering, Faith Ann tiptoed to the front door and picked up her backpack. By peering around the edge of the curtain she could see a parked police car at the curb. She put the backpack over her shoulder and moved stealthily to her bedroom. She eased open her drawers one by one and removed jeans, a shirt, and a hooded Tulane sweatshirt. Sitting on the braided rug beside her bed, she got dressed as quietly as she could. She finished and looked up to see a policeman standing outside her window. He cupped his hands like blinders, and as he started to press his wide face against the glass Faith Ann ducked.

"Don't see anybody," a man's voice reported.

Faith Ann waited several seconds. Then she slowly raised her head to look at the window, which was empty. Would they break in? She wasn't sure, but she didn't think they could enter the house without permission unless they had a warrant. She knew that cops had to get warrants from judges, but she had no idea how long that took: on TV shows, it only took a few minutes. She didn't have much time.

Slipping her old cross-trainers on and lacing them up, she grabbed the backpack again and crawled out into the hallway. She sneaked to the front window. The two cops stood at the gate with their backs to her, talking to another policeman in another police car that had pulled up beside the one already at the curb.

Faith Ann moved back down the hall and, remembering the money, stopped long enough to get it from the pocket of her jeans in the hamper. She saw her mother's cell phone charging on the counter beside their computer and pocketed it. She also took the small Mag-Lite her mother kept beside the phone charger in case the electricity went out.

At the back door, Faith Ann looked out into the backyard, which connected to a city-owned basketball court. As she opened the door and stepped out, she heard the cops coming up the gravel driveway and saw a patrol car on the next street. Quickly, she pressed the locking button, eased the door closed, heard it snap, and slipped off the back steps. Then she pulled out the hinged lattice panel that allowed access to the space underneath the house but kept animals out. She crawled inside, then froze. Two pairs of uniform pant legs stopped inches from the crosshatched lattice panel.

"Watch this door until the detectives arrive. I'll get the car out of sight and take the front and side from around there."

Faith Ann crawled slowly and carefully toward the front of the house, the deep dirt absorbing the sound.

10

The patrolmen had searched the building and the streets for ten blocks around and there was no sign of Faith Ann Porter.

Manseur sat at the conference room table. The women's corpses had been processed in situ by Manseur and CSI, then rolled and examined again before being carted out by the medical examiner's staff. CSI was still processing the scene for fingerprints and other trace evidence.

Ten minutes before, a locksmith had popped open the safe and Manseur had gone through the contents.

As he mentally reviewed what he had learned, trying to finish building a clear picture of what had taken place around six-thirty that morning, he looked up to see Captain Harvey Suggs, the commander of Homicide, peering in at him from the hallway—leering was the most accurate description of the captain's expression.

Captain Suggs was heavyset in the way of powerfully built men whose steely bulk had shifted with age into thickly padded sinew. His wide neck supported a square head—hard features covered in red skin. The white flattop and bushy eyebrows added to the overall effect, which was that of a battle-scarred old Marine spoiling for a barroom brawl. His suit looked like it had been applied to him with a brush, and the buttoned collar and narrow tie looked in danger of choking him. On a daily, sometimes hourly basis, Suggs's facial expressions ran the spectrum from distracted to nuclear-powered raging. His rare smiles had nothing to do with any sense of humor or internal pleasure. If he laughed it was only because a superior officer told a joke.

"So, Mike," Suggs said, entering. "Give it to me in big spoonfuls."

Manseur hated being called Mike. His name was Michael. His parents called him Michael. His brothers called him Michael. His wife called him Michael. His partner called him Michael. Everyone else called him either Detective or Mr. Manseur.

The big spoonfuls took only a couple of minutes to lay out. Suggs listened intently and asked very few questions. Manseur went over what he had discovered in general terms. For ten minutes after that, he gave his boss the details, ran the film he had pieced together for an audience of one. He told Suggs that he was convinced that Faith Ann Porter had witnessed the aftermath of the killings, maybe even seen them happen, and might know who had done it.

Suggs had asked for the specifics leading to that conclusion, and Manseur went over that in detail.

"I see," Suggs said.

"Amber Lee had a warrant out for her arrest," Manseur said.

"And you know this how?"

"The sergeant told me. She embezzled from Jerry Bennett."

Suggs exhaled noisily. "Mike, I see how you got where you got to, but I have to say that I think it is far more likely that the kid is the perpetrator."

"I'm sorry?"

"She was here, and she didn't call 911. Her prints are on the safe in blood."

"They might not be her prints at all, sir. That has yet to be established."

Suggs leaned back in his chair. "I'm betting Amber Lee was there about the child. Maybe the girl was in trouble for something, and when Amber brought it to her mother's attention the girl snapped. Shot them and scrammed. She's out there armed and dangerous. I'm sure we'll find out she's unbalanced. You can't tell me that's *not* a distinct possibility. You postulate there was a professional killer who did this, but there's no proof. He was a good shot, you say. Or lucky. At this point it's just theory, and the theory you select now is going to affect the whole investigation."

"It's preliminary. Investigations change focus as facts come to light. I'm basing this on what I think is most likely at this moment."

"I know that Horace Pond was Porter's client, but there's nothing to tie that case to this. Some vague conversation that someone had evidence that would free some convicted murderer. That client isn't Pond, Mike. He's going to die tomorrow night. I was the primary on the Williams case. Everything was done by the book. We never laid a glove on Pond. The evidence was one hundred percent incontrovertible. I know Arnold and Beth Williams were your friends."

"I never imagined that client could be Horace Pond," Manseur said. He felt like laughing, but he couldn't definitely say that Suggs was wrong. Not yet, but he felt it wasn't at all probable that the girl had killed her mother and Amber Lee.

For ten minutes, he and his boss discussed the collected evidence and how it fit or didn't fit into each man's theory. There was no cassette tape on the desk, which Suggs said didn't mean one had been in the machine at all. Everything was supposition, but it occurred to Manseur that Suggs was systematically closing the doors that didn't mesh with his own interpretation of the homicides.

"I tell you what," Suggs said finally. "I'll make this easy for us both." He held out his beefy hand. "Notes?"

"I'm sorry?" Manseur said, confused.

"I want your notes."

"My notes?"

"You're not thinking right, Mike. You've been working a lot of cases and your partner is out of town. I'm assigning this one to Tinnerino and Doyle."

Tinnerino and Doyle? "It's my case."

"You're done with this one, Detective. I'm making it a direct order. Don't make me write you up for insubordination. You'll take the next case."

Manseur had no hope of winning. The thought of Suggs taking this case away from him was stunning, and his mind reeled from the blow. "You can't do that. I'm the primary. If I need a partner, I can work with Lieutenant Caesar."

"Can't spare her." Suggs smirked. "I think I understand

why you are looking at this from a skewed perspective. You have two daughters. It's difficult for you to imagine a daughter could murder her mother."

Suggs intended to give the case to two of the meanest, least intelligent, and most incompetent detectives who had ever carried a shield in New Orleans. The team of "Tin Man" and Doyle had the poorest clearance rate in the department and more complaints lodged against them than the rest of the squad combined.

"You can't do this," Manseur said.

"I sure as hell can. One more word and I will suspend you for insubordination. You want a vacation that badly?"

Manseur slammed his murder book on the table and stormed out of the office and down the stairs to the lobby. He went outside, climbed into his Impala, twisted the key, jerked it into gear, and punched the accelerator, squealing the rear tires.

11

The eavesdropper, Paulus Styer, had shed the hairpiece with its long gray ponytail and the loose-fitting clothes designed to hide his physique. He drove to Greensboro and flew to New Orleans first class, getting onto the airplane before the Trammels, who were flying coach.

Before boarding, Styer had taken a seat next to the couple in the terminal and had planted the C-13A long-range transmitter in the band of Hank Trammel's Stetson. Styer had asked the old guy if he might have a look at the hat, saying that he wanted to buy one like it for his father. As he had talked to Hank, Styer had slipped the tiny bug in place. The gray C-13A was smaller than an aspirin tablet and a quarter as thick, and Styer was sure Trammel would wear the trademark hat in New Orleans.

The Walkman in Styer's carry-on was turned to the transmitter's frequency. The receiver was armed with a Beatles tape in the event that the security officers wanted a demonstration. The officer had merely looked at the Walkman, asking him only to turn on his laptop.

Even if the Trammels had noticed Styer earlier in the restaurant they would not have recognized him at the airport. Now his hair was short and he was dressed in an expensive and professionally tailored suit. A driver's license identified him as Phillip Dresser, a thirty-eight-year-old from Chicago. His business cards, gold American Express, and MasterCard, supported the fact that he was the CEO of a company that sold commercial fire protection systems.

Of all the numerous characters he had created over the years, Dresser was a favorite, because Dresser traveled first class all the way. He often hired limousines, ate in the finest restaurants, and stayed in the best hotels. Most of his other covers made less money and lived closer to the bone than Dresser. All of the identities he had would hold up well enough under police scrutiny. In the unlikely event that he did get into a sticky legal situation, his organization would free him by whatever means required.

When the plane landed in New Orleans, Styer was among the first off. As he strode into the baggage area, he spotted his contact near the terminal doors holding a hand-lettered sign that read DRESSER. The man was short and stocky and wore a cheap dark blue suit. His square face sported thick lips, a nose that was no stranger to being broken, and eyes with irises like bullet holes. His white shirt looked as though it might have recently been stored in the glove compartment of a car. The knot in his too-short tie was the size of a lemon.

As Styer stood at the luggage carousel, he spotted the private detective, chewing on a toothpick, who waited outside the gate to meet the Trammels. Styer had obtained Green's driver's license picture by hacking into the Texas DMV. Green's hand rested on an ebony cane with a brass doorknob for a handle. The private detective wore a royal-blue jacket with white piping, a cowboy hat, and boots with high, sharply sloped heels. His eyes were hidden behind sunglasses. And he was completely hairless. Styer knew that Green suffered from a condition known as alopecia. Green's lack of hair and eyebrows gave him the permanent look of a man who had just been startled out of a deep sleep.

The intelligence file on Green was being updated now by Styer's researchers, arguably the world's best, since they had immediate access to almost any database—including channels into sensitive government agencies worldwide. The file had told him that Green had been kicked in the knee three years earlier by the enraged lover of a client's wife. The man had objected to the alienation-of-affection lawsuit that Nicky's investigation had made possible. The karate kick, delivered from the front, had destroyed his knee and given him a permanent limp, which is why he always carried a cane.

Green had spent his tour of duty as an MP, where he had learned investigative techniques, but his service record was merely average. According to his tax returns, Green had made one hundred sixty thousand dollars the previous year; not a bad living for a single man without bad habits.

Styer didn't expect any surprises. He could stay light-years ahead of men like Green and Trammel without breaking a sweat.

With the Trammels standing six feet to his left, Styer plucked his leather suitcase from the carousel. He walked briskly to the short man holding the sign. "I'm Dresser," he said curtly.

The man spoke without looking directly into Styer's eyes as he took the suitcase from him, using English that reflected his Eastern bloc heritage. "You are having a Range Rover. Your equipment is in it." He smiled broadly.

"That should be fine," Styer said in a perfect Midwestern accent.

In the short-term parking garage, the driver placed Styer's bag into the rear of an immaculate dark blue Range Rover and handed him the key.

The man handed over a slip of paper with a phone number written on it. "It's my portable phone number," the man said in Russian. "The aging Cadillac you wished to locate is parked now just over there."

Following the shorter man's pointing finger with his ice-blue eyes, Styer easily located Nicky Green's red 1965 Cadillac convertible some fifty feet away. "I will need you later, so remain available," Styer told him.

A silver Lexus 300 pulled up, and the stout driver climbed into the passenger's seat. "You have our number and we will wait for your call," the ill-dressed driver said, again in Russian.

After Styer watched the Lexus drive away, he sat in the Rover until the Trammels and Nicky Green appeared. He doubted Green actually wore such ridiculous cowboy clothes when he was on a job, because he was utterly conspicuous—a flamboyant spectacle, a hairless decorated monkey.

Hank carried his and his wife's suitcases. Nicky limped along using the cane to take weight off his damaged right leg. Styer took the fake Walkman out and put the earphones in place. He smiled as the voices of Hank Trammel and Nicky Green came up.

After paying the parking toll, Styer remained within a quarter of a mile behind the Cadillac, comfortably within the unit's listening range.

12

Faith Ann felt safe in the cool hide. It was easy to understand why a sick animal would come in there to die.

Soon after moving into the shotgun house on Danneel Street, Faith Ann had explored underneath it, and she had discovered a tin toy car and a few odds and ends abandoned in the dirt. In the cavity that had been formed when the concrete porch and front steps were poured, she'd found the mummified corpse of a small dog. She and Kimberly had dug a hole in the backyard and had given the animal a funeral, which included a hand-lettered wooden sign Faith Ann made that read HERE LIES A DOG, WHOSE NAME IS KNOWN ONLY TO GOD.

The under-porch was in effect a steel-reinforced bunker, with a cement ceiling and walls. Unless someone with a flashlight came inside the space, they wouldn't find her. Faith Ann sat with her back pressed against a cool wall. What she had seen in her mother's office came into her mind. She pulled up her knees and rested her head on her arms. And she cried, as softly as she could manage.

Faith Ann jerked upright when she heard a car pull up out front and two doors slam. Her watch said she had been hiding for two hours. Curious, she slipped out of the bunker and peered through the wood lattice, painted on one side the same dark gray as the house. Two men in suits strolled up to the gate, opened it, and came into the yard. The male patrolman came around from the side of the house where the small porch and the garage were.

"No sign of anybody, Detectives," she heard the patrolman say.

"I didn't think she'd come here," one of the men said. Faith Ann decided he was a detective.

"Maybe she's at a friend's house. Take your partner and go on," the other detective told the policeman. "We'll make the call if we need help. We have her keys and the warrant. We're going to search inside."

Faith Ann's heartbeat quickened. They had her mother's key ring. The idea of these people going through their things frightened her—but it made her mad too.

The patrolwoman came around, and the uniforms left through the gate. The detectives opened the door but didn't go inside. After several minutes, a new car, big and black, arrived and parked across the street. Faith Ann watched as the driver's door opened and a woman with long dark hair climbed out. Faith Ann was studying her when another figure came into view. Terror seized her because this man was the same man who had killed her mother. As he approached the gate, he combed his dark oily hair back. One of the detectives opened the front door as the pair approached the steps.

"She hasn't come back," a detective said.

"Where else is she going to go?" the other detective said. "Any adult she turns to is going to call the authorities."

"That's what we're going to find out," the killer said in his familiar Spanish accent. "To discover everything we can about her."

Faith Ann crept to the back of the house, fighting panic. Her chest was heaving, her stomach lurching. Above her, four sets of shoes battered the hardwood as they too moved toward the rear of the house. When she was near the grids covering the floor furnaces, Faith Ann could make out the voices, but she couldn't hear what they were saying. The killer knew she had his negatives and he was looking for them . . . and for her. And he was a cop.

She had to get away.

Faith Ann slipped out from under the house. Crouching low, she scooted into the open garage. Her and her mother's bikes were connected to a galvanized eyelet by a plastic-coated steel cable. Her fingers trembled as she turned the four numbered cylinders so the right combination showed. Faith Ann removed the cable and looped it around her bike's crossbar before snapping the lock in the loops to secure it. After putting on her helmet, she closed the kickstand and rolled the ten-speed slowly out through the side door, which opened directly into the backyard next door. She went around that house and, after pausing to tuck her long hair inside the sweatshirt and raising the hood over the helmet, she jumped on board and pumped the pedals furiously.

At the corner of Marengo Street, she turned left toward St. Charles Avenue. The cool wind blew into her face. Her skin stung a little because she'd cried so much. The backpack felt as light as a feather. School would be letting out soon, she decided. The sidewalks, buses, and streetcars would be filled with kids for the cops to check out.

When she passed a patrol car stopped at the intersection with St. Charles, she cut her eyes. The cop inside hardly even glanced at her. She guessed nobody had thought that she might be riding a boy's ten-speed.

13

Marta hadn't chastised Arturo for his mistakes. He hadn't had any reason to imagine that there was a young girl in the lawyer's office, and he wasn't sure the girl had seen him there. It was clear to the police that she had certainly been there *after* the killings, because there was concrete blood evidence of that.

Mr. Bennett hadn't said anything about there being negatives; just eight photographs, and there was no way to be sure that Amber hadn't hidden them somewhere before she went to the attorney's office. And Bennett told Arturo that according to the cops, there might possibly be a tape recording of the lawyer's conversation with Amber, since there were scores of recorded interviews in the lawyer's desk. The thing that caused Arturo's stomach to hurt was the thought that if the killings were recorded, his voice would be on it, because Amber had spoken his and Mr. Bennett's names. If there was a tape, and it wound up in anyone's hands outside the police department, they were in the worst possible kind of trouble. If that happened, none of Bennett's precious connections would be of any use at all.

The two detectives might have been thoroughly corrupt, but they weren't particularly energetic or enthusiastic. Having no real personal stake in this, they searched rooms lackadaisically. As Arturo was searching for information with an urgency fueled by multilayers of fear, he kept running into their backsides. As far as he was concerned, the two detectives were just unnecessary and potentially dangerous witnesses. While the short one dumped out the dead lawyer's jewelry box, the big one rifled through the refrigerator searching for a snack.

Marta called the detectives to the bathroom to show them that she had found the girl's clothes in the hamper. She pointed out the bloody knees in the jeans, the smears of blood on the discarded shirt.

The short detective took the jeans and found four blast-darkened .380 shell casings in the pocket. Those would match the handgun that Marta had planted beneath the clothes—the weapon which Arturo had used at the office. After noting that they had found it in the bottom of the hamper, the cops bagged it as evidence. They could collect the child's fingerprints and fix things so that a print would be discovered on the weapon.

Since the clothes were there, they went through the house again, looking for the kid.

Arturo and Marta searched for the negatives and the cassette tape. They found a file box filled with proof sheets and sleeves of negatives, which they took to pore over later. They found a dozen audiocassettes in a drawer. These Arturo put in the shopping bag along with the negatives. The cops collected all of the correspondence they found, including letters and bills, took the laptop computer and a lot of other odds and ends along with the girl's blood-soiled clothing, which they put in a paper evidence bag.

As Marta and Arturo drove away down the street, Marta looked into a cluttered yard and saw a bulldog standing up on its hind legs, its forepaws on its smiling master's stomach. In her mind the dog became a rail-thin, filthy, dark-skinned waif who was kneeling to unzip the trousers of a porcine policeman while a young, hungry boy watched from the window of an abandoned car nearby. She shivered involuntarily.

I had to do what I had to do, to survive.

14

Faith Ann spent three hours at the Audubon Zoo, wandering here and there, visiting her favorite animals, unable to take comfort from the familiarity. Occasionally she almost managed to forget what had happened that morning, but those terrifying memories kept returning, each time accompanied by gut-gripping fear and nausea.

She counted the money she had taken from her mother's safe and discovered that she had a thousand dollars. She bought herself a green cap advertising the zoo, curled up the bill, and kept it tugged down low to her brows. At four-thirty, as the sky turned gray and the wind picked up the scent of moisture, Faith Ann left the zoo. She put on her yellow poncho, covering her backpack. She unlocked her bike, climbed up on it, and started pedaling off just as the first drops of rain fell.

At six o'clock, after buying a Walkman at a Rite Aid, Faith Ann balanced herself on her bicycle at the pay telephone station, the last one of three mounted on the outside wall of the drugstore, and opened the yellow pages. The overhang protected her from the rain. Her heart sank. There were pages and pages of guesthouses. She didn't have any idea which one Uncle Hank and Aunt Millie were staying at, because her mother hadn't mentioned a name to her. How could she find them? A name floated into her mind. *Rush Massey.* A warmth filled her as she thought about her friend—sighted or not, perhaps the best friend she had.

Maybe Rush or his father knew where Hank and Millie were staying. If anybody did, she decided, they would.

Normally she and Rush communicated via computer using instant messenger or sent e-mails. Rush's computer was set up to vocalize his messages so he could respond on the keyboard. Faith Ann had visited with him on the telephone but all she could remember now was that his area code was 704. She took out her mother's cell phone and put her finger over the buttons, trying to recall which buttons she had pressed to get him. *704 . . . 79 . . . 704–795 . . .* And then her fingers remembered the entire number and she turned on the unit and pressed them for real. Leaning against the wall beside the pay phone, she listened as the cell phone rang.

"Hello?" the soft voice answered.

"Mrs. Massey, it's Faith Ann Porter. Is Rush there?"

"Well, yes, just a minute, Faith Ann."

After a few seconds, Rush's voice came on the line. "Hey, Faith Ann!" he said excitedly. "Did Hank tell you I said hey?"

She felt suddenly like she was on the verge of breaking into tears. She fought back the emotion. "No. Rush, I can't go into it right now, but I really need to find Uncle Hank right away. He's here in town, but I don't know where he is staying."

"He isn't staying at your house?"

"No. And I don't know how to find out where they are. I hoped you might know, because there's about a million places."

"Daddy and Sean were with them today before they left. I can ask if they know."

"Please," Faith Ann asked tightly. This felt like her last chance—a long shot.

Faith Ann wished she could tell Rush what had happened, but it wouldn't do any good. And she couldn't risk that he might tell his father. She didn't want to get Rush's father involved. Rush had lost his mother, like she just had, and he'd lost his sight in the airplane accident that killed her. At the moment, the fewer people who knew about all of this, the better. Hank could tell Mr. Massey later, when it was over. She only had twenty-eight hours before Horace Pond's execution. Hank could do something by then.

"Faith Ann, Sean doesn't know the name of it, but she said Millie said it's near Audubon Park. Does that help?"

"Yes." Faith Ann disguised her disappointment by infusing a positive lilt to her tone. "That will help a lot. Thanks and thank your mo . . . stepmom."

"Sure," Rush said happily. "Anytime. Sean says you and the Trammels are going to come visit us in Washington this summer. We can do all kinds of stuff. Make sure they say they'll bring you, okay?"

"I'll call you again really soon," she promised, hating to break off the conversation. It was the first time since early that morning that she had spoken to someone who cared at all about her. But she didn't have time to talk.

"Bye," she told Rush.

She ripped out the pages listing the guesthouses. She folded them and put them and the cell phone into the pouch in the front of her hooded sweatshirt.

A hand gripped her shoulder, causing her to lose her balance and slide down the wall as the bike's tire turned at a severe angle to the wall she was against. Her cap slipped so its bill covered her eyes.

"Well, well. What have we here?" a faintly familiar voice above her growled.

"A little criminal, right in our laps," a female voice added.

Gripping the bike's crossbar, Faith Ann pushed her cap up and found herself staring directly up into the faces of the two patrol officers who had been guarding her home earlier. Both were wearing rain slickers, and their peaked caps had what looked like plastic shower caps on them. Their cruiser was parked behind them. She'd made a terrible mistake. She hadn't paid any attention to the cars coming and going around her. They had her.

"Destruction of public property," the male cop said triumphantly.

"Vandalism," the female said. "We could run you in for that, young man. Put you in jail. What if somebody needs those pages for an important call?"

They don't know who I am!

"I'm sorry," Faith Ann said meekly. "I can put them back. . . ."

The cops both laughed out loud.

"Glue them in?" the woman said, snickering.

The male cop released Faith Ann's shoulder. He patted the top of her head. "Go forth, son, and sin no more," he pronounced, cutting the Sign of the Cross into the damp air.

"Thank you," Faith Ann said. She righted her ten-speed and, almost falling down as she started unsteadily away, rode off as fast as she could pedal.

15

For two hours, Paulus Styer sat in his stolen Rover as motionless as a turtle on a log taking sun. He was parked so he could watch the Park View Guest House, a three-story yellow and white mansion located beside Audubon Park, diagonally across St. Charles Avenue from Tulane University. As he watched, he monitored the conversations around Hank. The rain that had begun at four had fallen without letting up.

According to conversations he had overheard, Styer knew that Hank and Millie had stayed at the guesthouse on a prior visit to the city. Millie loved its tall ceilings, its ornate moldings, and the rooms decorated with antiques.

Nicky Green had brought the two Trammels there directly from the airport, and for half an hour he and Hank had sat outside on the front porch talking about old times and mutual acquaintances, but for reasons of his own Styer found it all of interest. Styer used his pocket telescope to watch them. Nicky wore the brim of his cowboy hat down to where his eyebrows should have been. He kept chewing up the tips of toothpicks then spitting them into the yard and putting in fresh ones.

Styer was listening to the conversation when Nicky said, *"I couldn't help but notice that you're packing a handgun, Hank. You think that's smart?"*

"I feel naked without it. You know. New Orleans can be a dangerous place."

The mention of a gun had Styer paying closer attention. He hadn't imagined that Trammel would be armed, and he figured the old guy must have had the weapon in his stowed bags. Styer would have to take that into consideration. He knew that Hank was a highly decorated Green Beret veteran who spent two tours in Vietnam. Styer was prepared for whatever opportunity presented itself that evening. He wore a double-edged dagger in an ankle holster, a .40-caliber Glock under his left armpit, and he carried a shortened, quick-snap noise suppressor in his jacket pocket.

Nicky continued, *"Well, strictly speaking, toting a hog leg isn't legal. You're not badged up anymore, and I doubt you have a Louisiana concealed-carry permit. How'd you get it past security?"*

"I had it in pieces in two suitcases. Let me worry about that. You've got a P.I. license. Tell the cops I'm your gun caddy."

"You don't need it. You know what I can do with this cane, and I don't have to dig under my clothes for it. Hell, I could knock a mugger out before he could stick out his tongue. This here cane's got a lead core and the knob's solid brass. I'd sooner explain konking some jerk upside the noggin than blowing a hole through him."

"If I need to shoot my gun, I won't mind explaining that to a cop, prosecutor, judge, or jury."

"Better judged by twelve peers than carried by six friends," Nicky pitched in. It took Styer a second to understand the reference to six friends. *Pallbearers.*

Millie stepped out onto the porch. "Hank, you need to come rest a little while before dinner."

"I'll meet you at the bar across from the restaurant at seven-thirty sharp for a pre-dinner cocktail." Nicky stood and he leaned over and spit into the flower bed. "I have a client coming by my hotel for a short meeting and I'll call a cab and meet you at the bar. We'll have a drink and go over to the restaurant, where I have us reserved up for eight sharp."

For most of the time before the Trammels left for their evening out, Hank's Stetson had been placed too near the room's television set for Styer to hear anything much but the programs and, when they were close to the cabinet, the sounds of them talking as they dressed. Styer had perfected his plan for the evening. He knew exactly how he would attain the prize beyond that—another checkmate.

He watched the Trammels get inside the black and white taxicab, which because it was headed the wrong way on St. Charles, would turn around to head uptown. Styer had the Rover started, the lights on, and was watching the cab in his side mirror. As the cab made the U and came back up the street, he pulled out into traffic to lead the way. Styer caught a flash of yellow in his headlights, and he had to brake hard to keep from hitting a young boy in a rain slicker who had come off the sidewalk and was riding his bike, hell-bent for leather, across St. Charles. The taxi bearing his targets shot past him. Lifting his cell phone, Styer called his helpers to tell them the time had come for them to earn their fee. One of them was in the Lexus, the other was playing taxicab driver.

16

Faith Ann had pedaled from the drugstore to an isolated gazebo in Audubon Park. Sitting on a concrete table, she went over the torn-out pages, calling the guesthouses she thought might be on a street near the vast city park.

After making thirteen calls without finding the Trammels registered, she read through the list again and one name struck her. The guesthouse was on St. Charles. She called it and asked the clerk if the Trammels were registered there. To her excitement, they were. She asked for the location and it was less than a mile away, so she pocketed the phone, jumped on her bike, and took off.

Within sight of the Park View, she barely missed getting hit by a dark SUV as she left the sidewalk to cross St. Charles. She swallowed the surge of fear the near-collision gave her. Dropping the bike in the grass, she ran inside.

Faith Ann's legs and feet were soaked from the rain, and inside the poncho she was perspiring. A skinny young clerk was on the phone and Faith Ann waited, feeling like she would scream. He finally completed the call and looked down at her. "Yes?"

"I just called to see if the Trammels were here."

"Yes."

"Can you tell me what room they're in?"

"They're staying here, but you just missed them. Do you want to leave a message?"

Faith Ann felt her heart drop into her shoes and her lip quiver as she fought back tears. "No I guess not. . . . Do you know where they went? How long they'll be?"

"I heard them say they were eating at Dot's Steakhouse. It's on—"

Faith Ann knew where it was, and she didn't wait for the address before running back down the hall and out the door.

17

The Trammels remained silent while the cabdriver complained about the bad condition of the streets, the rain, the Friday-night traffic, and the price of gasoline, which, since we "owned" Iraq, didn't make sense.

The cab's tires hit numerous potholes because in the rain they had become standing pools, indistinguishable from the pavement. Despite the weather, the restaurants and bars on the street were busy. Hank was pleased they had decided to use cabs so they wouldn't have to worry about parking or navigating.

"I tried to call Kimberly to see why Faith Ann called," Millie told him. "Maybe she called to tell us that they wouldn't be at home this evening or something."

"We'll see her first thing in the morning. I'm pretty sure

she's just excited about us coming," Hank said as the cab pulled to the curb outside the bar.

"If it was important, Kimberly would have called the guesthouse."

Hank climbed from the cab and he waited on the sidewalk for Millie to pay and exit into the protection of his open umbrella.

Together, they entered into the bar. Hank hadn't been there in four years, when he and Nicky Green had last been in New Orleans together. It seemed to him the crowd had been vastly different then—certainly much older.

"Reckon any of these people are legal age?" He had to raise his voice for Millie to hear him over the music and general din of socializing youth. "Times like this I can see how old I am without a mirror."

"We used to be this age," Millie said.

"I'll make a fast swing through the place to see if there's a table," he told her. "You stay here and feel free to stick your fingers in your ears if you need to."

Millie's expression was as unreadable as weathered-down hieroglyphs on limestone when Hank returned.

"There's one in the back, but it's in the line of fire, right near the speakers." He looked at his watch. "Nicky's running late."

"Can we go outside?" Millie asked.

When they went out under the awning, they saw that the rain had intensified.

"We could go across to the restaurant and wait there."

"You think? The reservation isn't for twenty minutes yet."

"Don't you imagine Nicky's a good enough investigator to figure out where we went? Surely he's smart enough to cross the street . . . to get in out of the rain." She laughed.

Hank frowned at her. "He's a good P.I."

"I'm sure a man ingenious enough to have a skunk on hand, then go about tossing it into a window, ought to be able to cross a street. A chicken can do that."

Hank had to laugh. "I suppose you're right."

A rain-drenched couple ran up to the doors laughing. They embraced and kissed before they entered the bar.

"Once we were like those kids," Millie said cheerfully. "In love in a bright fresh world."

"I remember." Hank put his arm around his wife, and she leaned against him. "That hasn't changed."

In a grand gesture, Hank pulled Millie to him and kissed her passionately before he leaned back to study her face.

He saw, but didn't see, the lines, the way her face had changed into that of an older woman. The gray in her hair mattered so little. To his heart, Millie still looked eighteen years old, with a face as smooth as polished agate. After almost forty years, he could still picture her as he'd first seen her—standing behind the counter in a department store selling perfume.

Millie looked over Hank's shoulder and tugged at his sleeve. "Look there. That child looks like . . ."

Hank turned. He saw a figure pedaling a bicycle furiously toward them. The helmet with the hood pulled up didn't disguise the familiarity of the drenched features. "Faith Ann," Hank finished.

The child leaned the bike against the wall and ran into the restaurant across the street. Through the restaurant's window they could see that the child, who looked exactly like their niece, was talking to the hostess.

"It's her," Hank said. He opened the umbrella, and they stepped off the curb. Immediately, Millie cried out and Hank knew she'd wrenched her ankle. She insisted she could walk just fine. So, supporting his wife and holding up the umbrella against the downpour, Hank looked up and down the street to check traffic. Not seeing any headlights close enough to be a danger, he walked Millie toward the restaurant. "What in the world is that child doing out in this?"

Faith Ann turned from the hostess and ran outside.

Hank asked his wife, "Where's Kimberly?"

"Faith Ann!" Millie called out.

Faith Ann saw them coming and her face filled with emotion. She waved frantically. Hank couldn't tell whether she was laughing or crying.

Halfway across the street, Hank heard an accelerating engine and tires on wet pavement as a car roared up the street behind him. There was no time to clear the thoroughfare, so he drew Millie close. Keeping himself between his wife and the onrushing monster, he formed the smallest possible obstacle and prayed the driver would go around them, since there was a world of room to do that.

He saw the child's pale, wet face—her mouth opening to scream and her eyes locked on his. He shook his head, praying for her to look away.

As Millie tightened her grip on his arm, he was aware of a sudden pressure and . . . the sensation of taking flight.

18

A single image had fueled Faith Ann's frantic dash to the restaurant. All the way over she pictured the Trammels sitting at a table in the restaurant, and she knew that, as soon as she saw them, she would finally be safe. She had almost burst into tears when the hostess told her that the Trammels weren't there, that their reservation wasn't until eight. With twenty minutes to kill, Faith Ann went outside intending to lock her bike and wait for her relatives to show. Then she spotted Hank and Millie across the street, waving at her and looking worried. Millie was leaning on Hank and walking funny. Barely able to contain herself, Faith Ann started over to meet them halfway but stopped abruptly when she heard the roar of an onrushing car. Hank froze in the middle of the street. Faith Ann glanced at the car, then back at Hank.

Unbelievably, the SUV didn't veer or brake. It just hit them. She heard the impact, saw her uncle and aunt launched up into the air, and stared after the dark vehicle, which sped off down the street.

For what felt like forever, Faith Ann stood frozen in the driving rain, stunned. Others ran into the street. Several people yelled, "Call 911!"

911. The police are 911.

Approaching cars skidded to a halt. People kept pouring out from the restaurant and the bar across the street, moving like a gathering mob toward the broken figures lying in the street.

Faith Ann reached Hank. A man wearing a jacket and tie was kneeling down beside him with his hand against Hank's neck. The man shook his head sadly, then went to kneel down beside Millie. Faith Ann looked down and saw that her uncle's left eye was open and rain was filling the socket. His face was sliced open and rosy water ran off it in sheets.

Feeling like she was being pressed under a great weight, Faith Ann left Hank and walked over to where her aunt was lying in the intersection, illuminated by the streetlight. The same man who had checked on Hank hardly touched Millie before he stood up, shaking his head. Faith Ann wondered if he was a doctor, because he didn't look all that affected by what he was doing.

Faith Ann stared down. Millie's features looked like

they had been mixed up in a red batter and poured onto her head. Her limbs were at impossible angles. Faith Ann realized that she was turning away—no, that someone was holding her by her shoulders, turning her around. The kneeling man wearing the tie was looking into her eyes and talking, but Faith Ann couldn't focus on the words. "Are you all right?" he said.

Faith Ann nodded.

"Darling, did you see the accident?"

She nodded again.

"Are you with those people?"

"I'm fine," she managed to say.

"Where do you live? Do you live near here?"

"Where are your parents?" a woman asked. She was holding an umbrella over the man in the tie, who was already soaked.

Faith Ann pointed back toward the restaurant where her bike was. It wasn't anything she thought about before she did it. She just didn't want to talk to the man any longer.

"She lives in the neighborhood," the woman told the man. "She'll be fine."

"Go on home," he told Faith Ann calmly. "This isn't anything for you to see."

She took a few steps, then looked back to where cars had stopped and people were getting out of them. Through the rain, she saw the strangest-looking man limping toward the intersection. He wore a long raincoat, a white cowboy hat, and matching boots, and he was using a walking cane for balance.

The man in the white cowboy hat removed his coat to expose a bright red suit with white accents. His belt was also bright white. He spread the coat over the body in the wet street as gently as a mother might cover her sleeping child, then went to Hank and knelt beside him.

A siren was wailing in the distance. Faith Ann turned back to the restaurant and joined the crowd on the sidewalk beneath the awning. She moved to her bike and put a hand on the crossbar. She tucked her wet hair behind her ears and snugged her hood.

She saw the blue lights approaching, but she remained standing there because she had absolutely no notion of what else to do.

19

Paulus Styer hadn't planned to run down the Trammels with the Rover. He despised the sloppiness of it. He liked precision, especially in his wet work.

He had the stolen taxicab waiting nearby with his driver, the second man. Up until the kid showed up out of nowhere, again, and screwed everything, the plan had been to see that Nicky Green never got to the restaurant. Then, when Green didn't show up, the Trammels would have called a cab, and Styer's taxi would have picked them up. He'd have met the cab a few blocks away and clipped them while they were still in the backseat. His stocky accomplice in the Lexus, two blocks away, was the plan's wild card—ready to do whatever Styer needed him to do. When Styer saw the Trammels come out of the bar and spot that kid, he knew instantly the plan was dead, so he'd pulled out of his parking space and mowed them down.

He was glad the child hadn't run out to meet them, because he would have had no choice but to hit all three.

After hitting the Trammels, Styer sped off, stopping only after he was far enough away to safely hand off the vehicle to his second accomplice for disposal. He had climbed out of the Rover and walked briskly on a parallel street back to the accident scene. Once there, he took a few seconds to admire his handiwork. The Trammel woman was obviously dead. Hank wasn't yet, but he would soon be.

Styer saw the kid in the overlarge yellow poncho across the street holding up her bicycle. Having her show up like she had had been a shock, and now that he was able to think it over he was certain she was the very same whelp he'd almost run over in front of the guesthouse thirty minutes earlier. He knew from eavesdropping that morning and through the afternoon that Faith Ann Porter was their niece, so this kid had to be the same girl. Styer had no idea why she was on a bicycle flying around alone in the rain, or why her lawyer mother would allow it. He wasn't really worried about her being a factor in his deal, because she couldn't have seen him through the Rover's dark windows.

Styer stood in the crowd under the awning of the bar watching the EMS technicians waste their time and energy trying to save Hank Trammel's life. Now that the Trammels were down and out of play, all he had to do was sit back and wait for his victim to come running into his web.

20

Detective Manseur had been at home, napping before eating dinner with his wife and daughters, when he got a call ordering him to respond to a vehicular homicide. Vehicular homicides were handled by Traffic, unless Traffic requested a homicide detective or the victim was a cop or a VIP capable of generating a lot of heat. According to Sergeant Suggs, this victim was in the VIP category. Still tired and upset over being pulled off the Porter/Lee homicides, Manseur parked short of the intersection, climbed from his Impala, popped open his umbrella, and surveyed the scene. Fifty feet beyond the intersection, where a corpse had been covered by a raincoat, an EMS unit was working on the other victim. Four patrolmen worked to keep the street cleared, the crowd back. Manseur walked over to the body, leaned down, and lifted the coat to look at the woman underneath it. Her crushed head was almost severed.

The detective looked up the street, trying to spot the point of impact; but due to the pelting rain he couldn't see any debris. He let down the coat and walked up the street to where the second victim, a silver-haired man on a cot, was being fed into the ambulance.

"How is he?" Manseur asked, showing his shield to the EMT.

"Has a very weak pulse," the tech, busy securing the gurney, answered impatiently. "We'll take him to Charity Trauma Center. Maybe they can perform a miracle."

Seconds later the ambulance pulled away, siren whooping.

A patrolwoman approached Manseur. "Sir, your eyewitnesses are under the awning over at the steakhouse." She handed Manseur two driver's licenses, which he read as she talked. "Henry and Mildred Trammel from Charlotte, North Carolina, were crossing the street when a black or dark blue Range Rover traveling at a high rate of speed struck them. All the witnesses agree that the driver didn't apply the brakes, just kept going. The driver never turned on his lights. Probably drunk. We're talking extensive front-end damage. Lots of glass back there." Manseur turned to look at the glass and orange plastic, much farther back than he had imagined it could be.

"Put a BOLO on the damaged Rover," he said, referring to a "be on lookout" alert.

"I already have."

"Good."

Manseur looked over at the restaurant and scanned the crowd clustered under the awning, then at the bar where another crowd was standing like an assembled audience. His eyes were drawn to a cowboy chewing on a toothpick, standing on the sidewalk, wearing a water-saturated red suit, and staring directly at him. As if he had been waiting for Manseur to see him, the cowboy limped out into the street. Raindrops splashed harmlessly on the stiff brim of his pristine white Stetson. It looked to be an expensive bonnet. Otherwise, the entire outfit looked like a stage costume.

"I'm Nicky Green. I'm a private investigator out of Houston."

Manseur hoped he was dealing with a trained witness. That would simplify his job considerably. "Detective Manseur, Homicide. You witness this?"

"No. I arrived a couple of minutes afterward. I was supposed to meet them here for drinks and dinner. I had a meeting at the Clarion that ran long, and I had trouble finding a parking space."

"Where were y'all staying?"

"I'm at the Columns. Hank and Millie are staying . . . *were* at the Park View. They're good friends of mine. I've known Hank since I was knee high to a jackrabbit and Millie since '73 or so. Hank was a U.S. marshal until he retired a few months back."

"That so?"

Manseur saw that either a cell phone or a handgun was pushing Green's jacket out slightly.

Green saw him looking at it. "I've got a carry permit," he said, opening his coat to expose a Colt .45 with yellowed stag grips. The right base cover was broken and the blue steel on the butt was scratched.

"Did you drop your piece?" Manseur asked.

"I reckon I did."

"I suppose it's registered to you?"

"To Hank."

Manseur knew the gun had been on Trammel when he was hit. It wasn't relevant, and he'd never be able to prove Hank Trammel had been carrying it. For a cop, carrying was a tough habit to break. He doubted it mattered. He noticed for the first time that Green wasn't just bald, as he'd thought. He didn't have any eyebrows or lashes either.

"Detective Manseur, Hank Trammel is a veteran who won a Purple Heart and a Bronze Star. He served the marshals with distinction for twenty years. You're going to find out that he has a lot of influential friends who'll be watching your investigation."

"Do you happen to know their next of kin?" Manseur asked, opening his notebook and balancing his umbrella by using his forearm to hold the handle against his ribs.

"Millie's sister lives here. Name's Porter. Let's see . . . Karen, no—Kimberly, I think it is."

Manseur looked slowly up from the pad into Nicky Green's shrewd brown eyes. "Does she have a daughter named Faith Ann?"

21 | Concord, North Carolina

Winter Massey sat at the table across from his son and, picking up one card at a time, appraised his hand. A pair of fives, an ace, a jack, and a three. Rush, who wore a ball cap pulled down low to make him look more like a dealer, set aside the deck. He lifted his own cards, fanning them so he could use his fingertip to read the dots located on the upper left-hand corner of the face of each card. He closed his hand and turned his head to his left, where Sean sat arranging her cards.

"Pot's right. Bet's up to you, little lady," Rush said flatly.

Sean lifted two chips and dropped them one after the other in the center of the table.

"Two to you, old fellow."

Winter contemplated his odds of drawing another five, then tossed in two chips. "I'll check to the dealer."

Rush placed his fingers on either side of one of his five tall stacks of chips and lifted up several of them. Without counting them out, he put them down on the felt and said, "Your two, and three more is the raise." Laying his cards down and lifting the deck, he said, "Cards, lady and elderly gentleman?"

"One," Sean said.

Rush said, as he handed her a card, "Okay, the little lady has two pairs . . . or might she be drawing to fill a straight . . . or maybe she is a card short of a flush."

"Three," Winter said.

Rush passed the cards to his father. "Read them and weep. Working on building two pairs or three of a kind, are we?"

"You're fixing to find out," Winter told him.

"This is my last hand," Sean said.

"Because I have almost *all* the chips?" Rush said, arching his brows.

"No, not merely because your father and I are both almost out of chips. Also because it's almost ten."

"I'll give you more," Rush told her.

"Absolutely not. I hate losing the same money twice."

"If Daddy wins, we play one more hand. Okay?"

"Okay," Sean said quickly. "Like that's going to happen."

"Dealer is standing pat," Rush said, laying aside the deck and lifting his cards. "Bets?"

Unbelievably, Winter had drawn a third five and a pair of sixes. *Full house.*

Sean bet five chips. Winter raised her a like amount.

Rush put in twenty.

"Perfect. I have only ten left," Winter said.

Sean pushed in her remaining chips. "I'll be light two." She laid her hand down. "Three aces," she declared triumphantly. "Beat that, Misters Massey."

Winter cut out three cards, which he put facedown on the table. He put down the other two faceup. "Beats my pair of fives."

"Read 'em and weep."

"What in the world do you call that?" Winter said, laughing. Rush laid down a hand devoid of any merit whatsoever.

"I was bluffing," Rush replied.

"You were trying to let us win," Sean accused.

Winter watched his son laugh. If you didn't notice the scar that ran from his temples, across both eyelids and the bridge of his nose, you would never guess that Rush was blind. Despite the limitations caused by his blindness, his son came as close to leading a normal life as most kids his age. Often it seemed that his other senses more than made up the difference. Winter hadn't thrown the hand to let Rush win because the boy was blind. He had thrown it because he didn't care if he won. He didn't at all mind coming in last in his home. Rush and his wife Sean meant everything to him.

"Did Mama call today?" Winter asked.

"No, Lydia hasn't called yet," Sean said as she gathered up the cards and boxed them.

"It's that new *friend,*" Winter said. "Distracting her from her motherly and grandmotherly duties."

"Her condo beau." Rush was grinning. "Gram calls about every single night. Think they'll get married?"

"Don't be ridiculous," Winter said.

Lydia Massey had moved to Sarasota, Florida, the week after Winter and Sean's wedding the previous March. She was dating a retired doctor who had a unit on the floor above hers. Winter had spoken to the doctor on several occasions and he seemed nice enough. It was just weird that his mother was dating.

"I have something for you fellows," Sean announced. "A present."

"What kind of present?" Rush asked suspiciously.

"A small one representing a very large one." Sean leaned back and opened a drawer in the Stickley sideboard and removed a thin, gift-wrapped package. She handed it to Rush. "Open it."

Rush tugged the ribbon off and removed the paper. It was a small silver frame.

"A picture frame?" Rush sounded disappointed. "So what's in it?"

"Nothing," Winter said.

"Why is it empty?" Rush asked. "What's it for?"

"That's where we'll put the very first picture."

"You bought a new camera?" Winter asked. Sean had

told them it was a small something representing a larger something.

"Nope. The first picture of the new baby," she said softly.

"A new baby? Holy shit!" Rush said.

"Rush!" Winter snapped. "Don't say that. Whose new baby?"

"Holy crapoly," Rush said.

Winter finally got his mind around what his wife had said. "Are you sure?"

"Absolutely," Sean replied.

"The doctor said so? That's why you've been sick?"

"You don't just guess at something like that," Sean said, laughing.

He stood and pulled Sean up out of her chair and hugged her to him.

"Winter, are you crying?" she asked.

"Of course I'm not. I'm happy!" He knew, of course, that he was crying. But they were tears of joy. "We need champagne!"

"We have champagne," Sean said. "In the fridge."

"Holy—" Rush started.

"Rush," Winter said warningly.

"Sorry! Do *I* get champagne too?"

It was a big deal for all of them. Winter didn't believe he could be any happier. He wished he could freeze that moment so he could have it to take out and relive over and over for the rest of his life.

The telephone started to ring.

"Let it ring," Winter said.

"Might be Lydia," Sean said.

"Gram is gonna freak out!" Rush said gleefully.

"I'll get it. I need to get some soap to wash out Rush's mouth with anyway," Winter joked. He rushed into the kitchen to answer the phone, certain that he was going to be able to share the news with Lydia.

"Hello," he said cheerfully.

"Is this Mr. Winter Massey?" The unfamiliar voice was heavily accented.

"Yes," he answered, still thinking of Sean and her news. *A baby.* "I'm Winter Massey."

Of course it *would* be a salesman, but for once he didn't care. From where he was standing, he could see into the dining room where Rush and Sean were actually dancing arm in arm. He wished he had a camera so he could capture the image. "So friend, what is it you're selling on this fine evening?"

"I'm Nicky Green."

"I'm sure you are," Winter said distractedly. "What's the pitch?"

"I'm a friend of Hank and Millie's."

Winter's mind downshifted and he started paying closer attention. *Why would he be calling? Maybe Hank put him up to something.* "Sure, I know who you are. Sorry, what can I do for you, Mr. Green?"

"Well, I hate worse than anything to have to call you, but I'm afraid I have some god-awful news. It's bad . . . I . . . I . . ."

The smile had left Winter's face, and ice-cold fear froze his mind. Hank's old friend couldn't continue because he was crying.

22

In the open pool cabana, behind the sleekly modern concrete-and-glass house, a fire dancing in the small metal-mesh wastebasket positioned on a slate bar top was mirrored orange-red in the lap pool's crystal-clear water. Marta Ruiz, who sat on a stool at the outdoor bar before a cassette player, was at the end of an hour spent going through the stack of audiocassettes she had taken from the Porter house.

"Not here," she announced.

Frustrated, she jerked the final audiotape out and tossed it into the wastebasket inferno. Arturo, standing outside the cabana biting his fingernails, uttered a long string of obscenities, then stomped around in the wet grass beside the rain-slick patio. Before listening to the cassettes, Marta had inspected each of the strips of negatives he'd taken from the dead lawyer and thrown them all into the same fire.

"I'm fucking cooked!" Arturo yelled.

"It isn't good," Marta agreed. "Let's stay calm. We don't know that *she* has them either. The negatives could be anywhere Amber was during the days she was missing."

"The tape . . ."

"If such a tape even exists," Marta said, trying to calm him.

"All the police saw was an open machine, right? Probably there was no tape inside it. But if there was, it has my voice on it, Amber said my name a couple of times! It has my voice! I think I said Mr. Bennett's name! It has the fucking *hits* recorded on it!"

"Unfreak, Turo," Marta said calmly. "There probably isn't a tape."

"That's easy for you to say! Your balls aren't in the vise."

"It's always counterproductive to freak. You are a professional. Anyway, Mr. Bennett doesn't know what might be on the tape, and the cops didn't find one."

"Oh, so now there *is* a tape," he said sourly.

"Whether there is a tape is not yet relevant to the situation," she told him. "What Bennett is most worried about is the negatives—"

"Negatives which he didn't mention," Arturo interrupted. "How dare that strutting rooster be angry with me, when he didn't bother to mention them in the first place!"

"Which also is beside the point. The tape can't prove anything against Bennett."

"Is *that* right? Oh, sometimes I forget you know *everything*."

"Insult me all you like, but I am the one by your side, Turo," she said. "Bennett is all right because what people say to each other about him isn't proof. Without those negatives to give those statements credibility and provide a motive for him sending you to kill them . . ."

"Well, if he *had* told me about the negatives, I would have made that stupid bitch tell me where they were before I killed her."

"Unfortunately Bennett won't be concerned with that," Marta said.

"But it isn't my fault!" Arturo yelled. "He didn't say a fucking thing about any fucking negatives."

"Watch your mouth," she scolded. "Foul language is the crutch of the ignorant."

"I'm sorry," Arturo said. "Mr. Bennett only said she stole eight pictures. Never once did he mention anything about any negatives. If he had—well, he didn't."

"Here is the problem as I see it." Marta's eyes were on

the flames consuming the tapes. "The negatives tie Mr. Bennett to a crime for which he can be prosecuted and perhaps executed."

"Executed for sure. Anybody sees what he was doing to those people, he's a dead man."

"That is his main concern, which for the moment overrides any others. I don't care about the negatives. It's a consideration, because one of Bennett's alternatives is to think that you have them and that you might use them to blackmail him. Another thought he is going to have is that you can tie him to the hits today and all of the jobs you've done for him in the past. And maybe he is going to worry because you saw his dirty little pictures.

"He will start thinking about cutting his exposure and punishing others for his mistakes. After this settles down, he's going to feel the need to clean up. I expect his police pals will help him do it. Or he might bring someone in. There's nobody local with the ability."

"He was stupid to make the pictures and to keep them. How can he blame me? Stupid . . . whore-painted face . . . potbelly . . . wig head!"

"Men like him don't ever think anything is their fault," Marta said. "We have to get the girl, because even if she doesn't have tape or negatives she saw you. And she certainly heard your name."

"Nobody saw anything. I didn't see her, and the place was small with nowhere to hide. I looked everywhere in those rooms, and I made sure nobody was there. I always check. The kid wasn't in the bathroom down the hall or anything. There were not any schoolbooks or book bag, which means she came in after. If she saw me from a distance outside the office, so what?"

Marta exhaled, and like a patient parent she said, "You say that all you like, but that girl knows about Mr. Bennett's crime and about his connections with the authorities. Maybe the negatives were somewhere in the office."

"I wasn't looking for any negatives."

She nodded. "It doesn't matter anyway. But somehow the girl knows, and if she has the negatives and the tape she is going to figure out someone to give them to pretty soon."

Arturo frowned. "She wasn't there. I bet she just came in and then listened to the tape. Maybe on the tape Amber said Bennett owned some cops or something."

Marta had to fight to keep from slapping Arturo. "A child who just finds her mother dead will not sit down at a desk to listen to some stupid tape before she calls the cops—before she runs for help. No. If the girl had come in from somewhere else after you left and discovered the body, she would have gone screaming bloody murder for help, or sat there in shock until the bodies were found. She's twelve years old, Turo." She pointed at her forehead. "Think like a twelve-year-old girl. That shouldn't be too hard for you."

"I can't think like a girl," he snapped. "Before you were twelve, you had killed a man already."

"Because the law didn't do its job."

"At that age you were screwing—"

"She is *not* like me," Marta cut in, suddenly furious. "Unless she knew that Bennett owned cops, she would have called 911 first. And because no decent mother would tell her child that sort of thing, Amber must have told the lawyer all about it and the kid must have overheard it. If there was a tape, and the girl knew about that, then she took it. If she saw the negatives she certainly has them. She was hiding in a cabinet, behind a curtain, under the desk, or stuck to the ceiling like a fly, or who gives a damn where she was. *You missed her!* She heard enough to know *not* to call the cops. That means she will have to tell someone else, and if she has the tape and the negatives she will give them to someone who isn't a cop Bennett can buy off. Maybe it will be another lawyer or a friend of her mother's. We have to find her first, or whoever is hiding her, and make sure that doesn't happen."

Arturo smiled and nodded. "Absolutely. Once we get everything and close the door on this, Mr. Bennett will trust me again."

"Comb your hair."

Arturo produced a comb and calmly put his hair in perfect order.

Marta watched Arturo, his pretty face painted by the dying firelight. She would find the girl and kill her. Then she would kill Mr. Bennett before he could have Arturo killed.

Whatever else happened, nobody was going to harm her Arturo.

23

Faith Ann slowed her bike, looked around, and realized that she had no idea where she was, or how she'd gotten there. After the police came she'd fled, just rode away as fast as she could go, paying no attention to where she was going. It had stopped raining, and her leg muscles ached. She quit pedaling, rolled to a stop, put her foot on the curb to prop herself up, and looked around at the houses. She read the street signs at the intersection, but the names didn't mean anything to her.

It occurred to her that she was tired, thirsty, and hadn't eaten anything all day but a zoo hot dog. She got off her bike and walked it across the sidewalk into the closest yard. Next to the concrete steps, she located a faucet and a coiled garden hose connected to it. She turned the faucet on, found the end of the hose, and drank for a long time. Her mother had never allowed her to drink tap water, said it was bad enough having to bathe in stuff that chemical companies up the river infused with all manner of foul wastes. But the cool liquid quenched her thirst and, for the moment, her hunger.

She had never imagined the world without her mother in it. Her Aunt Millie and Uncle Hank were old people, and she had known they would die. Later on. Now, in less than fourteen hours, she was utterly alone, an orphan with no home to go to. The legal paper her mother had drawn up giving her to Millie and Hank in case she died was meaningless now. There were other distant relatives somewhere, but her mother had never talked about them, so best Faith Ann could tell, Kimberly hadn't thought much of any of them.

Faith Ann felt more tired than ever before, and, under the poncho, she was soaked through from sweating.

She laid down the bike so it was out of sight of the street. Kneeling between two rose bushes, she pulled off the poncho and shook the water from it. She slipped off her backpack to get out the poncho's pouch and discovered the bottles of water, the ham sandwich, and the chips that were supposed to have been her school lunch. She removed the sandwich and chips, each in separate baggies. She felt the Walkman and the card containing four batteries that she had bought at the Rite Aid so Hank could listen to the tape as soon as she gave it to him.

The envelope containing the negatives and photocopies was dry, but the tape was unprotected in the pack. She wanted to listen to the tape to make sure everything was there but knew she couldn't open the thick plastic packaging that the new Walkman was sealed up in without scissors or at least a knife. She didn't have scissors or a knife. She might need a knife in case . . .

She had to protect the tape. She opened the chips and ate them slowly, savoring the familiar, dry taste. After emptying the baggie, she dropped in the cassette tape and sealed it. Then, unable to resist her pleading stomach, she opened the other baggie and ate the sandwich.

Light washed over her. Startled, she looked up: someone had switched on the lights in the house next door. A man in his underwear sat down on a couch in his den, turned on his big television set, and started flipping through the channels. He hesitated on the news, and Faith Ann glimpsed a picture on the screen of her mother's building. Police cars were parked outside it. Then a man talked into a microphone and a picture of her mother came on the screen. Faith Ann had to put her hand up to her mouth to keep from crying out. Lastly, the television showed one of her own school pictures. That one stayed on for a long time, and she thought there was a phone number under it. When the story changed, Faith Ann sat back down and had to wipe the tears from her eyes so she could see.

Sitting in the bushes, she thought about what to do. She wondered if the police were gone from her home yet. She needed to get some dry clothes, rest some, if she could, and figure out what she was going to do next.

She had to find someone she could trust who would also know how to take the tape and the picture copies to the right person and free Horace Pond, and it had to be somebody the Spanish cop wouldn't just kill. She was sure that after she did that, God would make everything work out somehow. She looked at her watch. *Twenty-four hours*, she thought. *I have to save Horace Pond. Help me, Mama.*

Faith Ann got back on her bike.

24

It was nearly noon when Manseur parked and went into the Park View Guest House. The clerk was reading a novel, which he set aside when the detective approached.

"You have a Henry Trammel registered?" Manseur flashed his badge and let the young man read it. He showed the clerk a room key.

"Sure. The Trammels are staying there."

"There was an accident. I'd like to have a look at their room."

"I don't know . . . You have a warrant or something?"

"I'm just looking for next-of-kin information. I can have a warrant here in an hour."

"I don't know . . . I should call my boss. . . ."

The call took only a few seconds. The clerk came around the desk and accompanied Manseur to the room. Manseur gave the key to the clerk, who opened the door. "He said I should watch you," the young man said. "To list anything you take away."

"Watch and list away," Manseur said.

Manseur looked around the room. The room was tidy, the suitcases beside the bed. The bathroom had used towels hanging on the shower bar, male and female toilet articles on the counter. There were some prescription bottles, an open dop kit, some makeup, a hairbrush, razor and lather, two damp toothbrushes bristles up.

He looked at the clothes hanging in the closet, then set the suitcases on the bed and opened them. The only thing he found of interest was a leather holster for a Colt and a partially full box of .45 +P ammunition in Hank's suitcase.

There was an address book and a cell phone in Millie Trammel's suitcase along with eight hundred dollars' worth of American Express traveler's checks.

"I want you to leave things as they are for a day or two in case I need to come back."

"This room is booked through Tuesday. I don't guess there's a problem there. We're like half full."

Manseur handed the clerk his card. "If anybody comes looking for them, or calls to speak to them, you'll call me?"

"Sure. There was a little girl here earlier."

"What little girl?"

The clerk shrugged. "She asked after the Trammels."

"She give her name?"

"No, I don't think she did. She was only here for a minute. Just after they left."

"Describe her."

"Tall, skinny kid. She was soaked. I told her they had gone out to eat. She ran out of here."

"Was she wearing a yellow poncho?"

"Yeah. You already know about her?"

"If she comes back, you call me," Manseur said, but he didn't think she would.

25 | Concord, North Carolina

The Masseys' home was a California Mission Revival, a yellow brick house with a red barrel-tile roof and arches defining the covered front porch. It sat in a line of other homes all built when F.D.R. was president. For the past hour, Winter Massey had sat out on the porch swing alone, looking out through the arch, but Sean, who had been taking periodic peeks out the window at him, knew he wasn't looking at anything that anyone else could see.

She had never seen her husband grieve, but she knew him well enough to know that he didn't require her company, hadn't invited it. Knowing that she was helpless to comfort him was painful to her. She had been fond of both Hank and Millie, but she had been closer to Hank because he had taken a bullet in his and Winter's effort to save her life.

Not being a relative made getting any information on Hank's condition impossible. Sean called a lawyer she had been using in New Orleans. She told him to tell the chief administrator at Charity Hospital that the Trammels had no relatives, just close friends named Massey, and that for certain considerations she was prepared to make a six-figure donation in the Trammels' name to the ICU. Twenty minutes after hanging up, a Dr. Russell, the chief of medicine, called her back. He told Winter that Hank Trammel had only a slight chance of living through the night. The physician said that if he made it through the first twenty-four hours, Hank's chances would greatly improve, although he would probably never be the same. Winter told Dr. Russell that he would be at the hospital in the morning.

Sean went back to Rush's bedroom, opened the door, and saw that the boy was sound asleep. Her stepson had been every bit as upset as his father and was also upset by the fact that Faith Ann Porter's mother had been murdered and Faith Ann was missing. It appeared that Faith Ann may have been there when it happened.

Neither Winter nor Sean could imagine why Faith Ann hadn't gone to the police or remained on the scene after Hank and Millie were hit. They agreed that Faith Ann was probably in danger, that the odds against the two deadly incidents being unrelated were astronomical.

Winter reasoned that whoever murdered Kimberly Porter must have run down the Trammels and was probably still after Kimberly's daughter.

Sean was in their bedroom when she heard the front door close, followed by Winter's slow footsteps coming down the hallway.

Winter entered the room, sat on the bed, put his arm around Sean, and pulled her close.

"You know, I'm really happy about the baby. I haven't seen Rush so excited in a very long time."

"I know," she said, hugging him. *From the highest high to the lowest low in a matter of seconds.* "Hank will be all right."

"And so will Faith Ann," Winter said.

"I want to go with you," she said, knowing exactly what his response would be.

"It isn't a good idea," he said. "Nicky is going to stay close to watch over Hank and be there in case Faith Ann shows up. I'm going to be busy from the second I hit the ground. I don't want to have to worry about you."

"I can take care of myself, Massey. Or have you forgotten?"

"I know that. But Faith Ann may call here. If she calls Rush you need to tell her to call me at the Pontchartrain Hotel. Or better yet, tell her to sit tight and you call me on my cell and Nicky Green or I will go to her."

"I just wish I could do more."

As he rubbed her shoulder gently, Sean looked over at Winter's packed duffel parked on the floor beside the dresser. Winter's cordovan shoulder rig—the straps spooled around the holster containing his SIG Sauer 220—resting on top of the bag reminded her of a sleeping serpent.

"You need to get some sleep," she said.

Winter stood, and Sean watched as her husband undressed. She pulled the covers back and he climbed into bed beside her, and without saying anything they held each other until sleep took her.

When Sean awoke before dawn, Winter was gone. She thought about how adept he was at moving around without making noise. She lay there thinking about him and his mission. She knew that he wouldn't have left her a note.

There was nothing he could say to her that she didn't already know.

26 | New Orleans, Louisiana

At daybreak, Detective Michael Manseur returned to the scene of the vehicular homicide and got out to walk it to look for things he might have missed. Only after the physical evidence had been gathered, photographs made, measurements collected, and witness statements taken had the street been reopened. Manseur wanted to take one more look in the light to make sure he had everything that was there to get.

On his scene schematic, Manseur had marked the point of impact to where the Trammels landed and the relative distances where incident-related objects had been found. Hank Trammel's Seiko, one of his boots, a twisted umbrella, a cell phone, a purse.

The broken turn-signal lens and paint chips were from a 2001 deep blue Range Rover, which had been traveling at approximately fifty miles per hour at impact. A matching Rover had been reported missing from long-term parking an hour before the hit-and-run. Its owner was a respected sixty-two-year-old heart surgeon with Oschner Clinic. Were it not for the Porter connection, Manseur would have figured it was most likely some joyriders, or a drunk had hit them and kept going to avoid the unpleasantness associated with bouncing people off the grille after having had a "couple of drinks."

A physician who had been in the restaurant described a child in a yellow poncho who had witnessed the accident, and the restaurant hostess said a child of the same description had asked for the Trammels seconds before they were run over. Manseur was certain the child was Faith Ann Porter, but he didn't make a note of that in his book, deciding to keep her listed as: *kid in yellow slicker—witness?*

The presence of the murdered lawyer's daughter on the scene, and the fact that the Trammels were relatives of hers, made this anything but a coincidental event. While he hadn't informed Captain Suggs of the connection, he would have to do that very soon or risk serious consequences for violating protocols. Under normal circumstances, since there was such an obvious probability of a connection, Manseur would have been involved in both cases. But there was something very abnormal about the Porter/Lee case, and if told the connection Suggs would probably hand this one over to Tinnerino and Doyle. Manseur suspected that Jerry Bennett's connection to the crime might explain the abnormalities.

Manseur read over his casebook to see if he had missed anything. He stopped at notes he'd made while interviewing a girl from the bar across the street who said she remembered the man because "that white cowboy hat and his mustache made him look like Wyatt Earp." Manseur looked at the list of found objects again. There was no cowboy hat.

While there were no cars driving by, the detective hurried out into the intersection, knelt, and scanned under the cars parked on the street. He spotted the hat under a Nissan truck and rushed over to it. Reaching under the vehicle, he captured the pale beaver-skin hat by its brim and pulled it out. Other than being soiled from its journey down the street and smeared with grease along the crown, it was a cleaning and a steam-blocking away from looking new.

The decorative band was a simple gray cloth ribbon. As he inspected it, Manseur noticed the slightest bulge in the seam. He peeled back the band and removed a plastic disk that looked like the head of a thumbtack with a loop of fine wire sticking out from it.

He didn't have any idea what the gizmo was, but he took an evidence bag from his coat pocket and dropped the object in. One thing he did know was that it hadn't come with the hat from the Stetson Company, and the fine wire looked suspiciously like an antenna.

Before he left the scene, Manseur put the Stetson in his car trunk and slipped the evidence bag into his inside jacket pocket.

27

Faith Ann locked her bike up in the tall bushes next to a tennis club two blocks away from her house and, careful to walk quietly, cut through the basketball court, stopping at the twelve-foot hurricane fence behind her house. She waited in the dark for fifteen minutes, listening intently for the sound of anybody who might be lurking in wait. After she was sure there was nobody in the rear, she slipped under the base, where there was enough play to allow her to bow out the mesh. Two doors down, her neighbor's dog started barking its fool head off.

She crept to the house, slipped under it, and crawled to her bunker. Faith Ann took off her backpack and placed it against the wall. Taking the flashlight with her, she crawled out of the bunker and checked for cops in the front and side yards. Satisfied, she hurried back to the rear panel that swung out, climbed out from under the house, and went to the back door. She tried the knob and found that it was locked. Reaching into her shirt, she pulled out her neck chain, on which she wore her house key. Carefully she unlocked the deadbolt, eased the door open, slipped inside, and gently closed it.

The familiar smell of the house soothed the sharp edges of her fear. She didn't dare turn on any lights, but she could see well enough to navigate because of a nightlight in the hallway of the shotgun-style three-bedroom house.

White-hot fear gripped her again, though, when she turned on the flashlight and looked into her room. It was in absolute shambles. Instead of a few clothes lying on the floor, which was often the case, all of the clothes she owned had been dumped from the drawers, themselves tossed around the room. Her mattress and box springs had been flipped off the frame, her clothes jerked from the closet, the plastic hangers still inside them. Glass from the broken mirror and from shattered picture frames glistened faintly from the layers of clothing. *Oh, Mama, why would they make such a mess?*

She spotted a cassette under her chest of drawers, the boom box shattered as if someone had stomped it. There was no label on it, but she knew that it was a tape of poems that she had written and her mother had put to music. Kimberly had often played it to hear her reading her goofy poems in a serious voice with god-awful icky romantic music in the background. She slipped the treasured item into her pocket, fighting back tears.

This chaos erased any notion she'd harbored that she could stay there. She scooped up another hooded Tulane sweatshirt and her pillow. She clicked off the flashlight.

In the kitchen she felt her way along the counter and took the scissors from the knife block. Kimberly had bought them from an eager salesman who'd demonstrated them by cutting a copper penny around the edge until he had formed a makeshift corkscrew out of it. She slipped them into her back pocket.

She went into the hall bathroom and closed the door. There was no window in there, so it was safe to turn on the light.

They had messed up that room, too. The floor was littered with hair rollers, towels, washcloths, and brushes, and they had thrown things from the medicine cabinet and the closet into the tub, breaking some of the glass bottles. Suddenly sick to her stomach, Faith Ann dropped to her knees and vomited into the toilet bowl.

Standing, she looked in the mirror and was startled by her own reflection. Her face was streaked with dirt, so she washed it. Her hair was a tangled mess. She looked down in the tub at the empty box that had contained the electric clippers that her mother had used to trim their poodle Luther's fur. Luther had wandered into the street and got himself killed weeks before they'd moved to New Orleans. Kimberly had kept the clippers promising they'd get another dog eventually. Faith Ann pulled off her sweatshirt, put a towel around her shoulders, and plugged the clippers into the outlet.

Taking a deep breath, she put the buzzing contraption under her hair at the base of her skull and slowly brought it straight up, stopping at the crown. Circling her head, Faith Ann repeated the upward strokes until only the hair on the top of her head was still long. Gathering the remaining hair together, and twisting it so she could hold it up, she was pleased that the plastic gap in the blades had left her hair a uniform one half of an inch on the sides and in the back. With only a vague idea of what a boy's haircut should look like, she set the clippers aside, got the pair of scissors from the dog-grooming box, and started cutting her way through the rope of red hair where it entered her fist.

After a few minutes hard at work with the scissors, Faith Ann figured she'd best stop where she was. Carefully she gathered up all the long strands of hair she could find in the sink, left on the towel and from the floor, and put them in the toilet. It took two flushes to clear the bowl. Turning on the tap, she carefully washed the shorter bits of hair down the sink.

As Faith Ann studied herself in the mirror, she fought back tears as she imagined how horrified her mother would be at the sight of her daughter looking like a baby chicken.

28

Marta and Arturo sat in her Lincoln Town Car, parked across the street from the Porter house. Marta was certain the Porter girl would return home, because she, like other normal children, lacked the skills to survive outside what was familiar to her. The kid had run straight to her comfort zone immediately after leaving her mother's office. Maybe she had seen the cops waiting here, but if she had, where would she have gone? Best the cops could discover, Faith Ann Porter didn't have any close friends.

There was no choice but to sit and wait like hunters in

a blind. If the cops spotted the girl, they'd call the two detectives downtown and they'd call Arturo and Marta. Problem was that there was no obvious trail to follow, no list of friends and associates. Marta glanced at the sleeping Arturo and could see the golden crucifix through his open shirt.

Marta thought religion was candy for superstitious idiots. She couldn't stand nuns or priests, crucifixes, statues, or paintings of the Blessed Mother or of Jesus with His cut-out heart suspended in front of His chest. The only thing the Catholic Church had ever done for Marta was to use an ancient padlock on their poorbox. Marta had learned to pick it by trial and error—finally succeeding when she bent an ice pick tip between two bricks and used it like a key.

As a child, Marta had lived by her wits and her ability to successfully read people and situations. She had learned her lessons by trial and error, and by observation. She'd watched foraging raccoons and seen how they worked tirelessly to figure out how to get to sources of food that people had done their best to keep from them. Because the raccoons didn't understand people and were greedy, the animals left a big mess, so the people they'd outsmarted always figured out a new way to thwart further looting. For several years she had robbed the poorbox of its offerings, never taking more than a small percentage at a time. Picking that first padlock took the patience and ingenuity of a raccoon. Like the animals, Marta knew if she were found out the priests would change the lock to thwart her.

Marta had learned that often when a job went this wrong, somebody got caught, and then that somebody talked. Once people like Jerry Bennett started trying to save their own skins, they'd throw out every name they could remember to the cops.

Normally, as a matter of self-preservation, she would

have already killed Bennett for his stupidity. Unfortunately, since this involved Arturo, she had amended her normal rules. She had to get the tape, which tied Arturo into this. And she would make sure there was no evidence in Bennett's possession that connected Arturo to any other wet work. Finding that out would only require having Mr. Bennett alone for a short time.

She had two methods of getting information out of a man. One was by using her sex. The other way, which involved her other skills, was infinitely faster and far more palatable.

29

Sean had made Winter's travel arrangements, so even though the plane was only half filled with passengers he flew first class. By the same token, he would be staying at a luxurious hotel. Left to his own devices, he would have flown coach and stayed at the first motel he saw. The truth of it was that nothing mattered but the task awaiting him in New Orleans. It was a bonus that he knew the city, had once been a resident, so he wouldn't need maps.

Winter spent the entire flight deep in black-cloud thought. He was in a dangerous mental place, suppressing an anger as intense as any he had ever felt. The closer the jet drew to New Orleans, the farther it was from his family and the blacker his thoughts became. How had this horror happened? Who was responsible? How would he deal with whoever was responsible when he got to them? Could he find Faith Ann?

Never had his job felt like a more futile enterprise. No matter how hard lawmen worked, seriously twisted people popped up faster than they could be chased down and dealt with. He was happy to let those who still believed they could win a lasting victory have it all to themselves. He would be content to simply protect his own.

At the end of his flight, Winter rented a gray sedan. After leaving the interstate and taking a couple of wrong turns because his mind was running in ten directions at once, he found a place to park on Tulane Avenue, a block from the hospital.

Charity Hospital was a concrete building constructed by the WPA during the Depression. The state-supported hospital owed its founding to infamous Governor Huey P. Long, whose philosophy, before his assassination in 1936, had been to give the common man what the rich had always enjoyed—or more likely just to convince the poor guys that such was his intention.

As he entered the building, Winter immediately spotted Nicky Green standing alone reading a folded newspaper. The private detective was easy to spot, since he was bald and wore a dark red leisure suit adorned with yellow piping and a cowboy hat. A walking cane leaned against his leg, a toothpick was clenched between his front teeth. Green glanced up, saw Winter, and folded the newspaper.

"Nicky?"

"You must be Winter."

"I am. It's a pleasure to meet you." Winter offered his hand and forced himself to smile.

Green gripped Winter's hand and shook it vigorously. "I been waiting for you to show up. The sons of bitches won't tell me what color the sky is."

"And Millie?"

"Morgue. Kimberly Porter's there too. Thank God Millie didn't suffer. The initial impact killed her. I expect they'd want to be buried in Texas with their people, but I don't reckon it's up to me to make a decision like that. I know there are cousins all over Texas, but I don't know any of them by name. I reckon somebody will have to look through the Porter house or something to find names."

Winter didn't know of any close relatives of either Hank or Millie, aside from Kimberly and Faith Ann. "I expect we can wait to see what Hank wants to do," he replied.

"I sure hope you're right. I should have told them I was related, but I didn't."

"Let me see what I can do about getting us in," Winter said. He went to the kiosk and gave the woman the administrator's name along with his own. She handed him a laminated red pass and told him that a doctor would meet him just outside the intensive care unit.

"I'll need one for Mr. Green," he told her. The receptionist eyed Nicky suspiciously, called someone, and gave Winter a normal white visitor's badge from a box on the desk for Nicky. Winter and Nicky walked to the elevator bank.

"They think you're family?"

"My wife has a way with people," Winter said truthfully.

The doctor was waiting at the double doors outside the ICU. He shook hands with Winter and Nicky.

Winter was glad the doctor used language he could follow without having a medical degree. "First of all, it's a miracle that Mr. Trammel is still alive. He is so broken up inside by the impact that we're forced to keep him in a drug-induced coma. The best we can tell from the tests we can safely perform, he has multiple fractured bones, most of his organs are certainly bruised, he has a serious concussion, and two vertebrae in his neck are broken. There's no massive internal bleeding that would call for opening him up. There's brain swelling we're dealing with, and we have no idea yet how the pressure will affect him down the road. If we do anything in the next forty-eight hours, it will only be because it is absolutely necessary to save his life."

"You mean like he might be a vegetable?" Nicky asked.

"I won't sugarcoat Mr. Trammel's condition. He could remain in a coma even after we try to bring him out, or have a stroke at any moment. Any number of things could bring about his death."

"We'd like to see him," Winter said.

The doctor handed them masks, and they slipped them on and followed him toward Hank's cubicle. Except for a symphony of machines, the ICU unit was as quiet as a chapel. A frail man who looked like he should be in a hospital bed of his own was seated by the bed of an elderly woman. He nodded impassively to the three men as they passed.

The rooms were arranged around a nurse's station so the medical staff could sit there and see each of the patients. The rooms were without windows or front walls. In the unlikely event that privacy was necessary, a curtain could be pulled.

What Winter saw lying in the bed broke his heart. Hank's swollen face had no more surface depth than a pizza—the texture of his skin was like the inside of a grapefruit after the pulp had been eaten. A plastic tube entered the islandlike tip of his nose. An I.V. delivered clear liquid to a needle taped to the back of his hand while cords carried electric impulses of information up into the monitoring equipment. The trademark mustache, if it still existed, was covered by the tape that held a breathing tube in Hank's mouth. His legs were shrouded in clear plastic braces that inflated and deflated every few seconds to keep blood clots from forming.

"Hang in there, Hank," Winter said softly. Beneath the calm words, anger boiled inside him. The taste of bile filled his mouth. Hank could die, and he was afraid of the hole that would leave in his life. When his own father had died, Winter had felt the sort of relief one gets at the end of a grueling weight-lifting session. James Massey had abandoned his family and had been living with a barfly in a flophouse in West Memphis, Arkansas, when he died of cirrhosis. Winter had only known Hank for seven years, but their relationship felt as if it had lasted a lifetime. Winter had transferred to Hank the affection his father had rejected, and Hank had treated him like the son he had lost.

He put his fingertips against Hank's shoulder. "Hank, you just get well. Nicky and I are going to take care of everything else. I promise you that."

30

Assumption Parish, Louisiana

Each time the battered pickup truck hit a low spot, a great gout of brown water erupted into the air and a wave of slippery mud covered the windshield of the Blazer with the light bar on its roof. The wipers could only swipe a couple of times before the truck launched the next curtain of mud. Sheriff Toliver cursed, and pumped at the washer knob until the reservoir was empty of cleaning fluid. The road looked as though great herds of feral pigs had rooted in it. In places, it came within inches of the sharply sloped bayou bank.

The sheriff looked up in his rearview and saw that the other county car, a prowler, was staying far enough back not to be splashed by his vehicle. His wife, belted into the passenger seat, kept telling him to hang back, but he was too mad to pay her any mind, and he wasn't about to admit that he *was* driving like an "damn idiot." Her sudden yelp brought his eyes back to the windshield, and upon seeing the red lights in front of him he slammed on the brakes, sending the Blazer sliding sideways. The sheriff barely missed slamming into the truck, which was no stranger to having its body smacked. The squad car trailing the sheriff stopped, and four deputies poured from its interior like hounds itching for something to chase after.

"You stay put," the sheriff said to his wife. He put on his cap and stepped out. "It's muddy."

She replied, "Make it fast, Buddy Lee."

"Won't take long. Wrecker's on the way."

"Yeah, right. I'm not kidding around, Buddy Lee."

They had been on their way to breakfast when the call came in. Helene Toliver peered out at the bayou like it was something that could attack her. She was not a patient woman; every time they were doing something together Buddy Lee always had some emergency call, and she became a prisoner of time, sitting like a lump in the prowl car.

The driver of the battered truck and his passenger looked like the same person at two different ages and weights. Father and son lacked meaningful chins. Their suspicious eyes, long pointed noses, pronounced overbites, and sloping foreheads gave them the profiles of small unpleasant mammals. The son's hair had a curiously crusty appearance. Both wore matching outfits with the overalls folded up into cuffs and flannel shirts with rolled-up sleeves. The Herberts—pronounced "Ay-bears"—were commercial fishermen and trappers, but their hands and clothes looked like they belonged to men who stood in close proximity to burning tires while they overhauled diesel engines.

"Where?" Buddy Lee asked the Herberts, wondering which of the father's eyes was the good one.

The lanky sheriff rarely spoke when a gesture would

suffice. His features were all sharp edges, the cheeks and edge of his nose trying to slice their way out, the bags under his eyes filled with something heavy.

"Ri-chonder," the father drawled, starting to raise his hand.

"Yonder," the son added. He jerked his hand up and aimed a finger out at the scummy water.

Standing among the knee-high weeds, the sheriff peered out at the wedge of metal breaking out through the algae. A cottonmouth as big around in the center as a quart jar glided along on the water's surface, unafraid of the men standing on the bank twenty feet away.

"Sa cah," the older Herbert said.

"Black 'un," the young man added in case his father wasn't believed.

"Appears somebody drove it off in the water," the sheriff said to the deputies and the Herberts. "Insurance fraud."

"Maybe he drove off and he's still in it?" a deputy suggested, almost hopefully.

The sheriff frowned, shook his head.

"Mine fi shoot dat snake?"

The sheriff turned to watch the older Herbert pluck a weathered shotgun from the cab of the Ford and break it to load in a single shell. "Okay, just don't shoot the damned car."

There was a boom and the water moccasin, halved by the blast, sank out of sight.

By the time the diver and the tow truck arrived, Helene Toliver's breathing had fogged all the Blazer's windows. All Buddy Lee could see was the suggestion of his wife's yellow hair, which looked like cotton candy.

The diver hooked a cable to the submerged vehicle.

The tow truck's gears ground as it dragged the water-filled Rover, on its left side, up the steep slope.

"It hit something pretty good," a deputy said, pointing to the damaged front end. He cupped his hands trying to see through the opaque windows. "Charlie, I'll boost you up," he told another deputy as he locked his hands to form a stirrup. "It looks to be all burnt up inside. Wait a minute. I can see something moving, but it's too dark to make it out. I need a flashlight."

The sheriff went to his Blazer for his Mag-Lite.

"Just a few more minutes," he mumbled. His wife had the look of a woman about to ask him to check the bottoms of his boots for what she was smelling.

Buddy Lee handed his Mag-Lite up to the deputy, who aimed the beam down into the Rover's interior.

"Sure was set on fire. It's a man in it, looks like a nigrah! His clothes was burnt right off his back."

"Was a bulletin this morning about a dark blue Rover involved in a hit-and-run in New Orleans last night," the sheriff said. "Said it would have front-end damage—a busted light and turn signal."

"What you saw moving?" a deputy called up.

"Damn, Roy, it was in the bayou, what the hell you think it is?"

The young fisherman looked at his father, raised his hands up and mimicked claws pinching the air. "Trabs," he said, smiling like the word made him hungry.

31

The Pontchartrain Hotel had stood at 2031 St. Charles Avenue, with its right shoulder against Josephine Street, since 1927. A large canvas awning extended from the front alcove out over the sidewalk to protect guests from being inconvenienced by weather.

Winter drove the rental sedan with Nicky's fire-engine red 1965 Cadillac convertible following behind. He and Nicky parked on St. Charles, a block down from the hotel. Winter carried his duffel by its shoulder strap. Nobody noticed him because Nicky Green's outfit effectively made his companion invisible. As they approached the desk, the clerk stopped what he was doing and stared at Nicky.

"Winter Massey," Winter said.

"Yes, Mr. Massey," the clerk said to Nicky. "Your suite is waiting."

"*He's* Massey." Nicky inclined his head toward Winter.

The clerk's face reddened, and he reached down for the electronic key. "Mr. Massey. Everything is in order," he said, meaning that Sean had handled everything with her typical efficiency.

The clerk signaled the bellboy, but Winter shook his head and took the key folder. "I think between Mr. Green and myself, we can find the room without assistance."

"Nice hotel," Nicky remarked as they entered the elevator.

"My wife picked it," Winter said truthfully.

Winter's suite had once been a luxurious apartment containing 1,200 square feet of space furnished with antiques. Other than the obligatory placard in a brass frame on the inside of the door, there was nothing to indicate it was a hotel suite. Beyond the living room there was a dining room and, beyond it, the kitchen. To the left was a hallway where the bedrooms would be located.

Winter took his bag with him into the hallway. After looking into all three bedrooms, he entered the largest of them, threw his duffel on the four-poster bed, and excused himself for a bathroom stop.

"This spread is pert' near big as my whole dad-blasted house," Nicky said when Winter came into the living room.

Winter spotted a folded *Times-Picayune* on the coffee table. The headline read: "Death Row Attorney Murdered." Winter lifted it and looked at the picture of Kimberly Porter, who bore a resemblance to her older sister, Millie. He had met Kimberly only once, when she had driven her daughter to North Carolina. Faith Ann had visited the Trammels for a month every summer since Winter had been in Charlotte. He scanned the story, which contained very little useful information. The word *ironic* was used five times to describe the murder. The reporter was implying that her killer had probably canceled out his best chance to avoid getting a "hot shot" compliments of the state.

The second victim, Amber Lee, was referred to as a client. The story mentioned that Ms. Lee, a nightclub worker, had been the subject of a warrant for embezzlement. It implied that Ms. Lee was in the office for legal representation. The police obviously hadn't given the media enough information to allow them to craft a real story, so they filled the space with unrelated table scraps.

There was a much smaller picture of Faith Ann on the lower section of the front page. The caption below it said the police were asking for help in locating the murdered woman's missing daughter. The copy stated that the twelve-year-old was "being sought for questioning" and for anybody who spotted her to immediately call the detective bureau. It gave a telephone number.

"Faith Ann is a suspect," Winter said.

"When I mentioned that Kimberly Porter was the Trammels' next of kin, the news hit Detective Manseur like a slaughterhouse sledgehammer. Manseur didn't say so, but he recognized your name when I said I'd best call you, since you and Hank are such close friends."

"What exactly did Manseur tell you?"

"Not much really. He said just enough to get me to thinking. I called somebody with local P.D. knowledge and they told me Manseur is a top investigator with NOPD. He don't look like much—reminds me of that old cartoon dog cop, Droopy, with the hangy-down face, and he talks real slow—but that old dog always gets the bad guy. The two detectives that were assigned to it aren't guys with Manseur's reputation."

"Did he say Faith Ann was a suspect?"

"Manseur's a pro. He didn't come out and say much of anything. While he was sort of vague about Faith Ann, he said if I saw her, I should call him *first*. I learned that he was the primary on the Porter double homicide, but he was pulled off it by his chief, a fellow named Harvey Suggs. Suggs is an ex-marine, beat cop who worked his way up. Made it through when they did that big corrupt-cop cleanup a few years back. Lots of high-profile cases under his belt. He might give you the facts."

"Most cops won't give up anything to a federal officer they don't have to, especially one without any standing. I'll talk to Manseur first. You have his number?"

Nicky took a business card from his shirt pocket and handed it to Winter.

Winter dialed the number and got forwarded directly to Manseur's voice mail. He left Manseur the name of the hotel, the room number, and his cell phone number as well.

"We hadn't talked about it yet," Nicky told Winter, "but I sure want to help you get to the bottom of this mess. I'm just a civilian snoop, and I know all about how good you are from Hank, but I can give a decent account for myself at investigating, and I'm a fair hand at knocking the stuffing out of people if they ask for it. I'll do whatever it takes to help you find Faith Ann and track down who ran down Hank and Millie. And if you won't, I expect we'll be stepping all over each other on account of I ain't about to let the bushwhacking bastard get away with it."

"Where're you staying?" Winter asked.

"Well, I was at the Columns till this morning, but I have to find a new place on account of I was only registered until noon today and they rented the room out from under me. I need to get checked into a new place."

"Unless you require more than two bedrooms, pick one of the two I'm not parked in."

"It makes sense for us to bunk together."

Winter rubbed his hands together. "Then let's get started."

"There's something I should mention," Nicky said, pointing to the paper. "Earlier at the hospital, I was looking at that picture of that little girl. I thought that maybe she looks familiar because she reminds me of Millie. I mean, I was real upset last night, but I'm thinking that maybe I saw Faith Ann there, at the scene. If it was her, she was standing around in the crowd wearing a yellow raincoat. She looked upset and, if it really was her, she had a good reason to be that way. But far as I know she didn't talk to the cops. Not while I was there, anyhow. I was thinking that, if it was the kid, why didn't she say so?"

"Why would *she* have been *there*?"

"I'm not saying it was her," Nicky said. "That photo just looks like that child I saw. Maybe. I'm not sure."

32

Faith Ann's favorite day of the week had always been Saturday, because it was a day she always spent with her mother doing pretty much what she liked. Either they went to a movie, the museum, a concert, or just walked around in the French Quarter dropping into galleries and shops. They had family passes for Audubon Zoo and the Aquarium of the Americas on the Mississippi River. Today would be the first different Saturday.

Faith Ann used the small Mag-Lite, as she needed it to see in the dark bunker beneath her home. She used the kitchen shears to free the Walkman from its plastic cocoon. She put in the batteries and slipped on the earplug-style phones. She put in her tape, rewound it, and pressed Play. The sound of her mother's voice coming through the earphones filled her with a deep, painful sadness. As the tape played, however, that emptiness changed into anger that she directed at the Spanish policeman who had killed her mother. After the tape ended, she turned off the player and took off the earphones. Without the earphones, the player just fit inside the sandwich bag. She laid out the poncho on the dirt and lay down in the darkness with her head resting on her pillow. She scrunched herself up into a fetal curl, buried her hands in the pouch of her sweatshirt, and stared into the shadows.

An image of Horace Pond formed in her mind. In a way, although he hadn't done the murders he was supposed to die for doing, he was kind of responsible for two. It seemed to Faith Ann that if her mother hadn't been Horace Pond's appeals attorney, she would be alive, because Amber wouldn't have ever called her. Faith Ann found herself wishing that Horace Pond had been guilty and that Amber hadn't had any evidence to prove he wasn't guilty of killing that judge and his wife. But Uncle Hank had often said, "What is, is." It meant that you can only deal with the reality of a situation. That reality was that she had to do something or Horace Pond would die that night. *But what?*

God, as you know, Mama and I don't spent much time in your church. Please bless my Mama, Uncle Hank, and my Aunt Millie, who are all up there with you in Heaven. Tell them that I love them.

You know, you and me are about the only ones that know Horace Pond isn't a murderer. And just us know that Jerry man told the Spanish policeman to shoot Mama and Amber. God, we both know they'll kill me if they can get hold of me and I'm really scared to get killed, but it isn't because I don't want to go to Heaven or anything because I'm sure it's really nice. Please, Sir, I really, really, hope you can help me out. Maybe you could send an angel who can help me. Amen.

33

From his desk out in the bull pen, Manseur could see—through the open door of his office—Captain Suggs sitting at his desk. Normally on Saturday, Suggs would already be sitting on the porch of his fishing cabin near Pass Manchac, sucking expensive hooch out of a plastic cup and casting bait out into the murky water, hoping to catch fish he wouldn't eat.

None of the detectives in the bureau had mentioned the fact that the Porter/Lee case had been snatched away from him, but Manseur knew that they were all aware of the slight. And even though it wasn't because of anything he'd done, most of them would still figure that the reason was based on some delicious failing on his part—or that it was because his partner, Larry Bond, wasn't there. When your close rate was as high as Manseur and Bond's was, the less successful couldn't help but pray for an occasional failure to even things out. Maybe the reason Manseur was so angered was that his successes gave him—if not additional height, fuller hair, a few less pounds or a more aesthetically pleasing face—a certain luster that camouflaged his physical appearance.

Manseur's phone rang. He lifted the receiver without taking his eyes from the report on his computer screen.

"Detective Manseur."

"Detective Manseur, this is Buddy Lee Toliver, sheriff in Assumption Parish. We met a while back when you were on the Teddy Trepanier murder. Mindy Trepanier was telling me the other day how decent you were to her during the case and how thankful she was that you brought her some peace of mind along with the justice."

Manseur remembered the small, frail woman whose only son had been murdered in Armstrong Park by a crack addict for a grand total of three dollars and a Shell credit card. "That was kind of Mrs. Trepanier. What can I do for you, Sheriff?"

"Well, I hope it's more in the nature of what I can do for you. I just fished a blue Range Rover out of the Bayou, and it seems you have a BOLO out on it. Involves a homicide."

"A fifty-seven-year-old woman—wife of a retired U.S. marshal. He's in intensive care at Charity and probably won't live. I don't guess you caught the driver for me."

"Maybe so. I meant it involves a homicide here. There's a guy with the vehicle, and maybe he was the driver who hit your couple. All I can tell you is that somebody set the Rover on fire with a man's body inside it, then pushed it off into the bayou using another vehicle. Only trouble was that the water was about six inches too shallow and some fishermen spotted the roof sticking up through the algae. There's tire tracks in the mud coming in and going out. I did get a cast of both sets, and one matches the Rover."

"What about an autopsy?"

"Well, he got cooked real good. I'd like to run him over to your M.E. We usually do that since we don't have a real pathologist. We make do with a retired pediatric surgeon who does autopsies because nobody in their right mind will let him operate on a live child. This corpse has a dented-in skull, and I don't need an autopsy to tell me he was murdered. Tell the truth, I'm hoping he expired over there in New Orleans and was driven here for disposal."

"When is he coming over?"

"I'll have the Rover towed to your garage so your people can process it. Corpse is ready to leave out of here now. I'll have him on a table in your M.E.'s suite within the hour. If he died here, I guess we'll work it, and we'll have better information to go on. With any luck he died on your side of the fence, and I'll read about you solving it in the newspaper."

"I hope he died here too, Sheriff," the New Orleans cop said bluntly.

Manseur suppressed a joyous yell. He dropped the receiver into place. His excitement was diminished by the sight of Suggs strolling across the bull pen toward his desk, carrying a steaming mug of coffee.

"How's the Trammel hit-and-run coming?" Suggs asked. "The old retired marshal and his wife."

"The Rover just turned up in Assumption Parish with a corpse inside it—torched and pushed off into the bayou. Body is already on its way over."

Suggs's frown deepened. "You mean somebody killed the driver?"

"Sheriff says there were tire tracks from a second vehicle on the scene, and his skull was crushed in."

"So, like maybe some kid out joyriding hit the Trammels. And he had a pal follow him out to get rid of the Rover and the perp killed him and drove his car back. Something like that, you think?"

"It might be," Manseur said cautiously. "It tracks that the driver killed the only person who could tie him to the event. Could be a kid, as far as I know. M.E. will give me an age."

Suggs's brow creased. "Kids are psychos these days. It's those damn video games. Did you know that Trammel fellow had some friends? I've fielded calls this morning from the assistant director of the USMS, and Texas congressman Ross Fulgam. Seems Trammel's father was a Texas Ranger, killed on the job. Trammel was a decorated veteran."

"I knew he was a decorated vet. I'll keep those VIPs in mind. You want to 'red ball' this one?"

"Not just yet. It's early. If you don't have it in the bag by Monday, we'll take another look. I'm just giving you a heads-up that there are going to be some people watching over your shoulder. I assured them both that you will get it cleared fast. Keep accurate records . . . just in case. We need to cover our asses on this one."

"I'll give it my undivided attention."

Suggs started away, then turned back. "I want you to know that despite our not seeing eye-to-eye on the Porter thing, I have absolute confidence in your ability. Bond will be back on Monday"—Suggs actually managed one of his pained smiles, which looked to Manseur like something a funeral home director would wear when a grieving family opted for the cheapest casket available—"but I expect you'll have this solved by then."

Manseur nodded impassively at his boss. "Sure looks

like you were on the money on the Porter/Lee. All that evidence they found in that house. More than you'd expect to find."

"Well, she's an amateur, and Tinnerino and Doyle are damn good cops who use old-fashioned police work. Girls that age aren't all like your daughters. The Porter gal is the sort of misfit other kids pick on—classic type to shoot things up. She was probably on her way to the school to even some scores and her Mom got in the way."

"Nothing like good old-fashioned police work." *Like picking a suspect out, then beating a confession out of him.*

"Tinnerino and Doyle are closing in on her," Suggs said. "Just a matter of time."

An alligator's lifetime, unless Faith Ann Porter climbs in through their open car window while they're asleep. Captain Suggs was the only thing that stood between Tinnerino and Doyle and dismissal from the squad for any number of just-cause reasons. The single positive consequence of the pair's laziness lay in the fact that, since they spent as little time around the office as possible, the productive detectives weren't constantly exposed to Suggs's rewarding their obvious incompetence with his praise and protection.

"Well, carry on," Suggs said.

"I am going to solve this one before Bond gets back," Manseur told Suggs's backside. Despite the lack of sleep he'd suffered lately, Manseur felt energized. He wondered if Deputy U.S. Marshal Massey was in town yet. With luck he would talk to Massey before Suggs did.

As Manseur watched the captain make his way back to his office, he felt a sensation of excited anticipation very like the one he'd had as a schoolboy waiting patiently for his teacher to open her desk drawer and find the grass snake he'd hidden there.

34

Winter sat on his bed and mulled over what USMS Director Richard Shapiro had just told him on the telephone.

He had expected more from Shapiro. Modesty aside, Winter had single-handedly saved the USMS witness protection program from disgrace. His personal investigation had brought down a rogue CIA-affiliated network of assassins—ex military cutouts, men with fictionalized identities. He and Hank had both been shot up during the operation. So, yes, Winter believed his director owed him and Hank a great deal more than a brushoff.

In the three minutes their conversation had lasted, the director expressed his sympathy over Hank and Millie's "unfortunate accident." He did agree that the appearance of a connection between the death of Hank's sister-in-law and the timing of the hit-and-run was troubling. But when Winter pressed him for help, Shapiro said that after the events of the year before, the attorney general had made it clear that all federal investigations in the future would be conducted by the agencies. The AG had reminded Shapiro that the U.S. Marshals Service was not an investigative branch of the Justice Department, and, no matter what the circumstances were, the USMS would never be endowed with the powers of investigation that the FBI, CIA, DEA, and the ATF had. Shapiro told Winter to let the local police do their job. If there was any investigating to be done, the FBI would handle it.

In any case, Shapiro went on, hit-and-runs were not federal crimes unless they involved federal property or a federal agent struck down because he was a federal agent.

Since Hank was not a marshal at the time of the event, and the event was not as a result of his official work, the FBI wouldn't become involved. He did say that the FBI director and the attorney general were both aware of the accident and would certainly monitor the investigation. Lastly, he told Winter that he had picked Winter's replacement. Winter couldn't help but wonder if perhaps the director would have done more to help if he hadn't resigned.

Because Winter was a United States marshal for the next two weeks, he could carry his weapon anywhere inside the United States and its territories and protectorates. What he couldn't do was operate in New Orleans under the color of federal authority. That put him in exactly the same position he had been in a year earlier, except this time his director wasn't even "unofficially" complicit. The one person who had been at his side during that life-or-death battle to save Sean was now lying in the ICU two miles away, and Winter Massey had no problem divining to whom he first owed his loyalty.

He changed into a button-down blue shirt, black jeans, and cross-trainers. Then, he slipped on his shoulder holster and picked up the lightweight leather jacket. Luckily it was cool enough that wearing it to cover his shoulder rig wouldn't be uncomfortable.

Nicky was still unpacking in the next bedroom. Winter stood at the door, looking in.

"You're originally from Mississippi, aren't you?"

"Originally," Winter said.

"What part?"

"Cleveland. It's in the Delta."

"When I think Delta, I picture cotton fields. Old blues singers sitting on rickety porches playing bottleneck to their neighbors and kinfolk, just a hop, skip, and jump from the mighty Mississippi. That the way it is? Sort of like an old movie?"

"Everybody there sings the blues these days. The plantations are mostly owned by corporations and farmed by machines. I don't get back there often. The rice farms around that area make porch sitting dangerous. Mosquitoes will tear you up," Winter said.

"Big, are they?"

"It isn't necessary that they be big. They fly in clouds."

"In Texas, we got clouds of skeeters too. But they're so big they can stand flat-foot and pleasure a turkey while they're draining it."

"That so?" Winter said, laughing.

Nicky took out his toothpick, tossed it aside, and put a fresh one from his pocket into his mouth. "In Texas most everything is bigger. I'm surprised Hank didn't ever explain that to you."

"Been my experience that it's just the bullshit is bigger."

"That's because the bulls are so damn big."

Winter saw Hank's gun on Nicky's bed, so he crossed the room and lifted it.

"A little worse for wear," Nicky told him. "I couldn't find the piece missing from the grip. The scratches can be buffed out. Hank had it on him when he got hit. I sort of figured he'd want me to hold it for him."

"This gun's got quite a history," Winter said, setting it back on the bedspread.

"Well, it might have more before I hand it back to Hank."

35

Faith Ann closed the bathroom door and walked down the dark hall toward the rear of the house. As she approached the den, she saw that the flickering light was from the television set. Faith Ann entered the room and saw that her mother was lying on the sofa. Kimberly was asleep, with her mouth hanging open. Faith Ann knelt and put her hand on her mother's cheek. Kimberly's eyes fluttered and opened and she smiled.

Faith Ann awoke in the dark and to the reality of her situation. The deaths of her mother, her uncle, and her aunt slammed into her, and panic swept over her like a wave of stove-heated air. She listened intently for whatever had awakened her. She heard the sound of shoe soles on the concrete walkway, then on the steps, and then on the slab over her head. The door to the living room opened with a squeak of hinges and then closed. Faith Ann lay in the bunker atop her poncho listening to the sound of someone's shoes on the living room floor.

They're back.

She pulled the poncho around her and lay frozen in a fetal curl, safe in the bunker.

36

Marta didn't like Tinnerino and Doyle. The two cops were nothing but corrupt brutes with badges. People like them screwed everything up, and their bulldog, bulletproof mentalities made them a distinct liability.

She decided that she needed to get one more look inside the Porter house, to see if they had missed anything during the initial search. After that, she would ask the detectives if she could sift through what they had collected.

"Let's go in," she said.

"You think she's in there?"

"We're going to see. I'll come in from the back, you the front."

Arturo stretched his arms and climbed from the car.

Marta eased open the gate and closed it behind them, being careful that the steel lock didn't make any sound. While Arturo went slowly up the steps, she walked the length of the Porter house rapidly but quietly. At the door, she slipped off her boots then used her copy of the key to open the door. When she entered the den, she could see Arturo standing at the far end of the house.

Sunlight streamed in through the windows. The living and dining rooms, where Arturo had entered, were really one open space with a brick fireplace open around both sides. Then came the kitchen, also open, and past that was the hallway to the bedrooms and the hall bathroom.

Marta left the den, approached the mother's bedroom door, and eased it open. She scanned the disaster made by the detectives after she and Arturo had left. Hadn't she told them to be careful in their search—not to make a mess—in case the kid returned? Marta figured they'd done it because they resented her telling them how to do their jobs. Too late to worry about that now.

The master bath was also a wreck, but no sign of the kid. Marta came out and shook her head at Arturo, who had positioned himself in the kitchen.

Faith Ann's room was in the worst condition of all. The bed was overturned, the contents of the drawers and the closet strewn everywhere. The bastards had even shattered the mirror and broken the framed photographs.

Marta, who had caught herself feeling jealous of the girl the day before—perhaps because her mother had taken such good care of her—felt a pang of pity for a motherless child who was friendless and frightened as she herself had once been. This changed things. If there was any way possible when the time came, Marta would end the poor child's life with as little physical pain as possible—providing the girl willingly handed over what she had.

Marta moved down the hall to the other bathroom door and pushed it open. She turned on the overhead light and surveyed it. Her eyes ran over the counter and to the tub and the open closet door. She noticed that the toilet seat was up. That seemed more obscene of the cops than destroying things. *This was a house of women. Good women caught up in something they had no way to prepare for.* Marta squatted and picked up the hair clippers from the floor. She remembered seeing them during her search of the bathroom. They had been in their box then, which was now empty on the floor. As she studied the instrument, she thought that there was something different about it, but she couldn't quite put her finger on what it was.

"You should take those. You get tired of preaching to everybody, you can clip rich ladies' froufrou doggies," Arturo said.

"Let's go," Marta told him. "She won't come back."

"You think she's been back since we left?"

"Yes."

"Maybe we should burn this house down," Arturo said. "If the tape is hidden here, it will be destroyed."

"If she has anything, she has it with her. Anyway, the fire department would just put it out and I'm sure someone has seen us. The neighbors must know about the lawyer and her daughter. I doubt Bennett's cops can protect us if there are a lot of questions."

"How do you know she was here again?"

"I know it here." Marta put her hand low on her stomach where she believed her instincts were centered. That was where she first perceived warnings—where she first knew when something wasn't right. She believed that, in men, instincts were housed in a lower region. Marta remembered vaguely that she had returned to the shack where her mother had been murdered and had hung around there because it was all she knew.

After they went out the back door, Marta closed and locked it. As they rounded the corner, something caught her eye that she had somehow missed minutes earlier. The bottom of the last of the lattice panels was out of alignment. And in the flower bed, Marta saw impressions—the patterns left by a shoe and a hand—in the damp soil. Leaning down, she could see the sharp tips of the screws sticking through the wood where the panel was hinged to the sill on the inside. The hinges had been attached, for aesthetic reasons, between the panel and the support beam. If the panel hadn't gotten hung up as it closed, it would have been difficult to see that the panel was designed to give people a way to get under the house.

Marta looked at Arturo, who smiled and nodded to her.

She handed Arturo her cap before she slipped under the house.

It was cool under there, and Marta could see all the way to the front; the light coming in through the lattice dimpled hundreds of white diamonds on the soil. She followed the scrapings and shoe prints she knew the child had left. The numerous support columns and the fireplace foundation blocked a complete view, so she crawled toward the front of the narrow house, checking the shadows. She could see Arturo's legs, in diamonds, as he walked slowly along. It was nice having a partner you didn't have to explain everything to—someone who protected your back because he loved you. She never doubted that Arturo loved her as much as she loved him, but the difference was that he depended on her. And she wanted it that way.

She had just about decided that Faith Ann wasn't there

when she spotted a dark square, which turned out to be an opening left when the concrete porch had been poured. With growing excitement, she moved over the soft dirt, her senses focused on the opening of what she knew was Faith Ann's hiding place. She crept up to the opening and saw a yellow poncho that was pulled over something three-dimensional. *A sleeping child.*

"Don't be afraid," Marta said soothingly. She slipped out her folding knife and slid inside the bunker. "I'm not going to hurt you."

Marta reached over, took a corner of the poncho, and lifted it. Then she cursed softly. Inside there was only a pillow and a flashlight. She turned it on and, looking around, saw the packaging for a Walkman and a plastic container with two of its original four batteries remaining. She lifted the sweat-damp pillow and put the slip case against her cheek, to her nose. The child had been there very recently. Marta couldn't help but smile. The kid was lucky—or something.

Very soon now. Your luck can't last forever, Faith Ann Porter.

37

Faith Ann had felt secure in her hidden concrete annex. While she was in there she could almost convince herself that she was still in touch with her old life. She decided to remain there until the visitors upstairs left, and she would have done just that had an inner voice not ordered her to flee. Her mother had always told her to listen to her feelings.

So she grabbed her backpack and climbed out of the

bunker. She crawled to the rear of the house and pushed out the panel. She remained crouched as she scurried to the back fence. She had to take off her backpack to get under, pulling it after her.

Four neighborhood boys were playing basketball on the city-owned courts. Two of them glanced at her—but a skinny kid squirming under a hurricane fence was a whole lot less interesting than a Saturday-morning game. She put on her Audubon Zoo cap and lingered there near a group of loitering teenagers so she could watch her house.

She saw the killer and the shorter woman from the day before as they came out of her back door. Both glanced at the basketball players; Faith Ann dropped her head hastily so the bill of the cap hid her eyes. Seconds later, she looked up and watched the pair turn the corner of her house. She watched in horror as the woman slipped under and the killer began to walk slowly up the side of her house. She knew the woman would find her hideout, and she knew that she was alive only because she had fled when hiding had seemed safer.

She turned on her heel and strode off down the street toward the tennis club. When she got to the thick privets where she'd hidden her bicycle and helmet, all she found of them was the combination lock, its hasp cut cleanly in half.

Now she was on foot.

38

Winter never judged people by their appearance, and Nicky Green had told him that Detective Manseur, despite his appearance, knew his business.

"Pleasure to meet you," Winter said, shaking the policeman's clammy hand when he arrived at the hotel.

"I'm sorry about your friends," Manseur said sympathetically.

"Come and let's us have a sit-down," Nicky said. "Coffee? Water?"

"No thank you," Manseur said as he sat on the front edge of the chair across from Winter like he thought he might have to spring up and run. "I'm a little pressed for time. First off, let me say that I hope whatever I tell you remains between us. I'm sticking my neck way out already, and I like my occupation, which supports my family."

Winter nodded, accepting the detective's terms. "Nicky mentioned that you were taken off the Kimberly Porter case."

"Yes. In fact I caught the Trammel case later from the man who relieved me of the Porter/Lee homicides. Captain Harvey Suggs."

"Do you know why?"

"Because I didn't interpret the evidence so that it pointed to the captain's conclusion."

"Which was?"

"That Faith Ann Porter murdered her mother and Amber Lee. Believe me, it didn't seem to point that way at the time, but it seems to be fitting nicely now. A bit *too* nicely."

Winter listened as Manseur went over the evidence that pointed toward Faith Ann's guilt. Manseur told the two men what he knew about Amber's connection to Jerry Bennett and what Bennett's value to the city administration and the police department was.

"This Bennett a crook?" Nicky asked.

"He is a slippery but tough businessman for sure, and a little eccentric—a virtue in New Orleans. I understand that he worked hard for everything he has. He built the Buddy's Fried Chicken franchise from scratch, sold it for a bundle, and he still gets a million dollars a year as a consultant for like twenty years, and he furnishes them the special sauces through another company."

"But do you think he might be involved in the killings?" Winter asked.

"All I know is that Bennett accused Amber of embezzlement and swore out a warrant after she'd been his *special* friend for years."

"But why would Kimberly Porter handle a case of embezzlement?" Nicky asked.

Winter said, "I thought her practice these days was strictly appeals for death penalty cases. That was her area of expertise."

"As far as I could tell from her papers, Porter was focusing strictly on capital cases. Her assistant told me that there was a woman who'd called the office and claimed to have proof that one of the men on death row was innocent. If Kimberly knew which inmate, she didn't tell her assistant. It is possible that Amber Lee had that information and that might be why they were both killed. Amber might have had information on any of the eleven guys on death row Porter represented."

"What did Suggs say when you told him that Kimberly was Millie Trammel's sister?"

Manseur exhaled loudly. "I didn't tell him. I couldn't risk him handing the case to the detectives he already gave the Porter one to. I'm pretty sure he wants to control the Porter case, and if he believes they're connected he sure as hell won't want me running this one into that one."

"You think whoever killed Kimberly ran the Trammels over?"

"Don't you?" Manseur asked bluntly.

"Of course I do. But what I think isn't proof. Faith Ann telephoned my son the afternoon Kimberly was shot. She was trying to find Hank and Millie. Sean told her that they were staying at a guesthouse near Audubon Park, but not which one."

"She found it," Manseur said grimly. "And the clerk there told her where they went to eat. I believe she saw the hit-and-run, because people saw her there. A doctor on the scene said she had on a yellow poncho and she seemed upset." He looked at Nicky. "Did you see Faith Ann there?"

"I saw a kid in a yellow slicker," Nicky admitted. "It could have been her. Might be I just think it is, now that I've seen a picture of her."

"I am sure it was her," Manseur said. "I put in my notes only that there was a child in a slicker who went to both the guesthouse and the scene of the hit-and-run, and perhaps she might be related to the Trammels. The doctor on the scene thought the child was male. The clerk swore it was a girl, but he didn't get her name."

"Where's your investigation now?" Winter asked.

"A fisherman found the Rover, which was stolen from a long-term lot at the airport. There was a body in it that someone tried their best to burn. Fortunately they pushed it into a shallow bayou. I'm hoping they miscalculated how long or how hot the fire needed to be to completely destroy identifiable features. I'm betting it's either a hired killer, who was killed to make sure his employer never got identified, or the killer did in his accomplice for the same reason, or maybe so he wouldn't have to split the fee. I'm hoping the medical examiner can help me figure out whose body it is."

"You thinking Bennett might have hired it done?" Winter asked quietly.

Manseur shrugged. "I have no reason to talk to Jerry Bennett on the Trammel case. But there's no reason you can't ask questions about either case. Bennett's office is at the River Club, and he's there most of the time. Lives in an apartment on the second floor, and also out on the lakefront in a luxury boathouse."

Winter said, "If I talked to this Bennett, he might tell someone on the force about it, and Suggs could have the connection between the two cases. Of course, if Suggs did make the connection through Bennett . . ."

"Which I think is about the only way he could at this point," Manseur said, smiling. "I can tell Captain Suggs it's all news to me," he said. "And he can't prove any differently unless you tell him. If he takes me off the Trammel case, I'll know for sure he's dirty and that Bennett is calling the shots."

"In which case?" Winter said.

"You could interest the media in both cases. Hand them the right questions to ask. I seriously doubt Bennett owns the media."

"They sure love to get into the mud," Nicky said.

Winter smiled. "I like the way you think, Detective. Nicky and I will try to find Faith Ann first. You know why she might be hiding from you?"

Manseur shrugged. "If she has a reason, it might be due to something she saw or heard in the office. She was definitely there around the time her mother was killed. I think she saw it. Suggs thinks she did it. The murder weapon was found in a hamper with her clothes along with the four spent cases. I don't know how the weapon got there, but I'm willing to entertain the idea that it was planted there by the real killer. I had a patrol unit at the Porter house as soon as I could get one there. Faith Ann was already gone. As far as I know the patrolmen were there until the detectives took over the scene. The detectives found the weapon."

"You think the detectives could have planted the gun?" Winter asked.

"I suppose it's possible the killer beat us there and did it. Or maybe he dropped it at the crime scene, and the girl picked it up. It doesn't mean she used it. Who knows what a twelve-year-old thinks."

Manseur reached into his pocket and removed a clear plastic evidence bag. "One more thing that might be significant," he said. "I found this in Hank Trammel's hatband. The hat was under a truck."

"What is it?" Winter said as he reached for the bag.

"It's some sort of a spy bug," Nicky said.

"Looks like it." Winter nodded. "Why would this be in Hank's hatband?"

"I've seen some small ones," Nicky said, "but that critter there sets a new record for compactness. I doubt it has much range."

"I'm going to have it looked at by a friend who's in the electronics business and see what it's capable of doing. Sometimes he lets me borrow sophisticated devices that the NOPD can't afford."

Manseur pocketed the plastic bag, stood abruptly, and started for the door.

"I appreciate the information," Winter said. "More than I can tell you."

"Based on your reputation as a man who isn't afraid of facing Goliaths, I believe that confiding in you is the right choice—perhaps Faith Ann Porter's only chance of getting cleared. Be careful, Massey. Whoever we're dealing with here won't hesitate to give me more work."

39

When Captain Harvey Suggs's private line rang, he was clipping his fingernails. He let it ring three times because that was how long it took him to complete the work on his right hand. He lifted the receiver and grunted into it. "Uh-huh."

"It's J.B.," the familiar voice said.

Suggs straightened and swept the nail crescents from his lap. He checked the space outside his office door to make sure nobody was within hearing range. "What can I do for you?"

"You can do what you are supposed to do, Harvey."

"I'm handling that," Suggs said, trying not to sound irritated, which he was.

"My employees asked me about a cell phone."

"A cell phone?"

"One registered to the Porter woman. You see, if the phone wasn't at the office, it might still be in *family* hands."

Suggs furrowed his brow, thinking. "We're already running all the phone records. I'll get on the cell trace."

"Would you?" Jerry Bennett's voice had taken on a decidedly hard edge. "She had one. Everybody has one. For Christ's sake, Suggs, what are you doing on this, twiddling your fat thumbs?"

"Just a minute," Suggs said. He picked up another phone and dialed Tinnerino's cell phone.

"Yeah," Tinnerino answered.

"Porter's cell phone. You find one?"

"No," the detective said.

"Did she have one?"

"Matter of fact . . . I don't know." There was a short pause while he asked. "Chief, Doyle says there were bills for one."

"Have you gotten a list of the calls to and from all of her phones?"

"We're on that now," Tinnerino said, obviously lying.

"You'd better be. I want that cell phone number ASAP."

Suggs disconnected the line and picked up the one

where Jerry Bennett was waiting. "Porter has a cell phone, and it isn't accounted for."

"Well," Bennett said, "if I were you, I'd put a trace on that phone and I'd figure out how to pinpoint its location. You can do that, can't you?"

"Track it? Yes, of course we can do that."

"*She* might be using it. Harvey, don't expect me to do your job for you. Let me know as soon as you get a fix on that phone. And my people will handle the pickup."

"Of course I'll do what I can—"

"You understand how important it is for your people to keep my people in the loop?"

"She'll use the thing and we'll get a fix on her location."

"I know that, Harvey!" Bennett snapped. "I watch television. If I were you, I absolutely would not disappoint me."

40

Winter rode in the passenger seat of his rented Dodge Stratus, thinking as Nicky drove up St. Charles Avenue.

Other than what Nicky Green and Manseur had told him, Winter had no information to go on. Until there was evidence to the contrary, he had to assume that Faith Ann was alive and in hiding and that she had a good reason for not seeking out the police. He could accept that either Faith Ann knew, or believed, that there were cops involved in the death of her mother. Maybe she was correct. At any rate, it was her perception that mattered, not what the facts were. She was only twelve years old. If there was corrupt police involvement, then Faith Ann was in danger if the cops did find her. That would certainly explain why

Suggs wanted her declared the suspect in the double homicide. The public would assume she was guilty—just another killer child, the stuff of adult nightmares. And if such a killer dies during apprehension, who's going to look too closely?

For the present, Hank was beyond his help. Winter's priority was to find Hank's niece and make sure the child was safe.

Winter trusted Nicky Green because Nicky and Hank were close friends and Hank's judgment of people was accurate. Nicky was also a professional, even though he was a strange-looking one.

Winter didn't know Detective Manseur, and he had no idea if the detective's actual reasons for not telling his chief about the connections between the two cases were what he claimed. But Winter did believe their interests—when it came to Faith Ann Porter—did in fact coincide. It wasn't relevant to Winter yet whether Manseur's prime objective was to find Kimberly's real killer. Maybe he wanted to prove Faith Ann's innocence, or maybe Manseur needed to prove he had been taken off of the Porter case for "dirty" political reasons—not because he actually wasn't competent to handle it.

Winter was taking a chance. He desperately needed Manseur's help as a navigator—without it he had nothing at all to go on and no way to see inside the investigation. But he wanted to make sure he had exhausted his options before he put Manseur in Suggs's sights.

There was one person who might know something that would be of help. He dialed his home number. Sean answered, and he told her in detail what he had learned.

"So I need for you to talk to Rush," he concluded. "Explain this to him and ask him to think hard and try to remember if Faith Ann ever told him about any of her favorite places or named any close friends here in New

Orleans. Call me back with anything. Anything at all." Winter hung up the phone.

"We've got company," Nicky announced, glancing in the mirror. "Two cars back."

"You sure?"

"Absolutely. He was parked outside the hotel when I went out to my car for my gear. His car was one back from me. When I looked back at him, he turned his head."

"Lose him," Winter said. "Let's see how good he is."

"Belts on, ladies and gentlemen." Nicky jerked the wheel at the next cross-street without signaling. His tires squealed, and the oncoming car he cut off honked in furious protest. Nicky completed the U, took a swift right, and floored it. He was an amazingly skillful driver. He coordinated the wheels, the accelerator, and the brakes effortlessly, and the sure-footed car moved as though it was on tracks.

"You know," he said, "with a few tweaks here and there, some minor work on the suspension, this wouldn't be a bad car. It ain't no Caddy, but it ain't bad." He tilted back his cowboy hat and looked in the rearview. "Mission accomplished. Our tail is gone."

"Why did Manseur have us tailed?"

"Manseur?"

"Who else knows we're around?"

When Nicky slowed for the next light, something touched their bumper.

"Jesus Christ," Nicky murmured, looking back.

Winter turned in his seat and saw that the car they thought they had lost now had its front bumper resting against their rear end. The driver, a man with a crew cut, relaxed his grip on the wheel enough to wave his fingers.

"He looks like a cop," Nicky told Winter.

"Pull over," Winter replied. "Let's see what the deal is."

Nicky pulled into the parking lot of a bicycle store. The

sedan parked so that the driver was shoulder to shoulder with Winter, four feet away.

Winter zipped down his window. The driver did the same.

"Hi there," Winter said pleasantly. "Is there something we can do for you?"

The driver turned and stared at him. "Maybe there's something I can do for you."

"Like what?"

"I could tell you why Roy Rogers there didn't shake me."

"Okay."

The driver held up a laptop computer. On the screen was a blinking dot positioned on a street grid. "I put a C-2 Tracker behind your visor."

Winter flipped down the visor and unpinned the dime-size disc with a smiley-face decal stuck on it.

The driver raised his hand above the window, and the badge case in his hand fell open. "Special Agent John Everett Adams," he said. "Maybe we should sit down and talk."

Except for his eyes, which were light blue, Adams's features were almost bland. The FBI agent's closely cropped hair was light brown, and his fingernails were clipped so the ends appeared to be uniform in the amount of edge showing. His teeth were bright and so perfect that Winter wondered if they had been veneered.

"About?" Winter asked, handing Adams back the tracker.

"We could talk about anything you'd like. Sports? I'm a Redskins fan. Games? I play checkers and shoot pool. Or we could talk about Hank and Millie Trammel. You guys hungry?"

"I could eat something," Winter said.

"Follow me," Adams said. He backed up and pulled into

traffic. Three blocks later he turned into a diner parking lot and got out of his car. Winter and Nicky did so too.

"You like omelets?" Adams asked. "This place looks like shit, but the omelets are to die for."

Winter wondered if it was possible that the health department had not been informed of the existence of the diner. The space was long and narrow with booths along the left wall and stools at the long counter, behind which food was grilled in plain sight of the customers. The putty-colored paint on the walls and ceiling had been dulled years ago by airborne grease, and the floor tiles were stained and chipped. The three men took seats at the first booth, Winter and Nicky facing Adams, who kept his back to the door. They sat silent until the waitress took their orders. Adams ordered a cheese and mushroom omelet, Winter asked for black coffee. Nicky ordered a hamburger, which bought a scowl from the woman.

"Try a seafood po'boy," Adams suggested.

"I'd rather take my chances with red meat," Green said. "Medium rare."

"State won't let us make ground beef but one way," the woman muttered, walking away.

"So, what do you think of the place?" Adams asked. "It was recommended by a local agent when I was here a few years back. The seafood po'boys and omelets are the best in the world."

"Probably half the stuff they serve will kill you," Nicky said. He put a napkin over a sticky spot on the table. "I hope that's syrup."

"Deputy Massey, I expect you're curious as to why I'm here."

"I'd love to hear that. And why you're wiretapping us."

"I'd like to know that too," Nicky said.

"Well, when my director got this last night, he had a conference with your director, and my director told him that a hit-and-run wasn't anything the FBI could officially investigate, but that for reasons known well to you, he'd take a look from the sidelines. My director dispatched me to watch out for you, knowing you *might* try to interfere, and if that was the case, to unofficially give you aid if that became necessary. If it turns out that the hit-and-run had roots to what you and Chief Deputy Trammel were involved in last year, I can insert myself officially, and if need be I can call in necessary assistance. I have two associate agents a couple of hours away."

"If the hit-and-run was related to the past, by which I assume you mean that fracas last year, what does Kimberly Porter's murder have do with it?" Nicky asked.

"That I can't tell you. I know only what you know about it. I know what Manseur told you guys."

"You have my hotel room bugged?" Winter wasn't surprised.

"I used a device to capture the sound in your suite straight from the windows. You should be happy about it," Adams said. "It saves you from having to bring me up to speed."

"Were you already watching Hank?" Winter asked.

"What? Oh, because of that bug? No, it wasn't us. I'd like to have a look at it."

"About the size of collar button, but thinner. Gray, with a thin wire loop."

Adams nodded. "Definitely not ours."

"So does it look like these two incidents are related to *old* business?" Winter asked.

"Not on its face. But these two incidents are almost certainly related. It's not much of a stretch to imagine they are connected through Hank to the past—perhaps to you as well."

"You think I'm tied into this?"

Adams shrugged. "Well, even if it's totally new business, when you stick your nose in you could be in danger."

"That's probably true," Winter conceded. "What's your take on Manseur?"

"He seems to be a decent enough sort. Family man. We looked at him when we were poking around for crooked cops a while back. It's possible he's playing a political game of his own and you two might wind up in the middle of it. He appears to be clean, but then so does his commander Captain Harvey Suggs."

"I'm thinking I have to go at Bennett," Winter said.

"His name has come up from time to time, but if he's involved with organized crime, we've never seen proof. I'll go with you."

"Welcome aboard," Nicky said. "The more badges the merrier."

"Aboard? We don't need your help, Mr. Green," Adams said.

Nicky looked at Winter. "What's this *we* shit? You got worms?"

The waitress delivered the order. Adams cut into his omelet and tasted it tentatively.

After she was gone, Nicky said, "I'm thinking I have some say about it."

Adams shrugged and swallowed. "Say whatever's on your mind, Mr. Green. I couldn't care less. I don't want this omelet to get cold."

Nicky said, "I don't know you, Agent. Hank's about my closest friend. He's also Massey's friend. I'm not stepping aside to let some sneaky, funeral-director–looking Federal snot-wad who isn't Hank's friend—and who I doubt very much has ever had one—push me out. You smell like trouble to me, Adams. I wouldn't trust you to park my damn car. You push me out and I'm going to keep on sticking my nose in this until I know who killed my friend and why. And you can't help Massey and stop me both."

"Nothing personal. You're out of your element," Adams said. "This isn't some cheating husband you can sling a skunk at, and I can't worry about what you do or what happens to you. Massey is a trained law enforcement professional, and I know he can more than handle himself. That's just the way it is."

"And what am I: Swiss cheese?"

"Since you asked, you're physically handicapped. That, coupled with the way you dress, and you might as well be going around waving a red bedsheet on a pole. Plus if there's gunplay, I don't want to be responsible for the innocent bystanders. Nor do I want to catch one of your rounds in my back."

"I can change my clothes," Nicky said. "And this cane, which I don't require for mobility, does more than steady me. Maybe in the future I'll show you what I mean."

Adams shot back, "It's more likely I'd make that cane a permanent part of your anatomy."

"Nicky stays," Winter said.

"Listen, Massey—" Adams protested.

"That's the way it has to be," Winter cut in. "I trust Nicky. You, I'll have to get to know. Since *I* haven't been spying on *you*."

41

Detective Manseur stood beside a raised stainless-steel table in the autopsy suite in the city's morgue. A combination of intense fire and immersion in warm water teaming with carnivorous scavengers was responsible for the condition of the "Rover" body. The corpse's skin was like that of a brisket that had been left sitting on a very hot grill for several hours too long. The face was a hideous mask, and the hardened lips were curled back like the man was snarling at Death. The cadaver's torso stood open and the colorless but moist internal organs, after being weighed and sliced for sampling, were in a garbage bag, which had been reinserted into the cavity to await a suturing. The top of the skull had been set beside the head like a partly shattered bowl; the damaged brain rested in a stainless steel pan on the nearby counter.

Dr. Lawrence Ward, the Orleans Parish Medical Examiner, struck a match to light a cigar the size of a baby's wrist. His massive hands had white hair on the backs of them that showed through the tight latex gloves and matched the mane of hair sprouting on his watermelon-shaped head. Ward's watery eyes focused on his notes, made readable by the glasses perched on the tip of his bulbous nose.

"Your John Doe is approximately seventy inches in height, one hundred and sixty pounds. He's Caucasian. I'll have to do some further tests, but the only dental work, a bridge, is probably European. Age between thirty-five and forty-five. Died within past twenty-four hours. Lack of burning on his backside means he was sitting up during the fire. Safety belt melted to him. He was stripped down to his skin, probably to make our jobs harder. He's got some old injuries that could indicate a life of violence, race car driving, or an athletic background."

Manseur scribbled the information into his notebook.

"The fire was postmortem. No water in the lungs or fire damage to the throat," the doctor said through the dense cigar smoke that obscured his features. He turned to the X-rays on the light box. "Homicide."

"I sort of guessed that. Exact cause?"

"Somebody struck him over the left ear with a blunt object using enough force to fracture his temporal bone and put splinters into his brain. Wound is almost circular. Maybe he caught the end of an aluminum baseball bat. I'm pretty sure he was hit first, because of the bleeding inside the skull and swelling in the brain. Then somebody snapped his neck by twisting his head. That twist stopped his heart, which in turn stopped the inner cranial bleeding."

"Whoever did that was extremely strong?"

"Wouldn't have to be any Charles Atlas if Mr. Doe was unconscious from the blow, which he most likely was. I'd say the killer knew how to induce the injury. They teach that advanced stuff to Special Forces soldiers—SEALs, Rangers, and the like. I'll do a full body X-ray series and see what else I can pick up."

"Between the fire and foreign dental work, an identification is going to be a bitch," Manseur said. *Why foreigners?*

"You're in luck," the coroner told him. "The fire didn't completely destroy two of his fingertips, because those fingers weren't totally exposed to the heat." He made a loose fist that put two fingers against the palm of that hand. "I might have lifted enough detail to get you enough for a partial match. Maybe. Who knows?"

The doctor turned to pick up an index card from the table behind him. When he handed it to Manseur, the detective saw that there were two inked spots with lines, grooves, and clearly visible swirls.

Manseur put the fingerprint card in his pocket, then looked at the gurneys lined up against the far wall. "Dying to get in," he said.

"We've never needed to advertise."

"You autopsied the Porter and Lee women?"

"Sure did."

"Could I see those reports?"

"I gave them to Tinnerino and Doyle. You're not working that case, are you?"

"Just curious. Mind if I peek at the originals?"

"If you want."

"I want."

After Manseur had read over the reports and the medical examiner had answered his questions, Manseur left. As he stood in the elevator, he sniffed his coat, wondering if he smelled like he'd been hanging out in the kitchen of a barbecue joint.

42

Faith Ann took a streetcar downtown. From its window she saw cops in three separate cruisers going about their Saturday-morning business. One police car raced up St. Charles Avenue with its siren and lights blazing and frightened her, but it didn't pull over to wait at the next stop, so she relaxed.

When people looked at her, they paid no particular attention. One of them had bumped into her, looked down, and said, "Excuse me, son." Being mistaken for a boy made her smile to herself. She had hoped that her slim body enveloped in a bulky sweatshirt and jeans would disguise her budding breasts, and the half-inch-long hair gave her an added measure of safety. She had looked in the bathroom mirror after cutting off her hair and decided that she thought she looked like a boy but hadn't been sure others would think so.

Faith Ann walked self-assuredly with her shoulders slightly hunched to imitate the way boys her age carried themselves. She even occasionally cupped her hand to push up on her imaginary male genitals.

On Canal Street she looked into a newspaper dispenser and saw her mother's picture and her own. She crossed Canal and strode into the French Quarter, which was wide awake.

43

Captain Suggs had been busy since Jerry Bennett called him. He had revised the BOLO for Faith Ann Porter, adding that the "unstable" preteen had murdered two people and was probably armed and dangerous. He added that any policemen who spotted her should not approach her but keep her in sight and call it in directly to him. At that point he would call Tinnerino and Doyle, and they would clue the Latinos, who would handle the girl. Any complications—because he had no choice—he would handle. If Bennett went down, so might he and a lot of others up and down the chain.

He glanced down at his desk at the phone sheets listing two weeks' worth of calls for Kimberly Porter's office phone, home phone, and the missing cellular phone, which he assumed the daughter had in her possession. Now when she used it, he would be notified within seconds of her exact location. He was awaiting the list of the owners of the telephones that Kimberly had called and those who had called her in that time period, which the departmental researchers were gathering and had instructions to hand-deliver ASAP.

Suggs had often weighed Bennett's generosity—there was no disputing his largesse—against the damage he could do him if he ever decided to unburden himself. Suggs realized that if Bennett kept proof of his own guilt in murders, who knew what evidence of his payouts, and what he got in return for them, he had in his possession. Now he could turn rat and buy himself a lot of slack—maybe a life sentence instead of the needle. It was a disturbing thought. Suggs looked up to see a policewoman in his doorway holding up an envelope.

"You were waiting for these?" she asked. "Telephone records?"

"What do you think?" Suggs said curtly.

She placed the envelope on his desk. Before she was out of the office, he had it in his hands and had slipped out the pages.

The information for each of the three phone numbers was stapled together. Each list of numbers had, as its cover page, the names and addresses of the people the lawyer had called, followed by the names and addresses of those who had called her.

Suggs stared at one of the names in stunned silence. He rifled through all three covers and the number was included on all three lists. The name was H. Trammel, 1233 Post Road, Charlotte, North Carolina. There was another name in the same area code and this one struck a sour cord in Suggs's memory. It was Winter James Massey, Concord, North Carolina. That was a name he knew. It had been called from Kimberly Porter's cell phone two hours after she was dead. *Did Kimberly Porter know Winter Massey?*

Manseur's hit-and-run investigation involved Henry "Hank" Trammel. Suggs remembered Massey's partner in the shoot-out last year was named . . . Trammel. "Shit!"

44

Winter went into his bedroom to call Hank's doctor for an update before he called Sean to pass on what he had learned. He also talked to his son about Faith Ann Porter. He asked Sean how she felt. Talking about the baby put him in a better, healthier frame of mind for a few moments. When he returned to the living room, Adams, in a tailored gray suit, white button-down and striped tie, sat reading the sports pages of the newspaper. The suit jacket, laid over the back of a chair, had been tailored so that the gun rig beneath it was imperceptible. Winter noted that the federal agent's high-top, dull-leather shoes with solvent-resistant crepe soles were designed for a man who understood what being sure-footed was worth. The .40-caliber Glock in his shoulder rig was a utilitarian choice—a thoroughly dependable, highly accurate all-weather weapon, more plastic than steel. Winter's SIG Sauer 220, in the same caliber, was more steel than plastic, and Winter preferred the thinner grip posture the German weapon offered. In the right hands, both guns would drive nails at twenty-five feet. Truthfully, Winter thought Glocks looked like toys hewn out of blocks of chocolate. Winter saw that instead of a handcuff pouch, which he always carried, Adams had two three-magazine carriers so he was a walking arsenal. The ankle holster carried an odd choice in a backup weapon. The quick-release holster held a folding knife with a composite handle.

Nicky Green had changed out of his formal Western attire. He was wearing black denim jeans, a knit shirt, and suede cowboy boots, and he had swapped the cowboy hat for a plain blue baseball cap. "I pass the audition?"

Adams glanced at him over the newspaper, folded it, and set it aside.

"That's better," Adams said.

Winter took a seat on the couch. "Faith Ann doesn't have any close friends my son is aware of. He said her favorite places are Audubon Zoo, City Park, and the aquarium. Our best hope is she'll call him again. Sean is going to call me as soon as she does."

Adams said, "If she's still alive."

"She was alive last night," Nicky pointed out.

"I'm going to assume she is," Winter said.

"Well, we can't cover all of those places and hope she shows up," Adams told them. "The cops searched her house, so I expect the detectives working this have her address books, phone logs, computer files, correspondence."

"We need to get in that house too," Nicky said. "Maybe they missed something."

"I agree," Adams said. "Got to start somewhere."

Winter's cell phone rang.

"It's Manseur," Winter said.

"I think Captain Suggs has made the connection," Manseur told him. "He just called me and told me to report to his office. He sounded pissed. Doesn't mean he knows anything."

"How you going to play it?"

"Seat of my pants. I just wanted to tell you that the BOLO on Faith Ann has her classified as armed and dangerous. If she's spotted, instructions are to call Suggs and not to attempt to apprehend her."

"We're going to try and get a look inside the Porter house," Winter said.

"You can try to, but I don't know where Tinnerino and

Doyle are or what they're up to. What are you going to do if they catch you?"

"I'll play it by the seat of my pants," Winter said. "By the way, just so you know, I picked up another man."

"That right?"

"Yeah, an FBI agent. He's a card I can play if need be."

"That's good," Manseur said. "By the way, the M.E. got partial prints from the Rover body. I'll go over the report with you later. After I talk to Suggs, I'm going to run them and see what I get. The body was burned, and unless the prints hit I'm not sure it'll help you. I wish I could do more. And the M.E. told me Kimberly and Amber's killer used a silencer, which as far as I know wasn't found with the weapon."

"I think we're going to do doing some pot stirring."

"You have my number. Keep me apprised. I'll do the same."

"Thanks," Winter said.

"Good luck," Manseur said.

"Okay, fellows, we'll take two cars. I should call the chief deputy here in New Orleans and get some radios. Chet Long is an old friend of Hank's. I'm sure he'll be happy to assist."

"Not a good idea," Adams objected. "Fewer people we involve, the better. I've got the electronics end covered. I just need to stop by my room and collect some encrypted radios."

Winter scribbled an address and handed it to Nicky. "You and Adams go do that, then meet me at the Porter residence."

Winter called Chet Long before he had driven a block. The year before, Chet had supplied Winter and Hank with encrypted radios, long guns, and a Blackhawk helicopter to ferry an assault team comprised of U.S. deputy marshals. He wanted to check in with his and Hank's friend and alert him that he was in town. Out of habit, Winter checked his mirror for tails but didn't see anybody following him. Adams hadn't mentioned any partners, the norm for field agents, but that didn't mean he didn't have backup.

When Winter asked for Chet Long, he was informed by the receptionist that Chief Deputy Long was out of the country. She asked if he wanted to speak to anyone else and he declined, asking that she tell Chet he called.

45

When Manseur arrived at Captain Suggs's door, the chief detective was talking on his telephone. He motioned for Manseur to sit down while he finished his conversation. Manseur caught sight of what looked to be a phone log with some of the names highlighted in yellow, and he knew how Suggs had made the connection between the two cases.

Trying not to eavesdrop on what sounded like a personal conversation, Manseur let his eyes wander to the only framed picture on his boss's desk. It was a portrait of Suggs's German shepherd, Heinzie, who was a dreadful, constantly molting animal with severe gastric problems and the charm of a piranha.

Suggs dropped the phone into its cradle and turned his cold eyes on Manseur.

"Nothing on the Porter girl yet?" Manseur asked.

Suggs didn't answer the question. Manseur noticed that the tops of his chief's ears were turning crimson. "So, how's the Trammel case coming? I'm getting calls from all over on it. You haven't requested help."

"Haven't needed any yet. It's still preliminary."

"You look at the Trammels' room at the guesthouse?"

"Nothing there. I sealed it for the time being."

"Did Trammel make any calls from the guesthouse?"

"No sir."

"He have a cell phone?"

"His took a bath in a pothole. Hers was there, but the last number she called was U.S. Air. The techs are supposed to try and retrieve the stored numbers from the chip, if they can. They're backed up."

"I see. What did the Rover yield?"

"They just started going over it. But anything useful was burned up. Body's been autopsied."

"And?"

"Burned up too. Not much to go on. No I.D. Some dental work. Head crushed in, neck broken manually afterward. Homicide. Looks like a professional job."

"That's your take now?"

"Like I said earlier, there were at least two vehicles, so at least two people involved. Maybe our stiff's the driver, maybe the partner. It looks like it could be a professional hit and the killer covered his tracks. Or something else. Hard to tell with what I have to work with."

"Motive?"

"None that's obvious yet. Trammel was a U.S. marshal. Who knows?"

"You notify next of kin?"

"Not yet. His friend said he thought Mrs. Trammel had a sister living here and that the Trammels were going to see her today. I hoped to get that this morning from the marshals office, but it's Saturday. I asked the clerk at the guesthouse to call me if anyone inquired about them. If they were supposed to see the sister today, she'll call their guesthouse. The staff at the guesthouse will forward any inquiries to me," Manseur said.

"Well, we withheld the Trammels' names until notification," he continued. "The friend, that P.I., called a pal of the Trammels' in North Carolina who is supposed to come in today and handle things until we locate Mrs. Trammel's sister. I haven't spoken to him yet. He's supposed to call when he gets in."

"Are you saying that you're at an impasse?" Suggs asked.

"At the moment all I can do is wait for everything to come in. I don't see anything breaking before Monday. Bond will be back, and we can hit it hard," Manseur answered.

Manseur had held Suggs's stare since the conversation started. He noticed beads of sweat had gathered over his chief's upper lip—a sign that he was nervous. Manseur tried to imagine how his superior was going to play this. Suggs didn't know Manseur knew that the cases were linked, because Manseur didn't have the Porters' telephone records which established their link to the Trammels. He didn't believe that Suggs could afford to inform him of the connection yet. He knew Suggs had no solid reason to take the Trammel case away from him, unless he exposed that link and could justify taking the case on some pretext, as opposed to having Manseur, Tin Man, and Doyle working as a team. Down deep, Manseur was enjoying Suggs's discomfort. He wondered how Winter Massey's appearance would affect his comfort level.

"Have you considered the possibility of old enemies? Perhaps this might be connected to that mess last year Trammel was involved in."

"What thing is that?" Manseur asked, feigning confusion.

"The shootout between the marshals and the FBI, with

Manelli? You might consider revenge. Maybe some gangster spotted him?"

Manseur managed a look of surprise. "The Sam Manelli thing? You mean that's the same Trammel? It never occurred to me, and the P.I. didn't mention it." He touched his palm to his forehead.

"You didn't know it was the same Trammel?"

"No. It could explain some things. Like you just said—it's a motive."

"An obvious motive," Suggs agreed.

"Mob revenge. A mob angle," Manseur said. "There was another marshal who was wounded. What was his name?"

Suggs seemed to be leading Manseur close to the Porter case. Maybe he was trying to trap Manseur, believing that his detective *must* have already made the Trammel/Massey connection, and possibly even knew what the Porter/Trammel connection was.

"Massey," Suggs said, "guy has a reputation for attracting violence. He killed three men in Tampa, years ago. . . ."

"Who were trying to free a drug lord in the federal courthouse."

Suggs nodded. "And here, fourteen months back . . . Well, you know all about that one."

"He still out of North Carolina, you think?" Manseur took the casebook from his pocket and made a show of turning pages slowly as though he was reading through his notes. "Jesus," he said, tapping a page with a fingertip, "sure is. Winter Massey. I can't believe I didn't put it together."

"After you speak to Massey, I want to be filled in on his plans. If that marshal goes off on some sort of vendetta and creates any sort of havoc . . . I won't stand for that. You warn him about that. Be firm."

"I'll sound him out. Maybe he knows who might still want to pay Hank Trammel back for all that . . ."

"Unpleasantness," Suggs said, wiping the sweat from his upper lip. "Just keep me in the loop, Manseur. Whatever you get, pass on to me. If you talk to Massey or the missing sister, I want to know what they say ASAP."

"Soon as I talk to them. Frankly, Chief, I have some other cases that I need to check in on. I thought this one was in limbo at the moment. I've been running without sleep."

"Do what you can. Being Saturday and all, Monday should be when you can get your teeth into this one. Okay, no biggie. Just keep me in the loop and if you need anything, just ask. We have to wrap this one up. Big brother looking over our shoulders and all that happy crap."

"I will," Manseur said, standing. "How's the Porter/Lee case coming?"

"Tinnerino and Doyle are working it from several angles. They're getting closer to the girl."

"Someone told me the BOLO said she's armed and dangerous."

"We have reason to believe that is the case."

"But you have the murder weapon."

"She could have another weapon. It's extremely possible she had help. Maybe an older boyfriend. You're familiar with the Charlie Starkweather case from the fifties."

"So you think some Starkweather-type boyfriend might have given the kid another gun?"

"That's what Tinnerino thinks."

"Was the silencer found with the gun?"

"Silencer?" Suggs's eyes opened wide. "Who said anything about a silencer?"

"The M.E. on the Rover stiff mentioned the Porter and Lee wounds had strands of steel wool in them. Naturally I assumed it was from a silencer, since steel wool is commonly packed inside the baffle sleeve to absorb sound.

The gun that killed Porter and Lee was a .380 automatic, wasn't it?"

"A Taurus."

Manseur knew they'd have the serial number, which would make it difficult for anybody to swap the weapon with another, nonthreaded piece. Ballistics had matched the gun to the bullets. "Must have been evidence that a noise suppressor was attached to it. I bet the inside of the barrel is threaded."

"I'll look into it," Suggs said.

Manseur stood. "I'm sure Tinnerino and Doyle know how unusual it is for a twelve-year-old to have access to that sort of equipment. I'd love to know who the girl's accomplice is. I'm betting you'll find out he's a professional."

Manseur walked from the room, wondering if he should have dropped that silencer information on Suggs just yet. At least Suggs was on notice that he'd have to be very careful about what happened from that point out. It would give his chief something else to occupy himself with. The more pressure that was put on Suggs and his detectives, the freer Manseur would be to work under their radar.

46

The knowledge that Horace Pond's time was growing shorter by the second propelled Faith Ann Porter's steps. It was early afternoon when she crossed North Rampart Street and made her way up the sidewalk beside the brick wall that protected Saint Louis Number One, the most famous cemetery in the country after Arlington, from unauthorized visitors. Faith Ann had visited voodoo priestess Marie Lebeau's tomb in there.

She turned the corner and strode down the street that separated the Iberville housing projects from the cemetery. Her mother's friend, Sister Ellen Proctor, lived in a unit in the projects her Catholic order kept there for the sister's ministry to help the underprivileged. If anybody could help her now, the world-famous Sister Ellen could.

She didn't know which building Sister Ellen Proctor lived in. She had been there twice with her mother to pick up the anti–capital punishment nun, who was the spiritual adviser to several Death Row residents and wrote books on how bad the death penalty was. On both occasions, the nun had been waiting on the sidewalk for them to pick her up. Both times there had been people waiting there with her. Even though she was white, Sister Ellen liked living there instead of in a convent, and she'd told Kimberly that she wasn't in any danger in the all-minority projects. Kimberly had told Faith Ann that the people in the place loved the nun and protected her. Some of the automobiles parked on the street looked nice, while others like they belonged in a junkyard.

The two-story brick buildings stood lined up on land that was mostly bare dirt divided by sidewalks with a few shade trees scattered around. Some of the units had sheets of weathered plywood covering their doors and windows. On several of the concrete porches and around the buildings, people congregated, enjoying the autumn sunshine. Some were already drinking beer, while others seemed to be outside to keep an eye on the children, who were playing noisily.

As Faith Ann crossed the street, she was aware that people were watching her, as if trying to decide whether she might represent a threat. Faith Ann had assumed that since Sister Ellen was a resident and accepted as a friend of the community, that she would be too. As she approached a group of teenagers however she learned she was wrong.

A skinny boy of perhaps sixteen, whose crisp jersey and new denims would have fit someone twice his size, turned from his friends and faced her head-on. His reddish hair was in dreadlocks, his skin was almost as light as her own, and freckles dotted the bridge of his nose. His eyes reflected an arrogant surliness. And his front teeth were veneered in gold.

"You looking for something, zoo boy? You looking for a hookup?"

"Yes," Faith Ann replied, stopping five feet short of the red-haired teenager.

"What it is? Chronic? Somethin' lil' heavier?"

"I'm looking for Sister Ellen."

"Never heard of her. Y'all know no sistah name of Ellen?"

The others exchanged looks; the fattest one giggled nervously.

"You packin' any presidents?" the leader asked her.

"Yeah," the heavyset boy joined in. "What you gone buy rock with?"

"Rock?" Faith Ann really wanted to turn and run, but another sullen boy moved up behind her.

"You lookin' to score, or what?"

"I'm looking for Sister Ellen Proctor, the nun. She lives here."

"White lady?"

Faith Ann nodded.

"Sheeeeet. This look like a place for white nuns?"

"Maybe he thinks this is a Catholic school." The fat boy stepped closer.

"Maybe I was wrong," Faith Ann said, feeling scared.

"Maybe you got the wrong projects." The leader held out his hand. "Let me hold your lid for a second."

Before Faith Ann could respond, he jerked off her cap and was studying it.

"How much you give for this here?" the red-haired leader asked her.

"Twelve dollars."

"I'll sell it back to you for five."

"That's a good deal," the fat boy piped up. "Cute-ass hat like that gots to be worth twenty."

"Keep it," Faith Ann managed to say.

"I don't want no zoo hat. Zoo hats for faggots. I look like a fag to you?"

"He called you a faggot," another boy jeered. "You gone let him do that?"

The blow came out of nowhere, and Faith Ann was surprised to find herself sitting on her butt, looking up at the boys, the one in dreads smiling malevolently, showing her his fist. "You fall down, zoo boy?" Faith Ann felt the numbness where the sharp knuckles had connected with her cheekbone. She had never before been punched in the face and she was scared.

The skinny leader tossed the hat onto Faith Ann's chest, held out his open hand. "I said five dollars for the hat. That other was for calling me a faggot, faggot. You lucky I don't put one between your eyes." He put his hand inside his large shirt, suggesting he had a gun.

"What you got in the book bag, bee-otch?" the fat boy demanded.

"Nothing," Faith Ann stammered.

"Give me some money, zoo boy."

Faith Ann weighed her options. Nobody was going to rush up to help her, she couldn't fight them all, and she sure wasn't going to let them have the backpack because of what it contained.

"Okay," she said, standing, with the hat clasped in her left hand. "I'll give you some money."

The leader backed up, his bright eyes filled with anticipation.

Faith Ann faced the wall of boys, reached into her pocket and slipped her fingers around the wad of bills. She jerked her hand out, then tossed the currency that came out with it, where the breeze caught it and turned the wad into a fluttering cloud of bills. Faith Ann turned and ran.

"Come back here!" the leader hollered—like there was some chance of that happening.

Faith Ann didn't slow down until she was back across North Rampart Street and two blocks into the French Quarter. If Sister Ellen *was* in there, she was beyond Faith Ann's reach. Maybe she was at the prison telling Horace Pond that Jesus loved him.

47

Winter parked in front of the house next door to the Porter residence, a narrow wood-frame raised shotgun. He climbed from his car and noticed a woman peering out at him through the screen door of the next house over. Most of the houses in the uptown neighborhood were attractive, the yards well kept. The Porter house was light gray with dark gray shutters, a burgundy-painted concrete porch, and a glass-panel burgundy front door. A picket fence stretched across the front, but the fence running down either side of the lot was of hurricane wire. A freestanding cinder-block garage beside the house was painted the same gray as the house.

"Hello there," he called cheerfully to the woman.

She opened the door and came out on the porch, wiping her hands on the apron she was wearing to protect her cotton housedress. She was thin, probably in her late sixties, and wore her hair in a bun. She had a noticeable mustache.

"Can I help you, young man?"

He opened her gate and stepped into her yard, which unlike the Porters' was filled to bursting with raised flower beds, enough plants to fill a nursery. Dozens of flower pots cut the porch's usable sitting space down to the rocking chair she occupied.

"I'm U.S. Deputy Marshal Winter Massey. Can I talk to you for a moment?"

"I expect you want to ask about Mrs. Porter," she replied, shaking her head. "Nice lady. Her daughter is a sweet girl. Y'all find her yet?"

"When did you see her last?"

"I saw them both a couple of days ago. I always speak to them, and they are friendly enough, but they kind of stay to themselves. Faith Ann is sweet and very smart. Most kids her age aren't nearly as nice or able to have conversations with adults. I sure hope she's okay. It's just horrible what happened. I told the other police that I'd call if I saw her."

Winter said, "I'm a friend of Kimberly's sister and her husband, and Faith Ann is a close friend of my son's. I'm trying to find her on my own."

"Are you sure . . . Are you really a policeman?"

"I'm a United States marshal."

"Could you show me?"

He came up to the porch and handed her up his badge and I.D.

"Thought you might be a reporter. Several been by to ask me a lot of questions too, but I couldn't help them.

Truth is, I only made small talk with the Porters over the fence, how neighbors do. I gave her a recipe here and there. Faith Ann was the one who generally cooked, because her mama wasn't interested in it. I know Mrs. Porter worshipped that girl and vice versa." She smiled. "They would sit on the porch and talk and laugh and went almost everywhere together. Close, don't you see. Like best friends. They liked keeping their own company."

The woman handed Winter back his badge case. "I'm Clara Hughes."

"Nice to meet you. So, how many policemen searched the house?"

"Let me think . . . First, yesterday morning, the regular police came in a police car, but they didn't go in. They just walked around looking in windows. I thought that was odd, but it wasn't any of my business. I didn't know what it was about then. After a while, the man officer got in his car and he must have parked it somewhere else, because he walked back around the corner from Marengo Street, and those two sort of watched over the place.

"Later on two police detectives came, and the uniformed police left. Then the detectives went inside, and this other pair pulled up in a big Lincoln Continental and they went in too. The second bunch left after maybe forty-five minutes. They took a shopping bag with them. The two detectives stayed longer. I heard all kinds of racket in there like they were breaking things. I wasn't trying to listen, you understand. My windows were open to catch the breeze."

"They were probably other detectives," Winter said, making a mental note to ask Manseur about the couple in the Lincoln.

"They weren't dressed in suits like the other two. The young man was very handsome with his hair combed straight back like a movie star. Not tall as you, sort of thin, and he had a long black coat on. She was dressed up kind of fancy."

"She? Fancy how?"

"Sort of, I don't know . . . almost like fashion models."

"Glamorous?"

Clara nodded. "She was shorter, and she had black hair in a ponytail. The cap, boots, jacket, and the tightest pants you ever saw, all black leather. My husband would have said she got poured into her outfit. I've never seen police wearing any outfits like that. That pair came two times. The last time, he went inside by the front door, she went to the back. And they both came out around from out back. What was funny was, the woman crawled right under the house. Now, why, I thought, would somebody all dressed up like that get under a house with all that dirt and who knows what else? Anyway she came back out in a few minutes and then they left in their big black car."

"When was the second visit?"

"Early this morning."

"Did they talk to you?"

"I didn't talk to anybody but two detectives. The big one gave me a card with his name and number on it."

"Could I see the card?"

The woman went inside and returned with a business card. The name on it was Detective Anthony Brian Tinnerino, NOPD. There was an extra number added in ink.

"That's his private number," she said. "Said to call anytime night or day. I didn't like that man one little bit."

"You didn't?"

"He was a condescending jerk. Surly. Maybe that's police detective nature or something. You'd think they would be nicer to people they want help from."

"You'd think so."

"Catch more flies with honey. You'd think a policeman would know that."

"Seems like it," Winter agreed.

"Didn't make me want to help them at all. It's no wonder they don't solve more crimes than they do. If you call them, sometimes they don't even come unless it's a big house on St. Charles Avenue. Then they sure come running—you bet they do."

"Clara, if I give you my phone number, could you call me if you see Faith Ann? I'll help her. I'll make sure they don't pull anything on her after all she's been through."

"Like make me think that sweet little girl could have hurt her mama? He didn't come right out and say it, but that was what he wanted me to believe. Like that could be true, or something. That big one told me not to talk to her or anything—just call him and he'd take it from there."

"I just think somebody who cares about Faith Ann should know what the police know. In case she needs anything."

"And I shouldn't tell the other policemen?"

"I'm not advising you not to tell the police what they asked you to tell them. Unless there's some good reason, you should always help the *legitimate* authorities with official investigations. I'd just like to know. Maybe you could call me first, if you'd feel comfortable doing that. If not, I'll understand."

She fixed Winter with her stare, then nodded slowly.

"I don't see why not. You *are* a policeman." She smiled. "And you're a polite young man."

"I always try to be, Ms. Hughes."

"There is one thing . . ." she said. "Late last night, I woke up and—my bed's on this side, and after the rain it was so restful with the windows open. Well something woke me up, you know how it does sometimes when you hear something and you aren't sure about it. So I wasn't sure what woke me, but at the time I thought it was the sound of their toilet flushing."

48

John Adams pulled up to the curb near the Monteleone Hotel, just inside the French Quarter.

"I'll be back with the radios in two minutes. Think you can keep the car from being stolen?" he said to Nicky before he climbed out.

"I reckon I can manage it," he replied. "If you get lost in there, just fire that Glock three times in the air and I'll come get you."

Nicky Green watched the FBI agent worm his way through the weekenders cluttering the sidewalk and vanish through the doors. The agent moved with a fluidity that added to Nicky's doubts that Adams was what he claimed to be. Nicky was sure that whatever Adams's purpose was, it wasn't what he had claimed. Adams had the eyes of a predator, not a cop. If Massey was as good as Nicky thought he was, he didn't believe Adams's story either. How had Adams gotten to town so fast, located them, and bugged the car?

Nicky decided that he needed to learn more about the man. After Adams had been gone for thirty seconds, Nicky climbed out, made his way into the hotel, and strolled to the bell captain's kiosk. The bell captain was middle-aged, dressed in a navy sport jacket with the hotel's logo over the pocket, starched white shirt, and striped tie. Telephone to his ear, he was jotting down notes. Nicky placed his hand on the desk and parted his fingers to reveal a one-hundred-dollar bill. The bell captain saw the bill but didn't acknowledge its presence.

"How may I help you, sir?" he said, hanging up the phone.

"A minute ago, a man named John Everett Adams came in here. You might have seen him. Gray suit. Five-ten, one-sixty-five. Crew cut."

"I don't know the gentleman by sight, sir," the bell captain said.

"Well, see, I'm hoping he's registered under John E. Adams."

"He might be. And?"

A couple approached.

Nicky stepped aside.

The bell captain listened to their question about jazz clubs on Bourbon Street, which he answered by scribbling down the names of three he told them had good Dixieland. They left five dollars lighter.

Nicky returned to front and center. "Adams isn't exactly what he seems," Nicky said.

"Is that so?"

"He is a married NASCAR driver. He is meeting with an actress whose name is a household word. I just need to know what room he's in so I can see if it is possible to set up a camera to see in the window."

The bell captain inhaled deeply. Then he turned his sad gray eyes on Nicky. "You want to give me a hundred dollars for the room number of a guest so you can photograph him from a nearby rooftop while he's in bed with an actress?"

"That's about the size of it," Nicky said, holding the man's gaze. "A tasteful picture of her at the window with him would do."

"Private investigator?"

"Did I say that?"

"I should ask you to leave the hotel." He cut his eyes at

the front desk, sniffed, put his fingers between Nicky's, and slid the bill out. Sighing, he flipped open a book and at the same time slipped the bill into his pocket. He ran a finger down a list, then snapped the book closed.

"I would be fired if I gave you information on this John Everett Adams. It's against hotel policy. At any rate I cannot help you because, even if I told you he was in room four-sixteen, there is no place from which you could see into that room unless you get on our window-washing platform, which isn't available for that sort of tomfoolery."

"Damn it!" Nicky frowned like he was disappointed, then turned and walked away. Greed was so predictable. Nicky crossed the lobby to the front doors, passing by a ten-foot-tall grandfather clock as he went.

He got back to the car less than a minute before Adams appeared carrying a small leather satchel.

Nicky pulled down the bill of his cap to make it appear that he had been napping. Adams opened the driver's door and, tossing the case into the backseat, climbed in behind the wheel, cranked the car, and swung it easily into a gap in the traffic.

Nicky lifted the cap. "I see you didn't lose your way."

"Breadcrumbs," Adams replied,

49

The lock on Kimberly and Faith Ann's back door was a deadbolt, so it took Winter, not exactly a Houdini, over a minute to pick it and enter the utility room, which was open into the den. He found nothing there but saw where the computer had been, an empty space next to the printer and scanner. As he moved up the hall, Winter was appalled by the senseless mess the cops had made in the master bedroom, that small private bath. What could have been the point of the destructive behavior of the searchers? Faith Ann's bedroom was upside down. There had been both aquarium and Audubon Zoo posters on the bedroom wall, now torn up and scattered over the floor. A shattered boom box, ripped-up stuffed animals, glass shards . . .

It struck him that the men must have done this so they could say that Faith Ann had done the vandalism herself, the girl running amok while still in a fit of rage after murdering her own mother. It made sense to stack up as many pieces of evidence against her as possible. Framing someone was like painting a canvas—only talented artists knew precisely when to put the brush aside, before one more stroke diminished the painting. Tinnerino and his partner were certainly not artists.

In the hallway bathroom he surveyed the chaos and spotted the dog clippers. There was something else—something very interesting. On the floor beside the counter, on one of the white towels, were several long hairs. He pulled one of them off to inspect it. *Smart kid.* He folded the hairs into a towel and placed it in the cabinet under the sink. He inspected the plastic gap on the clippers and judged the length of her hair. He wondered if the other searchers had made the same discovery and prayed they hadn't. If he was right, the pictures of Faith Ann would not accurately reflect the child who was now running from them. It was a small thing, but it was an edge—it meant she was thinking like a survivor.

He took a quick look around the kitchen, dining and living rooms but found nothing useful. Winter went back out, locking the deadbolt behind him. Locking it took forty seconds. He wanted to see why the woman had gone under there.

Upon turning the corner, he spotted the movable wood

lattice panel because it hadn't fully closed. Winter went the length of the house and found the concrete porch with its square opening. It was pitch-black inside, so he took out a disposable cigarette lighter he always carried in his pocket, thanks to not having one a year before when he had needed a source of light. He flicked it to life and, holding it inside, spotted the yellow poncho. Bracing himself, he slid inside the cool damp enclosure.

In the flickering light he saw there was something under the plastic. His heart fell, thinking Faith Ann's curled-up body might be concealed beneath it. He lifted the edge of the poncho and discovered a pillow. He studied the plastic shell that had contained a Walkman, looked at the shears and the pair of batteries remaining in the packaging. He thought about the empty cassette recorder in Kimberly Porter's office Manseur had mentioned to him. *There was a tape . . . and Faith Ann has it.*

He put the pillow to his face, caught the distinctive odor of stale perspiration, and thought he detected moisture. She had been there since Nicky saw her the night before, and he was sure she had cut her hair and flushed the toilet during the night and taken the pillow then. The woman who'd been under there hadn't found Faith Ann, because Clara Hughes would have noticed her being taken away. He didn't think Faith Ann would come back here. It saddened him to imagine the frightened child lying in the dark space listening to the tape recording of her mother's murder. Reliving it, because if Manseur was right she had witnessed it. He felt a heightened sense of urgency in finding her.

He was behind the other searchers—hundreds of cops and perhaps the killer, or killers. Perhaps one of those cops was also the killer. He was afraid that if the cops got to her before he did, she wouldn't be alive long enough for him to save her. Shaking something loose by the selective use of a heavy hand was his only hope to get ahead of the others, cutting down the timeline. He would talk to Jerry Bennett. If the cops learned that he was on their tails, *maybe* they'd make a mistake, and just *maybe* they'd think twice before harming Faith Ann. He didn't know what else he could do.

Only once before in his professional career had he been looking for someone in order to save her—Sean. He had succeeded, and against insurmountable odds. And the odds of success had certainly been a lot slimmer then. *I will find Faith Ann,* he vowed. *And God help the bastard that harms one hair on her head.*

50

Marta and Arturo sat in Jerry Bennett's office, waiting for him to join them. She wondered what the idiot thought he was accomplishing by making them wait—wasting their time when they were all that stood between him and a death sentence. He acted like it was just a day like any other. Marta didn't know whether he was in some fog of denial or just couldn't alter his normal patterns for fear that he would trigger some avalanche that would bury him. She was thinking about something she'd seen in a movie. She thought she would enjoy cutting him into small pieces, starting with his toes. She'd feed them to hungry pigs while he watched—his stupid eyes lit with fear and pain.

Marta studied Arturo's profile as he chewed his fingernails. She felt the familiar desire, the need to protect him—to cradle him to her breast and comfort him. She knew him as well as she knew herself, knew that he depended on her, perhaps even loved her as she loved him.

Men were a different sort of creature—another species entirely.

She had taught him English. She had taught him her trade, but he didn't understand the nuances that would elevate him beyond being a plain-Jane killer. Arturo liked killing—almost too much, which wasn't the same thing as using it as a tool, a means to an end. She didn't know how she could teach him judgment, patience, or any of the thousand things that he needed to understand and be able to call upon to rise to the level she was on. He was loyal and as fierce as a jaguar, but he lacked the necessary instincts and the ability to see a much larger picture. He thought strategically, but only in the limited sense of a predator. For Arturo, the future was no further away than tomorrow. He was concerned with comfort, with showing off, with satisfying his passions. Unlike Marta, there was no fire burning in his soul that demanded feeding. He was beautiful and he was all hers.

The door swung open soundlessly and Jerry Bennett entered. He reminded Marta of a clown. The pancake makeup that she supposed he wore to give himself a tanned appearance had stained the collar of his shirt. He wasn't feminine, but he still made Marta think of an old whore who was dependent for her livelihood on the filtering effects of liquor, poor lighting, and makeup to keep her viable. At what must have been a young age, Marta's own mother had also resorted to those tricks to camouflage the effects of a hard life, abusive men, constant worry, and childbearing. She shuddered at the sudden memory of her mother lying dead on a dirt floor with a pool of her blood swelling out from under her head, her neck laid open by a man the law had not bothered to punish. She remembered the small bloody footprints where a frantic child, barely out of diapers, had paced around the room for hours before people had come in.

Before that day, her own life must have been hard, but she didn't remember it that way, because the orphan's dance that came after that had been so horrible.

"Well," Bennett said, exhaling loudly, "where are we at, people?"

"We are at your office," Marta said. "What I cannot tell you is why."

The fire in Arturo's eyes burned her, almost as intensely as did Bennett's.

"*Why* is because Mr. Estrada here made a mess of an assignment so uncomplicated that a retarded chimpanzee could have pulled it off. I want to ask you why you two *professionals,* if I can use that word with a straight face, haven't been able to locate one frightened child and retrieve my property."

"We will find her," Arturo said quickly. "Soon."

"Mr. Bennett," Marta said calmly, "if you have other *professionals* you can summon, perhaps you would like to do that before we go any further in this *mess*. It seems to me that if you had bothered to tell either of us that in the envelope we were to bring you, there were—besides the eight pictures you mentioned—negatives, Arturo would have checked to see that they were there. And Amber Lee would have come up with them. Since *you* failed to mention their existence, I don't think you should speak to Arturo so disrespectfully. I think you should be more considerate of the only people who can remedy your predicament. We will fix this problem, but insulting us is not acceptable. If I were you, I wouldn't do it again." The icy quality in her tone was as infused with warning as the buzz from a rattlesnake.

"I may have . . . I believe I misspoke. It's just that I'm under so much pressure. Of course you are doing the best you can. The best anybody on earth could do. And I failed to mention the negatives because I wasn't thinking about them. I assumed they would be with the prints. Well, there it is," he said, trying to smile. "So I am sorry if I insulted either of you, because that wasn't my intent. I mean, if you can't succeed, who can? The cops don't seem to be getting anywhere, and they're the cops, for Christ's sake. . . ."

The ringing phone in Arturo's pocket ended Bennett's stammering. He opened it, stared at the caller I.D., and put it to his ear. "Go."

As Arturo listened to what the caller was saying a smile appeared and started to grow. "Right now?" He turned his free thumb up and nodded. "Where? Just four or five minutes away." He stood and pocketed the phone. "The kid's using the cell phone. The aquarium just down the river."

"Remember my negatives!" Bennett called cheerfully, clapping his sweaty hands.

51

After the trouble in the projects, Faith Ann wandered the streets of the French Quarter, thinking hard. The sidewalks were now filled with pedestrians, and sometimes she had to slow to avoid running into tourists who had slowed to gawk at something they didn't see every day where they came from. She was still shaken up from her encounter with the gang, and her jaw hurt like hell. Eventually she found herself in Jackson Square in front of the cathedral, sitting around with older kids to look like she belonged, watching tourists and the performers.

Through the glass doors of every newspaper stand Faith Ann passed, Kimberly Porter stared out at her, reminding her of how important her mission was. *Unless you succeed where I failed, Horace Pond will die. It's all up to you, Faith Ann. You can do it. You must . . .*

She pulled the remaining bills from her jeans pocket and counted as she walked. Seventy-four dollars out of almost a thousand. Her escape had been expensive but worth every penny. She was starving, so she stopped in a fudge shop and bought a plastic sack of pralines for many times what they should have cost. She wolfed them down—the sweetness stinging the back of her throat.

She walked to the aquarium and stood near the entrance, watching people. She saw a mother and her daughter, hand in hand, vanish into the building. Taking off her backpack, Faith Ann found her mother's cell phone and dialed. When the familiar voice answered, "Hello?" she felt small and terrified and before she knew it she started crying.

"I . . . I . . . I. Rush . . ." she managed to say. "It's me, Faith Ann. Please . . . I need help."

52

Winter and Adams took Winter's Stratus, and Nicky followed driving Adams's Chevrolet. They arrived outside the River Club and parked in the lot. Nicky stopped the Chevrolet thirty feet away from them.

"Okay, Nicky," Winter said into his radio. "Adams and I'll rattle this buzzard's cage. I'll radio if we need you inside."

As the pair walked off, Nicky's voice came over the radio. *"Ten-four."*

Inside the foyer, the smiling hostess was bantering with a group of men, one of whom Winter recognized as the previous mayor of New Orleans, the son of another mayor long dead. As the local dignitaries were being led to a table, Winter and Adams waited for the hostess to return.

"Two?" she asked cheerfully. "Smoking or nonsmoking?"

Adams opened his badge case and showed it to her. "We need to speak to Mr. Bennett," he said.

"I'll see if he's in," she said, a pained smile freezing on her face. "Can I tell him what this is in reference to?"

"Shouldn't you see if he's *in* first?" Adams replied.

She lifted the telephone on the lectern and punched three digits. "Is the boss in?" she asked. After a short pause, she said, "There are two gentlemen to see Mr. Bennett. FBI agents."

She listened and looked back up at Adams. "Might I say what this is in reference to?"

"We'll handle that," Adams said flatly.

The hostess said, "Just go straight to the rear near the bathrooms. The iron gate will be open. His office is at the end."

Winter and Adams walked toward the rear, skirting the dining tables. He caught sight of two people who fit Clara Hughes's description cut across the restaurant from the office area and exit through a side door. Winter keyed the radio. "Nicky, the couple in the Lincoln are exiting the far side of the building. Follow them."

"I see them, and I'm so there," Nicky's voice replied. *"Leather lady and Stick climbed into a big bad black Lincoln, just like the neighbor lady said."*

"Stick on them," Winter said. "But don't get too close."

Now they would find out who the couple were.

"Well, that's an interesting turn," Adams said.

"Nicky, we're going in to see the guy. Radio silence unless there's an emergency." Winter shut off his cell phone as they passed through the ornamental iron doors.

Jerry Bennett's secretary was a plump, orange-haired

woman seated at a desk, blinking owlishly. Her face was as round as a pie tin, and her red lips were surrounded by thin lines, like metal fatigue cracks. Her irises were the color of mud, and her eyelids seemed to be trembling under the weight of green eyeshadow. "Can I help you?"

Adams flashed his badge. "Special Agent John Adams. Jerry Bennett, please."

"He's expecting you," she said. She got up, crossed to a tall, solid oak door, and held it open for them.

Jerry Bennett's office was spacious and elegantly modern. Illumination was provided by hidden light fixtures. The club owner approached the two men and extended his hand, which, since neither man moved to shake it, remained suspended before him until he lowered it and sat down behind the desk. The thick surface of the desk was granite, the edges rough as though something with very hard teeth had chewed on it.

"May I see your credentials?" he said, focusing first on Winter and then on Adams.

Adams held his ID inches from Bennett's eyes. Winter pulled out his badge case, and Bennett read it silently. If the presence of a marshal meant anything to him he didn't show it.

"What can I do for you?" he asked.

"We're looking into something, and a name came up that seems to be connected to you."

"Please, sit," Bennett said.

Adams and Winter sat in the two chairs across from the club owner. Adams opened a small notebook and stared at what Winter saw was a blank page. He took out a ballpoint, snapped its tip out, and positioned it over the page.

"Amber Lee," Adams said after a few more seconds of silence.

"I didn't know that the FBI investigates murders."

"Did I say we were investigating murders?"

Bennett reacted by shifting in his seat and smiling sickly. "No, I guess not."

"That would be an NOPD matter," Adams said. "Unless it somehow wasn't being handled legitimately."

"Poor woman," Bennett murmured.

"Yes," Adams agreed. "Poor woman indeed."

"Unfortunate, what happened," Bennett said, lowering his eyes to the desktop.

"You filed charges against her," Adams asked, snapping the ballpoint.

"I didn't want to. We go back a long way, Amber and I. At one time, we were very close. I've known . . . I knew her for over twenty years."

"And yet she stole from you," Adams said.

"That was . . ."

"Unfortunate?" Adams snapped the ballpoint on, made a note, clicked it off, and looked back up at Bennett.

Bennett nodded. "Very. I've thought about it a great deal. It's very painful, as you can imagine. Maybe she needed money and was embarrassed to ask. I can't understand it, because I paid her quite well."

"How much?"

"I'm sorry?"

"How much did she steal?"

"I believe it was fifty thousand dollars."

"Fifty even?"

"Yes."

"Your bookkeeper caught it?"

"No, it was in my drawer."

"Fifty thousand dollars . . . in cash?"

"Yes." Bennett nodded.

Adams scribbled. Clicked the pen closed.

Bennett cleared his throat. "Of course, I had to file charges. My insurance requires I do that if they are going to pay on my loss-by-theft policy."

"Insurance company?" Adams clicked the pen and poised it over the pad.

"I'm sorry?"

"You filed a claim. I need the name of the company and the claims agent. So I can check it. Routine procedure."

"Well . . . I haven't filed a claim yet . . . I will. My insurance broker is Felix Argent at Argent Consolidated. I'm not sure which company he has that handles that coverage. He uses lots of underwriting companies."

Click. "So, Felix Argent advised you to file charges."

"A policeman did."

"The policeman who investigated the theft? It was investigated?"

Bennett nodded. "Look, I knew she took it. It was in my safe, she was the only other one in here who had the combination, and she left and it was gone." He held out his open hands. "I was actually advised to file charges by a policeman, a close friend of mine, who said I would need that to collect on that kind of policy. I'm not sure Felix and I have talked about it yet. I've been extremely busy."

Scribble. *Click.* "And no doubt grieving," Adams said.

Adams's delivery was so deadpan that he could have been reading the questions out of an instruction book. Winter didn't do anything other than watch in solemn silence. It was a technique like the way Adams clicked the pen to make Bennett nervous. A mysterious U.S. marshal and an annoying FBI agent.

Silence for fifteen seconds. *Click.* "The name of this policeman friend?"

"Suggs. Homicide Commander Captain Harvey Suggs."

"I see," Adams said, not writing the name at all. "That wouldn't be the same Captain Suggs who is overseeing the Porter/Lee murder cases?"

"Is he? I suppose he would be in charge of the detectives who are. You'd have to ask him."

"Yes, I would," Adams agreed. "I would indeed."

Winter studied the club owner, spotting the tells, charting the lies. Bennett wasn't a talented liar, His eyes rolled up and to the right about every time he answered one of Adams's questions. He drummed his fingers on his desk and swallowed constantly. He wasn't just nervous, he was afraid, and he had been totally blindsided by their sudden appearance. Adams was shaking his tree and the miserable creature across from them was holding on for dear life.

"Did you know Kimberly Porter?"

"Who?"

"The second homicide victim."

"The murderer's mother?"

"Suggs tell you the child was the killer?"

"Well, I just assumed it, I guess. I haven't spoken to Harvey. Not since it happened."

Adams wrote that down. "After your friend Amber is murdered, you didn't call to ask Suggs about it? Not even seek more of his valuable advice? So, you haven't spoken to him in . . . how long?"

"In two weeks. Since the theft."

"And you didn't know Kimberly Porter."

"No. I never met her, as far as I know. I talk to hundreds of people in the course of my businesses."

"Well, I guess you wouldn't have. Mrs. Porter didn't hang out in *clubs* like yours, probably didn't eat a lot of artificially spiced fried chicken. She was a *Death Row* appeals specialist, and a mother."

Something in Bennett's eyes changed. They hardened and he seemed to have gained control of his fear. He leaned back in his chair and locked his fingers across his stomach. "I may have read that she was a lawyer. I don't have much to do with people on Death Row."

"And did Amber Lee have much to do with people on Death Row?"

"I seriously doubt it."

"Then it must seem particularly bizarre to you that Ms. Lee would be meeting with her, doesn't it?"

"I wouldn't know what she was meeting with that attorney about."

"Are you aware that she had approached the FBI?"

"Lawyer Porter?"

Adams looked down and made notes on the pad.

"Would you know what information Ms. Lee may have had about one of Ms. Porter's clients being innocent—of knowing who the real killer was? Of having proof of it in her hands."

"Ms. Lee never mentioned having any knowledge of any murder case. But in the past few years, we weren't as close as we once were."

"How close were you two, in the years when you were close?"

"*That* is none of the FBI's business," he said, standing abruptly. "Gentlemen, that's the end of this conversation. If you want to discuss anything else with me, submit your questions in writing to my attorney."

Click. Adams closed his pad and pocketed it.

"There is just one more thing," Winter said.

Bennett stood rigid, staring indignantly into Winter's eyes.

"What do you know about Hank Trammel?"

"Who?"

"United States Marshal Hank Trammel."

"Never heard of him."

Winter exhaled, disappointed. If his internal lie detector was working, Jerry Bennett was telling the truth . . . about that one thing.

53

Nicky Green followed the Lincoln toward the Quarter, but either the driver spotted him or she was really in a big hurry: she out-negotiated him through the traffic. He got stuck between several vehicles at a traffic light on Canal Street, unable to follow. He decided that being so close to the Monteleone Hotel, there was something he could do while he was alone.

Nicky parked in a loading zone and, entering the hotel lobby from the rear, strode to the elevator bank. He took a car up to the fourth floor. As he approached Adams's room, Nicky opened his wallet and slid out what appeared to be a credit card. There was a DO NOT DISTURB sign on the knob. He slid the electronic device into the electronic lock slot, the red light changed from red to green and the lock mechanism clicked loudly. *Master key. Don't leave home without it.*

As he opened the door, Nicky looked down and spotted a small sliver of paper fluttering to the carpet. Adams had put it between the door and the jamb so he'd know if he'd had any visitors during his absence. The paper was close enough to the color of the carpeting that it wouldn't be noticed by anyone who wasn't looking for that trap. Not exactly something the FBI should feel a need to do. Nicky took the sliver and placed it inside the door on the carpet, planning to replace it when he left. He checked his watch, knowing he couldn't afford to spend more than five minutes inside the room.

At first Nicky didn't see anything unusual. An inexpensive suitcase was perched on the folding rack at the foot of the bed. He knelt and studied it. The thumb releases had been polished so that any finger oil would leave a visible print. Using a tissue as a makeshift glove, Nicky opened the case. It had been packed with precision. Moving as fast as possible, he memorized the positions of everything on the top layer, then exposed the next layer with the care of an archaeologist. The shirts, slacks, and undergarments were all new. There were no hidden compartments in the case. Disappointed, he replaced everything exactly as he'd found it. He looked under the bed, checked the closet, where there was a lone gray suit—a duplicate of the one Adams was wearing—hanging, but Nicky hadn't seen any neckties. A man who wore suits every day should have had several.

The bathroom gave Adams away. The toilet articles were all unused. This room was a decoy. Nicky knelt and studied the knob on the adjoining door and found that it was also polished clean, not something most hotel maids would think to do. He looked and spotted a single broom straw leaned against the bottom left edge of the door that opened directly into the next room.

Nicky opened the door into John Everett Adams's lair. Clothes were thrown over a chair. An open suitcase on the floor contained more clothes. There were two Brioni suits, two pairs of slacks, and an Armani sports coat. There was a suitcase beside the dresser which contained eyeglasses, mustaches, wigs, and makeup. The Halliburton case on the bed contained a foam bed cut out for two handguns, two knives, an array of bullets, a noise suppressor, and assorted electronic devices. Carefully Nicky moved the upper foam insert and discovered six envelopes there. He opened one of them and slid out a Swiss passport under the name Hans Krutz. The picture was of Adams, but with his oiled hair combed to his skull. There were credit cards and photos of him with a wife and two kids.

"Well paint my butt red and call me a baboon," Nicky whispered.

Obviously Adams, or whoever he was, was a professional, but what was he after and who was he working for? What was his interest in Trammel? Or was it Porter that he was interested in? Had he joined them to get to the girl? Was he covering Bennett's or the cops' backs—a safety in case Massey found her first? How could he know so much about Winter Massey and, for that matter, himself? He had to keep an eye on Adams, and first chance he got he would let Winter know that Adams was a fraud—a very dangerous one.

Nicky heard someone out in the hallway, so he returned the items and pocketed the envelope. It wouldn't be Adams, but he might have a partner staking out his hide. He pulled Trammel's .45 and closed the case.

Nicky saw the shadows of feet pass under the door to the hallway. He approached the door, held his breath, and waited. Someone pressed against the wood and he aimed the pistol at the door, bracing himself for someone to burst in. In his mind he saw the shots and his exact escape route from the scene—the corpse he would leave behind.

He heard voices, and he moved to the door and pressed his ear against it. He smiled as he identified two distinct voices, almost whispering. A man and a woman. It sounded to Nicky as if she was being pressed against the door.

"Let's go into my room," a male voice urged.

"What if he comes back and I'm not there?"

"He's with George and them. They'll be drinking for hours."

"I guess so. What are you doing? Damn it, Frank, not here."

"Come on, Betts, you're wet already."

She giggled. "Stop it. What if somebody comes?"

"*I'm* going to come. Feel that? It's about to explode."

"All right. Ten minutes and I mean it."

"I'll make it in five."

Nicky looked through the peephole and saw an overweight couple disappear into a doorway across the hall.

He retraced his steps, replacing first the straw and then the chip of paper as he left.

John Adams had dismissed him as an incompetent, crippled bum. Nicky Green knew the value of having people underestimate you.

Sometimes Providence smiles. Nicky was heading back toward the River Club when he spotted the black Lincoln Town Car parked on the edge of a public lot across the street from the Wyndham Hotel. He drove slowly by the car, making sure it was the right license plate. *How can it get any better than this?* He scanned the lot, looking for the couple, but didn't see them. *Well, they'll be back.* His radio coming to life startled him.

"Nicky, we're all done. You still on the pair?"

"I'm at the Lincoln. I got caught in traffic. They parked in the lot and they're on foot. I'm trying to spot them. You guys meet me here, and we can spread out and look for them."

"We're on the way," Winter said.

54 | Concord, North Carolina

When the phone rang, Rush Massey was sitting in the porch swing listening to the latest Harry Potter novel on CD over a portable entertainment center roughly the size of a breadbox that sat on a Stickley side table.

Nemo, who had been sound asleep on the tile floor beneath the swing, barked in alarm.

"Like I couldn't hear the dang phone, Nemo." He stood and went inside with the dog close behind him. The call wouldn't go on to the answering service until the sixth ring because Sean hated to have to run to answer it. At that moment she was across town grocery shopping. Rush would have let it ring but for the chance it might be his father calling with news about Faith Ann. More likely it was Sean with a question about something he might not eat. She was still getting accustomed to his tastes, so if he didn't accompany her to the store she often called for his food-related advice. He turned into the home office and, putting the book down, lifted the receiver.

"Massey residence," he announced. "How may I direct your call?"

He was stunned to hear the sobs and Faith Ann's fractured voice. "I . . . I . . . I. Rush. It's me, Faith Ann. Please . . . I need help."

"Faith Ann. We've been worried sick about you! Where are you?"

"Rush, Mama's dead. I saw him . . . So is . . . Aunt Millie and Uncle Hank."

She cried loudly, and his heart went out to her. "I know, but Hank's not. He's just unconscious—he's not dead. He's at the hospital where they have real good emergency doctors. Daddy went there when they shot him in the leg."

"He's not . . . dead? Are you sure? I saw him. I thought sure . . . But . . . Rush, I saw them run over them."

"He's not good yet, but he's alive."

"Who ran over them?"

"I'm not sure. Have you seen my daddy yet?"

"No."

"Well, he's looking high and low for you."

"Where?"

"In New Orleans."

"Where in New Orleans?"

"Sean knows the hotel name. She'll be back in a few minutes."

"Can you ask her and call me back?"

"I can call her on her cell phone. What's your number?"

As fast as she told him, he had it committed to memory.

"Faith Ann, Daddy said you didn't ever call the police. Why didn't you tell them about your mother?"

"One of them did it." She was crying again. "They're trying to kill me too."

"No, Faith Ann. My daddy won't let them. You know him."

"Will you call me right back?"

"Sure. But I'll call Daddy and tell him where you are. Where are you exactly?"

"I'm at the aquarium."

"Where is that?"

"Right by the Mississippi River."

"I'll tell him. You just sit tight and wait. Okay?"

"Okay."

"Why did the police kill your mother?"

"Because of Horace Pond."

"Just wait there, Faith Ann."

"Okay, I will."

"It's going to be okay, Faith Ann."

"Thanks, Rush."

"Good-bye, Faith Ann."

"Good-bye, Rush."

"And, Faith Ann?"

"Yeah."

"We love you."

"I love you too."

Rush took a deep breath, pressed down the button, and

dialed his father's cell number. There was no answer, just his voice mail. "Dang it."

Rush tried again, same result.

He dialed Sean, and she picked up.

55

Marta and Arturo approached the aquarium from the rear. "Remember, Arturo. No guns. She's seen you, so we let Tinnerino and Doyle get her, and they'll hand her over."

"What if people see them take her? How can they hand her to us after that?"

"They'll do what they're told to do."

"We don't know for sure that she saw me," he said sourly.

"You don't know that she didn't. So we aren't taking any chances. There are a lot of people around. We can't afford to do anything stupid. Remember that we have to get the tape."

"And the negatives."

"And those too. If we can."

"Maybe the two cops will get the negatives *and* the tape and try to keep them. Bennett would pay a lot more for them than he'll pay if they just hand her over to us. I don't trust them."

"If they try something like that, we'll handle them. We'll have to anyway, eventually. But we should plan everything so we get them all before they know what we're doing."

"That's cool. But when I take them out, I want them to know I'm doing them."

56

Winter had turned off his phone at the club, so he turned it on and called Detective Manseur to fill him in on the conversation with Bennett in his office. He described the couple: "Short woman in leather with long hair and a young dark-haired man in a black Lincoln Town Car. They were in Bennett's office just before we got there."

"They aren't with Homicide, Vice, or Narcotics," Manseur told him. "They could be uniforms on special assignment, but if they were working with the detective bureau, I'd know about them."

"I don't think Bennett had anything to do with the Trammels' hit-and-run," Winter told him. "He was easy to read because we came out of the blue and rattled him good. I don't think he ever expected to be connected to anything, because he didn't have a straight story and he mentioned his close friendship with Suggs. By the time we left he was almost under control, but I'm sure he's never heard of Hank."

"But it has to be connected to Kimberly Porter," Manseur said.

"Oh, Bennett's tangled up in that. Proving it is going to be a different matter. He'll lawyer up."

Adams, overhearing the conversation, nodded, agreeing with Winter's assessment. "He's a narcissistic jerk. He thinks he's bulletproof and smarter than everybody else. He'll get more pissed if you criticize his lousy office decor than if you accuse him of a crime," Adams said.

Winter said, "Amber didn't take any money from him, but she might have taken something worth killing her for.

That charade probably allowed him to get the cops to locate her. I'd bet Suggs helped him with that. Maybe Bennett found her, he went postal, and Suggs is trying to cover for Bennett."

Manseur said, "I don't think Bennett confronted Amber in Porter's office and there was an argument that escalated. The choice of the weapon says that whoever did it was there to kill Amber all along."

"If Faith Ann saw Bennett do it, and Bennett ran to Suggs—his pal—that could explain why Suggs immediately started stacking the deck against her."

"It's worth considering, but I can't imagine Suggs risking everything to cover up a murder for Bennett. Kimberly Porter wasn't exactly popular with our department."

Winter had an incoming call, so he asked Manseur to hang on while he took it. "Yeah?"

"Daddy," Rush said.

"I can't talk now, Rush. I'll call you back."

"But it's super-important." Rush sounded frantic.

"Okay, hang on and I'll be right back."

"But—"

He returned to Manseur. "I gotta take this other call," Winter told him.

"Keep me posted," Manseur said.

"We're going to meet Nicky Green. I'll call you back as soon as we get there."

"No problem," Manseur said. "Suggs knows you are coming this morning. I told him I was going to talk to you. So we've talked. You didn't tell me about Kimberly Porter, right?"

"No, I didn't tell you squat."

Winter switched back to Rush. "What's up, Rush?"

"I've been trying to call you, but I kept getting the voice message."

"I had it off for a meeting."

"Faith Ann called. I told her you'd—"

"When?"

"I don't know for sure. Maybe about fifteen or twenty minutes ago—"

"From where?" Winter interrupted. "Rush, where did she call from?"

"The aquarium. It's near—"

"I know where the aquarium is," Winter said.

"I told her Hank was alive. She didn't know. Daddy, she's real scared. She said a policeman killed her mother. She says the cops are trying to kill her too."

"I'm not far from there. If she calls back, tell her I'm on the way."

"I'll call her back."

"You know her number?"

"She has her mother's cell phone. You want the number?"

57

Faith Ann turned off the telephone and slipped it into her pocket.

Rush's father is looking for me! He's coming here!

Uncle Hank is alive!

I'm safe.

Standing at the top of the steps leading up to the aquarium's plaza, she held on to those thoughts. Like a sign, she used them to cover the memory of her mother's body, of Millie and Hank lying in the rain-soaked street. Hadn't Rush said Hank was going to be all right? She replayed the conversation, but she couldn't remember if he had said so. Mr. Massey would know. He could use the negatives to save Horace Pond. And the tape held the proof of who shot her mother and the other woman. *What was her name? Ms. Lee. Amber.*

She wondered how long it would take Mr. Massey to get there. Of course he wouldn't recognize her with short hair, but she'd know him on sight. She'd run right up to him and throw her arms around him. She knew how happy he would be, how relieved. And after he straightened everything out, the cops would be in big trouble, and the man who killed her mother would be where Horace Pond was now, in prison. Her mother had always told her that justice, while it didn't always work fast, averaged everything out in the end—like the scales the blindfolded woman was holding. Faith Ann supposed that the sword she held in her other hand was for people who didn't want justice to win. She was the sort of a no-nonsense angel Faith Ann imagined when she had prayed for one to help her. Winter Massey was probably some kind of an angel.

Faith Ann was watching the streets when she spotted a big car drive up and pull over on the access road beside the walled-in power station and the wall that ran beside the aquarium. As the driver stepped out, her feeling of safety, of being rescued, evaporated. A wave of terror filled her and washed away everything else. The driver of the sedan was the larger of the first two cops who had come to her house. Faith Ann moved across the mall and joined the line of people who were entering the aquarium.

Turning her head in the other direction to look for Winter Massey, she spotted the driver's partner coming straight toward her from the downriver end of the structure. She paid the $6.50 admission and was aware that the cell phone in her pocket was ringing, that Rush must be calling her back, but she ignored it.

The security guards manning the metal detectors inside the doors didn't so much as look at her.

The two detectives met up outside the doors and came inside.

She turned her head to see that the cops were talking to the male security guard.

Inside the lobby, she turned to see that the big cop was behind her; he was scanning the crowd, surely looking for her. She left the slow-moving crowd, and as soon as she was out of sight of the cop she ran. *Where is Mr. Massey?* The cop had looked directly at her, but she didn't think he recognized her. She could hardly hear the canned music or the people talking over the roar in her mind, the fear that filled her. She forced herself to pause to look at a glass wall, behind which fish of all sizes swam lazily. *How did the cop find her?*

Any second the cop could spot her and grab her, and he would take the tape and the negatives and then they would probably kill her because she knew too much. When Mr. Massey came, it might already be too late. If Mr. Massey started asking questions about her, maybe they would kill him too. Two days earlier, she would have thought that was impossible, but now she knew it wasn't. If they grabbed her, she could scream bloody murder and fight them, but who was going to go against the police to help her?

She tugged down the bill of her cap and moved rapidly through the Caribbean reef exhibit, colorful fish swimming on the other side of the glass wall. On the escalator she dared to look back. She saw the big cop coming behind her and she fought the urge to break into a dead run, knowing it would only call attention to herself.

On the second floor, she walked hurriedly through the rain forest, past the food court and down to the first floor. After passing by the jellyfish tanks and the Gulf of Mexico exhibit, she came alongside the glass tunnel for pedestrians that was under the shark tank. She had never been at the aquarium that she didn't go inside that tunnel. She always imagined that she was scuba diving, without the dangers or the wet.

She had to get out of the building, into the open.

Faith Ann slowed when she saw the smaller cop standing near the drinking fountain, close to the exit. He was looking hard at every kid who was leaving the building. If he studied her face, he could recognize her—a kid alone.

The phone in her pants began to ring again. She tilted her head down and ignored the rings. Using the bill of her cap to shield her eyes, she stared at the cop's feet and tried to look casual—like she was waiting for someone who was still wandering around in the building. Luckily there were tons of people for him to check out. She decided that her best route of escape was back out the entrance, because she doubted they would figure that anyone would go out that way, or have other cops hanging around there.

The bigger detective, now downstairs, approached the smaller one, and they started talking. Even though nobody seemed to take any notice of it, the phone ringing again in her pocket seemed to her to be a huge sound in the large space. Then it stopped.

She was moving toward the front doors when the phone rang again. Faith Ann was out of sight of the cops so she took it out of her pocket. The caller display showed a number she didn't recognize. She pressed the green button and put the telephone to her ear.

"Rush? Mr. Massey?"

As she listened for a reply, Faith Ann was aware of the sound of the canned music surrounding her, and that it seemed to be slightly out of sync where it entered her right ear through the phone. The caller's phone was picking up the same sounds she was hearing around her, sending them over lines or around a bunch of satellites before sending it to her ear. The echo ended when the incoming call shut off. *He's here!*

Faith Ann spun around, searching the figures and the faces, trying to spot Mr. Massey.

58

While Adams radioed Nicky to tell him to meet them at the aquarium, Winter dialed the number that Rush had given him. It rang several times and was answered by Kimberly's recorded voice asking him to leave his name and telephone number and that she would return the call at her earliest convenience. He ended the call.

"Hurry," he told Adams, who was already driving as fast as the heavy traffic allowed. Adams honked, but the only effect it had was to earn them a few naughty hand signals from other drivers.

After they crossed Poydras Street, a truck swerving to miss another car slammed its rear bumper into a minivan, and they both stopped, completely blocking both lanes. Adams started honking. The driver of the truck jumped down and stamped over to check on the van's driver.

Adams cursed and craned his neck, looking for an escape route. A policeman parked his motorcycle and started walking casually over. He glared at Adams, who held his open badge case out the window. The cop gave him a "just a minute" dismissive wave and approached the truck driver.

"I'm going to hoof it," Winter told Adams. "It's about six blocks. Park the car as close as you can to the aquarium—there a road on either side of it—and meet me in there."

Winter jumped from the car and took off running. Under his jacket the holstered SIG Sauer swung against his ribs like a metronome, keeping perfect machinelike time with each long stride toward the Mississippi River.

When he ran, Winter was in his element. If he hadn't been so nervous, he wouldn't so much as broken a sweat. He took out his cell phone, pressed Redial, and listened to it ring. *Answer it, Faith Ann!*

He dropped the phone back into his pocket and took out the radio. "Nicky, Adams, I'm almost there. Positions?"

"I'm getting close," Nicky's voice said. *"I'm on foot. I can see the building."*

"I'm moving," Adams added. *"Two minutes."*

"When you get there, you two watch the front. Adams, park close and, Nicky, watch the entrance. We'll go in and look for her. I'll bring her to the car out front and we'll take her straight to the hotel."

Winter pocketed the radio and extended his strides.

At the corner of Magazine Street, he turned right on Canal Street and saw the aquarium's distinctive glass tower, like a cake made of mirrors, its flat top canted at a sharp angle.

59

Marta knew that the girl had called somebody from here at the aquarium. After scanning the plaza, she stood in line patiently, paid the adult admission fee, then went through the newly installed metal detectors without incident, since her blades were ceramic. Inside, she immediately spotted Tinnerino and Doyle over by the exit to her right and saw that they hadn't managed to find the girl. In the lobby, Marta checked the women's bathroom, figuring the cops hadn't thought to do that and it was a good place for the girl to hide.

Back outside the bathroom, Marta took out her phone and a slip of paper. Reading the dead lawyer's cell phone number, she keyed it in and listened. When the girl answered, the cops would have a new fix on her, and they would know if she was still in the area. She heard a phone ringing nearby. Marta's eyes stopped on a boy wearing a hooded sweatshirt and a ball cap, who nervously pulled a ringing phone from his pocket. As Marta watched, he looked at the display, pressed a button, and put it to his ear.

"Rush? Mr. Massey?" Marta saw the boy's lips mirror perfectly the words she heard. She realized that the boy wasn't a boy at all, but Faith Ann Porter in disguise! Marta had to hand it to her—this was one bright little girl. Too bad she was living her last day on earth. It was a crying shame she had seen Arturo. If only she had been in school, where she'd belonged, and not in her mother's office. Such a thin child, with such a fragile neck. One swipe and within seconds those bright blue eyes would lose their focus.

Marta saw the child searching the crowd. When the girl's eyes met hers, they filled with sudden shock, then abject fear. Marta hadn't imagined that Faith Ann would know her—had ever seen her before. Marta looked up to signal the two detectives to move in, but they were no longer standing there. Cursing under her breath, she watched the girl take off, weaving her way through oncomers and going straight through the doors the wrong way, Phone in hand, Marta headed for the exit, hoping she would attract less attention by going out that way. It would cost her time, but the security guards, alerted by Faith Ann's run past them, might stop Marta for a lot longer.

Marta dialed Arturo's cell phone as she made for the exit.

"Cover the front entrance. She just ran outside." Marta

walked fast, but she couldn't risk being captured on video rushing out.

Marta exited the aquarium knowing that the audiotape was in the backpack the girl wore on her back.

Arturo came rushing up the side of the building. Tinnerino and Doyle came outside. They didn't know how to react to meeting Marta in a public place, so they smiled like idiots caught playing with themselves.

Marta told them all, "The girl is dressed up like a boy. She has very short blond hair and a khaki-and-green–colored zoo cap. Dark red sweatshirt, black backpack, and dark jeans."

"She didn't come this . . ." Arturo said. "I see her. She's headed around the corner of Canal."

Marta caught a flash of red as the girl vanished around the power-station wall.

The cops sprinted after Marta and Arturo, who reached the corner of the shaded VIP parking lot just in time to see Faith Ann dart into an opening in the side of the building where the ramp to the Canal Place concrete parking structure was visible.

"She's inside the parking garage," she told the cops. "You two watch the deck exit in case she tries to come out that way. Turo, you take the far street corner and watch the side exits in case she goes that way. We have to keep her boxed in. I'm going in after her."

Tinnerino tried to interrupt her, but she pressed on. "Just do what I say," she snarled. "She gets away, you two are screwed. She walked right past both of you once already. On second thought, call your boss. You build a blue wall around this whole block and cover every exit."

60

Knowing that the woman would come after her, Faith ran around the far wall of the power station, past a kiosk, and through a tree-studded parking area. Ignoring the door into Canal Place because there was a security guard there smoking a cigarette, she hopped over a low wall behind a bike rack. She ran straight up the vehicle ramp, which coiled up into the parking garage. She stayed to the left side, where a narrow raised walkway allowed her to avoid the descending vehicles.

Faith Ann had no idea how the woman got her cell phone number, but she reckoned the cops could find out anything they liked. How had the woman known to come to the aquarium? All Faith Ann could figure was that somehow they could listen in on it and they had heard her tell Rush where she was. She didn't think Mr. Massey had told the cops, because she had told Rush they killed her mother and were after her.

She knew they would search for her and watch the outside of the building. The Canal Place complex housed a hotel, shops, offices, a million places to hide. On the first parking level, located on the building's fifth floor, a winded Faith Ann had no more idea of where to go than would a rabbit being chased by hounds. Standing beside two cars, she looked down on the intersection below and fought back her fear.

Concentrate.

Okay, Faith Ann, stop being scared. You have to think. How can you stop them from catching you? You know why they are coming. You know what they want. How do you keep those butt cakes from getting it?

Faith Ann fought to figure something out.

Concentrate.

61

Just as Winter arrived outside the aquarium, Adams was pulling up and parking on the access street next to the power station near a police-issue Crown Victoria. He got out and joined Winter about the same time a limping Nicky arrived, carrying his cane.

"Keep your eyes out for her," Winter told Nicky. After showing their badges, Winter and Adams were shown around the metal detector by a security guard.

"Just a quick run-through," Adams told the guard.

"Who y'all looking for?"

"We'll handle it from here," Adams replied gruffly.

"Thanks," Winter told the guard. "We're just going to make a quick sweep through the building."

"Happy to help," the guard said. "You guys aren't having any luck finding whoever you've been searching for."

"I'm sorry?" Winter said. "You said, *been* searching for?"

"Well, yeah. First the NOPD detectives—Tinnerino and Dale or something—and now you federals. USMS and FBI spells escaped federal prisoner doesn't it? The NOPD detectives said they were looking for somebody. One of them walked through the place upstairs and down while the other watched the exit. Then they just hauled ass. I'm surprised they didn't run smack into you guys."

"When?" Winter asked.

"They came in about ten minutes ago. They just went

by the doors there two minutes ago. I saw them all heading toward Canal Street."

"All?"

"The two detectives that came in and a couple more people were with them outside."

"Short woman? Tall thin guy?"

"She was inside for a few minutes. Dressed in leather—you couldn't miss her. Some other guy outside in a long black coat."

"Did you hear them say where they were going?" Adams asked.

"No. They grouped up out there and went off the plaza toward Canal Street. I walked them around the metal detectors because they had gold detective shields. They said it was official business. I figure they're after whoever it is you're after. Sort of less than forthcoming and not open for questions, if you catch my drift. I did hear the shorter one call his partner Tin Man. Like in *The Wizard of Oz.*"

"We're looking for a twelve-year-old girl."

"There's been about a thousand through here this morning."

"This one has short blond hair, maybe five-five and ninety pounds," Winter said.

The security guard's eyes grew serious. "Well, there was a boy that went out through these doors in a hurry. Wore a hooded red sweatshirt and a baseball cap and had a backpack. It could've been a girl, I guess. And that was just before the cops took off. The kid ran out so fast, I didn't have time to respond. I figured—"

"Thanks," Winter managed to say before he and Adams left the same way they'd come in, this time through the metal detector, which sounded two distinct ear splitting alarms.

He figured that Tinnerino and Doyle were looking for

Faith Ann, and they had flushed her and were in pursuit somewhere close by.

As he ran outside, Winter's mind whirred. The detectives had gotten there before Winter even knew about Faith Ann being there. Either someone spotted her and called the detective bureau or they were just checking places the girl frequented on the off chance she'd be there. The detective bureau's number had been on television since the night before and was published in the newspaper that morning. But because of the timing, and the fact that the picture they were using was two years old and she was now disguised, it was more likely something else. To have responded so fast, they had to have learned she was there about the same time Rush had. The pair in the Lincoln had left Bennett's club in a hurry, then had parked nearby and joined the detectives, so they must have known about it too. Once again, the couple was connected to Tinnerino and Doyle.

"She's gone," Adams told Nicky. "The two detectives from that Crown Vic over there and that couple are after her on foot.

"You know," he said, "we can track her too. You have the cell phone number. I make a request of my intelligence people and we can get fed the coordinates when she makes a call or takes one. In real time."

"Damn!" Winter said when it hit him. "The cops have her cell phone number! That's how they found her. The minute she called Rush, they had her."

"If they have the phone number, they'll know pretty quick who she's called. I think Suggs and his men will know about the connection to you pretty soon."

"Then we can stop playing games," Winter said. "They haven't had time to get far. They went toward Canal Street after her. Adams and I will go on foot. Nicky, you take our car. Where's yours?"

"Back there around the corner." He handed Winter the key.

"Run a grid and look for them. You see them, radio us your position."

Winter and Adams took off toward Canal Street. As the two men turned the corner where the power station wall ended, the city seemed to come alive with the sound of sirens. Blue strobe lights poured onto Canal Street as scores of patrol cars converged on their location.

"Good Lord," Adams muttered. "Seems excessive to send in an army to deal with one scared little girl."

62

There were hundreds of parked vehicles on several levels in the enormous lot: it would have taken hours for Marta to physically look under every car in the place. If she couldn't flush the kid, she'd be forced to let the cops' K-9 locate her. She didn't know how the detectives would explain her being there to the other cops. They wouldn't have to explain Arturo, because he was hooked up in the NOPD computers with official clearance.

Marta, unlike Arturo, did her best to remain in as few computers and as far off official radar as possible. She was a United States citizen. Her papers claimed she had been born on the right side of the border, in Brownsville, Texas. It was a lie, her name stolen. She owned her house and the twenty-nine creek-front acres it was located on. She had both wholesale and retail tax licenses and a retail antiques business on Magazine Street through which she laundered her earnings. She allowed a knowledgeable dealer, whose wife Marta had "accidented" so the unfaithful homosexual husband could inherit her estate before she could divorce him, to act as her partner and use her shop to warehouse his overflow stock. The real sales were his—he took the money off the books—and she got the paperwork on the sales for her purposes.

Marta heard the sirens of the approaching cruisers. She was totally relaxed, almost casual, as she strolled up the ramp to the first parking level, hunting for the child.

Maybe she would find the little rabbit herself in the next few minutes, but, if not, Faith Ann would be captured, because unless she could sprout wings and fly like a bird across the river, she couldn't escape. Before the day was out, she or Bennett would have the girl's evidence in hand. And Marta would have the opportunity to make sure she never made an identification of Arturo or herself.

Marta's attention was captured by a bulky object sitting by a stairway door. She approached it and lifted what appeared to be the girl's backpack. She squatted, opened it, and examined the contents. Among the items she found was a wadded-up red sweatshirt and a two-tone Audubon Zoo cap. She put the shirt to her nose and imagined that she could detect fear-induced perspiration in the material. Of course, Marta didn't have the tracking ability of a bloodhound, but her sense of smell was every bit as remarkable as that of a wine connoisseur or a perfume-scent tester. She was tuned in to her prey and knew her target didn't behave under pressure the way a normal twelve-year-old should. Marta's own similar behavior at that age had been influenced by years of survival in a hostile, unforgiving environment—a place filled with predators of all kinds. A place where the bodies of children were often collected from the gutters with the other garbage.

Setting aside the sweatshirt to look farther down in the backpack, Marta found the girl's Walkman with a cassette still inside it. She popped it open to retrieve the tape, which she slipped into her jacket pocket. The earphones for the device weren't there. After wiping prints from the Walkman, she replaced it and set the pack back where she'd found it. Marta had to hand it to the kid. The girl was smart enough to imagine that by abandoning the tape, her pursuers might break off the hunt. The trouble was that the child *was* that smart. She knew Arturo had killed her mother and that Marta was connected to him. She would still talk to someone, she would testify, and she might be believed, which simply wasn't acceptable.

Let Suggs find out if she had Bennett's negatives. Maybe Amber had separated them from the prints before she went to the lawyer's office—holding back that ace.

She dialed Tinnerino. "She went into the stairwell. Give me a few minutes without interruption and I'll track her down. You'll find her backpack outside the stairwell door on level three. It would be a good place for you to start searching."

"I'd say five is the best I can do," he told her, sounding odd.

Marta cracked open the door and, stepping into the stairwell, took a knife from her jacket pocket. She closed the door, opened the phone with her other hand and dialed the kid's phone. She closed her eyes, tuned her ears to listen, and heard the phone ringing in the stairwell not far above her.

Marta almost started up, but something didn't feel right. Leaning over the rail, she looked up and then down. Her heart soared as she caught the sight of a small left hand, three floors below, sliding along on the surface of the painted steel banister as Faith Ann descended, noiselessly as only a child can manage.

Marta went down after her.

63

Faith Ann ran down the stairs from the top level, backtracking. She was several floors down when she heard a door above her creak open. Close to the railing, she peeked up and saw a sliver of black leather. It was the woman cop who'd chased her from the aquarium.

64

Marta hit the ground level and would have run into a woman pushing a stroller containing a sleeping infant if she hadn't leaped over it.

"What the hell are you doing?" the mother screamed.

Marta bolted through the glass doors and into the atrium of Canal Place. She caught a glimpse of a figure wearing a gray hooded sweatshirt and a red cap moving around a group of pedestrians then turning right into a shop called Georgiou. *Okay, little bitch, now I have you.*

Marta made herself slow down, not wanting to draw any more attention to herself than necessary. She stopped at the edge of the showroom window and peered in. At the rear of the store, the kid stopped at a display table, flipped through a stack of sweaters, selected one, and went back toward the dressing rooms.

Marta waited to enter until after Faith Ann was out of sight. She walked between the racks, focusing on the rear of the store.

"Can I help you find something today?" an Asian salesgirl who was hanging up blouses asked.

"I'm just looking," Marta said, smiling.

"Let me know if I can be of assistance."

"If I find something, I won't hesitate to let you know," Marta said.

Marta stopped at the table and picked up a pair of slacks. She went back into the dressing room and spotted her target in one of the cubicles, whose doors allowed her a view of the inhabitant's lower legs—tennis shoes and dark jeans. She saw a sleeve of the hooded sweatshirt when the occupant laid the garment on the chair. Marta slipped out her folding knife, opened the blade silently, and slipped her hand holding the weapon beneath the folded pants.

Marta waited until the girl was pulling on the turtleneck, then she pulled open the door. As the child's head was emerging from the neck of the garment, Marta reached out and put her hand on Faith Ann's shoulder, ready to drop the slacks, put the knife to the child's throat, and ask about the negatives. When she felt the hand, Faith Ann whirled around suddenly, and, eyes growing wide, emitted a surprised squeak.

Marta froze, her knife hand underneath the garment. It was a good thing, because Faith Ann wasn't Faith Ann at all. The young woman emerging from the sweater was roughly the same build as Faith Ann and had short blond hair but was in her mid-twenties, and she was pissed off.

"What the hell are you doing?" the woman spat.

"Sorry, I thought you were somebody else," Marta said, already thinking where she'd lost the girl. Was it possible she had been chasing the wrong person all the way from the deck's stairwell? All she had seen was a sweatshirt sleeve and a hand. No, it had been Faith Ann in the stairwell, but she had somehow slipped by her. She might have taken any of a dozen exits. Marta had seen the woman, and assumed . . .

The woman in the sweater straight-armed Marta back out of the cube, and Marta let her. She put the knife away, rushed back past the table, and tossed the slacks onto it as she passed by.

65

Winter and Adams approached the detectives who were standing at the entrance to the packing deck. The larger of them was preventing cars from entering the facility by waving off the drivers. The drivers of the exiting cars were rubbernecking, so his partner was able to visually check inside the vehicles as they passed by him. The cops had to know that it was unlikely that in the time she'd been in the building she could have enlisted the aid of anyone who would agree to sneak her past the local cops.

"Let me handle these twats," Adams said. As he and Winter approached the larger detective, Adams opened his badge case. "Special FBI Agent Adams. What's going on here?"

"Tinnerino, NOPD Homicide." The detective's shield was displayed—suspended from a chain around his thick neck. "We've got a murder suspect in there."

"That right?"

"Yeah. Armed and dangerous."

Patrol cars started arriving, and officers stepped from them. Tinnerino's phone rang, and he took the call. "I'd say five is the best I can do."

Doyle, a short, swarthy man with a five-o'clock shadow, started giving orders to the patrolmen to get the complex surrounded and await instructions. Winter overheard him giving them Faith Ann's description. "Skinny kid, short blond hair, dark red sweatshirt, black jeans, light brown over dark brown cap."

"Who's in charge?" Adams asked him.

"I am," Tinnerino said. "Just stay out of the way, agents."

"I'm not an FBI agent," Winter said.

"No, he's a federal fugitive specialist—United States deputy marshal," Adams said.

"This is NOPD business," Tinnerino said acidly, but he was flustered and sweating.

"We can help," Adams said.

"You can help by keeping out of our way."

"So, who did this little girl murder?" Adams asked.

"Two people. Her mother and . . ." Tinnerino's eyes changed, and he cocked his large head to one side as he realized that he hadn't said the suspect was female or a little girl.

"Amber Lee," Adams said.

"That's right." Tinnerino's mean eyes were like small black stones.

"You don't actually believe that," Winter said.

"I've warned you to stay out of this. You have no right to interfere."

"I don't see how we *can* stay out of it," Winter said. "The odds are too heavily stacked against her to be fair." He turned and started into the parking deck.

"He's right," Adams said. "I think we'll interfere. Stand down, Officer."

"Wait just a damned minute," Tinnerino bellowed at Winter's back. "If you step one foot into that building, I will arrest you."

Winter stopped and turned. "Listen, Tin Man," he said.

"There won't be any trouble as long as you keep your people out here. We're going to go in."

"Yes, we are," Adams said.

"I'm in charge here!" Tinnerino snapped. "You two have no authority here."

"Get your superior on the phone," Winter said. "Ask him if you can arrest us to stop us from entering that complex."

"Ask him yourself," Tinnerino said as a Crown Victoria screeched up to the curb, rocking on its suspension. A stocky man with white hair got out and, his radio in one beefy hand, strode up onto the sidewalk to where the trio was standing. His red golf jacket didn't cover the mother-of-pearl–handled, short-barreled Python in his side holster.

"What's happening, Detective?"

"Captain Suggs, we have the Porter girl cornered inside."

"That's what I understood." He stared suspiciously at Winter and Adams. "And?"

"These two are attempting to go inside against my orders. I was about to arrest them."

"No, we weren't *attempting* anything," Adams told him. "We were going inside. We have noted your detective's strong advice not to, but I think we'll be just fine."

"Let's see some I.D."

Winter and Adams opened their badge cases.

Winter saw Suggs's discomfort and uncertainty when he read his name.

"There isn't any federal crime here. We don't require, and I haven't requested, your involvement. To the contrary, I suggest you both stay back and let my men do their jobs," Suggs said. "Tinnerino and Doyle will go in first."

"Can we speak in private?" Winter asked.

Suggs followed Winter over beside his car. Adams stood behind Suggs, his back to Tin Man.

Winter spoke in a low voice so he wouldn't be overheard.

"I have known Faith Ann Porter and her family for years. My son and Faith Ann are close friends. Her uncle is a dear friend and was my boss."

"You know who her next of kin is? We haven't notified them yet, because we didn't know specifics about the Porter family." Winter read the lie in Suggs's eyes.

"You mean when Detectives Tinnerino and Doyle ransacked the Porter house, there were no letters, address books . . . phone records?" Adams said. "Now, I find that very strange that an attorney like her didn't keep records."

"What do you mean ransack? Of course they searched the house for evidence. And they found plenty."

"I'm at a disadvantage because I don't know what they found," Winter lied. "I know only that Faith Ann Porter didn't kill anybody. Maybe you don't know that, but if you knew that little girl you would."

"There's conclusive evidence that she is absolutely guilty."

Adams said, "I'd be very sure of that—not only of the evidence's authenticity. I was you, I'd be sure it'll hold up under the scrutiny of our forensics people."

"Very sure indeed," Winter added. "What I believe is that whoever did it also ran down her aunt and uncle, Hank and Millie Trammel. You are familiar with the Trammel hit-and-run case? Last night, uptown. Vehicle dumped into the bayou with a stiff inside it. You have the vehicle impounded. There was an autopsy on the body." Winter gave Suggs a suspicious look.

"Detective Manseur mentioned he spoke to you. He didn't say that the Trammels and the Porters were related."

"I didn't tell him."

Suggs's ears were turning red; beads of sweat gathered on his upper lip.

"I've been asking around," Adams said. "I was told Manseur was primary on the Porter case but that he was pulled off before he could get into it good. What I find curious is that Manseur is an exemplary detective, with a clearance ratio above average, while Tinnerino's and Doyle's reputations are less than stellar."

"There were extenuating circumstances. Michael's partner is out of town. It was a field decision I made because I wanted manpower in motion."

Adams nodded. "You should reconsider that 'field' decision, because it is highly suspect when viewed with certain evidence we've already obtained."

"If she shoots . . ." Suggs started.

Winter said, "Your men chased her here directly from the aquarium, where she went through metal detectors going and coming. We have good reason to believe Faith Ann is in danger from someone on your force, which is why Agent Adams is here. Whoever killed the child's mother is still after her and is getting real-time police intelligence.

"Agent Adams and I are going in there, and we'll escort Faith Ann out. I will be accompanying her *wherever* she goes from here on out, and nobody is going to interrogate her without her legal counsel, C. Errol Cunningham, present."

Suggs's eyes reflected that he was very familiar with the energetic New Orleans criminal defense attorney—a man with an unparalleled ability to make life a living hell for anyone who found themselves opposing one of his clients.

Suggs was trying to compose himself. Winter knew the wheels in his mind were spinning as he tried to figure out what to do. "My detectives are highly competent. They didn't make the connections, because you withheld next of kin information."

"I've been gathering information, not giving it out," Winter said. "I'll make this easy. I'm going in now. Unless we request your assistance, no officers will come inside."

Adams keyed his radio. "This is Number One," he said, knowing Nicky alone would be monitoring the radio. "Massey and I are going in. Watch the perimeter. Spot anything queer, let me know immediately."

Suggs looked around, probably trying to spot whoever Adams was addressing.

66

Winter dialed Faith Ann's cell phone as soon as they were inside. She didn't pick up.

"I'll take the main ramp. Take the elevator to the top floor of the parking deck and come down. And be careful. That couple is probably in here."

"Number One?" Nicky's voice said.

"Here," Winter said into his radio.

"I have Mr. Fashion outside Brooks Brothers, talking on a cellular. Okay, he's moving. Turned the corner, I think he's heading back to their car. What do you want me to do?"

"Is he moving fast?"

"No."

Winter couldn't be sure Suggs had informed him of their presence, but it would explain why he was retreating. "Then hold your position."

He put the radio into his pocket and started up the ramp. "Faith Ann! It's Winter Massey!"

He heard nothing but the plaintive whistle of the ferry at the base of Canal Street.

It was impossible to predict whether Faith Ann would

stay in the deck, maybe hide in or under a car, or if she had gone into the main complex, which was what he would have done. He didn't think the police could get her out of the building without Nicky seeing the activity, but he doubted Suggs would risk having the Feds catch them at it. Suggs was either going to be very cautious now, or act in the rash manner of a desperate man. Winter hoped the captain wasn't feeling desperate yet. But since he didn't know the man, nor how dirty Suggs's hands might be, there was no way to judge what he might do.

There were a lot of places for Faith Ann to hide, but if she tried to exit the building the cops would get her for sure.

On the first parking level, after he had yelled out several times, he spotted a backpack next to the stairwell door. There was nothing on its exterior to indicate that it belonged to Faith Ann, but he knew it was hers. As soon as he saw the dark red sweatshirt and zoo cap inside, he radioed to tell Adams and Nicky that Faith Ann had changed her clothes. He had no way of knowing why she'd abandoned the pack where it would be found, unless she'd decided that it had become part of the description of her that her pursuers were going by. He wondered if she had done it to lead her pursuers in the wrong direction. If she was older, more experienced, he would have assumed it was calculated misdirection.

There was nothing else in the backpack of help, and nothing to indicate that she had been lugging it for any reason other than to hold a change of clothes. He lifted out the new Walkman—the one whose packaging he had found under the porch. He opened the battery compartment and saw that the batteries were the same brand as the two she'd left behind under the house. He put it back. Before standing, he turned his head and spotted the earphones beneath a nearby car. He reached under and lifted them out. Why had Faith Ann thrown them there?

"Adams, if you spot her, don't frighten her."

After calling Faith's name out again, Winter dialed Kimberly Porter's cell phone again. This time Adams answered it.

"Third level. Inside the stairwell."

Winter ran up the stairs and found Adams holding the phone in his raised hand.

"It was just sitting on the steps."

"She left a false trail," Winter told the federal agent. "She's long gone. I think she planted the pack on the floor below, then came up to dump the phone and went out or doubled back. She could have gone into the building next door."

"She could be anywhere," Adams said. "We need a psychic."

"Exactly. Go down and tell Suggs we would like a K-9 and a handler."

67

The small-framed, wiry German shepherd walked beside its handler, a thin NOPD officer who could have easily passed for a high-school student. Adams walked behind them. Winter wanted to start at the last place Faith Ann had been, for good reason. While Adams went for the animal, Winter had gone back down, gotten her cap from the backpack, and brought it back to the second-level stairwell where Adams had found the phone.

"Deputy Massey, this is Patrolman Gale," Adams said. "And his partner Beaux-Beaux."

"He's got a great nose," the young cop said proudly.

Winter opened the door, reached in, and picked up the cap, which he had placed on the concrete floor. He handed it to Officer Gale, who held it down for the dog to sniff. Beaux-Beaux focused on the scent, made a quick circle, came straight back to the door, lowered his head and froze before the door, growling.

"He's alerting," Gale said.

Beaux-Beaux started up the first riser, then whirled and came back down.

On the first level, the animal stopped at the door and signaled to go out. He found Faith Ann's backpack and led his handler toward the ramp down.

Winter directed the handler to take Beaux-Beaux back into the stairwell, and the animal excitedly began a descent.

"She doubled back," Winter said.

At the bottom floor the dog led them through the double glass doors into Canal Place, but the dog didn't head straight into the area. He stopped at an unmarked steel door, put his nose to it, and barked.

Winter tried it. "Locked."

"Beaux-Beaux says she went in there," the handler assured them. "We can get maintenance to open it."

"Allow me," Adams said. "You better turn your back, Officer Gale." He reached into his coat and took out what appeared to be a fountain pen. He popped it open and poured a pair of lock-picking tools into his palm. Using one as a tension bar, he worked the other one carefully. Within seconds Adams opened the door, and Beaux-Beaux pulled his handler through.

The animal worked its way down two hundred feet of hallway and through several doors, finally leading the trio through a physical plant packed with pieces of machinery working hard to perform tasks required to keep the building supplied with air and water.

The animal took them on a curving course between water pumps and around vents and pipes before coming to a pair of doors. They entered a wide companionway where a janitor, working within some plastic warning cones, was mopping what looked like vomit from the tiles. Beaux-Beaux sneezed violently. The scent of bleach had interrupted his trail.

Winter looked up the hallway, past where passing people hugged the wall to avoid the filthy mop water.

"Hold Beaux-Beaux here," Winter told Gale. He and Adams walked down the hall and to an exit that opened into the lobby for the Wyndham Hotel. Faith Ann was nowhere to be seen.

Nicky's voice came over Winter's radio. "*Massey*?"

"Go ahead, Nicky."

"You alone?"

"Just me and Adams at the moment."

"I spotted the kid. I mean I think it was her."

"Where?"

"She crossed the street from the aquarium, went over to the ferry's pedestrian walkway, got onto the ferry. I went after her, but the boat was already leaving when I got there."

"Drive. Take the bridge over," Winter told him sharply. "See if you can spot her. We'll be there as fast as we can get loose without creating suspicion."

68

Faith Ann had slipped out of the hotel, made her way around the power station, and crossed the intersection near the aquarium. Police cars were everywhere, but the cops were focused on Canal Place. Crossing the intersection along with a noisy group of tourists, she passed by the concrete benches. She went up the staircase to the pedestrian walkway to the ferry.

She couldn't have timed her escape better, because as she hurried onto the moored vessel the ferry's horn blasted and the deckhand closed the steel-wire door. Within seconds she was down the stairs to the car deck, standing at the bow of the USS *Thomas Jefferson*, gazing across the river at Algiers Point.

As the cool wind evaporated the sweat from her face, Faith Ann went back over the escape. She had hastily switched sweatshirts in the parking deck. She had run up to the fourth level and left her cell phone there. They had the number and were somehow able to track her down when she used it. Instinctively, she knew she needed to slow her pursuers, to keep them busy trailing her without getting too close, while she figured out how to get to Mr. Massey. She had seen enough television shows to know the cops could listen in on calls if they had a number, and they could track the phone's location.

She had escaped for the moment, but there could still be cops waiting for her. She had the strangest feeling that an angel had guided her steps. She would call Rush again as soon as she was near a phone.

The envelope was tucked inside her pants, hidden by the thick, hooded gray Tulane sweatshirt. Carrying the negatives and photocopies around was too risky. She needed to hide them somewhere safe. She only had eight hours until Horace Pond was going to die.

Without any plan in mind, she closed her eyes and prayed silently. She was aware that several teenagers had joined the crowd at the bow. She looked around and saw that the boys and girls were obviously not related, and they had all come from a stretched GMC passenger van parked thirty feet away. The side door of the vehicle said UNITED

CHURCH OF CHRIST, HATTIESBURG, MISSISSIPPI. There were luggage cases in an aluminum cage on the van's roof and a ladder leading up from the rear bumper.

Faith Ann picked out a boy close to her own age and sidled over to him. "Hi there. You guys on a field trip?"

"Nah. A stupid Bible bee contest in Barataria, Louisiana."

"Bible bee?"

"Like a spelling bee, but only with words from the Bible." He shrugged. "Some trip to New Orleans. Like we go right to the French Quarter, and instead of going to see Bourbon Street or something cool, they march us through some church, get us some lame powdered doughnuts, then drag us to see a bunch of stupid fish. Now we're crossing the Big Muddy to enjoy some dumb scenery before the contest."

"That's messed up," Faith Ann said sympathetically.

"Tell me about it."

"Can you do me a favor, you think?"

The boy eyed Faith Ann suspiciously. "Is it anything I could catch grief over?"

Faith Ann shrugged. "I don't know. Maybe."

"Cool," the boy said, smiling.

69

Winter knew Faith Ann would beat Nicky to Algiers Point by a good ten minutes, but since the girl was on foot there was a chance he might spot her on the sidewalks.

As long as the cops didn't know she was on the ferry, Nicky had an advantage.

Winter and Adams returned to find Gale waiting with his dog.

"She exit?" Gale asked.

"She didn't go that way," Adams said with certainty.

Winter nodded his agreement. "Guy who's been there for the last fifteen minutes said nobody came through the lobby from here."

"Nobody saw her?" Gale asked. "She went into the hotel, right? I'm sure Beaux-Beaux can track her."

"I said she didn't go that way," Adams snapped.

The K-9 officer didn't protest when Winter suggested that they go back the way they'd come, to see where she'd pulled the last double-back on them.

Before they got to the parking deck, however, Adams stopped.

"Officer Gale," he said. "You did a great job. I'm going to see that you get an FBI commendation for your effort. A nice letter from my director won't hurt your career."

"She got away," Gale said. "I'm sure she went into the hotel."

"I am going to ask you to do me a favor," Adams said.

"What's that?"

"Unless your superiors ask you directly, don't go into specific detail about the tracking."

"Sir?"

"For your and Beaux-Beaux's sake."

"I'm sorry?"

"It's just that if it comes down to a question of whether we screwed up, or if Beaux-Beaux here isn't up to the job, or whether your handling was questionable . . . you know what we're going to put in our reports. And if we do, the Director won't be sending any letters or issuing any glowing commendations."

"But it was the bleach," Gale said defensively. "It killed the trail for a few seconds."

"I smelled it before we opened that last door," Adams said.

"Me too," Winter agreed. "We thought you'd pull the dog back to save his nose, but you went straight through the door." He knelt to pat the dog's head. "Tell you what, Gale. Let's just agree that the trail looped back in on itself, which isn't a lie. We'll forget your mistakes, or whatever."

Gale stared down at Winter.

"She just outfoxed us," Winter said.

Gale stood listening, his eyes unreadable.

"You can keep tracking. Start over and follow the trail from scratch. Try and pick up her scent around the building, while we do a search on our own. Maybe she went back through the atrium and through some shops or something. Radio when you find her. You can be the hero. It's fine with us. That way our asses will all be covered."

"But . . ."

"Go on. We'll buy you and Beaux-Beaux some time. We'll tell Suggs you're still looking."

"You sure?" Gale asked suspiciously.

Adams and Winter nodded.

"I'll just take that swing through and see if we can scare her up."

Winter and Adams watched as K-9 Officer Gale and Beaux-Beaux strode back up the ramp.

"That should buy us some time," Adams said.

"I'm glad you're on my side," Winter said. "Let's see how fast we can get across the bridge."

Even though they had taken Suggs by surprise and bluffed their way into holding back twenty itchy-fingered cops, there was no real proof that Suggs was intending to harm Faith Ann and nothing to tie Suggs into Bennett other than Bennett's words. Suggs knew he was under suspicion, but for the moment Winter needed to keep him and his Tin Man team guessing. Whoever the couple was, they were only tied into Tinnerino and Doyle and Bennett. Until he knew who they were, there was nothing to be gained in mentioning them.

When Winter and Adams came out, Manseur was standing near Suggs's car, between Suggs and Tinnerino. He didn't smile when he saw Winter and Adams.

"Well?" Suggs said. Winter thought he saw something akin to relief in his eyes.

"We lost her trail. Officer Gale is trying to find it," Adams said.

"So she's still in there?"

"If she is, she didn't hear me calling."

"Or maybe she isn't as innocent as you think," Suggs said.

"I believe she is innocent," Winter said. He turned to Manseur, whose face remained unreadable. "Detective, I'm sorry I didn't level with you and tell you Trammel and Porter were related."

"So am I," Manseur said sourly. He was a good actor, but all good cops are.

"Well, I'm going to remedy that. Since you are here," Winter said as he handed Manseur his card, "she'll be in good hands. I need to check on Hank and talk to some people. The K-9 officer will find her. When you find her I expect a call, and Commander Suggs has her lawyer's name. Call him too."

Manseur turned his eyes to Suggs. Suggs nodded.

"I suppose I can do that," Manseur said. "I'm sorry you don't trust us to do the right thing."

"We'll see what happens. You're alerted to our presence and we are going to be watching you."

Adams looked into Suggs's eyes and straightened the knot of his tie as though Suggs's round face was a mirror. "Captain, are you familiar with a man named Jerry Bennett?"

Suggs flashed a pained grin. "Mr. Bennett is very well-known in the community. Why?"

Adams smiled. "No reason in particular. Massey and I visited with him earlier. I'd be willing to bet you he's not half as well-known as he's going to be in the near future. He mentioned that you advised him to file charges against Amber Lee for embezzlement, and it happens that she was murdered, and you are in charge of investigating her murder. Faith Ann told my son that she did not call 911 because a policeman killed her mother and Amber Lee, and that the police are trying to kill her." There. It was all out on the table.

Manseur dropped the indignant look and adopted a perplexed one.

"That about all?" Suggs's grin was erased, his skin tone a bleached cotton white, which made his reddening ears stand out.

"Bennett told us you are very close friends," Adams said.

"I'd hardly call us friends, and I don't recall advising him to file charges against Amber Lee. Perhaps he was mistaken."

"I'm not telling you how to run your detective bureau, but I assume you'll want to bring Manseur here up to speed on the Porter/Lee case, since they *are* intertwined. I'd think someone like him should be in charge of both cases. Since he hasn't been mentioned by a person of interest in this."

Manseur fought back a smile.

"I had already decided that very thing," Suggs blustered. "I was just about to discuss that with him."

Winter and Adams left Suggs standing on the sidewalk and walked briskly toward their waiting car.

"You know, this is exactly how I felt back in high school

while I was walking away from the boys' bathroom knowing that the cherry bomb I just flushed was about to go off," Adams said.

70

When Arturo called to tell her what Tin Man said about the Feds showing up, Marta had just left Canal Place through a rear exit, walking past two hawkeyed patrolmen. She strode casually down Peters Street to the lot where her Lincoln was parked. She opened the driver's side door, climbed in where Arturo sat slumped, smoking a cigarette. She took the cassette tape from her pocket, tossed it into his lap, and said, "Let the window down. You're stinking up my car."

"So this is what it was all about?" he said, holding up the tape and looking at it as though it was a large diamond. "But she is still in there somewhere."

"I only saw her for a second. By the time I got down two flights of steps she was gone. There were cops all over the place. Let them find her. She isn't going to sprout wings and fly away."

"You lost her," Arturo said smugly. "They have their dog searching for her. And now there's two federal agents who are very much involved. You should have gotten a tape deck as well as a CD. Like I have in my Porsche."

"We can buy a player."

"Oh, good thinking," Arturo said smiling broadly. He tapped the cassette against his knee. "It is too bad that . . . you . . . lost . . . her."

Marta's pocketknife appeared. The white blade came to

rest in the space just over Arturo's Adam's apple. She held the double-edged ceramic blade with such perfect tension that it made an indentation in Arturo's throat but without enough pressure to open the skin. Arturo slowly turned his pleading eyes to her, and he saw the chill she wanted him to see.

"I didn't hear you," she hissed. "What did I do?"

"I'm sorry." When he spoke, his Adam's apple bobbed and the tip of the knife had just the necessary additional pressure to penetrate the skin. A thin red droplet rolled down his throat and disappeared inside his open shirt collar.

"Don't you dare mock me!" She saw anger replacing the fear that had just been in his eyes. "Have you already forgotten that I am here in the first place to clean up *your* mess? I am putting my life on the line for a simpering pussy who sits in the car smoking cigarettes while I am"—she drew closer to him and hardened her black eyes—"*losing her,* was it?"

"Um-hum," he hummed, clench-jawed. He didn't dare speak for fear the blade's tip would slide deeper into his throat.

"I got the tape for you. Now I am done. Straighten out the rest by yourself. The girl can identify you, so you find her and kill her. I'm sure *you* won't lose her, like *I* did. I am going to take a nice long vacation. Alone. Maybe I will come back to attend your funeral after Bennett has killed you. You are such an expert that you can handle this simple matter all by yourself."

"Um-hummm."

Marta took the knife from his throat and wiped the blade off on his cheek—purposefully smearing it on like rouge. She snapped it closed, then dropped it back into her jacket pocket. Arturo's right hand sprang to his throat, the other tugged a tissue from the package on the console.

He pressed the tissue to the wound, took it away, and stared in disbelief at the blood.

"I was only joking, Marta!" he blurted. "What is your problem? You ruined my shirt. It's silk."

"I was joking too," she said as she started the car. "Wipe your face before somebody thinks you are a whore."

"Why do you insult me like that? You know that I am a man. I have no fear."

"I know," she said, laughing. "But you are a macho dog, such an easy target." She waved her hand. "Turo, I have bigger stones than ten men."

"Then you aren't going away?"

"It depends," she said as she turned in her seat and backed out of the space.

"On what?"

"On many things. I'll make you a list after . . ."

"After what?"

"After I have destroyed this tape."

Marta put the car into gear and rolled toward the exit. She checked her rearview to make sure there was nobody following. She made a mental note to ask Tinnerino for details on the two agents.

71

Nicky called to say that when he got to the landing, the ferry was already on the return trip to Canal Street, that he never saw her, so he was waiting for them. Winter called Manseur but got his voice mail and left a message.

He said simply, "Call me."

Winter told Adams, "Suggs has been a cop for a lot of years, probably a crooked one for that long. He's smart enough to have made it through the anticorruption sweep back in the nineties."

"We ought to keep the pressure on him."

"He is going to figure out pretty fast that the best way to cover his ass is to hand this mess over to Manseur and get as far away from it as possible. He can say he misinterpreted the crime scene evidence and that he saw the error of his ways and brought Manseur back on. I'm figuring he'd rather look incompetent than conspiratorial."

"At his level, incompetence is a job requirement."

"Every time you dropped another piece of this on him, he about pissed his pants."

"He could see the writing on the wall. That's for sure." Adams laughed out loud. "Man, you know he thought he had this thing locked until we showed up. If he *was* helping Bennett, I doubt he's going to be much help from this day forward. You reckon Officer Gale and Beaux-Beaux will come back out today?" Adams added, bringing more laughter.

Winter's cell phone rang. It was Manseur's name and number. He put the phone on speaker so Adams could listen in.

"Detective Manseur," Winter answered.

"Man alive," Manseur said. "After you left, I had the strangest conversation with Captain Suggs I've ever had with anybody. He was going around in circles. When he said he knew about the connection between Trammel and Porter, I thought he was going to accuse me of holding back information. Instead he said he spoke to you and Adams and told me there was a federal task force on this already. Man, he was spooked. He said that I might have been right about some aspects of the evidence against Faith Ann. Why did you leave?"

"She was no longer there," Winter answered.

"Did you get her out?"

"She got herself out. I'll explain it later," Winter said. "Face-to-face."

"I'm on my way to meet the chief at the office to discuss this."

"Faith Ann told my son that a cop killed her mother and Amber Lee, which is why she is running from you guys.

"She said a cop? I think it's more likely a professional hit," Manseur said. "The silencer, the precision of the shots. Maybe it was a cop . . ."

"Get Faith Ann reclassified as a material witness only, and get the word out to the cops and the media. Let the patrolmen and detectives all know that she should be located and held for her own protection. Make sure you are the contact person. If Suggs gives you any crap at all, we'll toss another grenade under his chair."

"By the way, I'm waiting for a match on the partial prints on the corpse in the Rover. The sheriff who found the Rover said that someone near there saw a black and white taxicab with two people in it enter the highway from that dirt road. There aren't any cabs out there, but there was a taxi stolen in New Orleans last night two hours before the accident. It was recovered locally this afternoon. Wiped clean inside, mud on the underside, wheels. I'm waiting for tire tread impressions from the sheriff to see if they match the ones at the bayou, but they will. There were two empty five-gallon gas cans in the dumpster near the cab, so I'm pretty sure it was how the perps got back to town."

"Maybe Tinnerino and Doyle?" Winter wondered.

"Could be."

"Maybe the corpse they put in the Rover was supposed to lead any investigation down a blind alley. If the corpse had a criminal record, the investigation would stop there. Or the couple in the Lincoln could have helped," Winter said.

Winter told Manseur about seeing the same couple leaving Bennett's, and Nicky following them to the parking lot. He told him that Nicky spotted the male outside Canal Place.

Manseur said, "Green get a tag number?"

"Good question," Winter said. "Give me a sec."

He picked up his radio and called Nicky. "Nicky, you happen to get the tag number on the Lincoln?"

"Of course I did. Louisiana DX-2088."

"I'll run it," Manseur said.

"Don't waste your time," Adams told him. "Let the FBI do the walking through the yellow pages." He pulled over to the curb, reached down beside his seat, and flipped open a laptop computer. He started typing, and within seconds he had a Louisiana DMV screen. He entered the license number.

"Registered to the House of Antiquities, Box 2233, New Orleans, Louisiana. The address is 2231 Magazine Street," Winter read to Manseur from the screen.

"Let's see who owns it." Adams brought up another Web page. This time it was for the Secretary of State. He typed, and the screen showed the incorporation information for the antique business.

Winter read it to Manseur. "The owner is Marta Ruiz. The other two corporate officers are attorneys."

"Marta Ruiz? I'm not familiar with the name," Manseur said.

Adams was already typing, and suddenly the screen was filled with a driver's license picture.

"I've got her. Our Jane Doe is in fact Marta Ruiz. Address is Route 2, Box 223, Covington, Louisiana. Five-four, hundred and ten pounds, black hair and brown eyes."

"Does the FBI want to run her for a record?" Manseur said.

Adams was already typing. "Not so much as a parking ticket," he announced.

Winter said, "All it takes to keep your record clean is being connected to the right people."

"Around here, the art of back-scratching is a science," Manseur said sadly.

72

Suggs looked down at the caller I.D. and shoved the unit into his desk drawer. *Bennett!*

Jerry Bennett had called Suggs while Massey and Adams were inside Canal Place, to see if the girl was in custody, but the nightclub owner hadn't bothered to mention that an FBI agent and a deputy U.S. marshal had been to his club minutes earlier. They had dropped that little bomb on him at Canal Place. Suggs had told Tin Man to get word to Bennett that he would get back to *him* when he could. It was bad enough that Bennett was in the Feds' sights, but that arrogant little bastard had implicated Suggs when there was no imaginable reason to have done so. God knows what that suicidal idiot said to them.

If they took Bennett down, that little prick would turn on Suggs, dragging in Tin Man, Doyle, and God knew who else up the ladder. Suggs had never liked Bennett, had never trusted him, but he had never before seen their mutually profitable arrangement as a threat to his freedom. Over the past twenty years Bennett had paid him a tax-free fortune, but not enough to go to prison over. In his career, Suggs had seen scores of his fellow police officers go to jail, and it wasn't going to happen to him.

Mike Manseur had control of both cases, and he would

have to say that Suggs gave him everything he needed to solve them. Any evidence was open to interpretation, and he could justify taking the case from Manseur to his superiors.

Suggs had never killed anybody for Bennett—if you didn't count framing Horace Pond for two murders Bennett had committed. And Pond had been a nobody, human refuse, whose only accomplishment in life had been using his dick to add to the numbers of snot-nose nigger kids on the welfare rolls or populate the jails and prisons.

The only thing that Suggs had to do now was to make Bennett vanish so he could never talk. Suggs would have to do that deed himself, and in such a way that it would never point back to him.

That settled, Suggs felt the hollow burn in his stomach receding, cooled by the knowledge that all he needed was to calm down and devise a simple plan that would tie up the loose ends.

73

Thanks to Adams's amazingly efficient FBI computer hookup, which saved Manseur a couple of hours on his NOPD computer, Manseur knew that the woman in the Lincoln was Marta Ruiz. Now he needed to find out who her male partner was, which might explain how the pair had gained access to the investigation. They were clearly connected to Bennett and Tin Man and Doyle, but he needed to figure out exactly what that connection meant before he confronted Tin Man or Doyle. He had an idea on how he might discover who the man was, but his ringing phone interrupted him.

"Mike, Captain Suggs."

"Yes sir?"

"Can you join Detectives Tinnerino and Doyle in the conference room?"

"Sure."

The two detectives sat like surly schoolboys behind the boxes containing the assembled Porter/Lee evidence. Suggs sat at the head of the table and indicated that Manseur should sit opposite the other two—exactly where he belonged.

"Mike," Suggs started, "I have just informed Tony and Clint that you are going to be the primary on both the Trammel and Porter/Lee cases. I've explained the connection between the two cases, and they have agreed to work with you to solve them. When will Larry Bond be back?"

"He's supposed to be back tonight. He might be back already. I was planning to call him."

"Excellent," Suggs said. "Whatever you need, I'll okay. Manpower, overtime, whatever. Just ask."

Doyle's and Tin Man's resentful eyes bored into Manseur.

"First off," Manseur said, "I have issued a new bulletin on Faith Ann Porter listing her as a material witness pickup, and I removed the armed-and-dangerous tag. I also took the liberty of changing the contact number to my own."

Tin Man shook his head rigidly.

"Problem, Detective?" Manseur asked.

"Just that there's no evidence that she *didn't* clip her old lady and Lee."

"Detective Doyle, do you agree with your partner?"

"Absolutely. She did it. Look at how she slipped out of Canal Place. She ain't like any twelve-year-old I ever saw."

Manseur's phone rang. He looked at the I.D. and saw Massey's name and number. "I need to take this," he said.

As he listened, the other three men talked about Faith Ann's escape from Canal Place. Manseur listened to Massey, let him know that he couldn't answer his questions, and told the deputy he'd have to call him back. What Massey had asked him had put a hot, hollow burn in his stomach.

"I think Mike is on track," Suggs said, rubbing his chin thoughtfully. "We can charge the kid after we interrogate her, if it is warranted." He rose. "Gentlemen, I'll leave it with you. Whatever you need, Mike. You're in complete charge." With that, Suggs walked from the room.

"How do you explain the evidence we found?" Tinnerino demanded.

Manseur said, "Maybe it was planted there."

"By who? Nobody else was there between when she was and we were."

"I wasn't suggesting that *you* planted it, Detective. Might be that the killer, or killers, did. Maybe they came before you got there."

Tinnerino clenched his jaw.

"Faith Ann Porter told a federal officer that a policeman killed her mother and Amber Lee. It will be interesting to learn how she came to believe that."

"That evidence wasn't planted in that hamper," Tinnerino argued.

"Then maybe she picked the gun and empty brass up, in shock, and took them with her. Unless one of you saw her put the evidence into that hamper, it is possible someone else did it. Hand me over the firearms files on the murder weapon."

Tinnerino looked in the stack and pulled out the files. Manseur flipped through them, scanning them while the other detectives sat silently.

"The .380's barrel is threaded on the inside. The M.E. found steel wool in the wounds. What does that say to you?"

No answer.

"The Taurus .380 was one of twenty stolen from a dealer in Cherry Hill, New Jersey, nine months back. Two from that robbery have been picked up at crime scenes since. To me that indicates they were either sold by the dealer under the table or hijacked and sold to criminal types. That points to a professional. Not a twelve-year-old who merely witnessed the murders."

"That's bullshit," Tinnerino said.

"I say it isn't. And I am running this. If you want, I'll relieve you from the team. In light of the insinuation of there being police involvement in these homicides, it might be best to bring in all new people who have open minds."

"No," Tinnerino said, too quickly. "No, you're the primary. If that is how you want to read the evidence, that's cool with us. Right, Clint?"

"Sure," Doyle agreed.

"If you say she was framed, she was framed," Tinnerino said.

"Who ransacked the Porter house?" Manseur asked.

"Did what?" Tinnerino said. He and Doyle exchanged looks of surprise.

"You didn't?" Manseur asked.

"Of course not." Tinnerino was indignant. "We searched. Who said it was ransacked?"

"Adams, the FBI agent," Manseur said. "You met him at Canal Place."

"Then I bet it was some of those porch chimps that hang out at that basketball court behind the house," Doyle said.

Manseur ignored the slur. "I need to go over the evidence you've collected," he said. "I'll need your notes and the report you've written so far."

"We have a problem there," Tinnerino said.

"We had a detailed report all typed up," Doyle started. "But . . ."

"But what?" Manseur asked, bracing himself.

Manseur left the conference room bothered by Winter Massey's call. He had given Tin Man and Doyle busywork, and they would be at their desks retyping the missing report for some time.

Massey had mentioned Horace Pond, a name that filled Manseur with anger. Pond was guilty, and Manseur didn't believe this had anything to do with him. It was a troubling direction that Massey was walking in, and he had to nip it in the bud. He spent ten minutes calling up and reading through the police files on Pond's case on his screen. After that, he looked up Doyle's and Tinnerino's service dates. Neither of the detectives had been involved with the Pond case. Doyle hadn't even been on the force then, and Tinnerino was patrolling in the Quarter.

Satisfied, he remembered to find out who Marta Ruiz's male partner was.

74

Faith Ann reached into her jeans and took out the envelope and the audiocassette she had taken from her mother's office. She tore open the corner just enough so she could slip the cassette inside.

Looking around, she spotted her hiding place. She wedged the envelope between a folded canvas fire hose in a frame and the steel wall behind it.

While Peter, the Bible bee boy, stood outside the van

and engaged the driver in conversation, she slipped up the steel ladder on the van's rear, then onto the roof of the vehicle.

Faith Ann nestled among the duffel bags and equipment cases. When the ferry slowed a couple of minutes later, she heard people leave the bow to get into their cars or go back upstairs to the passenger deck.

She felt the van rock as the teenagers climbed back inside.

As the van drove off the ferry, Faith Ann looked up at the darkening sky. If the cops caught her before she got to Mr. Massey, and even if they killed her, Peter knew where the envelope was. She had told Peter just enough so that if anything happened, he would seek out Mr. Massey and tell him where she had left the evidence. *Justice will be served, Mama. I promise you.*

75

Marta put the batteries in the cassette recorder she had bought at an electronics place on Canal Street. She rewound the tape while Arturo blew smoke rings out of the open window of her Lincoln. The cassette was a ninety-minute version, forty-five to a side.

The tape player made a loud snap to alert Marta that the tape had rewound. Holding her breath, Marta pushed the Play button.

"I'm recording," a woman's voice said. Marta turned up the volume to hear better.

"And you fixing to die in a minute, bitch," Arturo muttered.

Marta punched him hard in the shoulder. "Shhhhhh!" she hissed.

"It's her. The lawyer," he told her.

"You ready?" the lawyer asked somebody. *"And, let's be serious. This is serious material."*

"It is not! *Why do you say that, Mother?"* Marta, who had been anticipating another adult's voice, was surprised to hear the voice of the young girl reply.

"Because these are your thoughts, Faith Ann. And they are important."

"Im-por-tant? Oh, Mother, please."

"Important because you wrote them. They reflect your life, your world. Someday they might be valuable because they are your words."

"Yeah, right," Faith Ann's voice said. *"This is so gay."*

"It is not," her mother countered. *"It's precious."*

"That's the lawyer bitch," Arturo said. "And that's her kid."

"Just shut up, Arturo!" Marta snapped.

He shrugged. "Kid was in the office."

"Someday you'll be so glad to have this tape," the lawyer said.

"And you'll use it to humiliate me," her daughter shot back.

"No, I won't. Cross my heart. Ready? First poem . . ."

"Okay, you'll start the music again when I wave my hand. Okay? Okay. The name of this poem is 'A Penny for Your Thoughts.' I wrote it about everybody having opinions about everything, even stuff they know absolutely nothing about." The soft strains of chamber music came up in the background.

"A penny for your thoughts, by me, Faith Ann Porter.
I think without stopping.
all Spring through to Fall
If you get them for a penny
they're worth nothing at all."

Marta snapped the Stop button and hit fast forward.

"I want to hear the poem," Arturo protested.

Marta let it run for several seconds, then she punched the Stop button. "You can listen to the poem *after* I hear the hits." She pressed the Play button.

"—or maybe it's the fact that your breath is bad or your feet stink sometimes—"

Arturo laughed. "She's talking about her mother!"

Stop.

FF.

Stop.

Play.

". . . but I never knew him, or if he really wanted a son, or if he liked baseball or basketball more . . ."

Stop.

Marta stared at the tape player, unable to speak. Anger enveloped her. Or maybe it was that she wasn't accustomed to being outsmarted, outstreeted by a kid.

"This is bullshit!" Marta snapped.

"This is maybe just stuff before Amber got there, that's all," Arturo said.

FF.

Stop.

Play.

"—because like maybe you meant to fly a kite, but never had the right string for it. And—"

Stop.

FF.

"Her poems suck," Arturo said.

Stop.

Play.

That fucking string music. Those stupid verses.

And so it went for almost the entire side of the tape.

"Turn it over," Arturo said.

The other side was blank.

"That little monster!" Marta raged.

"There was no tape of me," Arturo said. "Don't you see? This was what she took from the machine. This was the last tape in the machine. Her mother didn't turn it on for her." He sniggered. "A bunch of silly girl-shit poems about stinky feet."

Marta burned him with her best "of all the dumb shit I ever heard" glare. "The little bitch! I can't believe this."

"Well. If there is one, where is it? I say there's no tape."

"That little conniving shit!" Marta yelled. She shoved the cassette player off the console onto the floor at Arturo's feet, startling him. The cigarette fell from his open mouth. Marta's hand shot out. She snatched the butt in midfall, clenched it in her fist, and squeezed hard, extinguishing it. That done, she flung it through Arturo's open window. "She handed us a dummy tape! Damn her. Goddamn her!"

"How can you know that?"

"Because I know is how I know. She left this shit in that player, and she took the earphones because she knew it would take time to hear what was on it. She was playing for time. She knew that if we had the tape, we would be satisfied enough to lose our focus for a few minutes. And it worked!"

"She's just a little kid," Arturo said. "No way she put that together. There is no tape, Marta."

"She has it, Turo. I am telling you she does. I would bet my life on it. And she has those negatives too. This is not a child. This is a demon. She isn't running scared at all. And she is going to give them over to someone who will use them. And, when that happens, you are going to die. Bennett will kill you, or Suggs will kill you, or the state of Louisiana will kill you. I am going to find her and I am going to cut out her little black heart and feed it to a pig."

"Take some deep breaths," Arturo said.

Marta stared at him, just daring him to say another word. He shrank against the door.

She closed her eyes for fifteen, maybe twenty seconds.

"I only have one question," he said finally.

She opened her eyes slowly, pinning him with her glare. "What?"

"Where you gonna get a pig from?"

76

Vehicles exiting the ferry went up the ramp, topped the levee, passed by a statue of Louis Armstrong, then descended into Algiers Point. Nicky had parked at the base of the levee in front of the Dry Dock Café and Bar, and, when Adams parked, he slipped into the backseat of Nicky's sedan.

"As far as I can tell, she didn't walk anywhere," Nicky told them. "You sure she was on that ferry?"

"I'm as sure as I can be," Winter said. "She'll call Rush again soon. I just talked to him. He said Faith Ann mentioned her mother was killed because of a something pond."

"A pond?" Adams said.

"Wait a minute," Nicky said. He got out of the car, went to the Stratus, opened the door and reached inside and came back carrying a newspaper. Inside again, he handed the paper up to Winter. "Look down there, under the picture of Kimberly." Nicky leaned his cane against the passenger's door.

Winter scanned the article. " 'Kimberly Porter had most recently been working on several last-minute appeals for Horace Pond, convicted of the 1993 home-invasion double homicides of Superior Court Judge Arnold Toliver Williams and his wife, Beth, both sixty-three. Pond, who had been working as a handyman for the couple, was connected to the murders by physical evidence and a signed confession. Governor Lucas Morton, who was the Orleans Parish chief prosecutor during the Pond case, has steadfastly refused to consider clemency for any murderer convicted by "the good people of Louisiana." One week ago Governor Morton released a statement that said, "If ever there was a poster boy for the death penalty, that person is Horace Pond. The Fifth Circuit has refused to grant a stay, so the execution will go on as scheduled."' The execution is scheduled for ten o'clock tonight. If the woman who claimed to have evidence exonerating a client of Kimberly's was Amber Lee, and the client was Horace Pond, then maybe it isn't that big a stretch to imagine a cop was involved in the killings," Winter said. "If the cops framed Pond somehow . . ."

"The governor prosecuted him," Nicky said. "It might be politically embarrassing if his poster boy for crime was to be proved not guilty. Says in there that he's up for reelection."

"I seriously doubt the governor had Pond's attorney murdered and risked being on death row himself just so he could be reelected."

"Then you don't know Louisiana politics," Nicky countered. "You're not a Southerner, are you?"

"Not hardly," Adams said.

"Where are you from?"

"Pacific Northwest."

"I wonder who the detectives on the Pond case were?" Winter mused. He was still looking at the paper.

"You thinking Tin Man and Doyle?" Adams asked.

Winter didn't reply. He picked up his phone and dialed. Manseur answered on the third ring.

"Yeah?"

"Got a second?"

"Can I call you back in a few? I'm in a meeting."

"You with Suggs?"

"That's right."

"I need to ask you couple of a quick questions. Yes or no's."

"Okay, if I can."

"Were Tinnerino or Doyle on the Pond case?"

There was a long silence. Winter could hear people talking in the background.

"No. Why?"

"Who was?"

"I can't say."

"Was it Suggs?"

"Why do you want to know that?"

"Can you call me when you get clear?"

"Twenty minutes."

Winter closed his phone. "It was Suggs," he told the two men.

"Suggs framed Pond for killing a judge," Adams said. "Makes sense. But where does Bennett fit in?"

"Maybe Bennett found out about it and he's been blackmailing Suggs. Maybe the case was important to Suggs's career, and he framed Pond because he thought Pond was guilty and was under pressure to solve it fast. Maybe Amber learned about the frame from Bennett, got pissed at him, and threatened to tell. Maybe she wanted money for it and somebody decided not to pay in money. That would explain just about everything Suggs and Tin Man have been doing. Maybe Tin Man used his badge to get into Kimberly's office, or Amber said something about him being a cop and Faith Ann overheard, or saw it. If she can finger Tinnerino or Doyle as the shooter . . ."

"Or Suggs," Nicky suggested.

"Anything's possible," Winter admitted.

"So where do we go from here, boss?" Nicky asked Winter.

"We have to wait for her to call," Winter said, yawning. "It'll be dark in an hour."

"Adams, maybe you could call in some of your FBI buddies?" Nicky said.

"What for?" he said.

"To give us a hand, you know. Comb the town, watch Suggs, track down those people in the Lincoln."

"I've tracked the female."

"I'll just bet you have," Nicky said.

Winter couldn't believe his eyes when Nicky leaned forward and pressed Hank's cocked .45 against Adams's head.

"What the hell are you doing?" Winter demanded.

"Stay calm, Winter. Don't nobody do nothing at all but sit and listen. Mr. Adams here can't call in his FBI pals, because he don't have any."

"What?" Winter said.

Adams turned his eyes up into the mirror.

"Put that gun away, Green," he said softly.

"I don't know who this here feller is, but he sure as hell ain't *Special* FBI Agent John Everett Adams," Nicky said.

"Of course I am," Adams said.

"What makes you think he isn't?" Winter asked.

"Makes me *know* he isn't, you mean. If you so much as quiver, old buddy, I'll spread your brains all over the dashboard." Nicky reached his left hand into his left coat pocket and handed Winter three envelopes.

77

"What the hell are you thinking, Nicky?" Winter said, looking from the gun at Adams's head back down at the envelopes Nicky had just handed him.

"Open 'em up and see for yourself," Nicky said. "If the FBI knows who this bird is, it's probably because they're looking for him. That I.D. he's carrying might as well have come out of a cereal box."

"You're making a big mistake," Adams said.

"I doubt it."

Winter opened one of the envelopes and poured the contents into his palm. A passport. Four credit cards. Wallet-size pictures of smiling people, business cards for a chemical company bearing the same name as the passport. Three business cards from associates to show business contacts, a list of names and telephone numbers.

"Each one of those envelopes contains a complete identity, down to wallet clutter. I didn't take but half of the ones in the secret compartment in his traveling case, which included two handguns, one fitted with a noise suppressor. Adams here also travels with makeup, wigs, false eyebrows and mustaches, and eyeglasses."

"I can explain all that," Adams said. His face was white with anger.

"Let's hear it," Winter demanded curtly.

"Maybe you ask your pet cowboy to lower his weapon before he pulls a *Pulp Fiction* here?"

"No, I don't think I can." Winter reached into Adams's jacket and took his Glock. "So, let's hear it."

"If Green will get out, I will explain everything to your satisfaction."

"Yeah, right," Nicky said. "I'd bet you'd just love that. Being a professional and all."

"Who's paying you?" Winter asked. "Bennett? Suggs?"

"Neither. It isn't anything like that," Adams said.

"You kill people for kicks?" Nicky said.

"Nicky isn't going anywhere," Winter told Adams. "So let's have it."

Adams shrugged. "You might wish he had."

"Then I'll just have to regret it later."

"I'm not an FBI agent."

"No shit?" Nicky said. "I think I already established that. You're a hit man. What I don't know yet is for who."

"Did you murder Kimberly Porter?" Winter asked.

"No."

"Where were you when she was killed?"

"North Carolina."

"Even that's true, you know who did. Maybe those assistants you said you had handy," Nicky said.

Winter ignored him. "Doing what in North Carolina?"

"Watching you."

"Bull," Nicky said.

"I bet you were killing Kimberly Porter, posing as a cop. I bet you ran down Hank and Millie while you were trying to silence Faith Ann and then joined us so we'd find her so you could finish her. Who hired you?"

"I was in North Carolina," Adams insisted.

"And you arrived here when?"

"I was on the flight with you, Massey. US Air 443. I was in coach. Seat 23-A."

"I didn't see you," Winter said.

"You weren't supposed to."

"He's a lying sack," Nicky said. "You killed my friend

Millie, you son of a bitch." He pushed the gun harder against Adams's skull, tilting his head to the side.

"No, I didn't. But I know who did."

"Who?" Winter asked.

"The name won't mean anything to you."

"I just bet not," Nicky said. "Pick an easy one, like Doe or Smith."

"Paulus Styer," Adams said.

"And of course he's a foreign-coated professional killer," Nicky mocked.

"He was born in East Germany. Styer was trained from childhood by the Soviet KGB at their academy. After the country went broke, his handler for the KGB, Yuri Chenchenko turned the group of specialists into a for-profit business. These guys handle wet work for clients all over the world. The Russian Mafia gives them a lot of work," Adams said.

"So you're working with Styer?" Nicky said.

"Not *with* him. I'm supposed to kill him," Adams replied. "And I will if you don't sneeze and blow my brains out."

"Why did *Styer* kill Kimberly Porter?" Winter asked intently.

"He didn't."

"How do you know that?" Winter repeated.

"There wouldn't have been any point. Despite the odds against such a coincidence, I doubt the two events are related."

"But you said he ran down Hank and Millie," Winter reminded him.

"It's classified," he said. "I can't tell Green."

"I could lock you up in the USMS holding cell," Winter said. "Incognito for days. If you know anything about me, you know I always keep my word."

Winter saw that finally something frightened Adams.

"You do that and you're dead," Adams said.

"Threaten away, you two-bit . . ." Nicky started.

"Nicky is going to hear this," Winter said.

"It isn't a threat, it's a fact. Styer *will* kill you both. Paulus Styer is a different sort of killer. He is a temperamental kill artist who is as idiosyncratic and brilliant as Bobby Fisher. And he kills like it's all a deadly chess game. He hit Hank as a gambit—solely to draw his opponent to him."

"How much money does this super-killer get paid?" Nicky said. He saw the expression of impatience in Winter's eyes and shrugged. "Just wondering."

"Who is his real target, his opponent?" Winter asked.

"There was silence for a moment. Then Adams told Winter: "You are."

"He'll wish he had a checker player to kill," Nicky said, laughing. "Massey here will eat him alive."

"You are a worthy opponent for Styer, but you won't get a shot at him, Massey."

"Sniper, is he?" Nicky said.

Adams shook his head slowly.

"You've been running surveillance on me?" Winter asked.

"Yes," Adams said. "Audio bugs, phone taps, GPS trackers. But we've been careful to keep our numbers down so neither Styer nor you would make us."

"You've seen him watching me?"

"We've never seen him, but he has amazing sources for intelligence, and he's a master at disguising himself. We don't think he's been piggybacking our communications, but it is possible. That's why I communicate with my handler only through encrypted e-mails."

"How long have you been on me?"

"Awhile."

"Days?"

Adams nodded.

"Weeks?"

"Yes. Weeks."

"Your job is to protect me from Styer?" Winter said.

"Yes."

Winter was sure Adams was lying. "Why is he after me?" he asked.

"That is classified." Adams glanced up into the mirror at Nicky. "Lock me up. Styer'll kill you, and they'll kill me for letting him do it."

"How do you know he's after me?"

"We turned Styer's handler. The—"

"Who the pink fuck is *we*?" Nicky interrupted, exasperated.

"Let him finish," Winter snapped.

"The handler's a businessman. Yuri Chenchenko sold us Styer for enough benefits that it's a zero-sum decision. We want Styer because he kills people we don't want dead. He's an enemy of the state, so making a deal with his handler for him was a no-brainer."

"If you are who I think you want me to believe you are, you sure as hell aren't here to protect me. If you are assigned to kill this Styer, I'm your bait, so you owe me the truth."

"It might be because . . ." He shook his head slightly. "This is just between us, it has to stay that way."

"Fine," Winter said. "My word."

"Cross my heart," Nicky said.

"It could be sort of our fault that he's after you."

"Define 'sort of.' "

"Look, I know you aren't going to shoot me, Green. So aim that damn gun somewhere else."

"So far, you ain't bought yourself a thing but a .45-caliber hollow point. I hope you got extra gore insurance on this car when you rented it."

Winter opened the breech of the Glock he'd removed from Adams's pocket and saw the glint of brass. He pointed the weapon at Adams. "Put the Colt away, Nicky. He knows I'll shoot him."

"When a certain Russian mobster, who wasn't technically guilty of what he was convicted of last year, whom you helped the A.G. frame, made an attempt to hire a hit on the attorney general, the FBI intercepted the messenger and came to see us about it. We saw an opportunity to thwart that hit and to get Styer, someone we wanted. We offered Yuri a deal, and Yuri offered Styer an assignment to get you, which he took because of your stellar reputation, Massey."

Winter asked. "Why didn't y'all get Yuri to point him out to you—give you his hideout?"

"Styer moves constantly, keeps everything secret, so if there was a mole in his group, or someone gets turned, he'll be safe. He trusts Yuri, but even Yuri never knows where Styer is, so all he could do was send him to us like he did. If Styer survives and figures out he was set up, he'll go straight back to Russia and kill Yuri. He has independent ties into intelligence and helpers."

"Styer ran over Hank and Millie because he wanted Winter?" Nicky said, obviously stunned. "That makes you people responsible."

"Does my director know about this?" Winter asked.

"No. Nobody outside my group does."

"You're gonna kill this Styer?" Nicky said. "How?"

"When he comes for Massey, I'll be there. He'll be coming soon. He will want to take you man to man, pit his skills against yours. That's why he used Trammell. Styer wants you angry, motivated, so you'll be on your game."

"If he is watching, what effect will you showing up have on his plan?"

"He'll just think an FBI agent was sent in to evaluate

the Trammels' accident. He'll check up on me using his intelligence resources, and he'll believe it."

"What about my family? Will he go after them?" The Russians, like the Colombian cartels, were notorious for killing entire families as an object lesson.

"Not a chance Styer would do that."

"He doesn't kill women or children?" Nicky asked, sounding skeptical.

"It would serve no purpose."

"Last year I killed some men. Were any of them friends of yours?" Winter asked Adams.

"I don't have any friends," Adams answered.

"If you are who I think you are, you know who Fifteen is."

"He runs our organization."

"Your boss goes by a number?" Nicky asked.

"It's not his real name," Adams said.

"He like the fifteenth in line for the throne?" Nicky said. "This is horse dookie."

"Fifteen ran into a blowtorch while he was on a mission in East Germany during the Cold War. Fifteen hours is how long he was interrogated without talking."

"Can't be true," Nicky argued. "He's lying, Winter."

Winter handed Adams back his Glock.

The cutout made Winter uneasy, in the same way sharing the interior of the car with a coiled cottonmouth might. But since the agent was a specialist—something Winter was painfully familiar with—that uneasy feeling wasn't necessarily a bad thing. If Adams so much as sneezed wrong, Winter would kill him.

The cells run by Fifteen, the groups Adams was affiliated with, were ex-military Special Forces–trained cleaners, assassins called cutouts because their identities were fictitious. Fifteen was powerful. And he was at the top of the list of the most poisonous and frightening individuals Winter had ever met.

"Green," Adams said, "I'm going to give you this one."

"One what?"

"Breaking into my rooms and putting that gun to my head. I understand why you did it and, even though I would have done the same thing, the next time you aim that gun at me you'd better pull the trigger."

"If I feel called on to draw down on you again, that won't be a problem."

Adams laughed.

78

Hood cinched tight, hands clenched together in the front pocket, Faith Ann lay flat in the narrow space between the hard cases, duffels, and rucksacks piled inside the tall steel cage on the van's roof. The raised flat bars that comprised the floor of the cage allowed the air to come at her from above and below, adding to the chilling effect of the wind. If she could have huddled up more, it would have made the ride more comfortable. At least she was hidden. By her watch it had been two hours of driving up and down rural roads. How long did it take to get to a Bible bee? She ventured a peek. Peter had mentioned sightseeing before the contest, but not that it would take hours. Below her, the kids started singing. Their voices filtered up to her from the open van windows.

She might not freeze to death this time of year, but darkness would drop the temperature, and she was bone tired—not to mention that she had important things to do. Sometimes it was as if she had dreamed the murders, had confused real life with a scary movie, and that her mother was really at the office, or at home, and perfectly fine.

Faith Ann saw the approaching sunset as an accusation against her. Horace Pond was sitting in a cell in the isolated Death House Unit at Angola. Faith Ann imagined him praying with Sister Ellen, his small voice telling God that he didn't kill anybody. Maybe Sister Ellen believed him, but Faith Ann knew hardly anybody, except a convicted killer's family and maybe a lawyer like her mother, ever really believed people in Horace Pond's position.

With four hours to go, she imagined Horace Pond eating his last meal, which she thought was probably something he never got to eat in prison. She thought about Horace Pond's family, his wife and four children, and how sad and afraid they had to be knowing he was going to be dead in a few hours. Thinking about it made Faith Ann sad. The fact that he was innocent made her angry. Thinking about justice made her think about her mother.

Faith Ann thought about the fact that her mother died knowing that Horace Pond was innocent. Her mother knew that the only chance he had to live was if Faith Ann survived and told the truth to somebody who could make the state stop the execution. And Faith Ann had to make that happen somehow. *If I can't stop it tonight, they'll all be sorry to find out they murdered an innocent man. They'll have to quit murdering people on Death Row.*

Faith Ann realized that it wouldn't be just as good if people found out Horace Pond was innocent *after* he was executed. No matter what, she couldn't let that happen.

It occurred to her that she could have done something and hadn't. If she had run out the front door before he fired his gun, and the killer had chased her, knowing a witness was escaping he wouldn't have dared kill the women. She knew that the elevators always went back down to the lobby and waited down there until someone called them up. She should have raced down the stairs. Then she could have escaped and called for help.

Her mind wrapped itself around that scenario. Faith Ann could see everything. Sliding out from under the table. Slipping to the front door. Slamming it as she ran out. Straight to the stairwell. Through that door. Down the four flights of stairs. Screaming bloody murder. Out in the street, waving down cars. A police cruiser, a cab, a mother taking her children to school. Her mother calling 911. The killer trapped. Horace Pond freed. Her mother a hero. Herself a hero.

I could have done it.

I could have saved her.

Mama, I'm so sorry.

It's all my fault.

I was afraid.

I didn't do anything but lie there safe.

Now you are dead forever.

Now Aunt Millie is dead forever.

Uncle Hank will know it's all my fault.

Mama, I'm so sorry . . .

Faith Ann started crying.

The van slowed and pulled off the highway. It stopped beneath a corrugated steel awning.

The doors opened and the passengers started getting out. She smelled gasoline fumes.

I can get down and find a phone. I'll call Rush . . .

She sneaked a peek over the luggage and her heart stopped. A police car was parked outside the gas station; the khaki-uniformed cop leaned against it, holding a soda.

The kids were going into the station convenience store to get snacks while the adults put gas in the van. She lay there, her thoughts racing, unable to decide what to do. Now she knew how rats felt in a trap. She felt the van shift ever so slightly and she froze.

She sensed someone standing on the ladder and she looked up to see Peter.

He put a finger to his lips to warn her to stay quiet. He took off his leather jacket and tossed it onto her. He made a gesture of putting his hand in his pockets and climbed down.

Faith Ann slipped the coat on. Inside the pockets she found a bottle of water, two packages of peanut butter crackers, and a candy bar.

Thank you, sir. Mama always said angels don't always need swords.

79

Harvey Suggs sat at a small table in a private dining room at a family-owned restaurant he frequented. The police captain had decided that he needed a sit-down meal and a stiff drink or two so he could calmly examine this mess and figure out his escape opportunities.

Suggs wasn't in the catbird seat, but neither was he dumb enough to be standing around at the bottom of the hill waiting to catch whatever rolled down.

If he played this right, handled it himself, nobody could point a finger at him when Bennett vanished. He remembered the words of the famous Louisiana gangster Sam Manelli: "Three people can be trusted to keep a secret . . . if two of them are dead."

Manseur was going to have to cover a lot of ground before he could trace anything back to Bennett, which would be a dead end. The Feds had compiled a lot in a short time, but suspicion and proof were different animals. Suggs had never banked one dime of the money he'd gotten under the table from Bennett or anyone else. The waiter brought his scotch, interrupting Suggs's worried train of thought.

"Ten minutes on the trout," he said.

"No hurry, Angelo. If you have any steak scraps . . ."

"Of course, Captain Suggs. A bag for Heinzie."

When the door opened a minute after the waiter left, Arturo Estrada and his girlfriend, or wife, or whatever she was, came in.

"What are you doing here?" Suggs demanded.

"We need some information," Arturo said.

"Meeting is not a good idea." Suggs was annoyed.

"Mr. Bennett says you won't take his calls."

Marta made Suggs very nervous. The woman was remarkably beautiful, and that was part of it, but he knew that she was as cold and as proficient a killer as any creature Nature had ever designed. Her big brown eyes were like wet river stones, and when she stared at him he was sure she was reading his mind.

"I can't talk to Bennett. Didn't Tin Man explain that?"

"Tin Man doesn't have the gift of explaining things," the woman said. "He is a dumb son of a bitch, who sees only his own small part of things. He mentioned two federal officers showed up to make trouble. Tin Man told Mr. Bennett that you put someone else in charge of the lawyer's and Amber Lee's deaths. Mr. Bennett isn't sure this is a good thing. He is a little bit nervous. He liked it better the way it was."

"Mr. Bennett doesn't get to decide how things are done. The Feds are all over this now. I had no choice. They know certain things that they shouldn't know. Remind Jerry that I had it all under control until that little hit-and-run. You shouldn't have run over the deputy marshal and his wife."

"What are you talking about?" Marta asked. "What deputy and his wife?"

"Uptown last night is what I mean. Your stupid hit-and-run brought in the FBI and Deputy U.S. Marshal Winter Massey. It turns out that Deputy Trammel and his wife were related to Kimberly and Faith Ann Porter. And the child was a close friend of Massey's son. She called the son and told him that cops killed her mother. That was how the Feds showed up at Canal Place."

"Cops?" Arturo said. "How did she think that? I *knew* she wasn't in her mother's office."

"*The* Winter Massey?" Marta asked, smiling.

"Tell Jerry I can't talk to him about this or anything else for a while." When Suggs said that, he had it all. His mind played out the scenario, ending with patting down the dirt over Bennett's grave. "Tell him that I have to talk to him face-to-face. Tell him to make sure he doesn't have a tail. Tell him to meet me at his lake house tonight at ten."

"Tell me more about the Feds," Marta said. "Winter Massey."

"Winter Massey is about the worst possible man to have on your ass. Ask Sam Manelli about it."

Marta nodded impassively. "What else?"

"What do you mean, what else?"

"Tell me everything you know about Massey and the agent. Where they are staying, what weapons they have, how they communicate. Everything."

"Why?" Suggs said.

"Because I asked," she said.

It didn't take long for Suggs to tell the killers everything he knew about Massey and the FBI agent.

Marta said, locking eyes with Suggs, "Sometimes I wonder about things. Like why would the spying FBI agents all stay out of sight after Agent Adams told you about them watching? And I wonder why you would have Mr. Bennett go all the way out to the boathouse when you could meet closer?"

"Sometimes I wonder about things too," Suggs shot

back. "Like what has Bennett done to get rid of any incriminating evidence? He did tell you that the Feds came to ask him questions? He must have told you that he didn't do very well in the interview. He mentioned my name to them. I am sure he would never give them *your* names."

Marta held Suggs's eyes for a long time. Icily, she smiled. "Maybe near the lake is the safest place for Mr. Bennett to meet you. We should all be thinking about our safety. And our futures."

"Maybe we'll see each other again real soon," Suggs said. "I like the way you"—he tilted his glass to her in salute—"think."

80

Winter and Adams went straight to Charity Hospital while Nicky stopped by the hotel to give the clerk a letter Winter had written, and an envelope. The letter said that if a child came looking for him, the clerks were to give her the envelope. It contained his phone number and a key to the suite. Faith Ann hadn't known where he was staying, because Rush hadn't known when they talked. If she called back, Sean would send her to the hotel and call him. He chose the hospital because there was a chance that the girl might show up, knowing Hank was there.

Winter was bothered by the amount of time that had passed without Faith Ann calling Rush. While he visited Hank in the ICU, Adams sat out in the waiting room, perhaps watching for the superkiller.

The young doctor assured him that Hank was showing signs of improvement as measured by the phalanx of machines that were charged with deciding such things. "We unhooked the respirator because he's breathing on his own now. I think we are going to set the bones we can set tonight and start bringing him out of the coma after the procedure. I wouldn't be surprised if he regains consciousness during the night."

To Winter, his friend looked even worse than he had the last time he'd seen him. The facial swelling looked worse and Hank's skin, where it wasn't abraded or bruised, seemed to have turned to a light gray.

Winter suddenly felt the weight of the hours of worry and stress settling on his shoulders. He was accustomed to long stretches without rest, and although he couldn't think about sleeping yet, he needed to eat something and fill himself up with hot coffee. When the doctor left him, Winter slumped in the chair beside Hank's bed, put his elbows on his knees, and closed his hands over his eyes. He thought about Sean, Rush, and the baby that would soon join his family.

When Winter opened his eyes, Detective Manseur was in the room. The bags under the cop's eyes seemed to be larger and to have turned a darker brown in the two hours since Winter had last seen him.

"How's he doing?" Manseur asked in a soft voice.

"Doctor says much better," Winter said. "I wish I could see it."

81

"In the city with the finest restaurants on earth we're eating in a hospital cafeteria," Winter said. "So where do we stand."

"The transmitter I found in Trammel's Stetson," Manseur said, "is an audio and positioning combination. My tech friend has never seen anything close to that size. Thinks it could be European. Probably a three-mile range. The body in the Rover had European dental work. That's about as far as I can go with that until we get I.D. on prints. I copied Interpol as well."

Winter didn't let on that the dental work or the bug's origin being European were of specific interest to him. It added credibility to Adams's story about a Russian assassin targeting Hank and Millie to lure Winter to New Orleans. If that wasn't true, the two crimes were just one very large coincidence.

"I found out who the male half of the Latin couple was, without letting Suggs or Tinnerino know that I knew about them." Manseur handed Winter a copy of a driver's license.

"Arturo Pena Estrada. How'd you find him?"

"There was no criminal record on the woman. But I ran her home and business addresses through the database and I got a separate hit on her home address. She owns the property. Estrada uses that address for everything, so he likely lives there."

"He's not a cop?"

"A licensed private investigator, works out of the same address. He's in our files as a key consultant to the NOPD.

In fact, despite his youth, he's been carried on the NOPD computer as a terrorism expert for three years."

"How are the two of them connected?" Winter asked.

"With Bennett?"

"To each other."

"She seems to be an antiques dealer. Seven years older. Could be married, lovers, business partners." Manseur shrugged. "I've been going over Tinnerino's and Doyle's handwritten notes. They said they've been typing up a report as they went, but when they tried to retrieve it, it wasn't there."

"The old dog-ate-my-homework excuse."

"They obviously intended to write a report after they knew what had to be in it," Manseur said. "They aren't much, but they *are* survivors."

"So let's talk about motives," Winter said.

"Porter/Lee or Trammels?" Manseur wondered.

"Trammels' hit-and-run might not be connected," Winter said.

"They're connected," Manseur said. "Both were professional hits. Porter/Lee was a silenced weapon, tight grouping, killer cool as a mint julep. Look at the sophisticated bug in the hat. The Rover corpse's old injuries and the European dental work, and the way he was killed. I don't see two separate pros doing this. The Trammel hit-and-run was planned, and so were the Porter/Lee hits. Faith Ann at both scenes . . ."

The Styer information presented a problem because Winter couldn't explain it to Manseur without risking bringing out everything Adams had told him. He would have to go into things that were not ever supposed to be talked about, because the authors of the weasel deals that made it possible—all cosigners being powerful and some certainly dangerous—wouldn't let them be known. It was bad enough that Nicky knew, but he trusted Nicky to keep it a secret.

"Any link to what happened to Hank and Millie Trammel probably sprang from the kid being there," Winter added automatically. "To get rid of the witness. Trammels were collateral damage."

Manseur nodded thoughtfully, sipped coffee. "Doesn't explain the bug in Trammel's hatband."

"You didn't tell me if Suggs was involved with the Pond case," Winter said. "Was Tinnerino or Doyle?"

"You mean the Williams case," Manseur said, visibly stiffening in his chair. His features hardened. "Tinnerino and Doyle weren't. Suggs was the primary."

"Your reaction to the name Horace Pond makes me think you have some connection to him too. Did you get on scene first or something?"

"Arnold and Beth Williams were close friends of mine. They lived near my parents. I mowed the judge's yard from the time I was ten until I went to college. They treated me as an equal, they introduced me to people, gave me advice. They were very dear people. If I could have gotten my hands on Pond the night he was picked up, we wouldn't be waiting for any execution."

"You believe he's guilty," Winter said.

Manseur burned Winter with a look of undistilled anger. "Pond violated Beth Williams with the barrel of his twelve-gauge, and he wasn't gentle. All the while Arnold, trussed up like a turkey, was forced to watch. Then Horace Pond blew their heads off."

"That's tragic," Winter said solemnly. Kimberly Porter may have believed her client was innocent, but Manseur was going to resist helping to save Pond. "Look. Just for the sake of argument, let's say Pond didn't do it. Let's say Suggs made sure the evidence fit Pond. He had a record.

So Pond was interrogated by Suggs and his partner. Anybody listen in?"

"Billy Putnam was his partner. It was a closed interrogation."

"Recorded?"

Manseur shook his head.

"So no witnesses. That usually means creative interrogation techniques. How long did his interrogation last?"

"Maybe twenty hours," Manseur said. "I know what you're thinking, but the physical evidence was overwhelming. They found the weapon hidden where Pond said he put it. They lifted his fingerprints in the house and off the weapon. Fingerprints on the gun were made in their blood. A box of shells behind the seat in his truck matched the hulls from the scene, the firing-pin strike was a match."

"Could the blood have been added to the prints *after* they were collected? When you fake a bloody print you can't duplicate what a bloody finger does when it comes into contact with an object—how the blood relates to the lands and grooves. If the blood was added to an existing print that was lifted from somewhere else, they can tell that now. Years ago, they couldn't. You're a detective. You going to tell me *you* don't have the technical expertise to frame somebody?"

"I could do it. That doesn't mean he was framed. He signed a confession."

"Bear with me. Suggs has a lot at stake if he and his partner framed Pond—even if they *believed* he was guilty, he might not be. They had the power to take an illiterate man with a record and tie it all up for the D.A. with the confession. The D.A.'s career gets a big bounce from the conviction that helps put him in the governor's chair. The D.A. certainly wanted Pond to pay for slaughtering a judge and his wife. Pond probably got a lawyer who didn't want the case but had to take it. I'd bet Pond's attorney didn't try very hard."

Manseur looked at his watch. "In four hours it will be a moot point. The trial was fair," Manseur said. "I was there, I heard and saw it all."

"Define fair," Winter demanded. "An illiterate black yardman with a criminal record who signs a confession to raping a woman with a shotgun while her judge husband looks on. Done with that, he then blows their lily-white heads off and goes to trial swearing he didn't do it—he was framed, he was deprived of sleep and didn't know what he signed was a confession. He testified and the D.A. ate him alive, tied him in knots. The media worked the community into a blood fury. Come on, Manseur, you should be shocked they didn't stick a needle in him on the spot."

"Debating this is a waste of time."

"Okay," Winter said, spreading his hands. "We both know the profile is all wrong. It seems to me that the foreign-object rape and murders were carefully planned sadistic acts designed to make the Williamses suffer as much humiliation and pain as possible. The perp violated her to torture *him*. What do you imagine the judge did to Pond to make him hate him to that extent? Give him a chance to earn a living? The D.A. said the motive was robbery, right? Home invasion gone bad?"

Manseur nodded.

"You're a homicide detective. Does Pond really make sense? If he wasn't guilty and he was framed, it means somebody else did it. And that sadistic psychopath is probably still out there."

"How would Suggs know where the murder weapon was if Pond didn't tell him?"

"Good question. Ask Suggs's partner."

"Putnam's been dead for six years. He retired right after

the trial, and during the departmental cleanup he ate his gun. The M.E.'s report had his blood alcohol level at 2.6."

"Who found him?"

"Putnam did it in a fishing cabin he and Suggs owned together. Suggs found him."

"So, if Pond didn't tell Suggs and Putnam where the shotgun was because he didn't know, who did? Someone Suggs knew and agreed to protect in return for something else?"

"Okay," Manseur said. "Like who?"

"I'll cut through the tall grass," Winter said. "Did Judge Williams ever do anything, personally or professionally, to piss off Jerry Bennett?"

82

Tinnerino had followed Detective Manseur from headquarters to Charity Hospital and watched as the detective parked near the FBI agent's car on the street. Five minutes later his cell rang.

"What, Doyle?" Tinnerino said.

"I'm at the hotel. There's some bald guy staying with Massey. I figure he's another Fed, maybe undercover FBI working with Adams. Five minutes ago I spotted the bald agent driving Massey's car. He went in for maybe a minute and came back out. I'm trailing him toward downtown."

"Yeah, he's headed to Charity. There's a powwow shaping up here. I'm parked on Tulane. Just meet me here."

Ten minutes later the bald guy had parked near Manseur's car and waltzed into the hospital. While Doyle watched the building's entrance, Tinnerino used a flat bar to jimmy open Manseur's Impala. He planted a transmitter under the dashboard. They had to keep up with what the opposition was up to, and since they couldn't wire the detective or go inside the hospital, the car was the next best thing. Suggs had accessed Manseur's computer to see exactly what files he had been looking at. Suggs wasn't pleased with Manseur's snooping, but that was the extent of what Tinnerino knew about it. Tin Man hated Manseur, and anything he could do to fuck him up was fine with him. Doyle didn't care much one way or the other, but Tin Man's partner was always in for a penny, in for a dollar.

Tin Man locked Manseur's door and, holding the jimmy bar inside his jacket, strode back to his car and got in. He drove a block away, parked, and after calling Doyle to tell him he succeeded, he put on the headset and waited for Manseur to get back to his car. Doyle was watching the entrance: he'd call when he saw Manseur.

Tinnerino called Suggs's private number and brought him up to speed. "Chief," Tinnerino said, "so we got three vehicles and there's two of us."

"Call in the Spics."

"You sure?"

"Oh yes. Absolutely certain."

Tinnerino dialed the number.

83

Faith Ann lay in the darkness between the bags and cases, just about frozen from the wind washing over her. Nobody had told her that the thirty-minute ride to the Bible bee would involve a three-hour detour to allow some no-stopping-to-get-out sightseeing. When the van finally slowed and turned, and gravel crunched under the tires, she leaned up on her elbow to see that they had pulled up in a large gravel lot next to a church building with a tall steeple. The van doors opened, and the kids and two adult chaperones spilled out. All of the kids, delighted to be somewhere, started horsing around in the parking lot below her perch.

A male voice rang out. "Okay, gang! Take the cases down. They go inside. Your bags all go in the van. Let's get cracking. We're on the Lord's time!"

To Faith Ann's immense relief, Peter was first up the ladder. He pointed at the left side of the van and held up two fingers, warning her that the two adults were down there. He untied the first duffel and tossed it down to someone on the ground. With Peter on the ladder, there was no way anybody else could see her unless he moved aside. It seemed that the others were happy to let him do the high-altitude work.

"You okay?" he murmured. "You must have just about froze your nuts off."

"Yeah, just about. The coat sure helped. Thanks," she said, handing it to him.

"Okay," he said, looking off to his left. "Mr. Lander is headed inside the church. Ms. Forest isn't looking this way. Everybody knows about you but them, so come around me and go down the ladder. Just stand down there while we unload the crap and they'll think you're one of the local yokels. Jesus, j-e-z-i-s."

Faith did as he said, holding onto the rail and edging past him. As she hit the ground, the teenagers crowded around to cover for her. After the things were offloaded, Faith Ann wandered into the church with Peter. The competition was being set up in the sanctuary. There were about seventy kids and at least twice that many adults—mostly parents and siblings of the contestants. Faith Ann doubted anybody else would want to sit in on this if they didn't have to.

"What're you gonna do now?" a voice asked. She turned to find herself face-to-face with another boy.

"I need to make a long-distance call. I guess I ought to go find a pay phone."

"This is Ashe," Peter said. "He's the best speller we have."

"Nice to meet you," Faith Ann said, shaking the boy's hand.

Ashe's brown eyes were serious. "You're a girl, aren't you?"

Faith Ann nodded.

"I told ya," Ashe said, punching Peter's shoulder. "I knew I saw breasts when the wind blew her shirt against 'em."

"I knew that," Peter said indignantly. "She's way too pretty to be a guy."

"Unless you're turning queer," Ashe said, laughing. "Which you probably are. You're that girl the cops are looking for, aren't you?"

Faith Ann felt the heat rising to her cheeks. She didn't know what to say, what the boys would do. "Yeah."

"Cool," Peter said.

"You can use this, then." Ashe held out a Nokia cell phone painted with red and yellow flames. "My mom gets pissed if I rack up roams. Talk as long as you want."

The two boys high-fived.

"Thank you, guys," she said, kissing each of them in turn on their cheeks. She felt like yelling.

"Anytime," Peter said.

"Guys, what's the name of this place again?"

"Church of Christ. Barataria, Louisiana."

Faith Ann dialed Rush's number and held her breath while it rang.

84

Tinnerino saw the four men strolling from the hospital's main entrance stopping at Manseur's car. Tinnerino heard the sound of Manseur's car door opening over the receiver. Manseur had just opened his door when the marshal answered his cell phone, stepped away a few steps to talk. Massey was on the phone for a minute, before he took out a card and scribbled on it. Massey waved the other two men into Manseur's car.

Through the earphones Tinnerino heard the men getting into Manseur's car and slamming the doors. He opened his pad to make notes because making a tape of this wasn't smart.

"That was Sean. Faith Ann just called her," the deputy's voice said.

"Where is she?" Manseur asked. *"Did she say?"*

Massey was silent for a few seconds. *"She's about thirty miles from here and she's freaked."*

"You direct, I'll drive," Manseur said.

"I have to go alone. If she sees anyone besides me, she'll bolt. Last time she called, the cops showed up before I did. I'll get her calmed down and explain things and I'll bring her back. Sean told her the police weren't trying to arrest her, but she doesn't believe it."

Manseur said, *"I'm interested in this alleged evidence. Does she have it or not?"*

"She doesn't have the evidence with her. She hid it after she escaped the parking deck. You can wait at the governor's hotel and I'll bring her straight there. You can get the governor to

put a hold on the execution. You can see it when we show it to him, and we won't waste time."

Manseur said, *"I won't bother the governor, attempt to stop Pond's execution, until I see absolute proof that he's innocent. I'm not believing Suggs was involved in a frame and cover-up until I see proof."*

"She has an audiotape of the killings in the office and negatives and photocopies of pictures that show the real killer doing it."

Manseur said, *"And you believe that sort of evidence exists—that somebody was stupid enough to take some sort of incriminating pictures and keep them? That girl has a vivid imagination."*

"Maybe not," Massey said.

Manseur was silent for long seconds. *"Okay. So what do we do?"*

Massey said, *"Nicky and Adams will go to my hotel and wait for me to bring Faith Ann there. You said a few minutes ago you hadn't seen your family in two days, so go home. I'll call you when we get the evidence and we can meet and you can see the stuff and make your call to the governor."*

"I get the feeling you don't trust me," Manseur said.

There was a long silence in the car.

"Okay. Meet me at the ferry landing at Canal Street—an hour, an hour and a half," Massey said. *"I'll pass on the evidence envelope."*

Tin Man heard three car doors closing.

The Impala's engine came to life and Tin Man heard Manseur call his wife to tell her he was swinging by the house to say good night. Then he turned the car radio to some opera crap and Tinnerino turned the volume on the receiver down.

"Who the hell are we following?" Doyle asked over the radio. *"They're leaving in three separate cars."*

"Nobody," Tin Man said. "Let them go."

"*What?*"

"I know where they're going. We can give them all the space in the world."

Tin Man dialed Captain Suggs. And he smiled because he knew their plans. He also finally knew exactly what the girl had and what all that lovely knowledge was going to be worth down the road. Suggs would put together a plan to snag the evidence. Let the Spics handle the heavy lifting. Tin Man didn't want to actually kill a child, or be in a shoot-out with Massey. When Manseur sent him and Doyle out, he would be handing them alibis on a silver platter.

85

Passing under a banner proclaiming a "Bible bee," Winter went into the Church of Christ in Barataria, Louisiana. He declined a program sheet offered by a man in a knit shirt with winglike collars and entered into the sanctuary, stopping at the top of the wide center aisle.

On the riser, teenagers sat in rows of folding chairs. A skinny girl with frizzy red hair stood at the pulpit. "Armageddon," she said into the microphone. "A-r-m-a-g-e-d-d-o-n. Armageddon."

"That . . . is correct," a voice announced.

Someone in the audience shouted out, "Praise His holy name!"

The girl raised her hands in the air in triumph.

A camera flashed.

The crowd applauded.

Winter recognized the skinny, short-haired boy with a bruised cheek who walked briskly toward him from the back corner of the santuary. Faith Ann grabbed his hand and squeezed it hard. Outside the front door Faith Ann looked up at him, her lower lip quivering.

"It's going to be all right," Winter said, putting his arms around her. "I'm here, Faith Ann. Everything is going to be fine."

He felt the sobs wrack her thin body. He understood that it would be a while before she'd be able to speak. He knew what sort of relief she was feeling, because he shared it. It was almost over.

86

When his cell phone rang, Harvey Suggs was walking away from the Verdict, a restaurant located around the corner from police headquarters, where he had explained to Tinnerino and Doyle what he expected from them. The captain's seriously shaken confidence had returned to normal. He had thought every angle through to its most likely conclusion. Everybody knew exactly what to do.

Peace of mind was going to cost Suggs a promotion each for Tinnerino and Doyle, and he'd toss the Spics a few thousand dollars. Tinnerino and Doyle would make sure that Manseur ended in such a way that he was discredited, so that whatever he had might have shared with the FBI agent and the private investigator could be more effectively denied. The Latinos were capable of the more difficult task of making the evidence vanish. They'd take care of the meddlesome Massey and the Porter kid. Without the evidence, no matter how loudly anybody howled, it would all fade away.

"Hello," Suggs said, not recognizing the number spelled

out on the caller I.D. He strode toward his car, parked a half block away. Tinnerino and Doyle sped by in separate cars, Tinnerino nodding once in greeting.

"Harold?" the somehow familiar voice said. *"This is Parker Hurt."*

"Parker Hurt?"

"Governor Morton's assistant."

"Sure, Parker. I knew your voice was familiar. It's been a while." Hurt had been an assistant under Lucas Morton when he was the Orleans Parish district attorney.

"It has been a while."

"What can I do for you?"

"Well, I just had an interesting call, and before I talk to the governor, I thought I should talk to you."

Suggs's trouble antennae were fully erect. He stopped short of his car and fingered his keys. "Sure thing," he said cordially, although his blood had turned to ice in his veins.

"I got a call from a Michael Manseur a few minutes ago. I believe he's one of your homicide detectives."

"Well, he's *presently* one of my homicide investigators," Suggs replied, his mind aflame with the implications. "Can you tell me why my detective called you?"

"Manseur wanted me to tell the governor that he was about to come into possession of evidence proving that Horace Pond is innocent."

"So he wants to stop the execution." Suggs added a tinge of sadness to his words. "You know . . ."

Suggs knew he had one chance to find the exact words that would nip this in the bud—and cover his own ass. And he realized that given the close gubernatorial race and Manseur's recent behavior, it was going to be a breeze.

Harvey Suggs finished his conversation with Parker Hurt, climbed into his car, and allowed himself a few moments to savor his masterful manipulation of the political animal Mr. Hurt.

If the evidence ever somehow found its way to the police or the press, Hurt wouldn't ever dare mention he took the call from a discredited, deceased cop—and failed to mention it to his boss.

As long as the evidence didn't surface, and Suggs knew it never would, Pond would just be another state-sponsored corpse. There would be nothing to connect Suggs to anything that happened, and everybody still living would resume life as usual. In two years, Suggs would retire and live out his life with his twin pensions. He'd also have the money Jerry Bennett had paid him over the years as filler for those little things a man appreciated. If by some miracle the Bennett negatives ever did surface, Suggs could blame his own dead partner—say Billy Putnam had gotten the location of the murder weapon from Pond when Suggs was out of the interrogation room. Ten years after the fact, who could prove differently? The fact that Billy had committed suicide would further support that the man had a guilty conscience.

And it wasn't like Bennett would be around to dispute anything. Suggs was meeting Bennett at the businessman's boathouse, supposedly to fill him in on the status and discuss future plans.

Suggs just hoped Bennett's cigarette racer had a nice heavy anchor on board.

87

Faith Ann sat in Mr. Massey's car, feeling dazed, staring out through the windshield at the church van. Mr. Massey had called a detective and told him they were on their way to get her envelope on the Canal Street ferry.

After he hung up on the cop, Mr. Massey made another call, telling someone named Adams that he had "the package" and was "rolling." As soon as that was done, he called Rush's mother and told her he had Faith Ann in his car and said he'd call back when things were settled. Before he hung up, he asked, "You want to tell Rush anything, Faith Ann?"

She shook her head. Not because she didn't want to talk to Rush, but she wasn't in a talking mood at that particular moment. How could Mr. Massey trust the police after what she'd told him about what they did to her mother? She'd made a terrible mistake in trusting him. "Can I talk to Rush later?"

"Sure."

When Mr. Massey hung up, he pocketed the phone and drove out of the parking lot.

"You were talking to a policeman," she said.

"I was."

"You can't trust the police, Mr. Massey. The police killed Mama."

Mr. Massey took a piece of paper out of his pocket and handed it to her, flipping on a map light so she could see it. Faith Ann's hands trembled as she looked at the image of a driver's license that portrayed a smirking man with swept-back hair and eyes that burned with pure evil. The picture belonged to the man who'd shot her mother.

"Is that him?"

"Yes." The name on the license was Arturo Estrada. "He's the policeman who killed . . ."

"He isn't a policeman, Faith Ann."

"He is too! He was at my house with the lady who chased me this morning at the aquarium. With those other two policemen."

"I know he was at your house. Those two policemen are crooked, but Detective Manseur isn't one of them.

He's going to help us get your mother's evidence to the governor."

"No! Please. *She* said we can't even trust the governor," Faith Ann blurted out, her level of fear growing. He still didn't understand.

"Who said you couldn't trust the governor?"

"Amber Lee told Mama that. It's on the tape in the envelope. Governor Morton is a friend of Jerry's, Amber Lee said so. Arturo said *Jerry* sent him to get the pictures she had. I'm sure of it!"

"Ms. Lee was mistaken. You can trust Detective Manseur. And you can trust the other men helping me; Nicky Green and Agent John Adams. And you have to trust Governor Morton, since he is the only person who can stop the execution at this late hour. He'll do the right thing here because he has no choice."

"Why are you so sure he will?" Faith Ann hated the wobble she heard in her voice, but she couldn't help it.

"Because Detective Manseur called him and told him the evidence that proves Horace Pond is innocent is coming to him in a little while. If he let an innocent man die, he'd have the devil to pay. That's politics."

Faith Ann was sure Mr. Massey believed what he was saying, but she wasn't nearly as sure of his judgment in this instance as he seemed to be.

"Did he run over . . ." She couldn't get "Uncle Hank" and "Aunt Millie" to come out.

"There's no evidence of it. None."

"You don't think he was looking for me and . . ."

"No," he said, firmly. "I really don't think he did it."

"Did you arrest him?"

"He'll be arrested as soon as he shows his face."

Mr. Massey knew about such things, she told herself. He *was* a U.S. marshal, just like her uncle Hank. That was even better than being a policeman, because it was being a policeman for the federal government. She had always enjoyed studying her uncle's badge, loved the smell of the mink oil he rubbed into his leather belt and holster, running her fingers over the yellowed stag grips on the Colt that had belonged to his father, who died on duty. She had never ever told her mother that he had let her shoot it at an indoor range one summer afternoon—it would always be their secret. Even with the ear protectors it had been loud, and the gun had almost jumped out her hand.

Faith Ann watched Mr. Massey as he drove, noticed him checking the rearview mirror. He drove fast, but he kept both of his hands on the steering wheel like her mother, and like her mother he didn't turn on the radio. No distractions.

Faith Ann was relieved that Mr. Massey had come to get her, and she knew she should feel safe, but she just couldn't believe that it was really all over and that Horace Pond would stay alive.

"Mr. Massey, can I go see my uncle as soon as we see the governor?"

"Let's wait and see what time it is," he told her. "I'm sure you could use some rest after what you've been through. Your Uncle Hank is going to be just fine in time. I spoke to the doctor earlier and he told me Hank is being weaned off the coma medicine, so he should start regaining consciousness anytime now."

"So when will he be well?"

"Well, I don't know. I suppose it depends. He's going to be in the hospital for a while before he can be moved to Charlotte, and then he'll need lots of therapy. He's going to need you to help him get well. We'll help you."

Faith Ann leaned back, crossed her arms, closed her eyes, and pictured herself on the rear deck behind her aunt and uncle's house, sitting in a lawn chair beside

Hank's wheelchair, watching his quarter horses running across the fenced-in meadow. Living in North Carolina on the little farm would be nice. It wouldn't be the same without Aunt Millie, though. Or without knowing that her mother was waiting for her to return. . . . Tears welled up under her closed eyelids and threatened to spill out.

Mr. Massey interrupted her thoughts. "Faith Ann, you know what I was thinking—and you don't have to make a decision right now—but we, Sean and Rush and I, we all really hope that you'll come live with us for a while. At least until Hank is back up on his feet again. And only if you want to."

"At your house?"

"Sure. We have a little corner bedroom that'll fit you like a glove. We might have to paint it a color you like. That's up to you. Any color you like *except* pool-table green. I could never stand that color on walls."

"Thank you for coming," she told him softly, because her mother had taught her to let people know she appreciated their kindnesses. "I was so scared."

"It's all over now. Just trust me on that. You're safe now."

"The cops want to arrest me."

"Detective Manseur fixed that. You know, just a few cops are bad," Winter said. "The good cops will take care of the bad ones."

"Do you believe that?" she asked him.

"I sure do, Faith Ann."

She smiled politely and yawned, covering her open mouth with her hand. She hoped he knew what he was talking about. She really did.

88

As Winter started down the Algier's Point ramp toward the waiting ferry, Faith Ann tried to make out the skyline across the river through the growing fog. She had studied fog in science class, and she knew that it happened when cold air came in over warmer water. The temperature had really dropped since the sun went down, and she was thankful it hadn't been this cold when she was riding on the roof of the church van.

There were a dozen vehicles in line with them for the less-than-ten-minute ferry ride between Algiers Point and Canal Street, maybe a mile's distance. The wait while the ferry loaded stretched the time of travel to more like twenty-five minutes. The twin bridges, just a couple of miles upriver, were a faster way across, but a lot of people still liked the ferry better. A ratty-looking pickup truck filled with pieces of salvaged wood and steel scraps was right behind them. A silver BMW, which had swooped past them before they made it over the levee, was in front of them.

"Which fire hose case?" Winter asked.

"Around on the other side," she told him. "Near the front. The stern."

"The bow," he corrected. "Bow front, stern rear, port is the left side and starboard is the right. I think the last two are correct, but I might be wrong." He smiled.

"So port side would be the side where we drive on?" she wondered out loud. "Port wine stern?"

"I think so," Winter answered.

He didn't get her joke, she knew, because he was distracted. Sometimes when her mother was thinking about something or reading, Faith Ann could get her to agree to things she later swore she hadn't. More than once she had taped her mother agreeing to something like putting a cotton candy machine in Faith Ann's bedroom if she made an A in Science—her best subject. It had been funny. Thinking about it now made her sad, though.

Winter followed the silver BMW sedan around the ferry's central structure and parked on the starboard side facing the stern. The vehicles parked in the lanes that circled the center structure so that the first vehicle on would be first off. Female deckhands wearing orange vests directed traffic. One of them smiled and waved at Faith Ann, so she waved back.

"That's the fire hose holder I put it in," she said, pointing out her window as the car passed by.

Winter nodded, took a radio out of his jacket pocket, and pressed the button once. "Nicky, we're on the ferry."

"Got it," a voice replied.

Winter put the radio in his pocket, looked up at the rearview mirror and then through the windows at both side mirrors.

"I'm going to get the envelope now," he told Faith Ann. "You sit tight. Lock the doors when I leave."

After he opened the door and stepped out, she locked it by pressing the button. People were moving from their cars to the railing to enjoy the wind in their faces, the view from the railing. As Winter walked back toward the hose holder, Faith Ann undid her belt, got on her knees on the seat, and watched him in the side mirror.

Faith Ann's heart pumped furiously as Winter stopped at the hose case.

Yes! Now it was done. *Now Horace Pond will be free, Mama, and the man who killed you will be arrested and . . .*

When Faith Ann noticed a figure step out from between two cars behind Winter, her chest filled with ice.

That woman!

He doesn't see her!

Without thinking, Faith Ann jerked up the lock, threw the car door open, and leaped from the car waving her arms. "It's her!" she screamed at Winter. "It's her!"

The smile vanished from Winter's face.

"Hold it there!" a voice yelled from behind Faith Ann.

The woman, aiming the gun at Winter, didn't fire. Faith Ann saw the woman's eyes shift from Winter, light on her, then look behind Faith Ann for the source of the yelled command.

In a motion so fast it looked like a blur, Winter reached inside his jacket, crouching as he turned.

A hand grabbed Faith Ann's sweatshirt and jerked her off her feet, dragging her around between the BMW's trunk and the Dodge's grille.

"Friend," a voice connected to the hand said.

She gasped, looked up at the man who had pulled her to safety and at the other man in a suit with short hair, who had yelled and who now stood next to the wall beside the BMW. His gun was aimed at the woman. A walking cane was leaned against the Dodge's grille.

The bald man kneeling beside her, gun in hand, looked familiar, and she remembered that the man without any hair or eyebrows had been on the street the night Hank and Millie were run over. The cane was his.

"I'm Nicky Green, a friend of Hank's. That's Agent Adams. You're safe, stay down and let us handle this." He winked at her, then peered at the stern area through the BMW's windows.

"Put down the gun!" Agent Adams hollered.

Faith Ann saw Adams take a step toward the woman, his gun still aimed at her.

"Now hands against the wall, Marta!" she heard Winter command.

Faith Ann ducked to look under the cars toward where Winter was standing.

Nicky straightened suddenly and aimed his gun over the BMW's roof. Faith Ann turned and looked under the BMW.

She was aware of the bald man ducking down . . .

A series of quick, deafening explosions . . .

Empty brass shells spattered the deck like they had been poured out of a box.

Glass shards rained over both her and the bald man.

She watched the two-tone shoes until they vanished around the corner.

Faith Ann had never heard a machine gun before up close and real, but she knew that was what destroyed the BMW's windshield. And, she recognized those shiny two-tone shoes.

The man who had killed her mother had just shot at Mr. Massey.

89

After the Stratus joined the line of vehicles, Arturo had joined the other passengers as they came onto the passenger deck through the sliding steel-wire door on the vessel's port side. He remained near the staircase leading down to the vehicle deck. Marta told him she'd wait until the ferry pulled away. Then she'd get to the marshal's car, use a silenced .22 to clip the two occupants, and get the evidence. Arturo would come down the staircase and make sure she succeeded. Once she was behind the wheel of the Stratus, Arturo would get into her car and follow her to the dump site.

Arturo had no idea anything was wrong until he came

down the stairs and turned the corner to see that Marta had walked straight into a trap. He had a clean shot on the FBI agent, whose back was to him, and he raised the Uzi only to see the bald-headed investigator suddenly rise from between two vehicles and aim at him. Arturo fired at the bald man, saw that he couldn't shoot the FBI agent or the marshal without hitting Marta, whirled, and ran up the stairs.

There was no plan to cover this mess.

Arturo broke up onto the passenger deck only to see a redheaded young man wearing a white shirt with epaulets come out of a door marked AUTHORIZED PERSONNEL ONLY. At the sight of Arturo's raised Uzi, the young man made a squeaky noise and froze.

Arturo jerked him away from the door, slamming him into the bulkhead. Racing into the stairwell, he hurried up the narrow steps. Flinging open the door at the top of the stairs, he lunged into the lit wheelhouse and aimed the weapon at the pilot, who had turned from the console—his face becoming a fright mask.

"Take me downriver," Arturo snarled, "or I'll kill you and drive this friggin' boat myself."

Arturo quickly checked out the doors on either side of the pilothouse. Outside the doors, short staircases went both to the roof and down to the passenger deck. The doors didn't lock, so the crew could come and go anywhere on the vessel as necessary. He was vulnerable from three directions. The Plexiglas was probably thick enough to stop a non-magnum handgun round. He hoped the marshal and his two pals got Marta in cuffs so that all three of them were free to come for him. Because if they were confident enough to turn their backs on her, cuffed or not, Marta would be back in play.

Arturo's main goal now was just to get away alive. As long as he controlled the boat's movements, he could increase his odds of escape and the men would have no choice but to come up to stop him.

"Go faster!" he screamed at the terrified pilot.

Arturo saw the door lever move ever so slightly as someone tried it. He fired a horizontal burst across the veneered wood and was rewarded with the sound of a body falling. *One down*. Arturo pulled a fresh magazine from his pocket, reloaded the Uzi, and buttoned up his coat to take full advantage of the ballistic lining.

90

Detective Manseur leaned against the grille of his Impala, parked in the shadow of the World Trade Center building near the railing on the southern corner of the Riverwalk Plaza. He was, as the crow flies, perhaps a hundred feet from the Canal Street landing, and he had a commanding view of the dock, where the eighty-five-foot-long ferry would moor. Through binoculars, he watched the USS *Thomas Jefferson* pulling away from Algiers Point, well over a mile away. When he became aware of someone standing next to his car, he looked over to see Tinnerino staring at him.

"You and Doyle are supposed to be at the Porter house. What are you doing here?"

Tin Man smiled at him. He leaned with his beefy hands splayed on the left fender. "I was just passing by. Saw you over here by yourself and I wondered what you were doing."

"You were passing by and saw me here?" Manseur knew that his position was invisible from the street. "I'm boat watching—to relax."

"Wouldn't be watching for a ferry bringing Massey and the Porter kid over, would you?"

"What makes you ask me that?"

"Because I bugged your car while you were inside the hospital, and Massey's too. Doyle and me have been right with you all along."

"Doesn't it matter that I ordered you to—"

"Your days of ordering anybody are over, Mikey."

"What does that mean?" Manseur asked, already knowing the answer. He and Tinnerino were both empty-handed, and getting to their guns would take some effort. *The Tin Man wouldn't be so cocky unless Doyle is close by.*

"We can't let that little envelope the kid has reach anybody that can stop the Pond execution. Big can of worms here, Mikie. Don't make any sudden moves toward that Glock in your coat. You and me ain't out here alone."

"So, I guess Captain Suggs sent you to silence me?"

"Yeah. That's about the size of it. Seems you been acting crazy. Buying meth from low-life dealers. Everybody knows how dangerous that is. Look at the bright side—the brass will cover up the drug thing at Suggs's suggestion, your wife will get your pension, Suggs will make sure there's a big, loud investigation. We'll pin it on some loser spook and make the streets safer in the bargain."

"Where is Suggs?"

"Had pressing business elsewhere. He's got this all figured out. That man is a strategical genius."

"Did he tell you Jerry Bennett killed the Williamses?"

"Yeah, he told us."

"You know why?"

"Doesn't matter," Tin Man answered, shrugging.

"Bennett paid Suggs to frame Pond. Bennett told Suggs where that shotgun was, and Suggs told the world Pond confessed. It was Bennett who sent Arturo Estrada to kill Amber Lee and Lawyer Porter. But you knew that, because you and Doyle have been working with him and his lady friend. We have evidence that proves it all."

"What does any of it matter? You think too much, Mikie. Your evidence ain't worth a fart in a hurricane."

"You'd do better to try thinking for yourself some. Do you really think Suggs can let you live, knowing what you do? He killed his own partner to keep the secret about Pond."

"Putnam offed himself. Man was a world-class juice head," Tinnerino said. "And I've got Doyle backing me to make sure nothing like that happens. Anything happens to me, my lawyer has a letter."

Manseur shook his head. He was aware of a second figure sneaking up on the other side of the car. Doyle held what appeared to be a .22 automatic. The bag containing drugs to plant on Manseur's corpse was probably in his overcoat pocket.

"Doyle," Manseur said casually, "before you do anything stupid, you should know that Larry Bond is up there behind me on that balcony over the ferry entrance. He's aiming his Tikka 30-06 at your head about now."

"Your partner's out of town," Doyle said.

"He came home early. I picked this place because it's where he could cover me best and shoot without risking harming any civilians. He's one hell of a deer hunter, a crack shot with his rifle."

"You're bluffing," Tinnerino said. But he was looking up, squinting.

"You walked right into it. Adams was checking the perimeter at the hospital and he spotted you getting into my car. Wasn't hard for us to figure out what you were up to. The conversation we had in my car back outside the hospital was strictly for your benefit."

"You're lying," Doyle said.

"I've already gotten word to the governor, and he's put a hold on Pond's execution. And—you'll love the irony—I'm wearing a wire right now. What you fellows heard on your bug was our plan to get you all to do what you just did."

"He's lying," Doyle said to his partner, now less sure of himself. "Get in the car."

"Not a chance," Manseur said.

"Enough jabber." Doyle raised the gun, but he didn't fire. Thunder rolled, and as a round from Bond's 30-06 shattered his right wrist the detective's .22 flew from his hand like a frightened bird.

Doyle screamed, considered his useless hand. Screamed some more.

Tinnerino stared dumbly up at the concrete structure, still trying to see Manseur's partner.

Manseur relieved Tinnerino of his Glock, cuffed the big detective's hands behind him, and took the .38 backup piece Tinnerino carried in an ankle holster.

"Okay, Larry," Manseur called. "I've got it covered. Come on down."

Tinnerino looked out at the ferry. "Listen, I can save Massey and the kid, for a deal. The Spics are on the boat to kill Massey and the kid."

Manseur walked over, picked up the .22 from the bricks and tossed it into the trunk of his car.

"Massey's car has a tracker on it," Tinnerino said desperately.

Manseur considered that. Massey's pals Adams and Green weren't at the hotel like the bad guys believed, they were on the ferry too. Manseur was sure the three of them could handle Estrada and Ruiz. He reached for his cell phone to call Massey just to let him know when a voice came over the tactical channel: "Transit Officer Davis. Shots fired on the Canal Street Ferry, in transit from Algiers Point. Officer needs immediate assistance. One perpetrator, armed with an automatic weapon."

Manseur turned toward the water. Halfway across the river, the ferry was making a sharp right turn.

"Okay, maybe it's too late for them," Tinnerino was saying. "What can you get me for flipping on Suggs?"

91

As soon as Arturo ran up the stairs, Nicky put Faith Ann back inside the Stratus. He told the wide-eyed girl to stay there and she'd be fine. As Winter was cuffing the woman, he ran after Adams, cane in hand.

"Stay behind me," the federal agent ordered.

Limping, Nicky trailed behind Adams, arriving up on the upper deck to find half a dozen passengers lying face-down on the floor near the bow windows.

"FBI!" Adams yelled.

"Freeze! Police officer!" a voice yelled out. Nicky saw the gun first, a Smith & Wesson Sigma aimed at Adams and him. The man who gripped it was dark-skinned. He wore a watch cap, baggy jeans, and a coat. A badge dangled from his neck on a chain, and his eyes were wild with excitement. Since he had a piece of toilet paper stuck to his shoe, Nicky knew where the dark-skinned man had been when the shooting started. The policeman came slowly toward him.

"Where's the shooter?" Adams snapped.

The young cop kept his gun on Adams, more or less. The copilot was cowering against the wall near the door. "Show me some I.D."

"Where's the damn shooter?" Adams repeated. But he dipped his gun so the barrel was pointed away from the cop, while reaching his left hand carefully into his pocket to bring out his credentials.

The ferry began swinging around, heading downriver.

The cop said, "I'm Davis, Transit Authority. I already called this in. The bastard has the wheelhouse."

"Obviously," Adams said. "We can probably flank him—"

"I gotta stop him," Davis interrupted. "God knows what he'll do, and there are civilians on board that I'm responsible for. I'm in charge here. No offense, but this ain't no white-collar FBI crime. People could get killed."

Adams said urgently, "What's the wheelhouse layout? How many doors? Access to them?"

"No time to waste making a plan. This is too fluid for that—too immediate. Look, I know this vessel, I'm trained to handle this—you two just make sure my flanks are covered. One of you keep guard on either side. He gets away from me, he'll come down one of the staircases on either side and nail you," Officer Davis said.

Nicky figured the cop was barely out of the academy. The rookie was determined to be a hero, and arguing with him was a waste of energy.

"We have the flanks," Adams told him.

Davis opened the door to the stairwell, looked up the steps. He started slowly up, holding his gun before him precisely as he had been instructed at the academy.

"He's a dead duck," Nicky quipped, taking a toothpick from his shirt pocket and putting one end of it into his mouth.

"We'll flank Estrada," Adams said. "You best be ready to take over the wheel, son," he told the copilot, who was crouching against the wall a few feet away.

The copilot nodded, smiled weakly.

"What's the layout?" Adams asked him.

"The stairs on either side go up to the roof, then after the smokestack there's another set up to the pilothouse. We—"

"How are they locked?"

"They don't lock, because the pilot might have to get

out fast, or someone get in. We've never had anything like this . . ."

"How many people in the wheelhouse?"

"Two of us when we're docking. One at the controls for the crossing. I was headed down for coffee. The pilot is up there alone."

"You best be ready to take over in case—"

A loud burst of nine-millimeter rounds fired into the stairwell sounded like hammer blows. Nicky peered in through the small window set in the door and saw the transit officer lying on the floor. His unfired weapon lay on the floor beside him, spattered with blood and brain matter. Nicky inched the door open, leaned inside the space, and looked up to see a dozen holes punched through the closed door.

"Dead?" Adams asked.

"Lying there dead with T.P. stuck to his danged foot—how embarrassing. Got it through the door."

"He wasn't trained all that well," Adams said. "If the shooter didn't see who was at the door, he's bound to be sure he got one of us. He'll think nobody in their right mind is coming up these same stairs."

"I'll go up these stairs on a double-stealth setting. He'll be watching the outside staircases, so when he sees you he'll open an outside door to shoot at you. When he does that, you dodge the bullets and I'll bust on in and smoke his ass," Nicky said.

"You're sharper than you look, Green," Adams said, raising a brow. "But let's do this my way. I'll go up the inside stairs and you circle around. Soon as he sees you, I'll kill the little freak, hopefully without hitting the pilot." He looked at the copilot, still cowering on the floor. "If we do, at least we have a spare."

Nicky spat out his toothpick, leaned his cane against the wall beside the door. He limped to the starboard wire door and, slipping the mechanism, slid it open. Reaching the top of the staircase, he saw Estrada looking out at him through a Plexiglas window. Nicky dived toward the smokestack located directly behind the wheelhouse. Arturo slammed open the door, pointed the Uzi out, and wasted most of what was in the magazine—precisely as Nicky had expected.

Nicky heard reports, saw muzzle flashes illuminate the wheelhouse like an electrical storm. A split second after the exchange ended, he put a toothpick into his mouth and climbed up the short rise of stairs to the pilot house.

The little room was filled with a fog of cordite. All three men inside were lying on the floor. Nicky aimed the .45 down at the prostrate killer as he moved to check Adams. "Adams, you still alive?"

Adams didn't move.

"Johnny boy," Nicky said, "you okay?"

Adams, who was beneath a narrow steel shelf under the window, sat up slowly and, according to his facial expression, painfully. "Lucky shots," he said hoarsely. "Couple in the vest. Think he got my right shoulder, though." Reaching his left hand across his lap to get the Glock from the floor beside him, he lifted it and set it down beside his left leg and covered his right shoulder with his hand to staunch the blood leak.

"That's a nasty cut on the side of your head," Nicky said.

"I hit that shelf on the way down. After I got him."

"Oh, I'm not so sure who got who." Nicky kept the Colt aimed at Arturo Estrada, facedown on the floor between him and the pilot's chair. "You can get up now," he told the pilot.

The pilot stumbled uncertainly to his feet. He stared down at the killer, whose blood was pooling around his head.

"Shouldn't you be driving this thing?" Nicky asked the captain. The pilot tore his eyes from the dead killer, then turned his attention back to the river.

Nicky picked up Arturo's Uzi, moved to the door, and tossed it out onto the roof.

"Nicky!" Adams yelled.

Out of the corner of his eye, Nicky saw Arturo rolling up, bringing a pistol out from under him, and getting to his feet.

Nicky dove out through the door. Arturo fired and missed. Knowing Arturo would immediately turn the gun on Adams, Nicky sprang back into the pilothouse behind Arturo, reached around him, and twisted the Beretta away.

"I give up," Arturo cried, putting his gun hand slowly to his neck wound. "I need a doctor." He took his other hand from his coat pocket and dropped it to his side. His face was ashen from blood loss, the floor beneath him slick with his blood. "Don't hurt me—"

By the time Nicky heard the switchblade snick open, Arturo had dipped his shoulder and was arcing the blade for Nicky's throat. Nicky caught Arturo's hand; using Arturo's inertia, he swept the blade slicing up and through the killer's throat. Arturo fell to the floor, convulsing.

The pilot made whimpering sounds as he began turning the boat back upriver.

"You all right?" Nicky asked Adams.

"Where'd you learn those moves?"

"In the Army." Nicky limped over and picked up Adams's Glock and, after turning to look out the windshield for a few seconds, came back and handed it to him. "Looks like a patrol boat's coming out. I reckon I'd best go see how Massey's doing."

Nicky took off down the stairs, stepping around the fallen transit cop. When he walked out of the door he leaned over for his cane. Reflected in the closest window he saw Adams come out of the stairwell, aiming his Glock at the back of Nicky's head.

"Ich denke Sie werde getan," Adams said as he squeezed the trigger.

There was no shot.

Nicky whirled, grabbing Adams's Glock with his right hand. Adams's eyes were bright with surprise.

"Like I didn't know what you were going to do, you dry-gulching son of a bitch," Nicky snarled as he slammed his cane's handle over Adams's damaged shoulder, knowing that the wound would keep him from blocking the blow. Then he drove the brass handle into Adams's temple.

As Adams toppled, Nicky was aware that Winter was coming toward him from the stairwell, gun in hand, unsure of what he had just witnessed.

92

After Adams and Nicky took off after Estrada, Winter went about the business of handcuffing Marta. He had thought it was possible but highly unlikely that Estrada and Marta would be able to make an attempt to stop him from retrieving the evidence. Nicky and Adams had been along the entire ride, watching his back, and they hadn't picked up on the Latinos' presence or they would have warned him. He figured there had to be a tracking device hidden on the Stratus, or maybe on Adams's Chevrolet.

"Okay, Marta, right hand behind your neck! Feet apart!"

"Sure," Marta said. "I am happy to spread my legs for a handsome man like you. Be gentle with me," she crooned.

"You should have stuck to antiques."

"I get so bored with old things."

"Right hand on your neck!" Reaching out with an open cuff, Winter snapped it around her right wrist so it was tight against her skin. "Other hand."

She seemed to be complying, but as her left hand started up, she spun into his side, elbowing him in the ribs. All sinew and cold intent, she clipped him again in the ribs with her elbow and, using the empty cuff at the end of the chain like nunchakus, slammed it into his temple. Seizing the hand holding the SIG Sauer, she came within a hair of taking the gun away from him.

Winter saw it hit the deck and skid under the pickup truck beside him, inside of which a heavy man sat, open-mouthed, gawking.

Fending off her focal punch, Winter hit her in her jaw with all his force. As her head snapped back, his second blow smashed into her nose, and blood spurted from her nostrils. He pivoted and slammed his shoe into her ribs.

Winter heard automatic gunfire coming from upstairs.

Winter's blows had amazingly little effect on Marta. She recovered instantly and came at him using her knees like pistons, uppercutting into his legs and stomach and then launching herself to uppercut his chin, driving him flat on his back.

She leaped up and descended, her right heel slashing down at his face, but he caught her boot and swept her left foot out from under her. As she went down, he rose, still holding her boot, and brought his right heel forcefully into her ribs. She somersaulted backward, ending in a ballerina-like pose, facing Winter. She held one hand high in the air, the other in front of her—holding her leather cap out by its bill—like a street performer expecting him to toss coins into it. She sneered and slung the cap away, exposing the short, wide, twin-edge blade in her hand.

Winter was aware of more gunshots from upstairs.

The ferry started turning, heading back upriver.

When she lunged, Winter jumped back, but he felt the knife's edge against his vest as it laid open his leather jacket. She didn't hesitate before taking a second swipe. Avoiding the bade, he clipped her shoulder with the heel of his hand, knocking her off balance, and he slammed the heel of his shoe into the small of her back, shoving her to the concrete. She hit the deck, rolled back up onto her feet, and sprang at him, blade dancing in the air between them. Now weaponless and winded, he was at her mercy—backing up as she came on—and out of ideas. Reaching back, he snapped off a car's antenna and swung it like a buggy whip at her, cutting the air viciously.

"I am going to open you up and you are gonna see your insides come outside. And after I have killed you, I am going to kill that little bitch and—"

He hit her in the shoulder, and although it must have hurt her he knew the slashing antenna couldn't hold her at bay much longer. She was going to take a hit soon in order to finish him.

Out of the corner of his eye, Winter saw movement. Marta saw it too, and she turned her eyes toward the motion for a split second. A small body popped up across the car hood, a fire extinguisher raised high. Marta reacted, swinging her left hand up to protect her face. When the cloud of vapor enveloped her, Winter drove his heel into her shoulder. The blow sent Marta backward, her skull striking the steel wall with a brutal thud. She bounced off and landed hard on the concrete deck, twisted and motionless.

"You cold-cocked her!" a voice exclaimed triumphantly. Winter looked up, breathing hard, to see a smiling Faith Ann, holding the fire extinguisher at the ready in case another blast might be necessary.

"Weren't you supposed to stay in the car?"

She frowned, shrugged.

Winter lifted Marta roughly onto the flatbed Toyota truck filled with salvaged junk and cinched the open cuff to a steel bottle jack partly buried in a pile of steel scrap the rear of the truck. Picking up Marta's ceramic knife, he hurled it out into the waves.

The truck's driver, a fat man in overalls, was staring out through the open window at Winter. "You a cop?" the man asked.

Winter nodded, walked over, and picked up Marta's .22 and his SIG Sauer.

"I used to be a law enforcement officer myself," the fat man said, getting out. "I was a state prison guard for ten years."

"Then you know how this works?" he asked the man, holding out Marta's gun.

"That's a Ruger .22."

"I'm a U.S. marshal, and I want you to stand here and watch her until I get back."

"Hellcat, that one is. Sometimes small ones are like that. PCP, probably."

"She's a professional killer. If she so much as looks like she might be trying to move, you shoot her. Can you do that? I'll be right back."

"She ain't going to go anywhere chained to that house-raising jack. Weighs about as much as her. But, yeah, dang straight I can shoot her."

"Stay back from her."

"I'll be right here," he promised, nodding at the .22 automatic in his hand.

"Faith Ann, follow me," Winter snapped.

He picked up the manila envelope, took the fire extinguisher from her, handed her the evidence, and opened the door to the Stratus. "I need to check on things upstairs. You *will* stay in the car this time!"

93

Faith Ann locked the doors of the Stratus, positioned the side-view mirror so she could see the fat man in coveralls holding the pistol and one of the unconscious woman's boots extending out over the side. Standing six feet away from the truck, the man with the gun seemed to be considering the woman lying in the debris-filled bed.

The notion that she had saved Winter's life warmed Faith Ann. Pushing aside her terror of Arturo and his murderous companion, she had crept from the car to take the fire extinguisher down from its place on the wall to help Winter. She wasn't sure what the chemicals would do to the woman, but Faith Ann knew that she was going to hurt him and she knew she couldn't let that happen.

She looked down at the soiled and battered envelope in her lap. Squeezing it, she felt the cassette tape inside and the sleeve containing the negatives.

She slipped out the tape and looked at the audio record of her mother's last minutes alive.

Faith Ann looked up, wondering how long it would be before Winter came back. The boat was heading for the Canal Street landing, the woman was locked up, and the man who'd killed her mother had to be arrested by now.

She thought about how many times since Friday morning she had believed it was all over, that she was going to die. But she wasn't dead.

Faith Ann put the envelope down in her lap, and looked at the mirror beside her. The fat man was still at his post, but he was looking at Faith Ann's reflection in the small side mirror—smiling and waving at her. She guessed being deputized by a U.S. marshal was a big deal for a scrap collector.

Faith Ann let her gaze drift to the side of the truck, expecting to see the woman's boot jutting out of the bed, but it was no longer in view.

She started to scream.

Before the man could turn, the woman moved in behind him and swung the steel bottle jack at him like it weighed nothing. The jack hit the man in the back of his head, creating a cloud of gore that spattered the rear window of the Dodge.

Faith Ann stopped screaming. She felt frozen in place as if some great weight was pressing her into the seat back. Her face twisted into a terrifying mask—the woman stood beside the door glaring in at Faith Ann. Faith Ann's fingers closed around the envelope on her lap. She watched the woman raise the jack. *I'm going to die, Mama.*

Faith Ann hit the horn, scrambled over the console, found the lock, and threw the door open. Mr. Massey was the only one who could keep her alive now.

Faith Ann was aware of something moving behind her, and then of being jerked off her feet. She hit the concrete hard, her left elbow cracking against the deck, sending a lightning bolt shooting up to her fingers. She realized that the woman had vaulted over the car to grab her. Before Faith Ann could do anything, the woman had Faith Ann back up on her feet, a leather-covered arm locked around her chest, squeezing.

"You gonna get wet," the woman said.

Faith Ann flailed and kicked—she screamed—but it had no effect on the woman, who held the jack by its handle like a suitcase and laughed as she dragged her young captive toward the stern.

94

Winter arrived at the top of the stairs just in time to see Nicky come out a door followed immediately by a battered Adams. Adams said something, suddenly raised his gun, and pointed it at the back of Nicky's head. Based on Adams's surprised expression, he squeezed the trigger without producing the desired effect.

Before Winter could do anything, Nicky ducked, knocked Adams's Glock aside with his left hand, and swung his cane's heavy handle into Adams's skull. There was a sickening crack, and Adams crumpled to the floor, his face hitting so hard it bounced. Winter vaulted up onto the deck, met Nicky's eyes, then knelt beside Adams. "What the hell was that about? He was going to kill you."

"I don't know," Nicky said, still gripping his bloody cane. "We took Arturo out. Adams was wounded, and I was coming down to check on you, but I never heard him coming. I saw the gun coming up in the reflection in that glass. Christ, why did he try to kill me?"

The sound of a car horn honking from the downstairs level ended the conversation.

"Faith Ann." Winter whirled, hurtled down the stairs.

Nicky lifted Adams's Glock, cracked open the chamber, and removed the piece of toothpick he had broken off in it minutes earlier in the wheelhouse to prevent the mechanism from firing.

He tossed Adams's Glock into the stairwell next to the dead transit cop, lifted his cane, and followed after Winter.

95

Faith Ann had only one thought. She still had the manila envelope and she needed to drop it so Winter would have it after Marta killed her, but she couldn't get her hand on it. Despite all her struggling, Marta's left arm remained locked across Faith Ann's chest. Faith Ann, a student of nature, immediately thought of a boa constrictor who had locked its muscles around its intended prey. The harder she thrashed, the tighter the grip around her became, crushing the air from her lungs. Her mind told her that in the face of such strength, any fight she could offer was hopeless, but her instincts were on autopilot.

As the woman carried her toward the stern railing, she spoke Spanish to her captive, cooing words into her ear that Faith Ann, who took Spanish in school, translated, and they were not terms of endearment. *"Mono dulce . . . niña del infierno . . . mi demonio hermoso." Sweet monkey . . . child of hell . . . my beautiful demon . . .*

Faith Ann saw the bloody jack, shaped like a giant steel Hershey's Kiss, that the woman was holding by the handle the handcuff was hooked to. The fat man with the crushed skull lay on his stomach, fingers still clenched around the pistol Winter had given him. She was aware of Winter coming down the stairs and coming toward them. *He will stop her!*

She stopped struggling, fighting now just to get one deep breath. She was aware of being lifted into the air as the woman climbed over the rail. For a second, Faith Ann thought she intended to climb into the emergency boat suspended there. The roaring grew in her ears. As her vision darkened, her mind screamed for air.

Faith Ann saw Mr. Massey's lips forming words she couldn't hear, saw him holding his gun out so Marta could see it.

Now it is going to be all right. Now she will let me go.

Faith Ann felt the reptilian grip around her relax slightly, and she filled her lungs with as much of the delicious cool air as she could suck in. Marta tightened her grip and started screaming at Mr. Massey.

Any feeling of relief that being saved from suffocation had brought the child vanished as her mind filled with new terror. Marta tensed the coil around Faith Ann's chest again. Faith Ann saw a look of terror wash over Mr. Massey's features. Refueled with oxygen, Faith Ann struggled once again, but Marta's grip was law, and they tumbled together over the railing into the river below.

Faith Ann knew two things: The boat was moving away, and she was sinking in the cold water like a coin.

96

The sight of Marta Ruiz dragging Faith Ann toward the stern railing horrified Winter. As he descended the final course of treads, he kept his SIG Sauer aimed at the killer. He didn't have to look back over his shoulder to know that the scrap man was dead, that too many years stood between the time when he was a prison guard and the present. Winter cursed himself for misjudging Marta's strength—her level of threat. Even now, the jack's weight had her listing dramatically, but still she held the struggling child up between herself and Winter's pistol like a shield. A shot would be impossible.

His mind was calculating the situation, figuring the odds.

This was a hostage situation—a grab bag of conflicting, self-interest-driven realities, probabilities, and variables—but far, far more than a mathematics equation to be worked out, for a child's life was at stake.

Winter was capable of putting a bullet into a very small target at close range, but this target was in motion and he needed a central nervous system hit, because if he only wounded her she could and would break Faith Ann's neck.

Knowing she had lost, Marta would want to escape. She would assume her partner was incapacitated: wounded, captured, or killed. She had no reason to harm Faith Ann, because the child was her only means of escape.

He watched Marta back into the steel railing and, using only her legs, go straight up to the top and drop, catlike, to the section of open deck behind it, Faith Ann imprisoned in her grip. She passed by the emergency rescue boat—a twelve-foot-long aluminum flat bottom with a thirty-five horsepower outboard motor.

Okay, Winter, now you can't shoot without risking her going into the river. Arresting her isn't your job. She has the upper hand. Just make her believe the truth—in exchange for Faith Ann, you will let her walk away.

Winter held the gun straight out to his side, knelt, and set it down on the deck.

"Okay, Marta, let Faith Ann go and I'll give you a pass." Faith Ann's frightened eyes were locked on his.

"What kind of trick will you use? What deception do you have in mind? Shooting me when the child is out of the way? I know what a famous shot you are, Deputy Massey."

"I'm not here as a cop, and I won't shoot you. You have my word on it. I won't try to stop you. I'll give you the key to the cuffs, and you can take that lifeboat. Your freedom for the girl, no tricks."

She laughed.

"What about Arturo?" she asked.

"Your friend didn't make it," Winter answered.

Winter was surprised at the change in her expression as she assimilated the news. Her black eyes glowed like hot coals, and her nostrils flared.

"Friend? Turo isn't my friend," she shrieked. "I don't have any friends! Now you people have killed all I had in this world. Arturo was my heart—my baby brother. My Turo was the last of my blood. It was her! This little demon bitch has ended my world. This little monster must pay!"

In his years as a cop, Winter had never seen such an instant switch from laughter to fury before, such an explosive display of hatred.

"Let her go," Winter pleaded. "She didn't do anything to you. You people killed her mother. This had nothing to do with her. Please, Marta, let her live."

Winter saw that Marta was thinking, so maybe he could get to her. "I can't bring back your brother, but I can give you your freedom. Your freedom for Faith Ann. You have my word on it."

"Words? Freedom?" she screamed at him. "What the fuck good is freedom without my Turo? I cared for him since he was two. I was his mother, his sister, his only friend. What the fuck do you know about freedom? You want to see what freedom looks like, Massey? This is freedom!"

And then she and the child went over the railing and were gone.

97

Faith Ann couldn't believe what had happened. The chugging of the diesel engine dimmed. She kept struggling, trying to break away, but this woman had no intention of sparing her. She would outlive Faith Ann, and when she did relax her iron grip it would be meaningless.

As they sank, both the cold and the pressure grew. Her ears popped. Faith Ann tried to bring up an image of her mother. She expected to see her any moment now, floating in the blackness, reaching out to take her to a better place. They would be together again. Faith Ann's chest felt like it would explode, and another, deeper darkness was closing in.

Don't breathe, Faith Ann, her mama told her.

Something brushed her and then squeezed her shoulder hard. Behind her, Marta started writhing violently.

Faith Ann's eyes were wide open but she couldn't see anything. She was aware of the woman's steely grip. She felt something brush against her and she knew that she was moving, but whether it was up, down, or sideways, she could not tell. She felt as if she was being pulled upward by some force, but she could no longer hold her breath. Although she knew there was no air available—that inhaling so would kill her—she no longer had a choice.

I'm sorry, Mama. . . .

98

Winter hit the water knowing instinctively that his only hope in the pitch-black cold water was to sharpen his angle of descent, increase his speed to close the distance between himself and the pair, and pray he would luck into them.

It seemed certain to Winter that he would miss. If he passed them by inches, he wouldn't know. Chained to the jack, the two had vanished from sight as if sucked under from below. His mind swarmed with doubts and self-incrimination as he kicked furiously and moved his hands before him. He had no way to know how deep he was when his hand brushed something; he clamped down on it and knew it was Faith Ann's wrist. The lack of movement in the appendage told him the child was unconscious. When he jerked the wrist, he felt Marta react to the grab—twist around to fight him, maybe just get a newer, deadlier grip. Marta was too late. Winter kicked away, heading for the surface.

Winter broke the surface first, let out a victorious yell, and jerked her wrist up hard to bring Faith Ann to the surface.

No!

It took his mind a second to digest the fact that the eyes he was looking at belonged to Marta Ruiz, as did the small wrist in his grip.

His mind filled with horror.

He released her wrist.

The police boat was bobbing beside them, a harsh spotlight illuminating her sneering face.

A cop beside Manseur aimed a shotgun down at the woman.

"Oops," Marta said, taunting him. She raised her hands to show him that the handcuff and the jack were no longer there. "I think you forgot someone."

Without hesitating, he took a deep breath and dove.

By now Faith Ann had inhaled water, was certainly unconscious, but he could still save her if . . .

The fury, the grief, drove him into the darkness, the pressure constricting his body. He'd promised his son he would keep Faith Ann safe. He was a madman, who believed that he could search a giant body of moving water for something so tiny. He kicked desperately. He grappled about in the icy dark until he was at the point of inhaling water himself. He broke the surface just long enough to inhale as much air as he could hold, then threw himself back into the depths again.

He lost count of how many times he dove. Finally, gasping, he came up for air and heard Manseur yelling at him from inside the nearby boat.

"Winter, it's been ten minutes! She's gone. Get into the boat. I've called for help. It won't help anybody if you die."

Winter knew it was over. His body was fatigued to the point of torture, his mind was filled with grief and pain and numbed by guilt. Tears of frustration filled his eyes.

Faith Ann is gone.

Dead and alone.

It is over.

"Get in the boat!" Manseur ordered. Winter looked from the detective to the policeman pilot standing beside him. Then, knowing he had lost, that he had failed both a twelve-year-old child and his son, he somehow swam the ten feet, reached up, and let the two men hoist him into the boat. There he sat slumped on the deck, his mind blank with failure.

The first thing he saw was Marta seated on the port bench, her hands behind her, a thin, taunting smile on her face.

Something is wrong. What?

On Winter's left, the young patrolman had laid his twelve-gauge across the passenger's seat, which had been left turned toward the driver's seat.

Suddenly his mind cleared and Winter realized that Marta had defeated the cuffs he had used earlier to join her to the jack. It was as if she was reading his mind, taking that moment to spring and grab the Glock from the young police pilot's holster.

Manseur had his back to her.

Marta shoved the pilot aside and was bringing the

Glock around to bear on Winter. When she saw the Mossberg 12 in Winter's hands, its dark eye staring at her, her own eyes widened in surprise.

The muzzle blast lit her against the darkness like a flashbulb—the buckshot erasing her features.

Winter's ears rang.

The wind swept the cordite away.

"It's over," Manseur said, gently wrenching the shotgun from Winter's iron grip. "There's the evidence. Pond is alive. Faith Ann didn't die for nothing."

Winter lifted himself up and slumped on the bench.

He knew that he would never allow himself to feel the slightest pang of remorse over shooting a child-killing monster.

"Faith Ann had the envelope on her," he told Manseur.

"We won't need it. They'll turn on each other."

Winter knew Manseur was right. Suggs, Bennett, and Tinnerino would all be tumbling over one another to cut deals.

Winter had never felt so completely defeated, so utterly empty.

99

As the speedboat raced toward the Canal Street ferry landing, Winter could see dozens of vehicles packing the ramp. Flashing lights—blue for cop cars and police department technical vans, red for EMT vehicles—washed the crowd standing on the balcony attached to the enclosed pedestrian walkway. There would also be media trucks in the street—their dishes elevated to send electronic signals to every television screen in the region.

How fast they react these days, Winter thought. *And why not? At first blush, taking a ferry at gunpoint must have looked like an act of terrorism.*

Law enforcement and EMTs swarmed the lower ferry deck, while another group was moving around on the roof near the pilothouse.

Nick Green stood solemnly at the stern of the USS *Thomas Jefferson* beside a deckhand, who took the line Manseur tossed, and Nicky helped Winter onto the deck. He handed Winter his SIG Sauer, but did no more than glance at the corpse in the speedboat, at the pool of diluted blood in the stern where her ebony hair floated, surrounding her ruined head like a storm cloud.

"It was all Marta Ruiz, Winter. It wasn't your fault."

"Yeah, I know," Winter said weakly. He wanted to vomit—to rid himself of the vitriol that filled him like a poisonous cloud. *I should have taken the shot I had on Marta. I might have wounded Faith Ann, but she might still be alive.*

"How soon can you get a search going?" Winter asked Manseur. "I don't want her in there any longer than—"

"Already under way. The Coast Guard will find her," Manseur promised. "They know exactly where she went in, and they have computer models, so it's just science to locate a . . ." He stopped when he saw the hard look in Winter's eyes. "Sorry."

"I looked all around," Nicky said. "I didn't see any envelope anywhere."

"Faith Ann put the envelope in her jeans. I saw it when she went in."

Winter looked at the Stratus, the shattered side window, the passenger door still open. A crime scene technician took a picture of something inside the vehicle, set the camera on the car's roof, leaned in, and lifted something out, dropping it into a clear evidence envelope.

"Hey!" Winter called out, striding toward the car. "What is that?" He reached out to take the bag. The technician straightened defensively but handed it over when he saw Detective Manseur nod his approval.

The technician said, "It's a cassette tape—no label. Was on the floorboard."

"You think it's her tape?" Manseur asked Winter.

"Yes," Winter said, looking at the cassette through the clear plastic. He knew that was the only thing it could be.

"That's great," Nicky said. "You've got evidence."

Winter nodded, seeing some light leaking into the situation. "If it contains what Faith Ann heard from her hiding place, it had Arturo implicating Jerry Bennett for sending him to get the pictures back from Amber Lee. It has the murders. It'll add weight to the fact that the negatives Faith Ann had were pictures of Bennett killing the Williamses. Don't tell Suggs we don't have the negatives. Play the tape to him and Bennett and one'll snap quick. At least Faith Ann didn't fail."

"She was something, that kid," Manseur said. "She cleared Pond single-handedly."

"Her mother would be very proud of her."

"Somebody cleared Horace Pond of something?" the technician said, looking up. "Too bad for him it wasn't of murdering the Williamses."

"What do you mean?" Winter asked him.

"Horace Pond is a goner." He glanced at his watch. "Well, he will be in about 25 minutes, give or take the speed of liquids snaking through the tubes. And damn good riddance, I say."

"The execution was called off," Winter said.

"No. It wasn't." The technician looked perplexed. "Who told you that?"

"It sure as hell *was* called off," Manseur said. "The governor's office will be announcing it any minute now."

"A half an hour ago the governor was on TV saying the death penalty was created for creeps like Pond, and his execution would serve all of the people of Louisiana, even those who oppose executions."

Winter saw the same confusion he was feeling reflected in Manseur's eyes.

"All due respect, Detective Manseur," the CSI tech protested, "you can walk up the hill to the first news truck and ask them. I mean, there's news coverage on every channel. Caption said it was live from the Fairmont. They had some kind of fund-raiser there. I know one of the patrolmen on the bodyguard detail at the hotel."

"The governor's staying at the Fairmont?" Winter asked. And when the perplexed tech nodded, Winter ran.

Manseur was close behind, the sight of the detective serving to get them past the cops on the ramp. From far behind Winter heard the tech yelp, "Hey! My tape!"

Winter arrived at the WWL van ahead of Manseur. On one of the monitors he saw the reporter standing outside the prison interviewing a woman under a KILL POND SCUM banner. A clock beside the monitor was counting the minutes down to the execution.

19:52, 19:51, 19:50 . . .

"What the hell is happening?" Winter demanded when Manseur reached him.

"I talked to Hurt, and he said he would . . . He didn't do it. Maybe they're just waiting for me to . . ."

"We've got to make sure," Winter said, looking down at the tape in his hand.

"George!" Manseur yelled at a police sergeant, who was standing outside a cruiser, watching over the cops who were holding twenty reporters and a crowd of the curious back from the ferry ramp. "We're taking your car!" Nicky was limping toward them.

"We gotta run," Winter yelled.

"Go!" a limping Nicky yelled, waving them off. "I'll see you at the hotel later."

100

Manseur and Winter erupted from the elevator into the hallway where the governor's suite and his staff's rooms were located. Badges out, they met the uniformed highway patrolmen, who had been alerted that the pair were on the way up. The patrolmen pointed them to a set of double doors set in an ornate facade at the end of the carpeted corridor.

As they approached, Parker Hurt opened the right-side door, allowing Winter and Manseur into the foyer. The governor's executive assistant were a red V-neck sweater over a starched white shirt, stiffly pressed khakis, and shiny black loafers with tassels. He looked like a college fraternity rush chairman.

"What can I do for you, gentlemen?" he asked.

"Why does the press think the Pond execution is still on?" Manseur blurted out.

"Why do you think it wouldn't be?" Hurt replied easily.

"Because you said the governor would call it off," Manseur snapped. "Hours ago."

"I said I'd tell the governor what you told me to tell him," Hurt replied. "I never said he would do what you wanted. Did I? That was before I spoke to Captain Suggs, your superior."

"You talked to—"

"And he told me all about your—"

Winter seized Parker Hurt by his cashmere sweater,

ending the need for Manseur's words and erasing Hurt's smirk. He had stood around far too long already talking to someone who wasn't the governor.

"We'll talk to the governor now," Winter snarled as he shoved the governor's executive assistant backward, throwing open the door into the suite using Hurt's narrow back as a battering ram. Four men in their shirtsleeves sat around a felt-covered table playing poker.

One of the men, a bodyguard, reached to his shoulder holster, but Governor Lucas Morton grabbed his arm to stop him.

A reporter, who had the illuminated ferry in the background, was showing on the large-screen TV on the wall.

"What in God's name is the meaning of this, Detective?" the governor asked, setting his cards facedown on the felt before standing. He waved his hand in the air, signaling the other three men to remain seated.

"Governor, my name is Winter Massey. I'm a United States Deputy Marshal. You know who Faith Ann Porter is?"

"Of course I do."

Quickly, Winter told the governor about Pond's frame, about what had happened over the past two days. He was careful to hit all of the important points. Manseur nodded, didn't interrupt. When Winter finished, Morton stared at him for long seconds, thinking.

Finally he spoke. "Let me see if I have all this. Jerry Bennett, who is a respected businessman and a friend and political supporter of mine, killed Judge and Beth Williams? Harvey Suggs, a decorated member of NOPD, fabricated Pond's case out of whole cloth? That alone is the most preposterous thing I've ever heard.

"And you say Jerry Bennett then sent a professional killer to murder Attorney Porter and this Lee woman—his mistress? Because she had in her possession photographic evidence that he murdered the Williamses. The child had the negatives and that tape, but not the pictures."

"The killer got those back. Faith Ann said he didn't ask about negatives. He probably didn't even know she had them."

"And tonight Commander Suggs sent two detectives to kill Detective Manseur here and two professional killers to the ferry to kill you and the Porter child. And both of those killers are dead, the detectives under arrest."

"Yes," Winter said.

"There are warrants out now for Bennett and Suggs," Manseur said.

"The ferry incident, all that gunplay, that was you two?"

"You have to stop the execution," Winter said. The time on the screen was now ten minutes to go.

"Bennett sent the killer to Kimberly Porter's office, which is on your audiotape," Morton said. "Marshal, if you had the pictures Faith Ann claimed to have, I would stop the execution this minute. That phone is connected directly to the death house." He looked the screen. "I've got just enough time."

"I only have the tape," Winter said, holding it out. "Faith Ann had the pictures and the negatives on her when she went in the river."

"So you said."

Winter said, "You can check me out by calling the A.G."

"Marshal, I don't have to call anybody to know who you are. Your reputation for leaving a veritable rooster tail of death and havoc in your wake is well-enough known hereabouts. Even if there are voices on that audiotape saying that Jerry Bennett sent a hired killer to Kimberly Porter's office, it doesn't prove who killed Judge Williams and his wife, unless Bennett himself confessed to it on the tape. You say Bennett's hired killers are dead. So who can prove the voice on this tape is this dead hit man? Or that he isn't lying when he says Jerry Bennett sent him? Or is it Ms. Lee or Ms. Porter who says that?"

"Faith Ann saw him commit the murders," Manseur insisted. "She was hiding under a table."

"She can't testify from the grave," Hurt said.

"I was a prosecutor for twenty-two years," the governor told them. "Emotion and hearsay aside—you have nothing but a wild tale."

"Stop the execution," Winter urged, feeling more desperate by the second. "Pond *is* innocent. Suggs *will* talk, and when he does, he'll implicate Bennett in the Williams murders. So will Tinnerino and Doyle."

Manseur said, "I'll get Bennett and Suggs."

Morton studied Winter's face. Then he said, "I prosecuted Horace Pond, and I know the evidence better than anybody. You haven't given me a scrap of proof that Pond is innocent. If Jerry sent a killer to Porter's office, it will take more than a recording of questionable authenticity to make me short-circuit a lawful execution. Only the child could have testified that the tape was authentic. Even if she was here with this tape now and I knew she had maintained the chain of custody, anybody who watches *Judge Judy* could keep it from ever seeing a courtroom. What is the sound quality? Who says what? How are the people identified?"

"We'd have to listen to it," Winter said.

"You haven't heard the tape?"

"Listen to it after—"

Lucas Morton laughed out loud. "Does the term *pig in a poke* mean anything to you? I'm sorry. If there is this picture proof and it turns up at some point, I'll eat crow, but what the jury and appellate courts decided on this matter is going to go forward. My stand on Horace Pond's execution is a matter of very public record."

"What could it hurt to put it off a couple of days?" Winter pleaded.

"Faith Ann Porter had the picture evidence on her," Manseur added. "With any luck those pictures will still be with the body when it is recovered and they *might* survive a dip in the river."

"*May* be, *could* be, *might* surface . . ." Morton was a political animal, so he was considering, measuring the probabilities, possibilities, and weighing his options. Winter saw his resolve swaying. For a long ten seconds, Lucas Morton stared over at the telephone, three steps and three words from saving an innocent man from being murdered. Winter was sure he had convinced him to at least postpone the execution and avoid any criticism should Winter be right about Pond's guilt. Morton took the three steps.

Then Parker Hurt spoke. "Sir, the election is being decided now, at this very moment. These men don't have one scrap of evidence. Stopping the execution will give your enemies ammunition that will pull undecided voters. Sir, you're within the two-point margin of error according to our own polls. You are playing with fire. You don't *have* to do anything."

Winter saw Morton's eyes change focus and, with his heart sinking, he knew the governor wasn't going to stop the execution. "The tape is useless," Morton told him bluntly. "Since you don't have those pictures in your possession, it is as if they do not exist. I will not override the judicial system on a maybe."

Manseur pleaded, "Call the chief. Check out what I've told you."

"No," Morton said finally, looking at his watch. "It's too late."

"You are making a big mistake," Winter said. "When Pond is proved innocent, when people know what happened on the ferry tonight, when they know you were told, when they know that a little girl died trying to save Pond and you turned your back on that, your career will be over. You will live the rest of your life with people pointing at you and whispering. That will be your legacy."

"Aw, hell, Deputy Massey. In a few days the election will be over. Who's going to worry about this last-minute maneuvering? Eighty-five percent of the people in this state want Pond dead. Go on back to wherever you came here from and make trouble there. We don't need your kind screwing things up around here like you did last year," Morton said.

Morton dismissed them by sitting down at the table, and picking up his cards. "This sounds to everybody here like a tall tale spun by a deluded detective who makes wild accusations against a quality citizen, and a deputy who shoots up the world. Who in their right mind is going to blame me for not accepting your words?"

Winter was done, and he knew it. He started to turn to leave. Then he saw something that almost stopped his heart. He pointed and said, "Well, I bet they'll believe *her*."

Manseur looked where Winter was pointing and cursed softly in admiration. "You're damned right, they will! Governor, look behind you. Your two-point margin of error just became the landslide that's going to bury you."

Lucas Morton whirled in his seat to face the television. Filling the screen, illuminated by floodlights, stood a very small, shivering figure wrapped in a blanket. The illuminated ferry was in the background, the angle telling Winter that the camera focused on Faith Ann Porter was set up on the plaza outside the aquarium.

"She's alive!" Manseur exclaimed. "Faith Ann's alive!"

The men at the table gaped at the screen. Since the sound was muted, they all missed the words, but Winter recognized the envelope she was opening up, and before the camera panned away from the soggy copy paper, they all clearly saw the photocopied images of murder she held in her hands.

"She has the negatives!" Winter yelled, picking up the phone's receiver and thrusting it at Lucas Morton. "You saw the pictures! Everybody in Louisiana saw the pictures. You keep watching because in ten minutes you'll see Manseur and me on that same screen explaining why you didn't stop the execution. Now make the call."

101

After Winter talked to Faith Ann over the telephone, she had given the negatives to Larry Bond, Manseur's partner, who delivered them to the photo lab and left two men he trusted to watch over the drying and printing of the negatives. Winter told Faith Ann he'd meet her at the hospital emergency room, where she was going to be taken for a medical check-over. He called Sean and told his wife as much as he could, promising to fill her in when she and Rush arrived in New Orleans the next morning.

He waited anxiously in the cruiser while Manseur stood outside talking on the phone to his people. Then Manseur joined Winter and pulled into the traffic, heading for Charity Hospital. Winter couldn't wipe the smile off his face. But Manseur was frowning.

"Something's bothering my astute associates," the detective said.

"What's that?" Winter asked.

"Adams got this serious, life-threatening concussion. Nicky Green told them Adams hit his head on a shelf in the wheelhouse, that as far as he knows he later collapsed on the deck downstairs from it."

"So?"

"The pilot confirmed Adams did hit his head and was wounded in the initial fray, but he claims Adams was fine when he left the wheelhouse. The pilot swears that Nicky Green, not Agent Adams, killed Arturo Estrada with his own knife. Adams was found unconscious just outside the staircase door. But the medical people say the side of his head was literally caved in, which made it impossible that he remained conscious after the blow. There was indeed a cut where the pilot said Adams hit his head, but it was the other side of his skull that was shattered."

Winter raised his brows noncommittally. He was going to have to let Manseur in on some things, but he wasn't sure it was going to have the desired effect of having the cop go against his instincts, training, and the nature of his occupation.

"And the copilot said he saw Nicky Green hit Adams with his cane. Said Adams was aiming his gun at Green's head at the time. He claims you saw it, too."

"That's true," Winter admitted. "I did."

"Uh-huh. An FBI agent tries to shoot somebody in cold blood. I find that strange, and very troubling. Needs some serious explaining. Attempted murder is serious. I'm going to have to find out why Adams tried to kill Green."

"You would be best served if you just forget it," Winter said.

"I don't see that happening," Manseur said, incredulous. "Tell me why I would even consider it."

Winter said, "You know how it is with icebergs. Only the tip shows. The majority of it is lying underwater, waiting."

"I saw *Titanic,*" Manseur said, irritated.

"Look, Michael, this is the best advice I have ever given anybody. You can take it or not. You are looking at the tip of one major, ugly iceberg. Let the FBI handle the Adams end. You thought he was what he claimed. Period. Who knows what a terrified pilot or copilot *think* they saw. If the Bureau asks for your help in clearing things up, want you to dig around and make a stink, do it, but if they don't—and they won't—leave it lie. I give you my word that Nicky acted in self-defense. That's all there is to it."

"If that's true, FBI agent or not, there'll be state charges. Adams tried to kill Green. And you saw it."

Winter exhaled loudly. "Okay, Michael. Adams isn't an FBI agent. I don't know *who* he really is, but I know what. The Feds'll take over the investigation and you'll never hear another word. If you get too curious, your superiors will discourage you from looking into it."

"I won't sit still for that."

"I said it was advice. Go after this case, and for the rest of your life you'll wish to God you *had* listened."

"What's going on here, Massey?"

Winter thought about what he should say. He remained silent until Manseur parked the car outside the emergency room, where scores of cops still waited, silent and grim-faced. Winter remembered that a transit cop had been killed and understood the vigil.

"Adams is a professional killer sent to kill me," he told Manseur. "My best guess is that he's a man named Paulus Styer, a German hit man. I believe Styer ran down Hank and Millie as part of a plan to get to me, but you'll never hang Millie's death on him, because there's nothing to prove it but what he told me and Nicky. I won't admit it to anyone else, and I'll deny I said even this much to you. Neither Nicky or I will ever admit we didn't believe Adams was FBI, and if you like your life the way it is, neither will you."

"Why?"

"Because you have only seen the tip of this berg, and the

base is a world of ruthless killers and people who would not hesitate to do *whatever* it takes to stay undiscovered."

"Arturo Estrada killed Kimberly Porter and Amber Lee for Jerry Bennett. What does that have to do with Adams—or the Trammels?"

"Adams said it was a coincidence, and I believe him."

"I don't believe in that kind of coincidence."

"Neither would I . . . normally."

"Who was the corpse in the Rover?"

"An accomplice—some loose end. Adams didn't care if it was found because he needed only a few days—had no reason to imagine you'd solve it before he was done and gone. I doubt the corpse's identity will lead to him."

Winter shouldn't have told Manseur what he had, but he had to warn him off. Winter knew better than anybody alive that the people in Adams's sphere had few rules, didn't want to be found out, didn't give warnings, and never left any loose ends. If Adams wasn't Paulus Styer—a target of the cutouts—he was almost certainly a cutout himself. Why Adams decided to kill Nicky was a mystery, but maybe he was making his move on Winter and didn't want Nicky in his way. So, if Adams was Styer, the cutouts would deal with him. If he was a cutout, they would cover for him. Winter couldn't afford to care, especially when the differences didn't matter.

Winter finally said, "What happened to Hank and Millie was about year-old business between me and the person who sent Adams, or Styer, after me."

"How do I leave Mrs. Trammel's murder unsolved?"

"Say Arturo and Marta did it. It'll stick. Look, Michael, I blundered into Adams's world and it's still costing me. I've got a life to get back to. My wife is going to have a baby. You have your family to think of. Let all of this bury itself."

"But if someone sent Styer after you, why won't they send someone else?"

Winter saw flashing lights, and an ambulance rolled past the cruiser and up the ramp to the doors of the emergency room.

"That's probably my date," Winter said. "See you around, Michael Manseur."

When she saw Winter running up the ramp, Faith Ann dropped the blanket and launched herself into his open arms.

"God," he said, "I thought you drowned."

"Well, I almost did. When I came up, I saw *her* getting pulled up into that police boat."

"You should have yelled. I was there."

"I didn't see you."

"I was underwater looking for you. Why didn't you holler at the boat?"

She looked up at Winter with disbelief in her eyes. "How could I know if they were good or bad policemen in the boat? They were helping *her*. I swam to a dock ladder and it wasn't easy. I didn't see you. I didn't know what the police would do, so I told the reporters who I was, about what happened, and I showed the pictures to the TV so the bad police couldn't steal them. Is Mr. Pond all right now?" she asked anxiously.

"He sure is," Winter said. "Thanks to you."

"That's good." She smiled. "So do you think we could go see Uncle Hank and then maybe go get something to eat?"

"Anything you want, kiddo. Anything at all."

Manseur came running up to Winter.

Winter introduced Faith Ann to him.

"We got Jerry Bennett," Manseur told him. "He was at his lake place, dragging Suggs to his boat for disposal. I have to go to H.Q. for the interview. We'll get your and Nicky's official statements tomorrow. I'll do it personally."

"You can do that?"

"Sure I can. This is New Orleans, remember?"

"The back-scratching capital of America," Winter said.

102

The emergency room doctor gave Faith Ann two shots of antibiotics and a bottle of more antibiotics he wanted her to take for a few days. Winter received the same treatment. It was going on midnight, and even though she was yawning and fighting to keep her eyes open, she told Winter that she wanted to see Uncle Hank. She really needed to see for herself that he was alive.

When Winter and Faith Ann walked into the reception area on the ICU floor, a man Winter said was Hank's doctor was writing on a chart. When he saw Winter he smiled. "You got my message."

"No, I didn't," Winter said. "What was it?"

"Hank Trammel's conscious. He's been in and out since we reversed the coma drugs. A nurse was at the bedside and he asked her for a scotch on the rocks, that he was thirsty. She said she'd get him water and he told her, not that kind of thirsty."

They followed the doctor to a cubicle where he drew back a curtain before hurrying off.

Faith Ann clenched Winter's hand and took a deep breath as they drew closer to Hank's bed. She stood there for long seconds, silent and white-faced. Her uncle's face was horribly swollen, the trademark handlebar mustache gone, and bandages covered the familiar gray hair. Both of his arms and his legs were encased in plaster.

"Uncle Hank?" she said softly. "You awake?"

There was no response from the man on the bed.

"The doctor said he was awake," she told Winter. "How can he still be asleep?"

"Beats me."

"Why can't he hear me?"

Winter shrugged.

"I'd give anything to hear him ask for a drink of whiskey," Faith Ann said. She saw a slight shiver run through her uncle. She leaned in closer.

"Uncle Hank?" she repeated, praying. "It's me, Faith Ann."

Her uncle's eyelids fluttered.

"Faith Anna-banana pants," he murmured. "Did I hear you talking about whiskey?" he asked her.

"They said you can't drink whiskey in the rooms," she said. She had never felt so absolutely thrilled.

"Faith Ann, you know what?"

"No, what?" she said.

"Of all the Porter women I've ever seen, you are the most beautiful. Nice haircut."

103

Michael Manseur stared through the two-way glass at Jerry Bennett. The nightclub owner was sound asleep, his head rocked back, his mouth wide open. Bennett's toupee looked like it was made from straw, his makeup was smeared. There was blood on his face and his shirt from using a baseball bat on Suggs.

"Looks like a man without a care in the world," Manseur said to his partner, Larry Bond.

"He said killing Suggs was self-defense. Says he didn't hire any killers. Doesn't know yet that we have the negatives. Let's wake him up and show them to him."

"Killing Suggs probably was self-defense. Get Ellen Caesar—you two handle it."

"You serious?" Larry asked him.

"As a heart attack."

"This is your case, Michael. It's a big fat juicy one."

"Yeah. Well, it's just a case. And I'm about done in from doing everything myself while you were off lazing about. Ellen's good with self-deluded fools like Bennett."

Manseur enjoyed the perplexed expression pasted on his partner's face. It was nice to surprise people sometimes.

Manseur accepted the congratulations from the other detectives as he moved through the bull pen. He stopped at his desk to get his coat. He probably would have spent the night with Larry interviewing Bennett, but for three things: first, Bennett was toast; second, he really needed to see, kiss his daughters and his wife; and third, the superintendent of police had told him that morning that he was going to get the slot Suggs's death had left empty.

He slipped on his coat and looked at Suggs's open office door. Inside, two detectives were searching files, paper by paper. Michael took one last look at his desk and saw a white envelope from the print lab in his in-box. *The corpse in the Rover*. He opened the envelope, pulled out the paper, and put on his reading glasses.

He read the name of the owner of the two partial prints three times, trying to figure how he had could have contaminated the request. Obviously he was looking at the wrong inquiry. Some technician must have put two things together somehow. It was simply impossible. The burned corpse in the Rover couldn't be who the FBI claimed it was. Somebody had to be playing a joke on him.

He read the name one more time, still thinking he was reading it wrong, that it would become something close to what it said, but not the same name at all.

Nicholas Green
101 Bobcat Lane
Houston, Texas
Licensed private investigator

Nicky Green.

Even though it wasn't possible, Manseur grabbed the computer keyboard and typed in a request for the Texas driver's license and P.I. license picture of Nicholas Green.

The screen showed two images of his Nicky Green. He stared into the eyes, studied the shape of the head, the jaw, and realized that, although the man he knew as Nicky Green was a dead ringer for the corpse Nicky Green, he wasn't him.

It hit him like a bullet in the chest. Winter Massey had it all wrong.

Manseur didn't know when the real Nicky Green had been killed—precisely when the switch had been made—but it had happened after the real Green left Hank and Millie at the guesthouse and before the new Nicky Green had appeared on the scene of the hit-and-run. He had either run them over himself or had someone else do it so he could take Green's place. The real Green's body must have been in the Rover when it hit the Trammels. An accomplice did drive it off and dump it because the fake Green—Styer—had been back at the scene taking Green's life over.

Winter thought Adams was the bad guy. Manseur grabbed his phone, called Winter's cell phone, then remembered he had ruined it in the river.

Massey was probably in the hotel suite with Nicky Green, the man who had been sent to kill him. Manseur dialed the hotel and asked to be put through to Winter's suite. Massey answered.

"Massey, thank God," he said. "Are you alone?"

"No. What you need?" Winter replied.

"Listen to me carefully. You are in danger. I got the burned corpse's prints back, and Jesus, Massey, you won't believe it . . . they belonged to—"

"Nicky Green."

Manseur was stunned. "You knew?"

"He's long gone, Michael. It's finally over."

104

Winter hung up the phone. Every muscle in his body ached, and he wanted to get into a hot bath to rid himself of any remaining trace of the Mississippi River.

Just outside the door, Faith Ann, wearing one of his T-shirts, was lying on the bedroom's couch, sound asleep. She had wanted to sleep close to Winter, and she had certainly earned the right to some peace of mind. Whatever the future held for her, Winter was certain it would be vastly better than the recent past had been. The child had amazed him and everybody associated with this, especially the bad guys. He wondered if she'd had any idea how terrible the odds of her survival and of getting the evidence to the governor had really been.

Winter lifted the note he had found on the bedside table in Nicky Green's cleaned-out bedroom, held in place by the Trammel Colt .45.

Winter,

I can't begin to tell you how much I enjoyed the exercise. I suppose sooner or later you will discover that Adams wasn't Paulus Styer, that I am. I regret what happened to the Trammels, but please believe me when I say it was for the game. You are alive because I was no longer obliged to kill you after I learned about my handler's deal with the CIA. I did stick around the rest of the evening to have some fun, which I certainly did, but I can't see the point in hanging around waiting for John Adams's pals to show up looking for me. While they might not have minded if I had killed you, I seriously doubt they will bother you now.

You know, Massey, you're a very talented man, but you have been elevated by that talent into a world of monsters where you do not belong. You should get out of the business before you find that out the hard way. Take care of the Porter kid, although going by what I saw, it may be she who ends up taking care of you. Don't think of trying to track me, figuring you might owe the Trammels some debt. If you and I ever meet again, I will not hesitate to finish what I started.

Wishing you and yours only the best.

P. Styer

Winter ripped the note into small pieces and flushed them down the toilet. He undressed and slipped into the hot water, sliding forward in the long tub until the water's surface brushed his chin. He leaned his head back, placed the wet washcloth over his face, and willed his mind to slow, to find a soft place to rest itself.

Epilogue

The dapper Phillip Dresser sat alone at a small table in a coffee shop, watching the passersby. The night before, he'd eaten dinner at Brennan's Steak House so he could monitor the Masseys and Faith Ann, who had been seated at a nearby table.

He had decided that the safest place to hide from his enemies, who would assume he was heading back to Moscow, was in New Orleans, at the Pontchartrain Hotel. He would repay his handler for the betrayal, without even lifting a hand. Yuri Chenchenko would spend his life in a perpetual cold sweat anticipating Styer's return—seeing ghosts until he died, hopefully many years down the road.

Styer looked at his watch.

Any minute now, he thought.

Moments later they came into sight, moving along the concourse. He smiled as he watched Winter, Sean, Rush, and Faith Ann strolling toward their flight to Texas. They were headed there to bury Kimberly Porter and Millie Porter Trammel. After that they would fly back to Charlotte. In a month, Hank would be able to return to North Carolina. Styer envied the old man. Hank would spend his last years surrounded by people who loved him. He wondered if these people really knew how lucky they were. *Of course they know.*

Faith Ann looked directly at Dresser. The girl couldn't recognize him—she, like Winter, had been far too preoccupied to have noticed him in the crowds, disguised and shadowing their party during the past days, listening to their conversations. She looked as skinny as ever, and her butchered hair was tousled and uncombed, but the happiness he saw reflected in her eyes warmed him. *You raised yourself a special daughter there, Kimberly Porter,* he thought. *She does you proud.*

Styer had an hour before his flight to Denver. He put a new toothpick in the corner of his mouth. The wooden pacifier was something he'd picked up recently—a habit he found oddly soothing.

About the Author

Upside Down is John Ramsey Miller's third novel.

His career has included stints as a visual artist, commercial photographer, advertising copy writer, and photojournalist. A native son of Mississippi, he has lived in Nashville, New Orleans, and Miami, and now resides in North Carolina, where he writes fiction full-time.

Visit him on the web at www.johnramseymiller.com

If you enjoyed
Upside Down, you won't want
to miss any of John Ramsey Miller's
electrifying thrillers.
Look for his debut, **The Last Family,**
and **Inside Out,** the white-hot
thriller that introduced U.S. Marshal
Winter Massey, at your favorite
bookseller's.

And read on for an exciting excerpt
from John Ramsey Miller's third
Winter Massey thriller:

SIDE BY SIDE

by

John Ramsey Miller

on sale in September 2005 from
Dell Books.

Author of *Upside Down*
JOHN RAMSEY MILLER
"JOHN RAMSEY MILLER KNOWS HOW TO GENERATE SUSPENSE!"
—*Kirkus Reviews*
SIDE BY SIDE
When you play both sides, no place is safe.

SIDE BY SIDE

On sale September 2005

Fast moving clouds were mirrored in the puddles of standing water left by a late afternoon rainstorm. Halogen fixtures set on tall poles spaced fifty feet apart painted the landscape an unholy orange blue.

A solitary figure dressed entirely in black slipped through a vertical slit in the tall hurricane fencing topped with loops of concertina wire. The fence surrounded a forty-acre lot beside a train yard where several hundred steel containers had been stacked and ordered with Mondrian-like precision. Here and there the painted steel skins of some of the boxes showed brown fingers of rust from years of exposure to the weather.

The man dressed in black, a thirty-year-old whose name was Patrick Taylor, slipped a hand-drawn diagram from inside his jacket and checked the inventory numbers on the closest container, then moved swiftly. Hours earlier, he had copied the coordinates from a scrap of paper he'd found secreted in Colonel Bryce's safe.

Opening his cell phone, he dialed a number he called only when he was alone and in a secure location. As he waited for the number to be answered he inspected the padlock using a small Maglight. The lock was substantial: it would take some coaxing to defeat.

When his handler didn't answer, Taylor assumed he must be on another call, and allowed himself to be routed to a voice mailbox. At the request to leave a message, he said, "This is Dog. I'm hooking up the thumper now. Just going to take a peek to make sure it's all in this box, then I'm leaving it up to you guys." He closed the phone and pocketed it.

He attached the GPS tracker to the steel foundation by means of a magnet. The tracker would allow the special task force to follow the shipment to its destination. Maybe that team would grab the receiving parties when they took possession, or perhaps they'd follow the cargo to the end users—terrorists all over the world and of homegrown militias with the resources to buy the latest devices of death and destruction. Taylor's sole responsibility was to stay close to the colonel, to collect the names of people the man met with, then report to his handler. Locating the first shipment of high-tech weaponry was a Godsend—icing on the cake.

Taylor had been undercover for eight long years; most of those spent building a faultless background and credentials for an operation like this. Eight years of being someone he wasn't just so he could be of use to his government. He had spent the last three of those eight years getting close to one man and gaining his trust. Three years to find out Colonel Hunter Bryce, a decorated hero, could actually betray his country for money.

Flashlight between his teeth so he could see, Taylor used his lock picks to open the padlock. As soon as he opened the door, he saw that the container was empty. Well, empty except for a sheet of plastic, which had been laid out like carpeting over the rough plywood floor.

The sound of breathing alerted Taylor to the fact that someone was standing just off his left shoulder, at his five o'clock.

"Lieutenant Taylor?" a familiar voice asked. "What are you doing here?"

Ice filled Taylor's stomach. He turned, already deciding what his next words were going to be. He had not expected to run into Colonel Bryce, but nobody could think faster on his feet than Patrick Taylor. The colonel's face was lit so Taylor could see the quizzical smile the colonel was wearing. Taylor put on a confident smile and started. "Colonel Bryce, I know you're—"

The razor sharp blade of the survival knife Colonel Bryce had carried during his years in the field severed Taylor's windpipe, his jugular vein and carotid artery. Taylor crumpled, landing hard on the floor of the empty container, the thud of his body echoing within the space.

Colonel Hunter Bryce used his gloved left

hand to wipe the fine droplets of blood from his face. He cleaned his blade on Taylor's pant leg before he replaced the weapon in its nylon scabbard.

The colonel retrieved the GPS tracker that Taylor had placed and put it in his victim's open mouth. Then he grabbed Taylor's collar and dragged him deeper into the steel container.

Before Bryce left, he stopped and spit on Taylor's face. Every man the colonel killed won his mark of disdain. Then he walked off into the shadows, whistling softly.

Two hours later, the ATF and FBI agents followed the GPS signal to the locked container. They noticed the fresh blood leaking from the closed door, pooling on the ground, so they opened it.

The night watchman told the agents he'd heard someone whistling in the darkness out beyond the fence.

"I think it was what the seven dwarfs in Snow White sang," he told them. "Whistle while you work."

Charlotte, North Carolina
Eleven months later

Twelve across.

Five letter word for good-bye.

A_D_I_E_U

Lucy Dockery put the paper and pencil down on the bedside table. She liked solving crossword puzzles, but filling in words from clues was too easy. She loved better to build them from scratch, putting her thoughts and feelings into short clues. After she constructed a puzzle she would file it away in her cabinet, unsolved. The inch-deep stack of pages was a journal of Lucy's life for the past year.

From her earliest memories, her parents always seemed to be working the crossword puzzles in the *New York Times,* other newspapers and magazines. Much to their delight, Lucy had begun crafting her own puzzles at an early age to entertain them. Their praise helped her build her self-confidence to bridge a painful shyness.

Later she made crosswords for Walter. She designed them so that he had to first solve the puzzle and then play with the order of the words until they made up a coherent message. She remembered the one that worked out to say, *Congratulations Sir after many fun years of playing around with that wand comma a baby is growing inside Lucy.*" Eight down was "_ _ _ _ *in the sky with diamonds.*" Although Walter loved a challenge, Lucy felt no need to make them complicated or too difficult.

She still wrote puzzle-grams to Walter, but he was no longer able to solve them.

As a child, she'd been told that anytime you say good-bye to somebody it could be the last good-bye. She had never really believed that something that happened in a fraction of a second could change everything in her life forever. You automatically tell a loved one to "be careful" until it becomes as meaningless as "see you later." Walter would often reply with, "But dear, I was looking forward to being reckless."

Lucy was bone-weary. Looking back, it seemed to her that her energy and enthusiasm for life had been boundless before the accident. And while Walter was beside her, she had felt invincible and filled to the brim with anticipation of a future—an ideal family nestled in a perfect world.

She knew other mothers of small children complained of tiredness due to washing, cooking and cleaning and all the million things you had to do daily, but the weakness Lucy felt was different. Lucy didn't have to cook, or clean, or even watch her own child if she didn't feel like it. And when did she feel like it? How many times had she—while propped up in her bed, or from lying on the couch—watched like a member of an audience while her son interacted with one of his sitters, her father, or the maid?

Lucy and her father shared the services of a woman who cleaned their houses three times a week. She had a list of competent baby-sitters to choose from. She subscribed to a gourmet service and once a week a chef prepared all of Lucy's and her father's main meals and put them into the refrigerator or the freezer, labeled.

Lucy had a very nice house, ten thousand

square feet of modern appliances and every convenience. She had a BMW X5 and a Lexus 420 sedan in the garage. There was more than enough room in the place for her and Elijah, and everything was paid for, thanks to Walter's obsessive desire to take care of his family. Her husband had carried a disability policy as well as one that paid all of his debts upon his death. He had a third insurance policy for two million dollars that carried an accidental death clause that doubled that amount. Thanks to Walter, Lucy had plenty of everything except what she needed most—Walter.

She'd been an odd-looking youngster, with big aqua eyes, a high forehead and a narrow chin. The boys in the first grade called her "alien." As she grew older that oddness evolved into "exotic." Even when teenage boys suddenly found her attractive, she had still felt like an odd duck. She had dated several boys in high school, gone steady twice, but she had never fallen in love but once. She knew that there was only one Walter Dockery, and anyone coming into her life after him would be less.

For three months after the accident, Lucy had lain in bed in the darkened bedroom she had once shared with Walter, crying and taking pills to make her sleep. For the year since, Lucy's depression had taken the form of apathy, chronic fatigue and difficulty making decisions. Her doctor said her depression would run its course as her grief lessened. He even had a list of the steps she could expect to pass through, like it was a disease with a progression of symptoms and even medicines to make it bearable.

Modern people took a pill to combat grief. Indians suffering the same pain took off a finger. Lucy didn't take mood-altering pills because Elijah was her most effective medication.

Since he had been an infant when Walter died, Elijah wouldn't remember anything about his father except what he was told.

At seventeen months her baby was walking and talking a blue streak. He used recognizable words, but mostly they came out embedded in a string of nonsense, which Lucy knew was his attempt to mimc conversation.

Elijah was a beautiful child, curious, affable, even-tempered, and, it seemed to Lucy, better coordinated than most of the children his age. He loved being read to, which Lucy did when she felt up to it. He watched more TV than he should—something Lucy had always sworn that her children would never do. But it was just easier to let the TV baby-sit. Some days, after Walter died, even little Elijah seemed too heavy a weight for her to lift.

Lucy rubbed her eyes and considered watching a late-night talk show.

Night, after Eli was asleep, was when she missed Walter the most. Sleeping alone was a problem because she had grown accustomed to having his warm, familiar body beside her. She missed having him to hold onto as the darkness closed in—to press her back against, or to spoon with, or to nudge when his snoring awakened her. She missed playing with him before they went to sleep and waking up to his fingertips tracing the line of her leg, stomach, and her breasts. Familiar lips nibbling on her shoulder, kissing her neck, her nose . . .

Lucy wasn't suicidal, but she fantasized often about waking up in paradise wrapped in Walter's embrace. Together for eternity . . . But that would mean that Elijah would be an orphan, a young man raised by his grandfather. Sometimes Lucy thought that might be best for him.

If a sitter was spending the night, Lucy could take a tablet to put her to sleep. Otherwise she lay in bed all night thinking, berating herself, longing for something she'd never have again. What if she took a pill to sleep and Elijah woke up and she didn't hear him cry out for her?

Life was fragile.

People could die.

It happened all the time.

Throwing back the covers, Lucy left her bed to look in on her son, to reassure herself that he was breathing. Since Walter's passing, she'd had a terror that she might go into the boy's room to find his little body wrapped in cold blue death.

The carpeting silenced Lucy's approach as she opened his door wider and slipped inside. At the side of the crib she reached down and rested the backs of her fingers on his forehead. The nightlight allowed her to study his chubby pink cheeks, his perfect lips, and the chin with the beginnings of Walter's cleft. His little fingers were curled tightly into his palms. His chest rose and sank slowly with the precision of a Swiss watch. Eli's fat little feet would grow narrower as they lengthened. His squat frame would stretch to six feet or better. His curly locks would straighten. Imagining him as an adult was easy since she was familiar with the genetic models he was constructed from.

She leaned over and kissed him gently, whereupon he shifted his legs and opened and closed his hands. She was tempted to pick him up and carry him to her bed, but she resisted, remembering Walter's admonition that such a tempting action was to be avoided for the child's sake. It had something to do with building a healthy self-image, a solid foundation for later independence. Walter had been raised in a large family of fierce competitors. Her husband had been the youngest of seven over-achievers. Walter was the best of the brood, and he'd achieved without seeming to try very hard, or allowing a drive to succeed to consume him in the way it had his siblings and parents.

Lucy went to her bathroom to wash her face and brush her teeth. When she turned off the water, she heard the sound of a floorboard or a ceiling beam creaking. The house, built in eighteen-eighty, made plenty of odd noises as it settled, or from changes in the weather. She heard Elijah fussing, and wondered if she had wakened him after all. She would have to stand beside the crib and rub his back to get him back to sleep.

She left the bathroom and went through her bedroom into the hallway. The nightlight seemed to have burned out again. She walked into Elijah's bedroom and looked down into the crib. To her shock, his crumpled blanket was there, but he wasn't. She heard him say "Momou" behind her and was wondering how he had climbed out of his bed, when she turned to see that her son was in the arms of a giant of a man who stood there in the doorway.

Lucy cried out in horror.

The huge man rushed from the room and Lucy raced after him.

"No!" she yelled out. "Stop! Give him back!"

She ran through the doorway. The man carrying her son was thundering down the stairs.

As Lucy passed the guest room there was a bang of the door hitting the wall as it was flung open and a powerful arm grabbed her around the chest and constricted her lungs. She was aware of Elijah screaming downstairs and the fetid breath of her captor on her neck. She screamed, clawed and writhed until a powerful hand holding a cold cloth covered her mouth and nose.

Chloroform!

Within seconds, Lucy Dockery fell into a silent darkness.